# Readers love the Long Con Adventures
## by Amy Lane

### The Mastermind

"This story is a prime example of a highly complicated long con complete with a family of the heart, a reunion of two souls destined to be together forever, and Revenge with a capital R."

—Rainbow Book Review

### The Muscle

"…Amy Lane has a way with surrounding herself with many characters and melding them into a great family… this book was no exception."

—Paranormal Romance Guild

### The Driver

"…Loads of bad guys, lots of feels, and perhaps best of all – the greatest found family I've encountered in MM romance."

—Love Bytes

By Amy Lane

All the Rules of Heaven
An Amy Lane Christmas
Behind the Curtain
Bewitched by Bella's Brother
Bolt-hole
Christmas Kitsch
Christmas with Danny Fit
Clear Water
Do-over
Food for Thought
Freckles
Gambling Men
Going Up
Hammer & Air
Homebird
If I Must
Immortal
It's Not Shakespeare
Late for Christmas
Left on St. Truth-be-Well
The Locker Room
Mourning Heaven
Phonebook
Puppy, Car, and Snow
Racing for the Sun • Hiding the Moon
Raising the Stakes
Regret Me Not

Shiny!
Shirt
Sidecar
Slow Pitch
String Boys
A Solid Core of Alpha
Three Fates
Truth in the Dark
Turkey in the Snow
Under the Rushes
Wishing on a Blue Star

BENEATH THE STAIN
Beneath the Stain • Paint It Black

BONFIRES
Bonfires • Crocus

CANDY MAN
Candy Man • Bitter Taffy
Lollipop • Tart and Sweet

DREAMSPUN BEYOND
HEDGE WITCHES LONELY HEARTS
CLUB
Shortbread and Shadows
Portals and Puppy Dogs
Pentacles and Pelting Plants
Heartbeats in a Haunted House

Published by DREAMSPINNER PRESS
www.dreamspinnerpress.com

Published by DREAMSPINNER PRESS
www.dreamspinnerpress.com

# The Suit

## AMY LANE

Published by
DREAMSPINNER PRESS

5032 Capital Circle SW, Suite 2, PMB# 279, Tallahassee, FL 32305-7886 USA
www.dreamspinnerpress.com

The Suit
© 2022 Amy Lane

Cover Art
© 2022 L.C. Chase
http://www.lcchase.com
Cover content is for illustrative purposes only and any person depicted on the cover is a model.

Mass Market Paperback ISBN: 978-1-64108-377-5
Trade Paperback ISBN: 978-1-64108-376-8
Digital ISBN: 978-1-64108-375-1
Trade Paperback published June 2022
v. 1.0

Printed in the United States of America
∞
This paper meets the requirements of
ANSI/NISO Z39.48-1992 (Permanence of Paper).

To odd couples everywhere. Mate and I have never looked like we belonged together, but all of our friends say they couldn't imagine us with anybody else.

# Acknowledgments

I READ a LOT of C.J. Box during the pandemic, and he, in turn, was simply fascinated by *The Egg Thief*. While the "murder bird" plot did not come from them, I was certainly inspired by his description of falconry and the oft-times amoral makeup of those who spend their lives in pursuit of the perfect bird.

# Author's Note

SO AFTER spending a couple of months listening to C.J. Box audiobooks, I really wanted to include falconry in my next Long Con story, but I needed something a little over-the-top and caperish. I stumbled upon a website talking about why we don't crossbreed falcons and eagles to create super-predator birds. I was as fascinated by the why as I was by the fact that it was totally possible, with a little captive breeding and a little genetic splicing. I just wanted to say that while the murder-bird depictions are completely my imagination, the fact that there really could be murder birds is within the realm of reality so don't @ me with hatemail about writing murder birds when murder birds could totally be a thing!

# Humble Beginnings

*Carl in Grade School*

CARL COX was nine when he realized his last name was going to get him teased on the playground. That didn't stop him from doing his duty as a class monitor, though.

"Put that back," he said, looking levelly at Johnny Clemson, who apparently had a name so unremarkable that he would never get teased about it ever. It didn't hurt that Johnny had been held back twice and stood head and shoulders above the other kids in the fourth grade—and unlike Topher Garrity, who was naturally genetically huge but had no skill or coordination, Johnny used *his* advantage to beat up the little kids and steal their lunch money.

Or in this case, taking books from the library without checking them out, then breaking their spines and ripping out their pages. Carl— who really loved reading—was not only the monitor from his class this week, he was also really irritated because Johnny had a book in his hand that Carl had been waiting to read.

"What're ya gonna do about it, Cox-sucker!" Johnny sneered.

Carl blinked. He knew the swearwords, yes, because he could listen to the big kids use them just like Johnny, but he'd never put two and two together.

He did now and made the sad realization that "suck" was going to be the operative word in this matter and then continued with his mission.

"Put that back," he insisted.

"No!" Johnny retorted. "Who cares about a stupid book!"

Carl scowled at him. "I do. It's about birds. Birds are cool."

Johnny scoffed and held the hardbound cover open like wings, letting the beautiful illustrations flap about in the New England autumn wind. "Then let's see if this book will fly!" he cackled, and Carl took the only option open to him.

He punched Johnny in the nose and caught the book as it fell. As Johnny howled and doubled over, clutching at his nose as blood spurted, Carl trotted to the library to inform the librarian that Johnny Clemson had tried to steal the book, but Carl was returning it, and he'd like to check it out after school if that wasn't too much trouble.

The surprised librarian—a sweet-faced older man who had never had children of his own and was often surprised to find other people's children responding so excitedly to reading—had reclaimed the book and was holding it to his chest when the vice principal strode in, looking baffled.

"Carl!" she said in exasperation. "Did you really punch Johnny Clemson in the nose?"

Carl turned to her and tried a smile. She was a handsome buxom woman in her thirties, sort of momish to the max, but with very stylish suits, and he'd noted that momish women *liked* his smile. Blond, green-eyed, with a choirboy's face, Carl could get away with everything from taking extra cookies at lunchtime to getting extra time on his math test by giving a pretty smile.

"He was going to tear the book, Mrs. Stewart. I couldn't let him tear the book! It's on birds!" The next thing he said was totally sincere. "Birds are cool."

Mrs. Stewart stared at him, dismayed because this was not a problem with an obvious solution, and Mr. Patrick, the librarian, held out the book in question.

"He, uhm, just returned it," Mr. Patrick said hesitantly. "The Clemson boy was in here eating, and I made him leave the library. The book was in the display of science books by the door. I didn't see him take it on his way out."

Mrs. Stewart scrubbed at her face with her hand. "Oh, Carl," she muttered. "What are we going to do with you? Johnny Clemson's father is furious—you punched his kid in the nose!"

Sadly, Carl *did* know the penalty for fighting. "Two day's suspension," he said glumly. "And you're going to have to call my parents."

She let out a laugh. "Maybe not *that* severe," she said. She met eyes with Mr. Patrick. "So, uhm, you like that book?"

"Yeah. I didn't want him to tear it up," Carl said.

"Well, how about Mr. Patrick checks that out to you, and you can read it in my office this afternoon. It will count as one day's suspension, and we can skip tomorrow's. How's that?"

"You mean I get out of PE?" Carl asked excitedly. Johnny and his friends would be there, and he was pretty sure his new nickname was going to make the rounds.

"Don't sound so excited, Carl," Mrs. Stewart said dryly. "People might believe this isn't a punishment."

Carl nodded soberly, but inside he was beginning to see the benefits of this law-and-order thing.

And spending the afternoon with the book still left him thinking that birds were cool.

*Carl in College*

ALAS, BIRDS were *not* cool enough to let him get a degree in ornithology, although if his college had had a good program, he might have gone for it anyway. But he *did* get to indulge his other fascination, spawned in part by looking at big picture books with antique illustrations—art history.

"Carl, baby, it's a very nice BA and all, but what are you going to do with it?"

"Get a law degree!" Carl said.

"Like your Uncle Roger?" his mother asked. "He makes good money."

"Like international law," Carl told her. "So I can be an art dealer." He had in fact completed his first semester of law school at Georgetown. He had grants, loans, and letters of recommendation. It seemed prestigious to *him*.

She shook her head, unimpressed. "Uncle Roger sues people. This other stuff I don't know about."

"Ma, it's a good degree, and I got lots of grants and stuff."

"So you got a degree in something useless and you're going to get a bigger degree in something even more useless?" his mother asked him, absolutely baffled. "Why don't you get your business degree? Then you can be like your cousin Jed! He got a degree in English and then a degree in business, and now he makes six figures."

Carl stared at her helplessly. Born in New Jersey, his mother had a wig of gold-and-brown hair piled high, a tight-fitting shirt straining around her bust with a fitted jacket over it in a leopard-skin print, and matching tight pants. A lifelong smoker, she had lines in her lips that could be seen in the lipstick prints on her highball glasses. She'd moved with his father to Maine but had refused to leave the accent behind.

Or the New Jersey.

"Because I don't *want* a degree in business," he said helplessly.

"You need to get a degree in something that pays the rent," she said, pulling hard on her cigarette. He really hated that she smoked, but like so much about his mother, it was something he'd been powerless against. "I'm moving to Florida, Carl. It's not like you can stay here."

"But I *don't* stay here," he argued. "I live in off-campus student housing!"

"I don't give a shit, Carl. You need to do something I can tell your Aunt Bessie about, because this 'My son's gonna die a student' bullshit is not gonna cut it. Do you want me to commit murder in Florida, Carl? Do you want me to? Because I'll kill that bitch, not to watch her bleed, but to please you because you wouldn't get a goddamned job to make your mother happy!"

"You're not gonna kill Aunt Bessie!" he told her.

"Well, you're gonna kill me," his mother retorted. They were sitting in the kitchen of the house he'd grown up in, and the yellow tile on the floors may have been cracked and the laminate on the table may have been peeling, but his mother, it seemed, was still as relentless as she'd been when he was a little kid. ("You got into a fight? Are you trying to kill me? Is this any way to repay me for cooking your dinner and buying your clothes?" Oh, he remembered it well.)

"I'm not gonna kill you, Ma," he said, trying to calm her down.

"If you don't get a real job for *me*, could you do it for your sainted father who's dead, God rest his soul? He wanted you to have a life, Carl. He wanted you to *live*!"

Augh! There was no arguing with that, because who *knew* what his father had wanted him to have? His father had been a quiet guy who managed a shoe store until it went out of business and then managed a Walmart until he retired and then spent most of Carl's recollection reading his newspaper in the middle of the living room, looking up very rarely to grace Carl with an absent smile. But for a guy who had been so very, very absent as Carl had grown up, he was very, very *there* when it came to throwing his weight in with whatever his mother wanted Carl to do.

In this case, it was apparently drop out of law school and find a real job.

"Fine, Ma. I'll look for a job in my field," he said, thinking that no, the only job he could get with a BA in art history was as a master's candidate so he could get a master's degree and then go on to get a PhD and teach. Or he could get that law degree and be an art dealer.

So hadn't *he* been surprised a few days later to see an ad posted at the student union for insurance investigators. All he needed was a background in art history and a willingness to take the required course in investigation and law enforcement. So easy! Seemed like a no-brainer. And wouldyalookatthat? Most of those courses doubled with his law school prerequisites.

For one of the first times in his life, he realized that his mother had been right. Getting a job *was* a good idea.

*Three years, one short marriage, and one law degree later, at the ripe old age of twenty-seven...*

"CARL, YOU'RE leaving for Europe again?"

Mandy Jessup, the secretary in charge of investigator assignments, smiled prettily at him over her desk. Carl had been flirting with her in a desultory fashion over the past few months, and she'd returned the attention. He'd needed the ego boost.

As it turned out, Serpentus Inc. had been more than happy to put Carl through the rest of law school as long as he worked for them for at least five years after he graduated. Once trained in some criminal justice classes with an emphasis on international relations, he'd been their perfect weapon: the polyglottal investigator with a background in international law and a degree in art history. He hadn't known it when he'd been going through school, but he had the credentials to be James frickin' Bond!

Sort of.

The fact was, the more he did this job, the more he wasn't sure he hadn't sold his soul to the devil at a bargain price.

A good example of that was the case he'd solved the month before.

Yes, it was true the client *had* stolen their own painting, but they'd done it to *pay the insurance company premiums* so their other paintings would be insured and they could keep getting a modest income supplement from in-home display. And they'd known they were in trouble. Hell, they'd offered to sell off the painting to pay the premiums, only to be told that there was a hidden clause prohibiting breaking up any part of the collection, and to do so would be to forfeit the entire thing to the bank. They'd offered to cancel their premiums and *then* sell the collection, only to be told that the collection was protected by their government as a historical find. They'd offered to abdicate the historical albatross that threatened to bankrupt their family, only to be threatened with prosecution and imprisonment.

In truth, a bit of discreet thievery hadn't been a bad option.

But Carl hadn't realized that when he'd seen that the security system was such that it could only be breached from the inside. And the look on the family patriarch's face when he'd asked, kindly, if perhaps one of the grandsons might have done it had… well, it had ripped Carl's heart out.

Unfortunately, by the time he learned the entire story, the damage had been done. The claims department had been alerted by Interpol, who had been there to assist in the investigation, and the company had impounded the tiny museum, the family livelihood, and three centuries of tradition to hide in their warehouse and hoard like the unscrupulous dragon they were.

As he'd boarded the plane back to America, his Interpol liaison, a *very* young policeman by the name of Liam Craig, had told him that the patriarch, Signore Marco Bianchi, had suffered a heart attack and been rushed to the hospital, but the prognosis wasn't good.

Carl had boarded the plane feeling like the angel of death.

When he'd gotten to his small DC apartment, he'd found the divorce papers from his fleeting marriage to a girl he'd met in law school waiting to be signed. She'd been *so* excited—two lawyers in the family! Mr. and Mrs. Esquire. She hadn't realized that he'd signed his soul away to Serpentus and he'd be expected to be on a plane three weeks out of every month as he put his knowledge to work.

So given the depression that had begun to set in, flirting with Mandy had proven to be good medicine. She was cute, didn't know any of his flaws, and knew he traveled. Win/win, right?

Besides, since she knew the score, maybe it would only be flirting on the table—flirting was free and fun, and it didn't lead to signing a ream of paper and then hearing your mother tell you that your Aunt Bessie always knew you'd take the one good thing in your life and fuck it up.

"So where are you going to this time?" Mandy asked, giving him that adorable side-eye. She had dark curly hair, big brown eyes, and apple cheeks. Everything about her was adorable.

"France, I think," Carl said through a yawn. His usual nightly scotch had turned into two or three the night before. Part of him was a little worried because that had been happening a lot, but the other part of him was thinking that at least he'd be able to sleep on the plane. "But it's a weird one. Apparently the museum suddenly had a priceless statue they'd never had before. Set up on display, no less. And since the statue had been insured by us and then had disappeared, they're wondering what to do with it."

"Uhm… thank their lucky stars?" Mandy asked, as baffled as he was.

"You'd think. But there was also a claim of theft," Carl told her. "From a private collector. When the museum said, 'Uhm, it turned up, but our provenance is the last to be notarized,' the private collector stopped talking. Anyway it's a mess, and they need someone who can look at stuff and sign things, and that's me." He gave a playful wave. "The stuff-looker and thing-signer."

Mandy giggled and waved him on his way.

When he got to France the next day, his first stop had been the private collector, who had been pouting his way through trying to make a claim. He'd filled out the paperwork—and even paid his premium—but the collector, a dour old man with no hair and a lip pulled up in a permanent sneer, could not be pinned down for a straight answer about where the piece had come from, or even who the artist was.

"So you don't have provenance?" Carl had asked finally, out of patience.

"I didn't say that!" the old man barked in French. "Here!" Stumping on his cane, he made his way to a giant dusty monstrosity of a desk and pulled a file from one of the drawers. "Here! Here is my provenance! See? It is signed by someone from your own company! Mr. Thomakins."

He practically threw the file at Carl, who leafed through it, eyebrows raised. "It looks in order," he said weakly—and it did. Every i dotted, every t crossed, right down to the watermark his company used to document provenance.

But Carl worked in a specialized field with relatively few players, and Carl had never seen the name Thomakins before.

Besides… it sounded like something from a "Puss in Boots" story. "I told you—"

"Wait," Carl muttered. "Wait. It says here the piece was a twenty-inch terracotta model of a John Flaxman memorial piece—the *Virgin Ascends*. But you weren't keeping it anywhere heat and humidity controlled. What, were you trying to age it like a pot?" He knew that keeping terracotta pots somewhere warm and damp was a great way to get the clay to change colors and appear vintage, but who wanted to do that to an expensive piece of art?

"That Thomakins guy complained about it too," the old man sneered. "But it sat in my solarium like it sat in my father's. I don't see the problem. He signed off on it, didn't he?"

*Yeah*, Carl thought resentfully. *Right before he stole it and took it to the museum.*

He didn't say that, though. Instead he smiled politely and went about getting as many details about "Thomakins" as he possibly could.

Then he looked at the setup and wondered why this man hadn't just put a "steal me" sign on his property. The pedestal looked great: marble, with a cushion of black velvet on which to display the statue. It had some mild security—motion detectors on the glass bell jar that protected the thing from dust and standard break-in security to the man's villa in general, but other than that? Any reasonably competent thief with steady hands could lift the bell jar without setting off the alarm.

And a man who had been inside to assess the security would have been in a prime position to insert a piece of tinfoil over a couple of window breakers to fool the basic system.

The only real wrinkle would have been the pressure point under the statue, but apparently their light-fingered thief had replaced the statue with a counterweight without even a hiccup.

Carl frowned, remembering that. "Can I see what they used as a counterweight?" he asked. There was almost always a clue in that— something in the soil if it was rocks in a bag, something in the fabric itself. Even carefully gathered lead balls held secrets of origin that could lead Carl to the perpetrator.

But when he saw what the man held in his hand, Carl's voice squeaked. "That?" The thing in the man's hand was *so* undignified.

"Bastard was *laughing* at me," the old man snarled, and Carl couldn't argue.

The counterweight was terracotta as well but obviously a more recent work, done by an immature if not juvenile hand.

"It's some sort of cartoon character," the owner snapped, and Carl nodded. He didn't have nephews or nieces, but the cartoon was everywhere. Even *he* recognized the Squidward character from *SpongeBob SquarePants.*

"That will be very helpful," he said dryly. "May I keep it?"

"Oui."

Carl took the thing, noting its weight, its texture. It really had been formed from terracotta, no matter how inexpertly, and it was almost perfect in dimension.

This Thomakins, whoever he was, was a very clever, very *unusual* thief.

CARL'S NEXT stop was the museum in which the original statue had appeared. Or *re*appeared, as it were. The Musée du Quai Branly in Paris was a creative mix of the traditional and contemporary, right down to the architecture. Half of the building was ivy-covered brick and glass with wide curving windows, and the other half was a colorful hodgepodge of various room-sized "boxes" rising from a wooden-shingled wall. A small strip of gardened walkways graced one side, but the aspect that faced the street was the dramatic contrast of new and old, chaotic and ordered.

Carl was more of a sucker for the Louvre, himself, but that was because he was never there on business. Quai Branly was not a small venue—but that's what made it so perfect for breaking into.

Which was where Carl's mind was *supposed* to be as he walked up the steps, only to fall in line behind two uncles, he assumed, helping a small boy up the wide steps.

They were singing together, in French.

It was the theme song to *SpongeBob SquarePants.*

Carl's heart thundered in his ears for a moment, that adrenaline-fueled thrill that meant he'd cracked a case, but he had to make himself sit for a minute. Could it be? These two perfectly nice men and the little boy between them were singing a song that literally millions of children around the world knew. It would be like accusing someone of theft because they knew the theme song to *Friends.* Even people who *hated* that show knew the song. It was a supremely dumb way to make a connection.

Then they started singing it in Italian.

And English.

And Spanish.

They hopped sideways on the steps as they sang, as though this was a game they played all the time. As Carl neared the front door, the boy began speaking in a patois of all three languages, and Carl felt secretly resentful. He'd studied languages since he hit high school, and he'd never be *that* good.

"Your mother will be out in a moment," the smaller of the men said in flawless French. He was… arresting looking, with curly brown hair, vulpine features, and teeth that were slightly crooked in the front. *European*! Carl thought, because Americans, it seemed, were the ones who stressed so much about slight imperfections in the smile.

"Where would you like to go for lunch?" the taller man asked. Bold and blond, with a radiant handsomeness and perfectly straight teeth, he spoke English with an American accent.

The boy began to babble. A series of café names bubbled out of his mouth until the smaller man told him laughingly that they would eat at the first place that served peanut butter and jelly and the boy would like it.

"Yes, Uncle Danny, I *would* like it! Make sure the bread is crusty, and there is butter too."

The two men exchanged glances—not of worry, so much, but of planning.

"Go," the taller one instructed. "Get food. I'll see what's taking so long."

"Oui," the shorter one said, and then they shared a touch—brief as it was—of hands.

And Carl rethought everything he knew about them again.

He had no excuse to linger on the steps, so he breached the door and stood for a moment, orienting himself and wondering how to speak to the head docent. As he was scanning the various corridors and displays, looking for the standard "offices" or something similar, he saw an exquisite woman rushing by, dressed in a pencil-thin black skirt and a red sweater, with her blond hair swept up almost like Grace Kelly by design. She turned a brilliant smile over her shoulder and spoke a quick patter of French, thanking the docent manager for being so very, very kind.

The man in turn called out, "Mrs. Thomakins, you and your husband may return any day. We are always so pleased to meet a donor."

She cast another dazzling smile at him and, as Carl watched, blew outside to snag the taller man by the hand. Together they rushed after the other man and the boy, off to find a peanut butter and jelly sandwich in a Parisian café, and Carl turned to the docent manager in a dream.

"Did you say Thomakins?" he asked the little man with the incredibly earnest face who was swishing his handkerchief after the exquisite blond woman with something like worship.

"Oui! Their family is so very gracious. They found a lost Renoir. Can you imagine that? They donated it to our museum. It will be ready for display in a matter of weeks!"

"That's, uhm, generous," Carl said, his mind racing. "I'm, uhm, Carl Soderburgh. From Serpentus?" They'd given him a cover name, and he used it whenever he was in Europe. He wasn't sure exactly what it did to keep him safe, but, well, company policy. "I'm here to look at your John Flaxwood statue, but would you mind if I looked at that Renoir as well?"

Both the statue and the Renoir were 100 percent authentic, although only the statue's right to be there was contested. Carl wasn't able to pay the client who'd contested, though. As he'd thought, nobody named "Thomakins" existed at Serpentus.

Carl was able to interest the company enough to give him some investigative leeway, which was where his obsession with the "Thomakins" family was allowed to take root and flourish.

Even after the trip to rehab and the sad, doomed affair with Danny Mitchell, fox-featured master thief who could sing the theme to *SpongeBob* in four languages to occupy a little boy, he would forever be grateful to the four thieves he'd seen at Quai Branly that day.

They helped make his life extraordinary.

# By Any Other Name

CARMICHAEL CARMODY had never liked his name—even when it was shortened to "Car-Car" since working on cars was what he did best.

Now that he had a new life, a new job, a new him—an out and proud *gay* him, working for people who gave zero shits about the gayness—he wanted a new name.

And he really wanted to try it out on a new person.

A specific person.

A tall blond-haired green-eyed Viking who wore sportscoats and spoke formally and always smiled at him and nodded when he borrowed the cars or boarded the planes that Car-Car... erm, Carmichael—wait, *Michael*—tended and kept ready to use.

Should the tall blond-haired green-eyed Viking ever smile at him specifically and say his name, Car-Car—*Michael*—wanted to be able to suggest the name change easily, as if it was butter and rolled smoothly off the tongue.

It didn't quite happen that way.

"Got your bag packed, Car-Car?" Chuck Calder asked as he wandered through *Michael's* end of the hangar, the part that housed Felix Salinger's planes and some of his other vehicles. Part of Michael's job was to make sure all the vehicles at the mansion were in top form. He tended to rotate them out once a month to service them—there was always something to do. If nothing else, the trip from the mansion in Glencoe to the airstrip in outlying farm country took up nearly an hour, and Michael had nothing to do there but drive those nice cars and let the breeze blow his hair back, listening to classic rock played at top volume.

It was like a little vacation at work.

He didn't need to go any of the places the airplanes went to be happy.

"Nobody needs me to fly to Belgium," Michael told Chuck. "Besides, I don't even know what *you're* doing there."

Chuck grinned. He was a handsome, raw-boned good ol' boy with a wicked smile and a divot in his chin. He and Michael had been lovers once, but that was long over, and now? He was a friend, which was good. Michael had grown up in Texas, and now that he was trying to make a new life in Chicago, he could use all the friends he could get.

"Honestly, they don't need me either," he confided. "They need Carl and Liam Craig. You don't know him. He's from Interpol. But Carl didn't want to go alone. I get the feeling he's spent a lot of alone time in Europe, and he's over it." Chuck shrugged, the action drawing his T-shirt tight against his broad chest. "Since *my* boyfriend is off making trade deals with China this week, I volunteered. That's what friends do."

Michael bit his lip. Chuck still felt like he owed Michael for some shit that went down a long time ago. Nothing could be further from the truth, but boy, Michael wouldn't mind cashing in on a little of that goodwill now.

"Uhm, Chuck?" he asked, smiling prettily. His teeth were the faintest bit crooked, but he knew he had big limpid brown eyes and an appealing smile. His ex-wife had told him often enough that he could get all sorts of things for the smile alone. Sadly he hadn't wanted those things from *her*, but she was such a sweet girl, she'd given him pointers for how to use that smile to get someone he could love the way he couldn't love her.

"Car-Car?" Chuck asked, as footsteps sounded on the far side of the hangar.

Oh, Michael knew those steps: firm in hard leather-soled shoes, with a long, solid stride. He'd been hearing them echo through his hangar for the last two months, ever since he'd started working for the Salingers and had gotten to know the other people who worked for them—or with them—as well.

"That's sort of what I wanted to talk to you about," Michael said, wincing. "See, Car-Car is someone you knew in Texas. Someone who went to jail. And he was… well, sort of a wreck. I was wondering if you could, you know, maybe call me something else?"

*Michael. Call me Michael!*

"Sure!" Chuck sounded all easygoing, but then he had to go and ruin it all by calling to the owner of those footsteps. "Hey, Soderbergh, get over here. We gotta find Car-Car a new name."

Carl Cox—Michael had no idea why people called him Soderbergh—changed the direction of his stride from the plane, which sat near the hangar's opening with the staircase descended, to the back of the hangar where Michael's area was neatly arranged, including an office toward the rear with a bathroom, a shower, and a little sleeping area he used maybe three times a week when he worked late and didn't feel like driving back into the city.

After his last accommodations, thanks to the state of Texas, the idea of having an entire airplane hangar without another soul nearby was almost like having God rock him to sleep on the sweet soft palm of his hand.

But having Carl coming back to this little personal area? It felt like he'd been called into Michael's living room, and Michael... well, he'd dreamed of inviting Carl to his place, the city apartment that their bosses, the Salingers, let Michael use. Not this little bachelor pad he'd carved out of an airplane hangar.

"Oh wow!" Soderbergh had cleared the cubicle walls set up to keep the office area private. "You've got a little apartment back here. I'm sorry. I didn't mean to intrude!"

Chuck blinked as if this had not occurred to him. "Are we intruding, Car-Car?"

"No," Michael said shortly. "But don't call me that." He realized that he sounded defensive and tried to make up for it. "Would anybody like a beer? I've got a mini fridge with snacks, water…."

"Water, thank you," Soderbergh said.

"Me too," Chuck said. "That's mighty kind of you."

"You flying too?" Michael asked Soderbergh, trying to make conversation.

Soderbergh shook his head and perched on the arm of the gently used couch. "Nope. I just don't do beer after a stint in rehab."

It took Michael a moment to get that. "You went to rehab?" he asked, thinking he couldn't have heard right. Rehab was where his family had gone when they'd gotten hooked on meth. It never took.

"Drank too much." Soderbergh shrugged, and while it seemed to be an old wound, Michael could sense a story there.

"That was a while back," Chuck commented. "That was before you and me met, wasn't it, Carl?"

"Yeah, 'bout eight, nine years ago." Soderbergh—Carl—gave Michael a smile, obviously hoping to turn the conversation. "So what did you want to ask me?"

"Car-Car here wants to reinvent himself," Chuck said, "and he was wondering about a name—"

"Call me Michael." Oh God. He'd said it. He'd actually said it. He'd promised himself that this job, these people, his new life would all be about reinvention. And he'd just taken his first step.

"Michael," Carl said, giving him a sweet smile. He had a square chin with only the hint of a divot, a square jaw, an almost Roman nose, and weary green eyes. A "sweet" smile was like a gift in that solidly male face. "Nice name. Well chosen."

Chuck let out a snort. "Are you sure? I mean, Car-Car has some character to it, right?"

"Car-Car has some *jail time* on it," Michael said, exasperated. "I… you know, want to be respectable."

Chuck grimaced. "You always *were* respectable, Car, erm, Michael. The jail time was mostly my fault."

Michael rolled his eyes. "The jail time was my stupid brothers' fault. They were the ones who'd hero-worshipped two assholes who were planning to shoot us all dead. And it was my fault for saying, 'Yeah, sure, I'll help you idiots rob a bank. Just don't beat the shit out of me like you been doing my whole damned life.'" He turned to Carl, wishing they were having a different conversation. Dammit, ever since he met the big broad-shouldered businessman, his dreams were always very… smooth. Very suave. Very urbane. Very *not* the redneck hick trying to reclaim his life. As he fetched the bottles of water from the mini fridge and gave one each to the guys, he reflected unhappily that this impromptu party in the hangar apartment was *not* what he'd planned.

"I'm sorry," he said resignedly. "I just wanted to know if, you know, I could make 'Michael' work."

Carl gave him another one of those incongruously winsome smiles. "I think it works great," he said. "And you know what? Making a fresh start in your life is nothing to be embarrassed about." He cracked the lid on the bottle with a wide-palmed hand. "Here's to fresh starts."

He said that like he knew what those were about.

"Here's to fresh starts," Chuck said, sinking into the couch. Michael had bought the furniture secondhand, but it was pretty comfortable, and he'd arranged everything in the "apartment" on area rugs. In a way, watching Chuck stretch his legs in front of him and yawn was sort of a compliment. He'd done his best to make the place homey.

"I'm sorry," Chuck added, after a long draught from the bottle. "I got in pretty late from Lucius's place last night. I know Hunter's got the first shift flying when he gets here but...." He yawned.

"No worries," Michael told him. "Look, I got to go around back and take care of my birds. How about you two rest here, okay?"

"Sure," Chuck said, yawning, but Carl, after giving Chuck a good-natured look, shook his head.

"I'll leave you to sleep." Carl stood up. He left his luggage, Michael noticed, but took his water with him. "What birds?" he asked, following Michael into the hangar. It was a good walk past the vehicles and the waiting plane toward the vast door of the hangar. Carl kept up with a long, swinging stride, which was something Michael had always found really sexy in a man. It had been Chuck's swagger that had attracted Michael to *him* three years earlier, and it had been Carl's easy hip-swinging walk that had made Michael look twice the first time he'd eaten at the Salingers and seen Carl "Soderbergh" Cox striding up the walkway to the Salingers' Glencoe mansion.

"A couple different kinds," Michael told him. As they cleared the door, the wind hit them, only softened a little from its journey across Lake Michigan, with a late September bite. Michael shivered in his hooded sweatshirt. "Wow, it's cold. Does it get much colder than this in the winter?"

Next to him, Carl choked.

"Oh my God, yes. Winter in Chicago is like seven layers of icy hell. Did nobody warn you?"

Michael grunted. "Well, winter outside of Austin is a lot like *this*. So no. Nobody warned me. I'm gonna have to get heaters for the hangar, aren't I?"

"The place should be heated already," Carl said. "But it's big and badly insulated, so that's not going to work so well. But if you tell the Salingers you're overnighting in your little apartment there, they'll probably spring for some space heaters and insulation and maybe even some swamp coolers for the summer. I don't know how you survived late July and August in there."

Michael gave a humorless laugh. "You kidding? There's big ol' fans in there, and even a cooling unit. Compared to my garage back in Texas, it was Shangri-fuckin-la."

"You don't miss it there?" Carl asked as they circled around the side of the building.

Michael had actually planned for this question—he had. He was going to say something smooth and urbane like "Not my kind of place, old son. No, I find Chicago far superior."

What came out of his mouth was not that at all.

"I'd live in seven layers of icy hell to fuckin' not go back there again," he said, with such deep loathing his voice shook with it. He took a breath and tried to rein it in. "And now that my ex-wife and kids are safe in Ohio, I won't have to. If I don't set foot in Texas again through my next six lifetimes, the seventh will still be too goddamned soon."

He heard a bark of laughter next to him and wanted to wilt into the shorn brown grass that hugged the hangar.

"Wow, Michael, tell me how you really feel!" Carl laughed through his fingers. "That was heartfelt."

Oh shit—way to impress this man with his style. "I'm sorry. I… you probably love Texas."

"Not particularly," Carl told him. "Although I save that level of pure hatred for Florida."

"What did Florida ever do to you?" Michael asked, lightening up a little. It didn't sound like he'd put the guy off any, so that was something.

"Nothing personally, although the humidity in the summer is sort of like being mugged by a sweaty manure truck worker with bad breath. But my mother moved to Florida so she and my Aunt Bessie could make each other miserable, and I'm telling you, I avoid the place like a shit-trucker's armpit. No. Just no. That much bottled vitriol is a *bad thing*."

Michael cackled outright, liking this moment very much. "I gotta work on how much I hate Texas," he said. "'Cause that's funnier than anything I've got right now."

Carl's laughter this time was warm: kind. And sort of rumbly: personal. It was personal laughter, for Michael alone. "I'll be sure to ask you when we return," he said. "Be prepared. I'll say, 'How much do you hate Texas?' and you'll have to say something funny back."

Michael looked at him from the corner of his eye. He had an open, happy expression on his face, and Michael's stomach tightened. Oh. Oh wow. This was even better than he'd imagined. Now they had a *thing*.

"Oh!" Carl said as they rounded the corner for the back of the hangar. Since the hangar faced the small airstrip, the acreage out back was mostly long grass. Michael could see some of it had been seeded as hay, and someone had come to mow and bale in early September. But that was a good mile away. The square mile behind the hangar was sage and prairie grasses, with a small grove of oak trees about two hundred yards behind the hangar itself. Michael had been drawn to the area when he'd first come to work; he'd taken his breaks behind the big building and had noted the rich wildlife population. He hadn't wanted to ask the Salingers, but he'd wondered if it was on purpose. A small stream, perhaps an irrigation ditch, wended its way through the trees and into the distant seeded farmland, and the result was a riot of fauna. Coyotes, prairie chickens, hawks, jackrabbits, feral cats—all of the creatures lived, mated, hunted, and died in this stretch of land, and Michael got to be an observer of it all.

He'd grown up on two hardpan acres in Texas and spent much of his adulthood working on the cracked pavement of a tiny town way outside of Austin. To him this sort of teeming animal sanctuary was something of a miracle.

"Nice, right?" Michael said with satisfaction.

"It's surprisingly wild," Carl said, smiling out into the prairie. The lines by his eyes crinkled when he did that, and his face softened a little, making him look like a young, blond George Clooney or a broad-chested Brad Pitt. This man knew how to smile, Michael thought, but he did it quietly and inside.

Carl looked back against the hangar and spotted the little shelter Michael had built for himself. Solid wood, it shaded him from the sun and kept out some of the wind. He'd built a cot that also served as a bench and a small bear-proof icebox to hold his lunch or dinner, a little wooden box to hold books and other essentials, and brought a camp chair because the cot got hard on the back. "I can see why you'd want to spend time out here. What's this structure here, next to—"

From inside what amounted to an eight-by-eight-by-eight wooden crate with a steel mesh front came an imperious shriek.

"Is that a *bird*?" Carl's voice took on awed tones, and Michael smiled, pleased. He'd been crushing on Carl something awful, but until this moment, the idea that they might share the same interests had only been a hope.

"It's a peregrine," Michael said, tugging on the sleeve of Carl's sport jacket to pull him in front of the mews. "See? I found him flopping out here, trying to scream his way past a coyote. Tore the shit out of my hand before I sacrificed a sweatshirt." He held up the hand that still sported a large bandage on the back, up past his wrist.

"Ouch!" Carl caught his hand for a moment, evidently to take a better look at it, and Michael almost pulled out of his grip.

Then he realized that this was the whole purpose of luring the good-looking guy in the businessman's suit to the back of the hangar.

He allowed Carl to peel back the bandage briefly to inspect the gashes—halfway to healing though they were—and for some of the warmth in Carl's big, well-manicured hand to seep into Michael's smaller, rougher one.

"They're getting better—I wear gloves when I work to keep them clean," he said shyly, warmth curling in his belly, and Carl shook his head and looked from the back of Michael's hand and wrist to the bird in the cage, currently wearing a toeless nylon stocking to hold his wings next to his body.

"Yes, but that's quite a sacrifice," Carl said gently. He rubbed his thumb along the knuckles and then lowered the hand but didn't let go. "The stocking's a good idea. Where'd you get that?"

"A bird-rescue site online," Michael said. He sighed. "They told me I should have hooded him, too, but by the time I got to that part, he'd started getting really ruffly and happy when he saw me, because he knew food was coming. I hope I haven't ruined his chances for going back into the wild." He liked having the falcon there, and he was proud of his part in helping the bird survive. But Michael had lived in a cage of his own for two years. He knew where that bird belonged, and it wasn't behind a load of pig-wire and plywood.

Carl studied the creature, frowning, and again the change in his energy when his expression altered was formidable. That frown could darken the heavens, although Carl didn't appear to know it.

The bird stood not quite twenty inches tall, and his breast plumage, visible through the stocking, was pretty—speckled black and white while the base of his sharp curved beak was an arresting yellow. His eyes, bright, passionless, analytical, studied everything about the two humans looking into his territory, and he opened his beak and shrieked, probably looking for food. Peregrines ate about 20 percent of their body weight every day. Michael kept a terrarium of field mice behind the mews, letting one or two loose on the feeding tray at a time so the bird could hunt even though grounded. But today he had a treat—for the falcon at least. Hadn't been so much fun for Michael, but then, he existed as a conduit for falcon food at this point, so he couldn't complain.

"Scuse me," Michael said, reluctantly freeing his hand from Carl's. First, he reached into his essentials box and donned a pair of Teflon gloves, the kind ladies wore to prune roses, he'd bought after the initial rescue—after the bird had ripped his hand open, of course. Then he went back to the critter-proof icebox and pulled out a dead jackrabbit he'd spotted off the service road that led out to the small airstrip.

"This here's super gross," he told Carl, apologizing. "You don't have to look if you don't want to."

Holding the rabbit carcass in one hand and opening the side of the mews with the other, he threw the rabbit on a big stainless-steel platter he'd affixed next to the falcon's perch, before dodging back outside. The bird shrieked and dove in, ripping at the jackrabbit and slashing with his beak, shrieking approval.

Carl made an *eww* sound and stepped back. "Damn," he said. "That's… that's terrifying."

"Yeah, I know." Michael shrugged. "I mean, I guess a bird's gotta bird. I *like* watching 'em fly, and even hunt, but still…. I'm kinda glad he's not doing it to the prairie chickens that live out back too."

"Prairie chickens?" Carl frowned. "Aren't those endangered?"

Michael held his hand out, palm down, and rocked it side to side. "Comes and goes. I looked it up, and this place out back is sort of protected acreage. I think that's why they don't hay it up like the rest of the area. I wonder if the Salingers did that?"

"I wouldn't doubt it," Carl said, suddenly thoughtful. "It's something they'd do, you know?"

"I know they've been nice to *me*," Michael said. Chuck had called them his new "crew" and had gotten Michael a job with them, but so far Michael hadn't seen anything crewish about them. They didn't *seem* to be bank robbers or thieves. In fact, Felix Salinger and his husband,

Benjamin Morgan, were almost local celebrities. Felix ran a cable network of news and movie stations, and Benjamin—whom Michael had heard called "Uncle Danny"—was a docent of some sort at the Art Institute. They lived together in a mansion with Felix's ex-wife, Julia, which would have seemed strange if you hadn't met the three of them. Julia was like the sister the two men had never had, and the young people who flocked to Julia and Felix's son, Josh, had been taken under Felix, Julia, and Benjamin's wings like fledgling birds.

Even Michael had been "adopted," he supposed. He'd been asked out to the mansion to eat four or five times in the past two months, and everybody at the table had treated him like a friend.

In a way it had been intimidating, all these rich people, all of them pretty, some of them even sort of famous—Torrance Grayson was a YouTube phenom, and he was there all the time—but it had also been... sweet.

Everybody had talked, their voices rising and swelling in a tide of chatter, and every voice had been welcome. If it hadn't been for the one thing that hung over the mansion like a pall, Michael would have said it was Camelot.

But there was that one damned thing.

"The Salingers are nice to most people," Carl said. "But, you know, not so nice to bad guys."

Michael gave a humorless little grunt, thinking about the day Chuck had saved his and his brothers' lives and gotten them arrested at the same time. The guys who would have killed him had been left dead on the bank's marble floor, and it was an image Michael would live with for the rest of his life.

But he couldn't get over the idea that he'd *heard* them plotting murder. He'd even seen proof that they'd been planning to sabotage the job and get out of it with the money. Michael's brothers had been dumb and willing, but Michael had been desperate. He'd had a wife and three kids, and the bank had been about to foreclose on his garage and then probably take the house his children lived in. Part of that had been because his brothers kept stealing from his business and he'd been too afraid of them to do anything about it, but another part had been that Michael had been in over his head in the business department.

He was so glad to get a second chance, and he couldn't regret having to walk over the bodies of the two guys on the bank floor to get it.

He had to side with the Salingers on this one—bad guys need not apply.

"Well, someone needs to get the bad guys, you think?" Michael asked, and was relieved when Carl nodded.

"It's hard to know who they are," Carl said, "but once that's clear, I think you're right." He let out a sigh. "You said birds? Your, uhm, savage friend here is only one."

The falcon was still ripping apart the jackrabbit, and they both winced at the sound of a particularly loud cracking bone.

"Yeah, well, the other ones are the prairie chickens. Look out there and you might see a few."

Carl turned so he could scan the empty acreage, and Michael heard his surprised chuckle as one of the distinctive round birds with striped plumage and red faces broke cover and ran, pell-mell, for a little huddle of shelter on the ground.

"Oh wow," Carl said, sounding charmed. "They're all over. That's amazing!"

Michael was so proud of this. "I sort of dug a little trench out from the irrigation ditch. You see?" He pointed toward the oak trees. "And I put some big pieces of plywood in the middle of the field on top of big prairie grass hummocks, like lean-tos for the birds. I figured if I could bring a little water to the area and give them protection from assholes like this," he nodded at the falcon, "I could make their protected land a little more protected."

Michael had been exposed, and he'd been helpless. Even when he was a kid and his brothers and mother put a crossbow in his hand and told him to go find something—bird, squirrel, something—for dinner, he'd always had more of an affinity for the hurt creature than the hunter. The first thing he'd vowed when he'd held his children had been to keep them safe. It was such a relief, here in this new home, to be able to care for hurt things, to show kindness to those silly chubby birds, and not to worry that it might get his ear boxed or his eye blackened because "real" men shouldn't be kind.

Something about Carl's smile, the way his eyes crinkled in the corners, the way they got shiny and bright, gave Michael more than approval—it hinted at sadness as well.

"That's wonderful," he said. "That's… that's so smart. It's…." Carl bit his lip and took a long, deep breath.

"What's wrong?" Oh. Things had been going so well!

"It's good to see people being kind for the sake of being kind," he said, his voice gruff. "Let's hope that's catching."

Michael frowned. "Why? What are you talking about?"

Carl grimaced. "Gah! I shouldn't have said anything." He shook his head and looked away, but inadvertently he looked to where the falcon was still savaging the poor dead bunny. He turned his gaze back to Michael almost like he was running away. "It's sort of confidential," he said, grimacing. "And there are enough sketchy things about it for me to not want you to know anything, okay?"

Michael scowled, hurt. "You know, I'm not a fainting flower. I did two years in prison. You know that, right?"

"Yes, I know that," Carl retorted. "And Chuck made it very clear to everybody that you were to be left absolutely in the land of 'plausible deniability.' Which I'm trying to do." Some of his irritation seeped out of him. "But the important part isn't the sketchy details anyway. The important part is that Josh Salinger isn't doing well, and we're hoping that the results of this trip to Belgium that Chuck, Hunter, and I are taking might save his life."

Michael sucked air through his teeth. "Oh. Oh no." Josh Salinger, Felix and Julia's son, had been the bright and brilliant light that attracted so many people to their house—including Chuck and therefore Michael. Michael had seen him declining in the past two months in spite of everybody's hope after each treatment for leukemia. Michael was always very grateful for the invitations to the house, partly because he realized that people were so damned worried about Josh, it seemed like Michael should be the last person on everybody's mind.

"Yeah," Carl said, the skin around his eyes tight. "I... I knew that kid as a little boy. I'm really hoping this thing we're doing works out."

"Will it hurt anyone?" Michael asked worriedly.

Carl shook his head. "No. No. Essentially what we're doing is asking an estranged family member for some bone marrow. Chuck and Hunter can fly, so they get to go, obviously, and I've got the law degree, so I'm going to negotiate."

"What about Hunter's boyfriend?" Michael asked curiously. Dylan Li—aka Grace—fascinated him, much like squirrels or bunnies were probably fascinated by cats. Grace was self-absorbed and rude sometimes, but he was also fiercely loyal to Josh and the rest of the family.

"He's staying here," Carl said. "He and Josh are… uhm, brothers, I guess. Best way to explain it."

"Yeah, but real brothers. My brothers are assholes I'm glad aren't talking to me. Grace and Josh sort of speak the same language."

"They do." Carl's attention was diverted by a black SUV pulling onto the service road to the airstrip. "And speak of the devil, that's probably Hunter." He turned back toward Michael and gave a tentative smile. "Thank you. For showing me this. I was *not* looking forward to the next couple of days, and this is damned cool. It's totally brightened my day."

Michael was so happy, he thought he might be glowing. "Birds *are* cool, aren't they?" He'd always thought so, even when he'd been hunting them. Falcons, hawks—sometimes they'd just spread their wings under the sun and ride the wind. He'd never had that kind of freedom in his life. Ever.

"I have always thought so." Carl's eyes crinkled warmly at the corners before he turned away and started for the front of the hangar. Michael made sure there was water in the little fountain he'd set up for the falcon before closing up the cage and following him, thinking the whole time, *He liked it. He smiled at me. He held my hand!*

And he'd called Michael "Michael" during their whole conversation.

Oh yes. Reinvention was possible. If only they could get the Salinger kid better, things would be looking up.

# Unspoken Among Thieves

MOST OF the people in the Salinger "crew" had day jobs. Pulling gigs with Felix and Julia Salinger and Danny "Lightfingers" Mitchell was fun—and surprisingly fulfilling from a philanthropy standpoint—but it didn't pay the bills, and if they were scamming all the time, they'd be too recognizable to pull any good cons.

Carl, who didn't really think of himself as a con or a thief, although he'd participated in both, was no exception. He continued to work for Serpentus, but after his trip to rehab eight years earlier, he'd insisted on picking and choosing his jobs, as well as on retaining some autonomy about how he handled those jobs. It didn't mean Serpentus wasn't a horrible bunch of human beings masquerading as an uber-rich board of trustees, but it did mean Carl could help minimize the damage done to some of their most vulnerable victims. Erm, clients.

And over the last few months, having a job—albeit mostly in a consulting capacity at this point—for Serpentus gave him the respectability the Salingers needed in order to keep some of their most outrageous adventures under wraps, covered with his shiny, respectable veneer.

Two months ago, when they'd helped keep Lucius Broadstone's shelters for battered women safe from some very powerful abusers, Carl had been onsite as a "hired security expert" to explain to the *non*local authorities what had happened.

Sure, it wasn't as exciting as thwarting a plan to blow up a factory or climbing through ventilation shafts to steal priceless gems or convincing really horrible people to spill their most terrible secrets on live television, but he liked to think he helped.

But the gig he, Chuck, and Hunter were currently flying toward wasn't what he was concentrating on as Hunter took off and started them on their first leg of the journey to Brussels.

"Penny for your thoughts," Chuck asked as Carl stared moodily out the window. The private jet was spacious and comfy, but Carl had always figured that flying was flying. Yes, it was nice not to be sitting in his neighbor's lap, and he could get up and make use of the wet bar or the kitchenette whenever he felt like it, but he was still enclosed in a small space hurtling in a tight concentric orbit around the earth. As far as he was concerned, he had time to do paperwork, time to nap, and time to listen to that Michael Connelly audiobook he'd been dying to catch up on, and that was pretty much it.

Or it had been before he'd become tight with the Salinger crew.

There was no such thing as uninterrupted time in your own head when you were in close quarters with people who actually gave a damn about you. Carl was having a hard time getting used to that idea.

"You'd get change for that penny," Carl told Chuck, smiling a little. He and Chuck *did* have some history, but then Chuck had history with a lot of guys. Take away the history and what was left was a bond formed by two guys who weren't quite content with the average everyday life the world had to offer and who had somehow found their way outside it.

"No, seriously," Chuck said softly, coming to sit across from Carl in one of the leather seats. "C'mon, talk to me." He gave a pretty smile that Carl knew for a fact had gotten him laid more than once. A couple of times by Carl himself. "I'll teach you to fly."

Carl frowned. "That better not be a euphemism—"

"No! I swear." Chuck laughed. "Hunter's doing the first leg and then napping, and I'm taking the second leg. I hate flying without a buddy in the copilot's seat. I'll go over the basics until you fall asleep. I promise it's not a come-on."

Carl chuckled, thinking about Lucius Broadstone, the one man apparently capable of making Chuck slow down enough to commit. "I believe you," he said mildly. "Your boyfriend thinks you walk on water. You're not going to do anything to fuck that up."

"See?" Chuck grinned and pointed to his temple and then Carl's. "You get me!" He sobered. "Now tell me about Car-Car—I mean, Michael."

Carl grunted, not sure he wanted to talk about Chuck's mechanic friend, but he didn't have anyone else he could really talk to about him, either. He thought of Michael, though—large, limpid brown eyes bright with excitement, collar-length brown hair slicked back behind his ears, and boyish, almost delicate features wide open and earnest as he pointed to the prairie chicken sanctuary he'd built with a little bit of ingenuity and an affinity for creatures that couldn't help themselves—and suddenly talking to Chuck wasn't optional. His chest gave a little ping, and he needed to say something, to sort out what that ping might mean.

"He's sweet," Carl said after a moment, surprising himself. "You told me a little about him but, you know, two years of jail. I didn't think he'd be so... so sweet."

Chuck let out a slow breath. "C—*Michael* was always sweet," he said, his voice a little sad. "That was one of the most difficult things about him. I mean, when I met him, he was married and nuts about his wife. Every way but sexually. I think he still is. I left him and his useless fucking brothers in good shape financially. I took the bank take, invested the shit out of it, and handed the three of them a clean million each, no questions asked. His brothers are still serving their nickel. For all I know, they'll blow that money on meth and hookers when they get out, because they were that stupid. But the minute Michael got those account numbers, he sent them to his wife. And I was thinking, 'Oh, buddy. She's going to take your money and run.' But she didn't. She took the money and got an apartment in a better neighborhood with better schools for the kids and started making arrangements to move the whole family out of state. I monitored those accounts—she didn't spend too much, and she didn't cheat on him. Not once. And I don't know what he said to her when he got out, but I know he's got plans to spend Christmas in Ohio with her and the kids and has asked them to spend some time with him next summer. I think he calls them every day. I...." Chuck blew out a breath. "I am actually jealous of the little bastard, because he's got more of a family with his ex-wife than I ever had before I met Josh Salinger, and then Lucius, you know?"

Carl nodded, the information comforting him somehow. "So he really *is* sweet," he said, his instincts confirmed but with a little sadness. Too sweet for Carl, anyway.

"Guess so." But there was something reserved about the way Chuck said that.

"What?" Carl asked. "What are you not telling me?"

Chuck let out a breath. "Look, some of this may be guilt. I told you how things ended with Michael, and it sucked. I was going to take him with me—blow that town and not go back—but he wouldn't leave his wife. I said we should tell his brothers that the other guys in the heist were going to double-cross them, but he knew they wouldn't believe him.

He was right. They'd been beating on him his entire life. They wouldn't have changed just because he heard the job was going wrong. I ended up turning them over to the police and leaving while the cops took down the guys who were planning to blow people away, and that doesn't sit right with me. But Michael? He hasn't shown a trace of resentment over that. And I know that, objectively, I gave him a better place in his life when he got out of prison than when he went in, but I just keep thinking… man, how bad, how fucking *miserable*, did his life have to be to think two years of prison was worth it so he could break free when he was done. And I don't like the answers. Now he made it perfectly clear to me when we started our little thing that he was never—*never*—leaving his wife and kids. And the more I think about that, the more I think it was a kindness to *me*, because it meant I didn't have to think about how to get him out of a shit situation with no way to win. I don't want him ever in that situation again. Ever. Him and me were never gonna be forever, but… God, the least I can do is keep him out of the family business, you know what I mean?"

Carl nodded, taking in every word. "I do," he said after a moment.

"But what?" Chuck asked.

"But nothing," Carl lied. "It's not my business. He's a sweet guy, but I'm probably some super-old boring asshole in a suit to him."

Chuck snorted. "Oh, buddy. Seriously. That's sad."

"What?"

"So sad. Like, 'forty years old without a blowjob' sad."

"I'm thirty-eight. What are you talking about?" Carl asked, genuinely puzzled.

"Oh, I can't even *tell* you how sad that is!" Chuck needled.

"Now you're just saying that to piss me off."

Chuck laughed softly and leaned back, lacing his fingers behind his head. "Sure, Soderbergh. That's what I'm doing. Just, you know. The next time someone asks you if you want to see their birds, remember that anything can be a euphemism for 'penis,' would you?"

Carl scowled at him. "He had a peregrine falcon in a mew behind the hangar and an entire covey of sage grouse in the field beyond. No penises to be seen," he said. "Until now."

Chuck laughed so hard, he snorted and then laughed some more. Carl tried—hard—to ignore him while he finished off his paperwork for the job he, Hunter, and Chuck were traveling to Brussels to perform.

But Chuck wasn't done with him yet.

"Everything in order?" he asked quietly.

Carl closed his laptop and leaned back. Ever since the beginning of July, when Josh Salinger had been diagnosed with leukemia, that tone of voice among any of Josh's family or friends could only indicate one topic of conversation.

"Yeah," he said. He remembered that kid he'd seen so long ago, singing the theme to *SpongeBob* in four different languages. Carl had spent that entire summer following Felix, Julia, Danny, and Josh around Europe. He'd seen Danny teaching Josh how to panhandle outside an Irish pub, and Julia teaching the kid math by counting windows in a castle in Bavaria. He'd been thoroughly crushing on Danny by then, but even his jealousy toward Felix hadn't been able to stifle his appreciation as he watched the boy ride his father's broad shoulders as they traveled the crowded streets of London. That whole summer, he'd tracked the family by tiny hints of crime—not enough evidence to prosecute, ever, but Carl could recognize Danny Mitchell's small, whimsical signatures in the dark. And Carl had witnessed their devotion to the little boy.

After Danny and Felix had fallen out and Carl had stumbled into Danny at a rehab clinic outside of Wales, Carl had felt Danny's devotion to the boy through a year of absence and half a world of distance.

Carl would never forget the morning he'd woken up alone, a small note on the pillow next to him.

As goodbyes went, there were worse things than a note on the pillow.

And Carl had known Danny was never coming back. It had taken eight more years for Danny and Felix to reconcile, but Carl had never been more than a footnote in Danny Mitchell's extensive effort to live without Felix and the makeshift family he'd forged out of a lifetime of loneliness and dreams.

When he'd run into Danny on an investigation back in March and realized his crew had expanded to Josh's friends too, he should have worked his damnedest to put them all in jail.

It never crossed his mind.

Danny and Felix had reconciled, it was true, but Carl had lived those empty years on the company dime, and he'd been... alone. So alone.

That night he'd run into the Salinger crew, Julia had asked him if he wanted to join their little gathering at the mansion when it was done. After some posturing and puffing—thieves liked to brag, he'd learned— he'd been welcomed.

They'd even filled him in on the job.

He'd helped them a few times since as the suit. The security guy. Their inside man. Not once had he done anything he'd regretted as much as half the things he'd done for Serpentus.

He'd be the Salingers' inside man as much as they needed him.

And being asked to do this thing in Brussels had been an honor. And one of the most important things he'd ever done.

"That shit you're working on," Chuck said, interrupting his thoughts. "That's going to make this binding?"

Carl grimaced. "We can't coerce this guy to give up his bodily fluids," he said. "In fact, Julia told us explicitly not to. She said Josh would never forgive her if we did this against his consent. This is just to establish dates, times, etc. Make sure it's all legal and the doctors can proceed as soon as he signs. I'm an expediter, Chuck, nothing more." His job was to put a legal face on things; he had no delusions of anything romantic or exciting, even as he broke the law.

Chuck nodded. "I know. I…." He let out a sigh. "Dammit. That kid—that kid gave me a new start. He gave all of us a new start, you know?"

Carl nodded, understanding. Yes, he'd fallen under the Salinger family spell long ago, but Josh had been part of that charm. Watching Felix, Danny, and Julia pour their hearts into the little boy had defined something for Carl Cox. He'd had a feeling—a vague, unclassified feeling—that the world was not as black and white as simply outwitting bullies, and that doing the right thing wasn't ever going down into the ledgers as a win in the plus column. But seeing the simplicity of adults interacting with a child? That had told him all he'd needed to know.

Do no harm.

He'd started bending the rules that first year, when he hadn't gone after Danny Mitchell, the man who would steal an already stolen statue and return it to a museum, leaving his adopted son's model of Squidward in its place.

Anything Carl could do, no matter how small, how undistinguished, to help restore the heart of the Salinger family, he would do.

He'd leave the flashy stuff to Chuck, to Hunter, and to Hunter's boyfriend, Grace. If all these people needed from him was paperwork and security, well, turned out that was his specialty, and he could supply it.

"I…." Carl had no poetry. He was an insurance investigator. That pretty much indicated his soul was a desert of practicality. "I need very much for Josh to recover," he said finally. "I know you're his friend, Chuck, but I saw him as a kid." Memories hit him hard and out of nowhere. "Danny and I have met a handful of times in the last nine years. Usually he was pulling a job and I was right behind him. But before we'd engage in cat and mouse—and the cat never wins those, believe me—we'd end up having a cup of coffee together, and he'd pull out pictures of Josh. I… I don't know how he got them. Josh at his birthday party or Josh onstage. Josh and Grace taking selfies at Willis Tower. Danny watched that kid grow up. And watching Josh grow up kept Felix alive for him. And I mean, I knew. I knew that if Felix was alive for him, I didn't have a chance. But that kid kept *Danny* alive. I don't have a wife. I don't have kids, and my mother is terrifying, but I had the promise of turning a corner in Prague or Antwerp and running into Danny and having a family. I need that kid to be okay. Do you understand?"

Chuck was looking at him unhappily.

"He's my friend," Chuck conceded. "But Carl, man, so are you. And I say this as your friend—you need a life. One of your own! You are more than just an adjunct performer in Felix and Danny's little play. I love them, don't get me wrong. And I'd die for Josh, and so would the rest of us. But I'm going to have some hope and envision a life in a year or so when Josh is all happy, fine, and the picture of health and off running jobs and getting laid. And when that's going on, I want to be in on the job, but I also want to be spending time with Lucius when I'm not. What do you want to do?"

Carl thought about it. "I'd like to have a cat," he said. "Or a dog. One of my own, in my own apartment. I sort of have an apartment right now, but it's sublet to someone who works in DC, and mostly I just keep my clothes in the spare room. I want to have an apartment and to be home often enough to have a cat."

"What about a boyfriend?" Chuck asked, sounding patient. "You want one of those?"

"Or girlfriend," Carl said, because that was also a possibility.

"Sure. Fine. Or a girlfriend. What about a *friend*, of the naked kind? A life. You want a life, Carl? One of your own and not borrowed from Danny Mitchell?"

"Sure," Carl said.

"I'm convinced," Chuck muttered. "C'mon, man. With some conviction!"

Carl snorted. "I'm not the guy who gets the guy," he said. "Or the girl. And the only conviction you should be worried about is a legal one. My job is to keep us from getting convicted."

Chuck kept staring at him, his broad face disbelieving, his sprawl in the swiveled seat deceptively tense. "I don't believe you," he said after a moment.

"What's so hard to believe?" Carl asked mildly. "I'm not that guy. I'm the suit. I'm an afterthought to the crew. I get it."

Chuck shook his head. "No, man, I really don't think you do." Frustrated, he pulled out his phone and sighed. "Look, I got another hour of shuteye before we fuel up in New York, and then I'm going to make you sit in the cockpit next to me while I show you how to keep this bird in the air all by yourself."

"Are you going to show me how to land?" Carl asked, eyebrow raised. "Because I understand that's the hard part."

"Sure. Sure I'll show you how to land. Whatever. But while I'm showing you all about planes in the air, I want you to think about something."

"What?"

"A bird may not be a penis to Carmichael Carmody, but if Mikey wanted to show you his birds, that's still something special to him. Which means he thinks *you're* special. So maybe find more ambition in your personal life than a cat and an apartment, okay? Maybe have a little faith that you're destined for greater things."

Carl swallowed a lump of frustration. "You can't have it both ways, Chuck. I can't be super exciting and destined for greater things at the same time I'm safe enough for your friend who needs security. Did you ever think of that?"

Chuck scowled at him. "You're making me tired. Take a nap and get ready. One way or the other, you, my friend, are going to fly."


CARL HAD to agree with Good Luck Chuck—flying was a *blast*. He was pretty sure he couldn't have crashed the plane if he'd tried; Chuck's instructions were far too succinct for him to accidentally push down on the controls when he meant up, and Carl was, in fact, a fast learner. He'd noticed that most of Danny's crew were "fast learners," which was code for "bloody geniuses" in most cases. Carl had often pondered that a select few criminals seemed to take up breaking the law as sort of a hobby to stave off boredom.

It was for Chuck, anyway.

"Yup," Chuck said as Carl mastered the stick. "Yup. Doin' great. Plane's sailing smooth. Nothing but blue sky. So blue. Blue as far as the eye can see. Very few clouds."

Carl slowly turned his head and gave Chuck a level look. "Are you bored, Chuck?"

Chuck smiled, all teeth. "I don't mind a little turbulence now and then."

As if in response, the plane bucked, very gently, and Carl let out a low growl. "If the plane gods decide to throw us against a mountain because you felt like fucking around, you're gonna have to find another cellmate in hell."

Chuck cackled. "Hunter'll room with me until Grace can break us out."

"Or the devil *kicks* you out," Carl added. "Now stop tempting fate!"

Chuck's laughter subsided, and Carl settled into the experience.

In a way, it was much like driving when the road was clear and traffic was mild. You had to keep your wits about you—keep to the fight path, keep the altitude consistent, literally stay in the lane you'd told everybody you'd be occupying when you filed your flight plan—but there was all that much-vaunted freedom and exhilaration that people dreamed about, and it turned out to be true.

The terrifying part was, of course, the different gauges, the three-dimensional space, and the margin for error. But once Carl had compartmentalized the margin for error, the rest of it fell into place.

The exhilaration shouldn't have surprised him, but it did. The ocean opened underneath them as they crossed the Atlantic, and while the air currents got frisky, knowing it was underneath them felt sort of vast and awesome, much like the openness of the sky above. Chuck took over for a couple of hours, and Carl watched him, answering his questions about gauges in his area, listening to his discussion of how to react to pretty much every flight contingency known to man.

When land came into sight, Hunter kicked Carl out of the cockpit and took over as copilot. Carl left the connecting door open and settled into the nearest seat so he could listen to their conversation.

"Hey, Carl!" Hunter called. "How come we're staying in Brussels when we're landing closer to Antwerp?"

"Because Danny's still fairly well known in Antwerp and he didn't want anybody's hackles raised. Besides, our hotel's in Brussels for the night, but the thing we're doing is closer to the airstrip. Better getaway potential."

Hunter grunted. "I hate the Sablon."

Carl shrugged. "It's okay," he said. "It's original." The hotel boasted "cocoons"—townhouse-style rooms with an upstairs loft and a downstairs sitting area. Julia had done the booking, telling Carl that she was choosing a highly recommended place that none of the Salingers—including Danny—had ever visited.

"It's just that if you're going to check into a place that charges like a palace, I want it to *look* like a palace."

Chuck shook his head. "I've been there," he said. "It's clean, spacious, modern—"

"Modern." Hunter put his finger on his nose. "Not really a fan."

"You like the antiques." Carl smiled a little. "I've been to your apartment. I wouldn't have guessed."

Like a lot of the crew, Hunter kept an apartment in the city when he wasn't sleeping periodically in the Salinger mansion. His was in a high rise, a loft surrounded by brick and enormous windows. Hunter used it mostly to work out and to think. It had comfortable furniture, a large bed in the corner, a serviceable bathroom, and soundproof walls. It also, Carl surmised, held an arsenal's worth of guns and weapons, all nicely locked up in secret caches. He'd spotted several false walls and ceiling tiles when he'd visited.

"Brussels is an old city full of art and history," Hunter said, making the adjustments to the plane that would start it on its landing path. "I just like to feel the old." Then he clicked on his headset and addressed the tower of the private landing strip they were using and the conversation was over.

THE DRIVE into the city was probably lovely. Carl knew there was a lot of farmland involved, but by the time they pulled their rental up in front of the 9Hotel Sablon, it was deep into the dark of the morning, and even Brussels was sleeping. Whether Hunter liked the décor or not, the hotel *was* one of Brussels' premiere lodgings. As Chuck, who had no problem adapting to rules of the road in any country, pulled the car past the neatly angled, big-windowed exterior, Carl looked wistfully at the lights and thought hopefully of a bed in the suite he knew had been reserved for them.

Those hopes were dashed when a young man with dark-brown curly hair and a neat slim-cut sports jacket over a red turtleneck sweater and slacks waved at them from the ashcan near the front of the hotel. He pulled guiltily at his cigarette one last time and ground the butt out before approaching their car.

Carl noticed him pulling a small hand sanitizer from his pocket as he walked, and he was popping in a breath mint before they even got out of the car.

"Poor boy's been caught," Chuck murmured before hopping out of the Renault Magane. "Should we give him shit about it?"

"Of course," Hunter murmured back. "Carl, got any fun statistics for us?"

Of course he did, but he wasn't going to share.

"Liam!" Chuck said pleasantly, extending his hand for the shake as the valets cleared out the luggage. "So good to see you again."

"Particularly when you're not disassembling an explosive device," Liam replied with a thin smile. He glanced at Carl. "You weren't there that night," he said, puzzled. His accent—British by way of East London— left a lot of consonants out of that sentence. "I didn't realize you were part of the crew until Julia contacted me."

"I was on coms that night," Carl said with a sigh. "Someone had to speak with the police in the museum and make it all look happy fine."

He extended his hand. "Good to see you again, Liam." He and Liam had worked together periodically. Liam was an up-and-comer in the property crimes division of Interpol—art theft was his bread and butter—but it went deeper than that. They'd worked together nine years ago, and Liam had been the one to gently poke Carl about the four-scotch-a-night habit that had snuck up on him when he hadn't been looking. Carl had gone to the rehab clinic Liam had recommended outside of Wales, unaware that Liam had actually driven Danny to the same place two weeks prior. The affair with Danny had ended, but the friendship with Liam remained.

Liam returned the shake. "The sentiment's mutual," he said before moving on to shake Hunter's hand. "I took the liberty of setting up a late supper in your suite. If we can have a brief discussion before you turn in, I'll let you sleep."

"Nice of you," Hunter said. "I could eat."

"Lord, me too," Chuck agreed, and Carl nodded in agreement. It was a kind gesture—finding food at the end of a late-night flight was always a pain in the ass.

The suite was a townhouse-style room, done mostly in white with bursts of color in the bedding and in the comfortable lounge-area furniture. The two bedrooms were upstairs, and Chuck grabbed Carl's suitcase along with his own.

"Carl, you and me can bunk together. I don't trust Hunter not to wake up, realize you're not Grace, and knife you."

"Comforting," Carl muttered. He glanced at Liam in time to see him smirking. "Does that mean Liam and Hunter are bunking together?"

"No thanks. I'll take the couch!" Liam said, holding his hands up in mock fear.

"Smart man," Hunter growled, coming down from his security check of the rooms.

When Chuck returned from his own check, he held a little device in his palm that wasn't doing anything exciting—but that, apparently, was the purpose. "Well, the bug tracker says there's nothing fun up here," he said. "So that's good to know."

"Security's pretty tight internally." Hunter scowled. "I'm not a fan of the giant windows, but at least they're tinted from the outside."

"It would be really obvious to stage a hit through the windows," Carl said. "The street's so narrow, a sniper couldn't come in at any sort of angle. Besides, who would know we're here? And why would they want to kill us? For once, we're not really doing anything wrong."

"You're *never* doing anything wrong," Chuck said.

"I don't know about that," Carl protested. "The truth seems to get awfully bendy when we're around each other."

Young Liam Craig grinned. "'E's right, Chuck. You bend the truth like a pretzel, pretty soon yer goin' when ye ought'er be comin'!"

Carl blinked at him. "I could swear that was English," he said blankly, and Liam smacked his own forehead with the flat of his hand.

"Forgive me," he said, pulling his accent under control. "I'm tired and a little punchy, and I've taken two days leave for this and I'm worried it might get back to my commander."

"All you need to do is stage the introduction," Carl said, trying to put him at ease.

Liam shook his head. "No, no," he said. "I'm afraid it's a little trickier than that."

Chuck and Hunter drew closer, and Liam gestured to the long rectangular family-style table in the kitchenette part of the suite. It was covered with plates of meat, cheese, crackers, olives, and fruit, in addition to a bucket of chilled bottles of beer, juice, and water.

"Give us a minute to eat," Chuck said, eyeballing the feast with relish. "And I'm sure we'll think tricky is a walk in the park."


NOT QUITE.

Carl hadn't been wrong—the mission was still to talk to a man about a voluntary medical procedure. But there were a couple of wrinkles.

The first was that the man was rather famous for a number of enterprises that were less than legal. As with any such gentleman of means and reputation in these areas, his home came complete with deadly security measures and a couple of high-profile mercenaries.

The second was that his estate sat surrounded by a vast acreage of gardens and horse pasture, with very few trees and almost no covert means of approach.

And the third wrinkle was that this estate, with all the unwanted visibility, was still the easiest way to approach him. His city apartments were like bank vaults. It would take a year to plan for the job that would crack those, and they didn't have a year.

They had, at most, a couple of months. Josh Salinger's health wasn't getting any better. If his body kept resisting chemo, very soon he'd be too frail to bounce back.

It had to be done the next day while people were coming and going to move their target to his winter home in Corfu.

"Has he hired any moving vans?" Hunter asked, all tactical.

"Yes," Liam said. "I'd thought of that. I've even got a line on some onesies for us if it comes down to it. But he's not moving the whole bloody place—just his kids' clothes and such for himself."

"He's married?" Carl asked, hating the idea of breaking in on a family.

"Divorced," Liam said, nodding like he understood the question. "The kids come and visit him when he's in Corfu, and he brings some of their favorite items by request. One small moving van—that's all they need. Four of us would be overkill, and most assuredly we all wouldn't be able to sneak past his guards." Four had been the agreed-upon number: Carl to present their target with the proposition and the other three to make sure nobody *shot* Carl while he was just trying to ask a hard-to-reach man a simple question.

They didn't want to hurt anybody, they didn't want to get hurt, and they didn't want to involve the authorities when neither party wanted scrutiny.

And suddenly something exceedingly simple was irritatingly difficult.

Carl grunted and laced his fingers behind his head, relieved to see that Hunter and Chuck were also looking grim. Short of just driving up and asking to speak to the man—which, given who he was, might not generate the results they were hoping for—this job was proving more difficult than they'd planned.

"Give us good news," Carl begged simply. "Liam, we're not even trying to do anything illegal here."

"I do have one thing to offer," Liam said, "short of going to my commander and getting a court order to burst in and talk to this man, which would not incline him to listen, I must tell you that."

"I'd shoot you on sight," Hunter grumbled. "No, we need to be better than that. What's your one thing."

Liam gave a slight grin. "I've got the plans of the house. Here."

With that, he unrolled a fairly impressive map of the estate, and Carl had to grimace. Liam had color coded the places that would be accessible during the move and the places where the master of the house would likely be located, isolated from all of the moving activity.

It really was like trying to break into a wardrobe from a freeway, wasn't it?

But Carl's expertise—and all the years he'd spent in his chosen, if hated, profession—was starting to percolate through his tired brain.

"Liam?" he asked, his voice coming from under layers of exhaustion and hope. "Do we know who insures his valuables or takes care of his estate while he's gone?"

Liam cocked his head, eyes widening. "We do not," he said. "But give me an hour after the crotch of dawn and I could tell you."

Carl nodded, hiding a yawn behind his hand. "Give us some rack time," he all but begged. "You're welcome to take the couch. I've got an idea, but I need sleep to brain words. Can we wake up early and try this again?"

Chuck hid a yawn against his shoulder. "Carl, buddy, I knew there was a reason we brought you along."


FIVE HOURS later, they were all dressed nattily in Italian-cut suits—even Hunter, whose suit jacket was his trademark Kevlar-lined leather. Packed into the Renault, a plan solidly under their belts, Carl and Chuck sat in the back making last minute contacts with their crew back in Chicago.

"I'm going in as a real estate agent who mistakenly thinks the place is for sale," Carl told Julia. He and Chuck had squeezed their bodies back-to-back and were wearing earbuds so Chuck could hold court with Molly, their young drama student who was going to be Chuck's tacky millionaire bride over the phone. Liam was the banker with the false papers of sale, which Carl had printed up that morning, and Hunter was their driver who was going to need a glass of water after Carl, Chuck, and Liam brazened their way through the front door.

The idea was on the fly and sketchy as hell, but hopefully Liam's plans, leading to the enclosed study where their target would be retreating that day, would help.

Julia nodded over the screen and daintily bit her lip. An absolutely stunning woman, with pale blond hair, pale blue eyes, and the exquisite features of Grace Kelly in her heyday, she had cut her con-man teeth on staying away from her father's heavy hand and cruel disposition. Carl had heard enough stories—many of them whispered—about Hiram Dormer's monstrousness toward women and children. Julia had ever looked the pampered princess, but she'd been trapped in her tower by a fierce dragon, and her unlikely saviors had been Felix Salinger and Danny Mitchell.

She'd joined hands with them and marched into the game, conning her father, protecting her then-unborn child, and forging a family with Felix and Danny. Once, Carl had resented her because her marriage to Felix had caused Danny so much heartache. But Danny hadn't let him feel that way, pointing out again and again that her resilience and compassion had survived what would have killed many lesser souls.

She'd been the one to invite Carl back to the mansion in Glencoe the night he had stumbled into one of the crew's first jobs together, and Carl had found himself beguiled and impressed.

"Good," she said now in response to Carl's summation. "I'm going to keep your room in reserve. That way if this goes well, you don't have to jump right back on the plane. We were going to have you fly to Munich. I'll keep that possibility open, but I like this idea of going in covert and then the big reveal." She flashed a smile at Carl that lacked its usual oomph, and Carl's stomach knotted.

"How's he doing?" he asked quietly.

"He'll be spending this treatment round at the hospital," Julia responded quietly. "The drive there and back is a little hard on him. We set up a cot there—he's never alone."

"Tell Grace that Hunter was an absolute asshole this morning and that he's missed."

Her smile picked up at the corners. "I will, thank you. It will make Dylan happy to know that."

It was, in actuality, a lie. Hunter may have communicated in grunts and monosyllables, but Carl had met—and occasionally awakened with—much surlier men. But Grace had been devastated by Josh's illness and torn when he realized that coming with them on this venture would mean he'd have to leave Josh's side. In the end, leaving Josh was something he simply couldn't do. Knowing that Hunter missed him would make him feel better, and Carl wasn't above the occasional lie to make that happen.

"I'll tell the others about the hotel—"

"And tell Liam to get on the plane if things get hot. We'll make a plan to drop him off somewhere should we need to."

"I will." Carl dropped his voice. "The young man was smoking. Is that something we're allowed to nag him about?"

Julia's eyebrows arched. "Oh. Oh my, yes. But after the job."

"Of course," Carl said, trying desperately to pinch his smile off at the corners of his mouth. "Understood."

"Good. Wish everybody luck for me," she said. "And be careful. Leon de Rossi isn't a monster, but he's no one to fuck with. I'm reasonably certain somebody has been censoring our letters and emails from him." Her face softened. "Matteo, his brother, lived in awe of Leon. But never fear. I got a feeling of protectiveness from Matteo's stories, not oppression. Be as absolutely honest as you can."

Carl nodded. He'd faced down the world's worst insurance scammers and the world's most cold-blooded insurance administrators. He had a fairly well-honed bullshit detector, and he'd become adept at diffusing tense situations. His international law degree may have been why he'd been tapped for this job, but those other skills were definitely a plus.

At that moment, Hunter turned off the main road onto a long straight drive. The mansion—literally on a slight hill—was plainly in sight, albeit probably a mile away at the least.

It was time to get his game face on.

"Julia, we're almost there. Gotta sign off."

"Tell Hunter to keep me on standby!" she told him, and Carl nodded before hitting End Call.

Next to him, Chuck had already removed his earbuds and relaxed into his patter with Molly Christopher, a budding actress, fierce tae kwon do fighter, and stunning con woman.

She was also one of Josh's oldest friends from high school, who along with her brother, Stirling, had moved into the Salinger mansion in spite of being in their early twenties. They'd been foster siblings adopted by friends of Felix and Julia's when they were fairly young, but they'd lost their adopted parents less than two years ago. Brilliant and devoted to each other, they also had the deep-rooted sense of amorality that helped all good con men in their jobs.

And Carl got the feeling that being a part of the Salinger crew not only gave them a community but also a chance to get back at the forces of life that had shit on them so often in so many small ways.

"Okay, sweetness," Molly was saying, her voice relaxing into a Texas drawl much like Chuck's. "You gotta show mama what we're trying to buy here so I know how much we're gonna spend." Her drawl disappeared. "Stirling, are you getting this? We need to know how much to spend."

Her brother—taciturn, quiet almost to the point of being antisocial—responded briefly.

"I've got the price tables up, Molly, and a list of people who've made offers on the property in the last five years. I'm not stupid."

"I know it," she said. "Sorry. This is just—"

"Don't worry about me," Stirling told her. "Just be fabulous and overbearing through the phone screen. You're good at it."

"I hope she is," Liam said from the front. "Because we're here."

"Whoo-ee," Molly said, her drawl firmly in place. "That is some special summer cottage, Charlie-bear. You and me are gonna have to shop to fill that thing with any *decent* furniture."

Carl and Chuck exchanged dry glances.

That "summer cottage" was a castle—or more likely a chateau, given that the words in Flemish and English were often interchanged.

It sat flanked by shade trees, part of about an acre's copse that stood out from the property of horse pastureland. They'd spotted the barns and outbuildings soon after they'd turned off from the main highway and had even seen a couple of Belgium's trademark draft horses, sturdy and majestic, trotting amicably along the fence line.

The insurance investigator in Carl was wondering who cared for the beasts when Leon de Rossi was away, but the kid who'd liked to look at animals in books thought they were just marvelous, glossy and royal, and left it at that.

But none of the nicely manicured greenery and stunning equine muscle prepared them for Leon de Rossi's "summer cottage." Tall and angular, a rectangle with three stories and an attic, judging by the graded windows near the top, the structure also sported three turrets and a gabled roof that avoided coming to a point by a bevel. It was built of stone, with a smaller outbuilding—recently adjoined—that was probably once used to shelter farm animals and horses but, according to the floor plans they'd studied that morning, housed an indoor pool. As they'd driven in, past the modern barn, they'd also passed an even more modern structure, obviously used for cars, that appeared to have an apartment on the top floor. Carl even saw someone—probably the chauffeur—polishing a luxury SUV with tinted windows that were probably bulletproof.

Against his will, Carl's thoughts wandered to Michael, and he wished Michael had been in on this job, for no other reason than Carl liked his company.

And the way he smiled.

And even the way he smelled, like clean laundry and motor oil and the wind outdoors.

With a yank, Carl hauled his drifting attention back to the matter at hand.

The chauffeur wasn't the only one out. True to Liam's prediction, a small moving van sat near the front entrance, and the great arching doors that stretched two-and-a-half times a man's height were propped open while men in cheap tweed suits moved items out of the chateau.

Unconsciously, Carl straightened his shoulders—and his necktie—before Hunter even started to slow the Renault. It was game time.

"Oh, darlin'," Chuck said into the phone. "Wait until you see what your Good Luck Chuckie's gonna bring home for you!"

Hunter pulled the car to a halt a good twenty feet behind the moving van and was out the driver's door almost before he killed the engine and opened the rear passenger door for Chuck.

Carl and Liam alighted simultaneously, and as Chuck kept up his patter with Molly, Carl started haranguing Liam as though they'd been having this conversation during the drive.

"So here we are, papers ready to be signed, our buyer and his bride *really* excited to take ownership, and does the seller know we're here?"

"Sir," Liam said, obsequiousness and cockney dripping from every syllable. "I promise you I had this bloke's secretary on the line and she *told* me he'd be here."

"We are ready to take ownership *tomorrow* and you're giving me some horseshit—" Carl stepped carefully around a pile of same (the animals were obviously allowed close to the house). "—about a *secretary*!"

Behind him, Chuck and Molly were making sweet, cooing baby noises at each other, and if Carl hadn't caught Hunter's eyes bugging as he tried to hold back his disgust, he might have broken his own character.

"Look, it's not even a deal," Liam defended. "Watch. Hey there, mate. You there!" Imperiously he summoned the biggest mob muscle to them, a man with a shaved head, no neck, and shoulders that gave the horses' hindquarters a run for their money.

The man demanded the Italian equivalent of "Who the fuck are you?"

"*Scusi*," Carl said smoothly and took over the conversation, asking for the master of the house. While Carl engaged No-neck, Chuck and Hunter managed to make it over the threshold, Chuck talking the whole time about how, yes, they could replace the baroque woodwork, nobody would miss it, and most definitely Hollywood Regency would be the way to go on the decorating scheme.

No-neck was in the process of telling him no—no, nobody could see the master of the house—when Chuck made a show of accidentally knocking a lamp over. Hunter caught it before it hit the ground, much to Carl's relief because it didn't look cheap, and Carl held up a distracted finger.

"Yes, yes, of course he's busy. He's up to his eyeballs in paperwork." Carl laughed, waving his file of copied papers that he'd spent the morning filling out by hand. Behind the sheaf of fake papers sat a sheaf of the real documents he needed de Rossi to sign, but he wasn't telling anybody that until they got their face-to-face. "Here, you're obviously busy. Let me go find him…. Charles, my friend, no, put that down!"

Not satisfied with almost destroying a priceless Louis XVI antique vase, Chuck was now holding it up for Molly to assess while Hunter manned the camera.

Their no-neck friend started calling urgently to the other mob muscle—Carl counted four in all, although Hunter might have marked more on the inside—but Carl's ruse had worked. Hunter and Chuck were inside, and Carl and Liam were striding over the threshold, loudly engaged in their previous dispute as to whether or not Liam had contacted the buyer and where he could possibly be in the house.

They knew where he was. Up the stairways on either side of the grand foyer, across the walkway, and around the back to the bedroom study that overlooked the forested part of the grounds.

There were two different ways to get there. Hunter and Chuck took the more ostentatious route, Chuck and Molly talking loudly as they went, Molly complaining about the stunning staircases and how she could *not* deal with walking up and down them in heels and how they'd have to be converted to ramps immediately, her voice tinny over the phone.

Liam and Carl took the quieter way, down the hallway on the ground floor, past the kitchen, and up the steep and narrow servants' stairs, their pretend dispute over Liam's incompetence going silent the minute they disappeared into the shadows of the hall.

Carl had the feeling they needn't have worried about making noise; everything about the servants' passage, from the antique runner on the wooden stairs to the tapestries on the stone walls, was meant to deaden sound, making the servants as invisible as possible.

"There's not even a place to dodge into for a quick fuck," Liam muttered, and Carl tried not to laugh.

"I'm sure there's a passage somewhere," he said softly. "In the library, behind a faux shelf, there's probably a small bowl of goose grease and some linen rags to wipe down with."

Liam grunted. "Have you ever tried to get goose grease out of trousers? I have. It's unpleasant."

Carl kept back a snicker. "And now I know more about your personal life than I ever wanted to."

Liam's blue eyes widened comically, and he clapped his hand over his mouth. "No!" he protested. "No, that's *not* what I was talking about!"

Carl kept laughing even as they broke past the winding staircase and into the grand bedroom, which had already been covered for the season.

"Nice bed," Liam said on a whistle. "Could do some damage in there, you think?"

Carl's cheeks pinkened as he did exactly that, picturing himself as the suave and seductive lord of the manner and Michael as the impressionable young servant.

*That fantasy alone should tell you what's wrong with this situation!* he told himself and quickly pulled his attention to the bedroom study. He could see partially inside because the door was open to the bedroom, probably to let some air flow through. The bedroom itself was not even dominated a little by a large four-poster bed and matching dresser, and Carl could *still* feel brisk September air flowing through the upper story.

Liam took a bold step toward the open doorway, but Carl, remembering Julia's words about how she didn't think Leon di Rossi was getting any of their communications, held him back and jerked sharply with his chin.

"And look here, darlin'," Chuck said loudly from the hallway. "It's like an office space attached to the bedroom. We got paneled walls, we got a rolltop desk, we got a…. Hello there, who's this?"

"This is Mr. di Rossi's study!" came a shrill, indignant male voice. "May I ask who in the blazes are you?"

"Dietrich, take it easy." This voice was urbane and deep. They heard footsteps and the mellow, pleasantly accented English saying, "Sir, I don't know how you got so far into my house but—"

And then a scuffle, as the outside guards obviously caught up with Chuck and Hunter.

"That's our cue," Carl murmured to Liam, and together they scurried in through the ignored bedroom door and shut it quietly behind them.

In the hallway, they heard a series of thuds, a grunt, Chuck hollering "Whoo-ee!", and a muffled scream, and Carl turned around in time to see a man he recognized as Leon di Rossi go to his desk for what was probably a very lethal munition.

"Please don't," Carl said softly. "We're not armed, and there's no reason for you to be. I swear, we only want to talk."

Next to him, he heard Liam Craig's sharply indrawn breath and remembered that Liam probably *was* armed, but he ignored that for now.

He was too busy catching Leon di Rossi's attention.

Mr. di Rossi was a wide-chested man of about forty-five, with a neatly cut goatee streaked with silver, and thick black hair, expensively cut, that had its own share of streaks. He was currently in his shirtsleeves, but everything about him—from the silk shirt to the lambswool trousers, belted at the waist with something black and expensive, to the shiny black men's loafers that cost more than Carl's apartment—screamed money.

"And who are you?" he asked.

"We represent the interests of Julia and Felix Salinger," Carl said. In the hallway doorframe, Chuck and Hunter stood, shoulder to shoulder, facing outward. They didn't appear to be threatening, but they were making it very, very clear that nobody was going to get past them.

"They've been sending you everything from email to registered letters for the past month. Have you gotten them?"

The way di Rossi frowned told Carl that he hadn't. Carl glared at the man standing at di Rossi's shoulder. A tall stoop-shouldered fellow with a thin nose and thinner hair, the man screamed middle management and suck-up from every pore in his body.

And he looked quickly away from Carl's angry stare.

"I can see that you didn't," Carl said flatly. "If you would call your men off and allow us to talk, I promise that in half an hour, we will either be an unpleasant memory or ambassadors to a member of your family you have not met yet."

Di Rossi's expression, which had been wary but accepting, turned to disgust. "If this is another baseless paternity suit—"

"No," Carl, Chuck, Hunter, and Liam all said quietly at the same time. "This isn't about *your* child," Carl continued. "And this isn't about money or privilege or any of those things you're thinking about. This is about your brother."

And in seconds, di Rossi's broad, darkly tanned, handsome face went from masterful and wary to vulnerable and sad.

"What about my brother?" he asked faintly.

"Sir," the man at his side, Dietrich, said angrily, "these men are nothing but con men and grifters, after some sort of scam—"

"I said, what about my brother?" di Rossi demanded, his voice taking on the timbre of a man so emotionally invested, one wrong word could spark a dangerous conflagration.

It was the doorway they'd been waiting for.

"Sir," Carl said softly, "if you'll tell your men to back off for a moment, I will tell you. This is a personal story, for both you and for us, and I know you don't want it spread beyond these four walls."

Di Rossi looked at his indignant aide, and then at Chuck and Hunter, who hadn't moved.

Then he looked back at Carl, who, Carl knew, had "deadly boring and yet honest insurance agent" written all over him.

Surprisingly enough, his expression softened when he looked at Carl.

"You do not look that dangerous," he said, shaking his head.

"Me?" Carl asked. "I'm an insurance investigator. My only danger is boring someone to death. But I don't think that's what's going to happen today."

DIETRICH GOT sent for coffee, which all of them needed. Chuck put down the telephone, although whether he had turned it off and ended the call with Molly remained to be seen. Carl hoped he'd at least had the sense to put her on mute.

After the muscle, including their disgruntled no-neck friend, were sent back to resume moving, the four of them made themselves comfy in the study. Di Rossi offered Carl one of two chairs across from the desk, and he resumed his position by the rolltop, swiveling so they could face each other.

The effect made Carl feel a little like an Italian don, about to make an offer di Rossi couldn't refuse, and he hoped heartily that was the case.

"So," di Rossi said softly. "My brother."

Carl nodded. "Let me tell you a story about an American girl," he said. "One who was vacationing with her monstrous father in Rome when she was not yet twenty. In an effort to attract businessmen—and their sons—the girl was allowed to dance in the marketplace and attend the functions for young tourists. It was there she met a young man."

"Whose father was also monstrous," di Rossi said, his eyes sad.

Julia had implied as much by saying Leon had been a protector.

"So she understood," Carl told him softly. "After a week, the young man was called away to marry—he was very frank—and she was left alone in a villa with a man who would beat her to death if he ever discovered the truth."

Di Rossi closed his eyes. "*Bastardo.*"

"Si. She got lucky, though," Carl said, mouth twisting into a smile, "because she was supposed to be the target of a con man—two of them, in fact. Lovers who wished to take from her father in retaliation for his abuse of the young women in his employ in the area. Their one rule was to not hurt the young woman, but when they realized her predicament, that changed to helping her instead."

Surprisingly enough di Rossi smiled, a broad, relieved grin that almost made the sun a little shinier and the world a little purer. Given that he was said to have taken over his father's "trading" business and was expanding it, that smile was quite a shock.

"It is like a fairy tale," he said, clearly charmed. "Is it true?"

Everybody chuckled. "Oh yes," Liam said from behind Carl. "It's true. The young man who'd posed as a visitor eloped with the young woman, and the two of them were visited by the other young man in short order. For the next ten years, the three of them pulled off the biggest grift of all. Two of them pretended to the world to be married. They raised the boy, they worked hard in the father's business, and they were a perfect family."

"But it was the two men who were in love," di Rossi said. His brow furrowed. "That would, I think, be very hard on the one who was hidden."

"It was," Carl said sadly, remembering the broken version of Danny he'd encountered in the rehab clinic. The funny, charming young man who had been vacationing with his family when Carl had first encountered the Salingers had almost—almost—been drowned in scotch and bitterness.

Watching that man reemerge stronger and more magnetic than ever had been a joy, even if they were destined never to connect again.

"You said ten years," di Rossi said softly. "My brother was in Rome before his wedding twenty years ago. I take it they are no longer together?" di Rossi asked softly.

"They have recently reunited," Carl told him. "But yes, they lost a lot of years to the pain of keeping that secret. And yet not once was the boy neglected. The lover who left visited him frequently—under the radar of course. You see, the four of them were still a family. A little fractured, a little imperfect, but that boy grew up knowing he was loved."

Hunter spoke up, surprising him. "He grew up so loved he reached out to other people to pull them into the circle. He grew up so loved he tries to look into people's hearts to see what they're made of. Nobody is irredeemable."

"He sounds like the best of men," di Rossi said, his eyes shiny. "Why would he need his father—or me—after all this time?"

They all swallowed, and Carl wondered which one of them could say it.

"He's dying."

It was Hunter, and the word looked like it cost him.

"Oh no," di Rossi murmured.

"Lymphoblastic leukemia," Carl said. "And while they're treating it aggressively with chemotherapy, what would really, really help would be—"

"A bone marrow transplant." Di Rossi nodded. "Of course. I'll make plans immediately. Where are you based? I assume America from your accents?"

Carl sucked in a breath, so relieved he hadn't been aware he'd been holding it. "Chicago," he said. "We can get you accommodations in the city, or if you like, you can stay in the mansion. Or we'll buy you a mansion. Or—" Liam's steadying hand on his shoulder let him know any cool he had ever possessed had simply evaporated.

"I will be traveling with the children," di Rossi said, a hint of a smile on his face. "I apologize. I can be there within a week."

Carl nodded and reached to the briefcase he'd left resting at his hip. "I have papers here for you to sign. I'm sure you have your own solicitor to look through them. They agree we will pay for everything— transportation, accommodation, even childcare if you should need it. There's an option for a stipend. It's generous, and the money would be in the bank before the end of the week—"

"I'll take none of these things!" di Rossi protested, as though slapped. "I know what I am, Mr....?"

"So, er, Cox. Carl Cox." His face flushed, and he resisted the temptation to glare at Hunter and Chuck. "My, uhm, friends call me Soderbergh."

Di Rossi's thunderous expression eased up. "I understand the need for a nom de plume," he said. "Mr. Cox, I should very much like to meet this young man, Matteo's son. That is all I ask for. My brother was...." He bit his lip. "He was too dear for the world he was born into." He blew out a shaky breath. "Our father was a monster as well, and Matteo was thrust into a loveless marriage with a woman who did not make his life easy. He was killed five years ago, as I'm sure you know."

Carl nodded. Julia had known, in fact. She, Felix, and Danny had kept tabs on Josh's father for many reasons, including contacting him should Josh ever ask.

"My father was killed the year before that, and Matteo was allowed to divorce his wife, and that year—that year was the happiest I have ever seen him. I have done the best to turn my father's business into something approaching legitimacy since then, but I will always regret my brother not having more time to be the man he should have been. I would give everything—my homes, my business, anything but my children—to see my brother's child and do what I can to bring him to health."

Carl could hear everybody's breath coming shakily. In his pocket, his phone buzzed, and he startled before checking it. "Oh," he said, thinking that Chuck must have left Molly on the line in his pocket, muted but still able to hear. "Uhm, Mr. di Rossi, this is Ms. Dormer-Salinger. Would you like to speak to her?"

Again, that sunshine smile.

Carl handed over the phone and tried to breathe through the feeling that everything just might be all right.

# The Life of Pawns

MICHAEL TRIED not to be too excited that Carl and the others were returning. They'd only been gone for a few days.

It was stupid, really, to feel a connection with a guy he'd seen a couple of times, maybe, in a social situation, and who had come behind the hangar to look at birds with him. But then, all Michael had needed from Chuck had been a well-timed wink and a sparkle from his green eyes before he'd known he could at least get some touch.

What he felt from Carl went way beyond touch.

Chuck was a good guy, but he'd been comfortable robbing banks long before he met Michael. Michael had only wanted what everyone else did. Security. Someone to care for him when he went home. Somebody he could talk to. It was great that Good Luck Chuck had a billionaire to charm and a crew that would keep him from being bored at the same time they kept him out of trouble. Chuck and Michael had never spent any time talking anyway.

Carl had listened to him go on and on about birds and thought they were cool, and the only person Michael had ever had that with had been his ex-wife, which is why he'd hung in there for so long.

And he just really, really wanted to see the man again. He had green eyes too—not sparkling like Chuck's, but flat and inward looking.

Michael would really love it if those eyes would look at *him*.

So when he got word from the tower that the plane would be taxiing in an hour after he was supposedly off the clock, he volunteered to hang back and see if anybody needed a ride.

He sort of knew they didn't, really. He knew Hunter had driven his own vehicle, and Carl and Chuck had arrived together, but well….

As if to confirm his hopes, he heard the brisk stride of hard leather soles echoing in the hangar when he knew for a fact the jet had not yet returned.

He pushed himself out from under the Roadster he'd been repairing, the wheels of the dolly so well oiled and balanced they didn't even squeak.

"Can I help you?" he asked, smiling like someone who *wanted* to help.

The man who'd entered was slick and moneyed, wearing a three-thousand-dollar suit and shoes that looked more expensive than Michael's first car. He was slender and conventionally handsome, with hair cut just so over his brow and kind hazel eyes.

"Don't mind me. I'm only here to see if they're back yet. I, uhm, was hoping I could spirit Charles away for dinner in the city tonight, since we're both in the area at the same time."

"Mr. Broadstone! It's so good to see you. No, they're not back yet. I'm sorry. Do you, uhm, want to wait here? I've got a little apartment and everything." Even if he didn't recognize Lucius Broadstone from seeing him on the news and in person two months ago, Michael would have remembered him from those dinners at the Salingers'. He'd often thought that if anybody could put a rein on Good Luck Chuck, it would be this kind, elegant man. There was something so intense about the way he carried himself—he wasn't coarse or rough like the men Michael had grown up with, but he sure could let someone know what he thought, sometimes with just the arch of an eyebrow.

"A place to sit would be so very appreciated!"

He didn't look around like he expected it to be covered with grease or anything. Now that was class.

"Here, let me show you the way. I got a mini fridge and food and snacks, if you want them. You can pull out your briefcase there and get some work done while you wait."

Lucius grinned tiredly at him. "Honestly, Carmichael, I'd really rather play the stupid little game on my phone, but don't tell anybody."

Michael grinned, not the least because Lucius was one of the few people who'd refused to shorten his name to Car-Car. "You can call me plain Michael," he said. "I figured if I'm starting a new life, I'll start with a new name."

"Michael's a very good one," Lucius said. "Lead on!"

Michael got him settled with a soda and some apple wedges and was about to go back into the hangar to work when Lucius stopped him.

"Do you mind keeping me company?" he asked. "I could use some conversation."

"Sure!" Uhm, that was a first. "Do you mind if I go clean up my workstation? I need to put my tools away. I'll be back in ten."

"Go right ahead. I'm sorry for imposing."

"No, that's fine. I just didn't expect… I mean, nobody ever really asked me for conversation before. It's sort of exciting. I'll be right back."

He made sure the tools were arranged against the workbench and the dolly was hanging from its pegs against the back wall, and then he spent about five minutes at the sink, soaping his hands. When he was done, he used some of the moisturizer that sort of appeared in the hangar by magic, along with toilet paper and air freshener in the bathroom.

When he returned, Lucius looked up from his phone almost guiltily, and Michael smiled.

"I won't get you into trouble, I promise."

"That's kind of you." Lucius pocketed the phone and gestured to Michael's little "apartment" of cubicle walls, furniture, and area rugs. "This is really charming, but I thought you were staying at Danny's old apartment."

Michael shrugged. "I am, some nights. It's just there's a lot of driving back and forth, and I like to drive, mostly, but I don't even have a cat at the apartment. Some nights, it's nice to stay here."

Lucius nodded thoughtfully. "I think Charles would like it if you stayed," he said. "Maybe you should think about getting a cat."

Michael bit his lip. "It's okay, then? Me being here in Chicago? I know Chuck says it's okay, but I also know I showed up here right after you guys got together, and that's sort of… you know. Weird."

"People have pasts," Lucius said with a shrug. "To me, it means something that Charles wants to make sure someone from his past is happy. He likes to pretend that he doesn't really care what's in his rearview, but I think you and I both know he likes to leave things better than he found them."

Michael nodded. "Can't argue with you there. He certainly left *me* in a better position."

"Indeed. So it would ease his mind now to know you're settled. You're happy. And he does like getting the chance to talk to you."

Michael's cheeks heated. "I… I didn't really have folks I could talk to at home. My ex-wife, but I didn't tell her everything either. It wasn't a real forgiving place. Not for people like me—uhm, us—anyway."

Lucius nodded slowly. "I imagine not," he said, voice soft. "I hope the dating scene is a little easier for you here." He brightened. "You do have people your own age who can show you where the good places to go are. I know when I was in college, a good scene was easy to find."

Michael couldn't help it. He tilted his head sideways, the way he did when his youngest child told him that eagles would fly through the sky, bring water to the masses, and save all the puppy dogs.

"Sir," he said, his voice full of pity, "I know you're trying to help, but I have the feeling that my twenties and their twenties are two very different decades."

Lucius's cheeks pinkened. "I would imagine so. Sorry."

He bit his lip then, and Michael thought, *Oh crap. Now I've gone and killed the conversation.* But Lucius apparently didn't stay cowed for long.

"You don't have to be an outsider here, you know," he said after a moment. "I know it might seem like it, but you might find you have more in common with the Salingers and their friends than you think."

Michael opened his mouth to deny it, but Lucius kept going.

"People don't always wear their pain on their sleeve, Michael. I know… I know you feel like you might still be wearing that orange jumpsuit from Texas, and everybody can see what your life has been like, but honestly, if Chuck hadn't had to confess his past to me—and if you hadn't been part of that past—I would have seen nothing but a rather nice man who is always polite and likes to work on cars."

Michael nodded, struck by that. "But I'm different. I've got three kids," he said. "And I'm not thirty."

"True." Lucius nodded. "But have you asked yourself why Julia Salinger looks so young? Her son isn't yet twenty-one, if I understand it."

Michael gaped. "But she can't be more than—"

"Forty," Lucius said, his eyes twinkling. "And barely so. So yes, Julia knows what it's like to be a young parent. As do Felix and Danny."

"I'd never thought about that before," Michael said quietly. "But about that orange onesie—"

Lucius blew out a breath. "You got that running a job with Chuck, right?"

Michael nodded.

"Chuck hangs out with the Salingers for a reason, Michael. The things they do for me aren't in the strictest sense legal. They help people, yes. But in my case, I'm hiding the vulnerable from the powerful. That can get you imprisoned very easily. You know that, right? It's not my job to tell secrets, but you may want to hold back judgment and loosen up your reserve. It seems to me that you're in a place right now in which people would understand you way more than you imagine."

Michael realized he was gaping and closed his mouth.

"Didn't think about that, did you?" Lucius asked smugly, and Michal recognized Lucius was jerking Michael's chain.

"You're very smart," he replied, his eyes playfully narrowed.

Lucius laughed, and Michael smiled back. Chuck's boyfriend was apparently not a bad guy.

"Hey," he said impulsively. "Wanna see my birds?"


A HALF hour later, he was telling Lucius about falcons and the Tom Cade method of inviting them back into the wild and how he'd been reading up on what it took to keep one when they saw the Salinger jet come in low for a landing.

"They're coming in hot," Michael said, a little bit of alarm in his voice.

"They're… oh, they're pulling up." Lucius, too, sounded concerned as the wheels barely brushed the tarmac before the plane rose once more into the air. "Are they circling around to try it again?"

This time the jet came in at a better angle and a more sedate pace. But when the wheels made contact with the tarmac, it bounced much higher than normal, and it came down hard enough to make Michael's teeth click together, and he wasn't even in the plane. But finally it was down and taxiing like a slowing snake winding across the tarmac.

"That was rough," Michael said. "But… oh, wait. They're sort of wandering around the airstrip."

"That was most odd." Lucius still sounded alarmed. "I've flown with both Hunter *and* Chuck, and they're usually smooth as silk."

"I'm just glad they're back," Michael said, practically wiggling in excitement as the roar of the engine dissipated and the jet circled to taxi back to the hangar.

Lucius, who had seemed interested and had been asking questions the whole time, particularly about the sage grouse and their endangered status, gave him a dry look.

"Anyone in particular you're excited about?"

"Oh, not Chuck," Michael reassured. "No, you're too nice a guy. I wouldn't crush on your fella."

Lucius kept his head cocked, his eyes sideways on Michael's as the plane eventually slowed its wandering and started a purposeful coast toward their hangar.

"And not Hunter," Michael added. "I don't know him well, but, uhm, his boyfriend scares me a little." Grace was unpredictable at best, and smarter than Michael in his sleep.

Lucius kept his head tilted. Michael realized that there were only three people on the plane, as far as they knew.

"So that leaves…?" Lucius began for him.

"Someone out of my league," Michael told him with dignity. "But he's real tall." *And safe. And kind.* "And a little older than I am." Michael had turned twenty-seven right before he'd gotten out of jail.

"Then that's a riddle I shall keep to myself," Lucius said, obviously keeping his amusement to himself as well. "Here, it looks like they've stopped. Let's go greet them, shall we?"

The jet came to a halt just outside the hangar, and Michael was surprised to see Carl and Hunter behind the controls.

Carl appeared to be yelling at Hunter at the top of his lungs.

After a moment the stairs dropped and Chuck came down them, carry-on in tow, laughing so hard he tripped on the last stair and almost stumbled.

"What in the—"

"Oh my God!" Chuck hooted. "That was the best ride I've had in a *while*. And I swear if Carl had a switch, Hunter wouldn't be able to sit for a week!"

"What was Hunter playing at?" Lucius demanded. "You all could have been killed!"

"Oh, Hunter wasn't playing at anything," Chuck told him between blasts of laughter. "Hunter asked Carl if he wanted to learn to land, and

Carl said yes. So Hunter set the jet on its course and went to the bathroom. That was all Carl!"

"But Carl doesn't know how to fly a plane!" Michael protested. He'd told Michael that himself three days ago.

"He does now!" Chuck howled. At that moment, Hunter came down the steps, walking sideways so he could hold his carry-on as a shield. Carl was attempting to beat him to death with his briefcase while towing his own luggage behind him.

"You colossal asshole!" Carl was shouting. "You went to the *bathroom*? You left me in charge of the jet controls while you went and got rid of something you ate in *Brussels*? Are you *high*? Do you have a death wish? What in the name of holy hell is wrong with you?"

"You said you wanted to learn!" Hunter protested. "How do you think I learned?"

"I assumed somebody *taught* you in the military! They didn't throw you in a cockpit and say, 'Hey, don't fucking die'!"

Hunter had gotten to the tarmac by now, and he turned and grabbed Carl's briefcase. "Nobody taught me," he said indignantly. "They needed somebody to land the plane, so I landed the goddamned plane! I thought you'd want the same courtesy!"

"I wanted to not crap my pants!" Carl retorted. "Jesus, Hunter. Didn't anybody tell you to choose life?"

Hunter turned to glare at Chuck, as though he was looking for backup, but Chuck was shaking his head and holding his hands out in front of him.

"No, no. Don't look at me. I've got my own shorts to clean, muscleman. I thought we were giving him a couple of lessons, not courting death by private jet."

Hunter scowled at him and then gave sort of a conspiratorial smile. "It *was* a good ride in, right?"

"It was the best," Chuck agreed. He looked at Carl and nodded. "I'm telling you, I haven't had that much fun since—"

"Since you wrecked two Bentleys in two days," Lucius said dryly. "I think you two should apologize to Carl and maybe promise not to leave him in the lurch the next time you're teaching him to fly." He shook his head in disgust. "Seriously, aren't you afraid somebody saw that? They could take away your licenses."

Hunter and Chuck stared at him.

"Licenses?" Chuck said blankly.

"That would be a trick," Hunter said, shaking his head. "All we ever told Felix, Danny, and Julia was that we knew how to fly."

"Well, I had one in the military," Chuck conceded, "but what I've got now is mostly forged."

"Augh!"

Carl yanked his briefcase out of Hunter's hands and got in a good wallop on the back of Hunter's head before Michael got between them and broke it up.

FIFTEEN MINUTES later, Hunter had taken off in the SUV he'd driven in, Lucius had left in his preferred Bentley, Chuck at the wheel, and Carl sat on the couch in Michael's hangar, washing down two ibuprofen with a bottle of cold water and some crackers.

"You're lucky he just got in that little slap to calm you down," Michael said soberly. "That guy looks like he could kill you with one hand tied behind his back."

"He could probably kill me with his thumb," Carl said miserably. "But he patted my back as you pulled me away. No, I think we're good. In fact if I had to guess, I think I was the victim of some kind of a macho bonding ritual reserved for someone who has passed a test of sorts."

"Yeah?" Michael sat down right next to him on the battered corduroy couch. "What makes you think that?"

Carl turned his head and smiled directly into Michael's eyes, and Michael had to remember to breathe. "Our trip went well, as far as we know, and I did more than sign papers. I think the land-the-plane thing was his way of saying 'well done.'"

Michael grimaced. "That's twisted. But you know, it's something one of my brothers would have done, but not as mean. Hunter, I'm talking about. He isn't as mean as my brothers. If I had to guess, I'd say someone was waiting in the wings to save your ass if it looked like you were really going to crash."

The sound Carl made wasn't quite a grunt, but it wasn't quite a laugh either. "You're probably right," he said, leaning his head against the back of the couch and closing his eyes. "I guess I should be grateful. I'm never anybody's favorite guy. I guess this really was better than a polite round of drinks in an overpriced restaurant and a 'Good show, chap. I really must run.'" He did the snooty accent too.

"Is that what you usually get?" Michael asked, curious.

"Nobody likes the investigator," Carl murmured. "I'm there to see if there was fraud, and a lot of times there is. And sometimes there's a damned good reason for it, because the insurance company is fucking draconian. I've seen people steal their own paintings to pay off mobsters demanding protection or stave off eviction. In America I've seen them steal their own stuff or set their restaurants on fire to pay off medical bills. Sure, some people are accomplished fraudsters, and those people I want to nail. But a lot of the time they're just desperate and sad, and it's a hierarchy-of-needs thing. They need food and shelter more than they need my good opinion or a piece of art they can't eat. But nobody wants to talk to me even if they're innocent. And the insurance company resents the hell out of paying me even if I find the fraud."

He sighed and held the cold water bottle against his eye, where the bruise from Hunter's slap was coming up nicely. "So having my colleagues fuck with me a little—that's almost a hand job and a beer right there."

Michael cackled, surprising himself *and* Carl. To cover for the inelegant sound, he asked, "So, this job you did, it went well?"

"Yeah." Carl studied his face. "Do you want to know what it was?"

"*So* bad," Michael said, nodding. "I get the feeling Chuck's been warning everybody off me, you know? Like keeping me in plausible deniability? But I haven't seen anybody do anything that looked… you know. Off the rails." He frowned. "Except that landing. God, they're lucky you had the smarts to lift the plane up and try that approach again."

"Smarts had nothing to do with it," Carl muttered. "Chuck was screaming at me from the passenger compartment to pull up on the stick and bank and try the approach again."

"I shouldn't laugh!" Michael protested, but he could hold his hand up over his mouth all he wanted and it didn't make it any less funny.

"Feel free," Carl said, waving his hand. "Now that it looks like I'll live, it does make a good story."

"That's sporting of you," Michael told him, and he meant it. "Now tell me! I really am dying to know."

So Carl told him about the mild bit of cloak-and-dagger they'd had to do to inform a less than reputable businessman that his brother's son was dying and he might be able to save him.

"Doesn't his blood type and shit have to match?" Michael asked, concerned. "I mean, if it was just a blood relative, I think Julia would have yanked the marrow out of her arm with a kitchen knife and not blinked. Don't you?"

"Without question," Carl said, grimacing. "But let's say Stirling—you remember him from dinner?"

"Yessir."

"He's good with computers and information gathering. We looked up those particulars before we even tried to make contact with Mr. di Rossi. He's most definitely a match."

"And he might not even have known," Michael said. "That's amazing." He smiled, feeling Carl's decency in his bones. "You guys making it sound all spy versus spy and shit. You were doing a good thing, weren't you?"

"I hope so," Carl said soberly. "I don't want to know what will happen to this family if Josh doesn't get better."

Michael patted Carl's knee. "You'll make sure that doesn't happen," he said. Then he looked at his hand. On Carl's knee. And felt the heat seeping through the wool slacks into his palm. He sat, frozen, unable to even snatch his hand back, and then Carl's hand covered his and squeezed.

The touch unfroze him. His eyes flew to Carl's, and Carl squeezed his hand again and then released it.

"I should go," he said softly.

"Where to? I know Chuck went to Lucius's apartment, and Hunter's got his own in the city. Where you going?"

"Glencoe," Carl said, obviously meaning the Salinger mansion. "We're having a tribe breakfast in the morning so we can talk about what's next. I didn't hear the particulars, but I gather Josh's uncle has a problem we might be able to fix. Oh!" Suddenly he sat up a little straighter. "And he's going to need help with his kids when he gets here. Apparently they're teenagers—thirteen and fifteen—and they're supposed to be on vacation in Corfu. Julia offered to entertain them. I'm pretty sure everybody's on deck for that, including you."

Michael looked at him questioningly. "I'm the mechanic," he said, feeling befuddled.

"Yes, but you have kids you talk to and who appear to like you. And I know Chuck and Lucius gave you a grand tour of Chicago when you got here, so you know what to show them." His animation dimmed. "That is... I mean, you're not obligated. I'm sure Julia and Felix will pay you more—"

"No, no. It's just...." Michael smiled a little, remembering Lucius's words about being involved, about becoming a part of a group of people who seemed to welcome him. "I'm just real honored to be asked."

Carl's expression went a little soft. "You're really nice to consider it," he said. "Come to breakfast tomorrow." He yawned again and his eyelids fluttered. "Sorry. I should go."

"Here," Michael said, standing up and offering him a hand. Carl took it, and when he was standing, they were chest to chest. Michael fought his instinct to step back. He liked the closeness. He wanted more of it.

"You can stay at my apartment tonight," Michael said softly. "And tomorrow we can go to the Salinger mansion for breakfast."

"Your apartment?"

"The guest room," Michael told him, knowing that no, it was too soon for that other thing but suddenly wanting it really bad. "You need sleep, and I need to...." This would sound stupid if he said it out loud.

"Need to what?" Oh, his eyes were so pretty. Green irises, yes, but the crinkles in the corners were also pretty. This was a man who knew how to smile kindly.

"Need to impress you," Michael said with dignity. "I'm not sure how to do that, but I want you to think well of me."

He actually heard Carl swallow.

"That's wonderful," Carl said gruffly. "But you need to know right now, I'm not the A-guy. Hunter and Chuck, they're the A-guys. I'm the almost-ran. The B-team. I run security checks." He rolled his eyes. "Oooh... scary."

Michael moved a little closer, close enough to smell sweat and tired man and an aftershave that didn't make him sneeze. Carefully, because he wasn't used to making moves like this, he put his hands on Carl's hips.

"Chuck's like riding a tornado. He'll fuck up your life one way or the other, but you're grateful for the ride."

Carl cleared his throat, sounding embarrassed, and Michael looked up to see a sheepish grimace on his handsome face.

"What?" he asked suspiciously.

"Uhm...."

Michael suddenly knew what he was embarrassed about. "No, really?"

Carl shrugged. "I think Good Luck Chuck was really a Good Time Charlie," he said, his face red. "I was trying to infiltrate a crew. They didn't just steal—they'd killed a couple of guards. Chuck had just been recruited, and he made me right away. Took me to bed, told me not to come back or I could be in real danger. I told him about the dead guards, and we both hopped a flight out of Sweden, spent a week together in Cairo because it was as far as either of us could think of before we changed our aliases, and went back to working our jobs."

"Him being a getaway driver and you being an insurance investigator?" Michael asked, nodding like he was making sure.

"Oh yeah," Carl said.

Michael leaned his head against Carl's chest and snickered.

"What?"

"I don't know who you think you're fooling about being the boring one, the B-guy, but you know what you are?"

"Everybody's least favorite party guest?"

Michael smiled slyly up at him from his position on Carl's shoulder. "You're sneaky. You are powerful sneaky. Being all quiet businessman. You landed a jet today. You might have saved Josh Salinger's life by being sneaky so you could go speak to his uncle. I mean, you don't *look* like you're sneaky. You're a freakin' giant with super broad shoulders, but that's what makes you sneaky. Nobody has really seen inside you, have they, Carl?"

Carl's hands settled on his back, right under his shoulder blades, and Michael closed his eyes and tried not to purr. "Not much there," he said, sounding sad.

Michael shook his head and fully committed. They were lined up, body to body, the heat between them counteracting the chill of nightfall in the big, big building. "There's plenty," he said softly. "There's a guy who thinks birds are cool."

He could hear Carl's rumble of quiet laughter, and it soothed him.

But they couldn't stay there forever. For one thing, Carl was almost dead on his feet. Michael pulled back and grinned. "Now I can sleep here on the little bed, but that couch will kill your back, which is why I bought the little bed. Let's get you to the apartment before you drop from exhaustion."

Carl yawned apologetically, and Michael wanted more than anything to fall asleep next to him. Michael led him to his vehicle and asked him if he wanted to stop for takeout on the way to the city.

"Oh wow, yes!" Carl told him. "Yes. I love a friend who feeds me."

Well, it wasn't hearts and flowers, but Michael would take it.

THE APARTMENT the Salingers kept in the city was pretty much the poshest place Michael had ever been in, besides their actual mansion. But while the mansion had young people and cats falling out of corners and stuff, the apartment was lots of angles and black marble columns with white marble floors. There was art on the walls—really nice stuff, mostly cityscapes featuring the river, not the nightmare scenarios that some people called art. Michael knew who Hieronymus Bosch was, and he never wanted to meet the man in this life or the next. The people who'd painted the pictures that adorned the walls of the apartment, though? He felt like maybe he could sit down and have a drink with them.

The living room furniture was soft-as-butter leather and smoothly polished wood, with bright throws hung on the arms to add a little bit of warmth. Michael had taken the smallest room as his own, since it was almost as big as the house he and his wife and kids had lived in before he'd gone to prison. "Uncle Danny" had been the one to show him around, and he'd invited—or rather insisted—that Michael fill the place with stuff of his own.

In fact, Danny had sat down with him and a computer and ordered the bedspread and some of the pictures and the furniture to fill it, since Danny had never used the spare room when he'd been there. He'd gaily waved off the cost, although Michael finally had money of his own.

"Consider it your payment for apartment sitting," he'd said, a foxlike smile dancing in his brown eyes.

"I don't need charity, sir," Michael had said stiffly, not sure what Chuck had told him about Michael's past.

"No, my boy," Danny had said, the smile fading. "You need welcome. You're all alone in a new city, and while you may think you've landed a great job and a great place, you still need people and comfort. Don't think I can't see it. Making a place your own, even if it's just a room in this apartment, that will make you feel a little less lost. Trust me."

The result had been that with Danny's help, he'd bought a sturdy wooden queen-sized bedframe and a cloud-lovely foam mattress to go on top. Michael had, for the first time in his life, picked out comforters and sheets, and he'd discovered he liked green and off-white a *lot*. He'd picked out end tables to go with the maple bedframe and a couple of chairs, some dressers, and a television.

He liked the results very much, although when it was all set up, he'd lamented that it hadn't gone with the marble floors and black trim of the apartment at all.

"Well, no," Danny had agreed. "But see? This is a staging area for the home you'll make yourself. You're practicing to find the Carmichael you plan to be in the future."

"You know I may have to move somewhere so my kids have a place to play by next summer," he'd said. "Can I plan the them *they* get to be in the future?"

Danny had laughed, eyes crinkled in the corners. "Are you kidding? By then, Julia will get her hooks into them, and trust me, we'll be having them at the mansion."

Michael had laughed along with him then, thinking Danny was kidding, but that was before he'd started to receive dinner invitations and had been subtly and inexorably made to feel welcome in a Glencoe mansion that was worth more than Michael could have made in a lifetime of fixing cars. Even the healthy portfolio Chuck had left him with didn't begin to touch the amount of wealth the Salinger family had. But not once had he been condescended to or made to feel left out.

Now, as he led Carl up to one of the pricier apartments off Chicago's famous Loop, his stomach fluttered with nerves.

Carl knew it wasn't Michael's place. Would he think it was too ostentatious? Michael's room too rustic? He'd never had company here before of any kind. More people had seen his little living space at the hangar than had seen this place, and he was... unsettled.

Carl, though, looked like he felt right at home. He put their takeout on the kitchen island—also done in black marble, which made Michael feel like he was on the set of a vampire movie—found plates, silverware, and napkins, then pulled up a stool and sat.

After a pause to lock the door and set the alarm system, Michael joined him, sitting kitty-corner because it was easier to have a conversation.

They'd gotten pizza and salad, and while before prison, Michael might have written off the salad as a distraction from deep-dish pepperoni, he'd learned to appreciate his greens. Michael watched as Carl put both on his plate, dishing everything up as if using nice china, and he did the same. At least once a week, he'd come here and cooked for himself, making something he'd always wanted to try or had tried and liked but nobody else in his house liked. He and Beth had enjoyed some fun conversations over the phone about how they'd discovered whole new food groups now that they'd moved someplace where nobody would give them shit for trying Thai food or sushi, and he was running with that.

He smiled a little, thinking about Beth's last experiment with Indian food, which she'd found entirely too spicy but he'd liked. Carl told him to share the joke.

He squirmed a little, embarrassed. "It's sort of dumb. My ex and I have been trying different foods. I told her about deep-dish pizza and how it's entirely different in Chicago than it is in Texas, and we started from there. It's like we both sort of cut loose after the divorce. Not boyfriend-wise, just, you know…."

"Exploring," Carl said softly. "Like you both got married because you were expected to live in a box, but suddenly you weren't in that box anymore."

"Yeah!" Michael smiled at him, relieved. "She was my best friend in high school, you know? And once she got over the sad part—"

"That you couldn't love her like she deserved?" Carl filled in, voice gentle.

Michael nodded. "Yeah," he said. That never got easier. "Once we pushed through that, and she knew I wasn't trying to leave her in the lurch, and I still cared about her and the kids—once we got through that, it was like… like I got my best friend back." He studied Carl unhappily.

"I hope that's not a problem. I mean, I would, eventually, really like to be more than friends with you. I hope the baggage isn't too heavy."

Carl shook his head. "No." He looked down and swallowed. "I, uhm, I'm pretty sure you'll change your mind, but your ex-wife, your kids? Those wouldn't be problems." He glanced up. "And anybody you're with should feel the same way. You get that?"

Michael blew out a breath but decided to ignore the pessimism. He had the man in his apartment after all. "So the baggage isn't a problem?" he persisted.

"It speaks well of you, actually," Carl said with a small smile. "When I got *my* divorce, my ex asked me to forget her name."

"Why'd you split?" Michael was dying to know. He couldn't imagine getting tired of that low, rumbly voice or those fathomless green eyes.

Carl gave a shrug. "The real question was why'd we get together. We met in law school. I was getting paid by the insurance company to get my international law degree, and she just wanted the Esquire by her name. She had this idea of Mr. and Mrs. Lawyer, and then it turned out that my job was a lot of traveling and chasing down petty criminals, and her job included a lot of people who liked no-strings liaisons. And I wasn't even mad about that, really."

"'Cause you were gay?" Michael said, to clarify.

"I'm bi," Carl told him mildly. "It was just… I would feel bad about the things the company asked me to do, and I'd balk on assignments or push back or get in the nooks and crannies. The company wanted things easy and quick, and life doesn't work like that. So I didn't make the money or get promoted the way she wanted, and I'd lost some respect for her because she wanted the money and the prestige more than she wanted the truth or to do the right thing. It wasn't a good match."

Michael stared at him, biting his lip. "Not a lot of people would take your way, you know that?"

"Chuck did," Carl said.

Michael nodded. "Yeah, he did. He could have left me and my brothers high and dry." He gave a humorless laugh. "My brothers probably don't see it that way, but they're gonna have some cash when they get out, so maybe that'll change."

"Are you going to visit them?" Carl asked.

Michael shook his head. "What for? So they can threaten my life for being a fag? No. No fun there. Fact is we could have all walked away from the job if I'd known they'd believe me. But they wouldn't have. Chuck knew it, I knew it. I was way more fun to beat on than listen to."

"That's a shame," Carl said softly. "You're a lot of fun to talk to." Then he ruined a perfectly nice compliment with a yawn.

"Here, you ready to go to bed? I can clean up—"

"I could honestly really use some stupid television," Carl told him. "I'm falling asleep in my plate, but my brain keeps buzzing, and you're looking awfully cute, but—" He yawned again. "—can we watch some TV?"

"There's a smaller TV in my room," Michael said. "The one in the living room feels like you're at a movie theater. I can't sleep with it on. You get your jammies on, and I'll clean up."

Carl nodded. "Only for a few minutes. I know it's a terrible habit, but it really does put me out like a light. I'd feel like a bad guest if I just curled up in bed with my computer, you know?"

Michael laughed softly and shooed him off.


IT TOOK five minutes for Carl to nod off sitting in one of the stuffed chairs in Michael's room. Dressed in a T-shirt and plaid flannel sleep pants, he looked helpless and dear, head back, snoring faintly, and Michael didn't have the heart to rouse him. So he shoved his shoulder underneath the big man's arm and they staggered the few feet to Michael's bed. Michael laid him out and covered him with the comforter before turning off the light.

He was going to head to the guest room to sleep when Carl mumbled, "I'll get up and go to my room in a minute."

"Naw, that's okay," Michael murmured, coming to the side of the bed. Almost against his will, he smoothed a shock of heavy blond hair off Carl's forehead. "You stay. I'll go."

"You could stay," Carl said. "I only snore a little."

"You trust your virtue with me?" Michael laughed. He'd made his intentions pretty clear, and Carl hadn't seemed to react. Michael wondered if all of Carl's looking inward was him studying to see what he really felt. Like all of his emotions were so deep inside he had to analyze them to know.

"Safe as a virgin bride on Fire Island," Carl said, then giggled at his own terrible joke. Or maybe it was that he was exhausted and Michael's words hadn't really made an impact. That was fine too.

"Says you," Michael told him, going to the other side of the bed and turning off the light. He'd already checked over the apartment; he'd had too many nights checking the house as a husband and father not to do that.

Too many nights as a convict not to enjoy the power of turning off all the lights and knowing he breathed free air not to do it either.

He crawled in next to Carl and turned on his side, studying Carl as he lay on his stomach, face turned toward Michael. It wasn't a big thing. Certainly wasn't a mind-blowing kiss or a hug or sex or anything. But it was... sweet. Like having the power to turn all the lights off, it was something to be savored. And Michael was exhilarated. This new person he was becoming, this Michael he'd made himself into, had boldly announced his intentions with a handsome, eligible man. Even though Carl was a little nonresponsive, he didn't seem appalled by the idea either, and look at them—in the same bed. Platonic or not, it was a big deal, and Michael was quite pleased.

Then with a groan Carl adjusted his position in bed and said, "C'mere. You be little spoon."

Heart beating like a trapped sparrow, Michael rolled over and backed carefully against that strong male body. Carl wrapped his arm around Michael's waist and mumbled, "Can't hurt, right? Just making the best use of the space, right?"

And then to make that a total lie, he buried his face in Michael's hair and breathed in, squeezing Michael snugly against his hard body.

"Right," Michael said, feeling a little faint. Oh wow. Wow. This was even better than he'd hoped for.

Behind him, Carl's breathing evened out, but the arm stayed possessively around his middle. He closed his eyes and smiled, falling asleep as happily as he ever had in the world.

# The Next Job

"WHAT?" CARL asked as he came into the apartment kitchen, ready to go. Michael was looking at him like he'd granted the man's dearest wish.

"Are those... *jeans*?" Michael asked, as if transported. "You are wearing jeans and a hoodie! Oh dear Lord!" He fanned himself, eyes fluttering back in his head, and Carl stared at him, befuddled. He was not sure what he had done to earn this sweet guy's regard, but damn if it wasn't starting to go to his head. Something about those big black/brown eyes staring at him like he was something made him really, really want to live up to that kind of faith.

"I go casual sometimes," he said, trying not to be defensive. "Brunch isn't really a suit-and-tie thing there."

"Good," Michael said, grinning. "Because jeans and a denim jacket are about all I've got. But you look real nice." He frowned, his eye catching Carl's briefcase, roller board, and a suit bag he'd been carrying in the roller board. "You going back to the mansion to sleep?"

Carl bit his lip, feeling shy and a little awkward. "I've got clothes in a room there," he said. "I'd really need to dry-clean my suit and get some changes of clothes, if, uhm, I was going to stay here."

Michael smiled like the sun had just come out from the clouds. "'Course. We can stop by the dry cleaners on the way there too." Then he cocked his head quizzically. "So you got a room and some clothes in Glencoe, and you said you got an apartment... where?"

"DC," Carl told him, not wanting to think about it. "I need to make a trip there to get my winter stuff and—"

"Why do you live there?"

"My company's based there," Carl said. "But I don't really *live* anywhere. I'm almost always between gigs." He grimaced, feeling like admitting to this was admitting to not being the guy Michael seemed to admire so much. "Until Julia asked if I wanted to stay at their place when I had downtime, I didn't have a home, really. And even if Felix sort of hates me—"

Michael's eyes shot open. "Why does Felix hate you?" he asked.

"He doesn't. Never mind. We should go if we're going to stop at a dry cleaner. Do you know where one is—?"

"There's one on the corner. I'll drop you off and wait for you on the curb. Why would Felix hate you?"

Gah! This was embarrassing. "Uhm, you know how Felix and Uncle Danny were broken up for a little while?" Ten years.

"Yeah?"

"Well, uhm, they weren't exactly celibate, right?"

Michael's eyes got really big, and for a moment Carl's hopes of ever having that sort of sweet enchantment he'd seen the night before— or hell, that morning as they'd woken up—aimed at him ever again dimmed.

And then Michael burst out laughing.

"Oh my God. You, I mean, you didn't have *me* fooled, but I bet you surprised everybody else. 'Not the A-guy' my *ass*. Now hurry up and let's go!"

Carl grunted and grabbed his stuff. As they cleared the doorway, he thought about the apartment building and how he'd run into Danny and the others while they were pulling their first job together in an apartment a few floors up. How he had, without thought, thrown in his lot with theirs. As he and Michael made their way to the elevators, he thought he might tell Michael that story in case he hadn't heard it before, mostly because he thought the description of Hunter and Molly practically maiming him in an effort to make sure he didn't ruin their con would make the younger man laugh.

He'd always known he wasn't the A-guy, but somehow not having any dignity seemed like less of a burden when Michael looked at him with that sudden delight. He might end up telling Chuck's ex-boyfriend *all* his embarrassing secrets, just to see him smile.


BY THE time they'd cleared the city and gotten to Glencoe for brunch, Carl had managed to stretch the story out and then describe how they'd taken down a rather awful woman who had raised a social media storm against Felix so she could take over his news station, which was the job that had pulled them all together, just that past March.

Michael had laughed—a lot—and as they pulled up the long driveway, he said, "You know, the way you guys talk, you'd think you'd been together a lot longer."

And suddenly Carl wasn't quite so jubilant. "Watching Josh get sick has brought us all together," he said. "I mean, we were probably going to end up together anyway, but…." He shook his head. "I feel like I watched him grow up. I need to see him get a lot older, you know?"

Michael nodded. "You got a good heart," he said as he parked the vehicle—one of Felix's, actually—a black SUV he was probably dropping off so he could take another vehicle back to the hangar to fix. For a moment they were quiet, listening to the brisk fall wind whipping around the cooling hood, and Carl couldn't help thinking of the moment he'd awakened, Michael on his side, gazing into his face. They hadn't kissed, but for a moment—a sublime moment in which Carl couldn't remember breathing or even hearing his own heartbeat—they'd both been so very, supremely aware of each other.

Carl had wanted to kiss him so very badly. Michael's slow sunrise smile had started his heart again in a big way, and sitting up to roll out of bed and go shower had been the exact opposite of what he wanted to do.

Carl wasn't sure what had started Michael's crush, or why the weight of it had landed on him, but Carl was starting to think there wasn't much he wouldn't do to keep that faith alive.

Now, looking at that wide-eyed faith, Carl swallowed, knowing his face was heating up and not able to stop it.

"What?" Michael asked gruffly.

"I don't know what I do to make you look at me like that," Carl said. "It's amazing. I need to know what I'm doing so you don't sto—"

Michael kissed him. Soft, gentle at first, and Carl…. Oh, he hadn't had that closeness in so long. He opened his mouth and palmed the back of Michael's head, bringing him closer, breathing in the clean smells of soap and aftershave and the faint tang of motor oil that never completely left.

Carl didn't care. That smell meant Michael, and he craved more of it. He lunged forward, taking the kiss deeper, until Michael melted against him, panting.

"Coming back to the apartment with me tonight?" he breathed.

"We're not sleeping together yet," Carl said, trying to sound like he knew what he was doing.

"Sure we're not. I just want to kiss you more."

"Absolutely." They were still close, breath mingling, and Carl felt a little savage, thinking they had to stop this moment and go do something that required brainpower and civility.

"Naked," Michael moaned, and Carl kissed him again.

Oh, this was not the way to discourage a crush.

Michael tasted like good scotch or something clearer, purer. Like gin. Sweet, heady, with an unexpected kick. Carl hadn't taken a drink in nearly nine years, but God, he could get used to tasting Michael.

And the little sound Michael made as he surrendered completely, put himself at Carl's mercy, gave Carl leave to plunder some more. It made Carl feel like the A-guy, the central player, the guy who ran the show, and he wanted to run it until they were both naked and panting and sated, and then he wanted to run it some more.

A sharp rap on the passenger window broke them apart. As Carl's heart thundered in his ears, he turned to see Hunter, smiling evilly and gesturing to the entrance of the house.

"We got work to do!" he called out, and Carl nodded and wiped his mouth with the back of his hand.

"Work," he croaked, and Hunter just stayed there, like a complete asshole, waiting for Carl to open his door.

"Friends are a blessing," he muttered, not meaning it. He had not been aware, until this moment, how little he knew of the bonding patterns of American males, but he was pretty sure he'd never had a friend who'd been as comfortable as Hunter and Chuck seemed to be about butting their heads into his life.

"They really are," Michael said sincerely, and Carl was going to give him an evil look, but he couldn't. God, those enormous black/brown eyes. And more than that—the sweet twist to his mouth when he smiled.

Instead, he sighed and threw open the door, gratified when Hunter hopped back before he got smacked with it.

Carl shut the door and glowered at him, and Hunter smiled with all his teeth.

"Have a good night?" he asked sweetly.

"Fell asleep in front of the television," Carl replied. Then, unable to sustain snark for long, he sighed. "And sadly that's the truth."

Hunter slow-blinked. "I am... disappointed," he said. Then Michael rounded the corner, and he gave a smile that even Carl had to say was sincere before leading them to the house.

The kitchen sat to the left of the foyer, but that was not the heart of the house. Hunter led the way through it anyway so they could all pay their respects to Phyllis, the housekeeper, a tart-tongued woman in her fifties who was grateful for her position as the Salingers' housekeeper because it meant she could pursue her passion for academics as the mood struck her and yet still be surrounded by people who cared about her and appreciated her for keeping their lives organized.

The men walked through the kitchen, waiting until Phyllis came to the other side of the kitchen counter to kiss her on the cheek. Gray corkscrew curls bobbing, she shooed them through to the dining room, which *was* the heart of the house, before going back to her two trainees, both of whom, she cheerfully admitted, could cook way better than she could.

Carl paused before going in. "Is Josh here?" he asked, the question weighted.

Phyllis nodded, the strain on her face doing the unforgivable and making her look her age.

"Still has his hair," she said, her voice cracking with the effort of keeping it light.

"It would be a shame if he didn't," Carl said diplomatically.

"You boys did good," she said, standing on her tiptoes to kiss *his* cheek. "Thank you."

Carl shrugged. "I just brought the legal papers," he said, but she shook her head and then turned away, obviously overcome.

He left, out of respect, and braced himself for what would meet him in the dining room.

The room itself was dominated by a giant carved maple-wood banquet table set up against the wall. The seats on the wall were bench style, so Danny, Felix, and Julia usually presided there. Danny and Felix were, of course, very comfortable with each other's personal space, but Julia had been in their lives for twenty years as a sister and friend. They had no compunction about climbing over each other to get out from behind the banquet table when the occasion called for it.

But by now, none of the people at the table had reservations about personal space.

"Stirling, if you pull my hair one more time, I'll wrap it around your throat and choke you with it," Molly said conversationally. In person, she was even more stunning than over the phone, her mass of curly red hair highlighted with neon dyed streaks, twirling their way through the mass. Buxom, with sassy hips, she had high cheekbones and milk-pale skin with unapologetic freckles that she only tried to hide when she was working a role.

Her brother—foster brother, although they squabbled like they'd shared a womb—was a little younger. Carl thought they may have graduated from high school at the same time because Stirling was that level of genius. He had the pale brown skin of mixed-race heritage, with eyes as liquid and brown as Michael's, but much, much warier. His tightly curled hair was cut short, although Carl had seen him go weeks without trying to tame it, and his face, when relaxed enough to smile, had a sharp-cut handsomeness that took the breath away.

"You wouldn't color it if you didn't want the attention," Stirling said, and while he wasn't laughing or smiling, there was a tilt to his lips that indicated he was teasing her on purpose, probably to keep the atmosphere around the table light.

"I agree," Dylan "Grace" Li said from Molly's other side. "But if you pull *my* hair, I will steal all the mother thingies from your computers, and I may not know what they do, but I know you'll be very upset."

Stirling gave Grace a look of fear that may have been genuine, and Grace—Asian American with a pointed chin, tawny eyes, and showy, exquisite male beauty—smiled with pointy teeth.

"Don't worry," Grace said, sounding magnanimous. "I'll only do it if you pull my hair."

Stirling relaxed a little. "I will never, ever touch you if I can possibly help it," he said, nodding sincerely, and Grace turned to Molly as though making conversation.

"You need to be a better thief," he said. "It gives you better things to threaten with."

Carl could see it because Molly had once lifted *his* wallet, and he knew what to watch for as she smoothly passed Grace's billfold to Stirling, whose eyes grew overlarge as it landed in his lap.

Carl bent down and put a hand on Molly's shoulder. "If you didn't tease him unmercifully, he wouldn't pull your hair," he said patiently, as though talking to a child. While he spoke he pulled the wallet from Stirling's fingers and held it behind his back while Hunter grabbed it.

Carl straightened and turned to Michael, who was watching the entire enterprise with big eyes until Carl put his hand in the small of Michael's back and steered him to the end of the table, where he could sit at the head with Chuck and Lucius on one side and Carl on the other.

"Hey!" Grace said as they sat. "Who gave *you* permission to be the thief?"

Carl looked up quickly to see Hunter grinning like the cat who had stolen the wallet.

"Not my fault you're off your game," he said, going in for a kiss.

Grace was still working on an expression between outrage and hurt before the kiss landed, but as soon as Hunter touched him, he seemed to melt, the agitation, which colored the space around his body like an aura, calming down.

"He *was* off his game," Chuck murmured, his casual sprawl belied by the quietness in his green eyes.

Lucius gave an imperceptible nod toward the opposite end of the table, where Josh Salinger sat, wearing sweatpants and a hooded sweatshirt with CSU on the front. The hoodie now hung off his shoulders like they were coat hangers. His dark-brown eyes were enormous in a sheet-white face that was all points and angles, and Carl had an aching moment to wonder if they'd ever be treated to his dimples again.

God, if the kid lost another ounce, he'd be able to see light through Josh's paper-thin frame.

"How long until his next round?" Carl asked, stomach knotting.

"A week, and then a final round," Lucius said. "Then the bone marrow transplant to replace what all the chemo destroyed."

Carl took a deep breath, and next to him, Michael did the same. Michael had a good heart. He may not have been close to Josh Salinger, but he was a father, and he seemed to understand what everybody was so upset about.

Suddenly the object of everybody's attention spoke up. "He'd better not be off his game," Josh said, his voice rusty. "He's got some serious work to do in the next two weeks. Did you hear that, Grace? Pay attention!"

Grace pulled back from the kiss, obviously centered by Hunter's presence enough to resume the snark that made them brothers.

"I don't know what you think I'm doing while you're in the hospital, Cancer Boy. We all know you have control of my cortex. If you're not in the field, I'm not in the field."

Josh gave a snort that looked like it might launch him off his chair. "Oh no. There will be no sitting here watching Josh die. I'm getting the chemo and sleeping and barfing without any company, thank you. And you all are going to go out and take care of the family business."

"You're not dying," Stirling snapped, surprising Carl. "You're between healthy spurts."

Molly nodded solidly at her brother and held out a fist to bump. "He never speaks out at the table," she said. "You can't contradict him."

"Okay," Josh said with a thin smile. "Not dying. Particularly not if my long-lost Uncle Leon shows up in a week and gives up his bone marrow. Then I'll just sleep for four-to-six months and hate you all for partying without me."

"Hate us now," Chuck drawled. "'Cause you missed Carl landing a plane for the first time, and whoo-ee if *that* wasn't a party."

"That was a party in my *pants*," Carl argued, "and not the fun kind. I'll never get those shorts clean."

Grace's eyes locked on Carl and Chuck with undisguised gratitude. Josh and Grace had been brothers of the heart since grade school. If Josh didn't get better, only Hunter had any chance at all of pulling Grace back from the spiral Carl could see him descending into without Josh Salinger to anchor his heart.

"You landed a plane?" Grace asked suspiciously. "I'm not sure I believe that. Tell me why you're not dead?"

"Mostly because Chuck here was sitting in the passenger compartment screaming, 'Pull up and circle around and try again or we're all gonna die,'" Carl told him honestly. "But also because Hunter spent a good hour explaining how to land the plane before we got to the airfield. I just didn't think I was going to get a pop quiz."

Grace turned his head and scowled at his boyfriend. "Wait—where were you?"

Hunter gazed at him without compunction. "The bathroom."

"*You* are the stupidest asshole on the face of the planet!" Grace yelled. "Why would you leave Mr. Suit Man to crash the plane and kill you just so you could go to the bathroom?"

"Two reasons," Hunter replied, unperturbed. "One, the bathroom is the safest place to be in case of a crash, and two, with Mr. Suit Man behind the stick, I wanted the option of *not* shitting my pants!"

There was a stunned silence around the table while people tried to decide whether or not they got to laugh at that, until a rusty cackle issued from Josh.

"Now *that's* my kind of party!"

"No," Julia Salinger said, speaking for the first time since they'd entered. "If you didn't look like death, I'd smack you for that. That's insane. Hunter, Chuck, you're grounded!" She turned to Carl, her wide blue eyes gentle. "I don't know what to tell you, Carl. That's reprehensible. I'm ashamed of you, Chuck! Hunter, how could you?"

Both men were looking down at the table like errant schoolboys and not full-grown men.

"Aw, Julia," Chuck said in his best twang. "You know we wouldn't have let him crash the plane. Hell, we were *on* the plane! He needed a little instruction, that's all. We thought, you know, it was a long flight. Having one more person who could fly would give us more sleep time."

Julia narrowed her eyes. "You just wanted to haze Carl so he didn't get too confident because he absolutely *ruled* that job!"

Chuck shrugged. "Awkward sincerity is his schtick!"

"Besides," Hunter said, "he beat the hell out of me with his roller board—"

"It was my briefcase!" Carl defended.

"He's completely one of us now. He didn't try to get me arrested or anything."

"Please," Carl snapped back, trying to hide how warmed he was. "If I was going to get you idiots arrested, I would have done it months ago."

"Yeah," Hunter said as though this hadn't occurred to him. "Live and learn."

"Well," Danny said from between Julia and Felix, "We're so very glad you all lived."

"Are we?" Felix asked, his dry humor making an appearance. "Are we really?"

Felix Salinger had dark blond hair that hid any silver at the temples and piercing blue eyes. He was a lion of a man, tall, distinguished, easily the most eye-catching person in the room. He and the exquisite Julia really had looked to be a perfect couple while married, and if Carl hadn't seen that brief touch of hands between Felix and Danny at the very beginning, he would have made the same assumption.

But part of that believability lay in that Danny wasn't golden or leonine or anything close, which for Carl was the root of his appeal. A slight, slender man with curly brown hair, a vulpine face, and the golden-brown eyes of a fox, Danny "Lightfingers," aka Benjamin Morgan, didn't *look* particularly imposing. But given enough conversation and a mission, he could definitely dominate a room.

Carl watched him speak with a quiet ache, their meeting in the rehab clinic nine years earlier haunting him still. He wasn't in love with Danny Lightfingers anymore, but he did hold a deep pocket of gratitude for the man because he'd taught Carl how to care about something beyond his own needs, how to love someone more than himself.

Seeing him pull the disparate parts of his makeshift family together, Carl was reminded of Danny's appeal, but with Michael sitting close enough to bump knees with him, Carl experienced a deeper, stronger tug toward this one unassuming man.

In nine years he'd never known anything that trumped his hopeless crush on Danny Lightfingers—until now.

"Thank you, Carl," Danny said, tired eyes twinkling kindly. "I mean, *I* knew you had it in you, but it's nice to see you've proved yourself to these other assholes, because I'm sure it was your life's goal."

Chuck and Hunter snickered, and Carl hid his own laugh behind his hand. This moment here actually made the whole 'Oh my God, I'm gonna die!' moment sort of worth it.

Danny paused, allowing the laughter to soothe and to heal, and then went on. "And I'm sure you'll all be happy to know that we spoke with Josh's doctor, and if the transplant goes well, his prognosis improves dramatically." His voice cracked on the word "prognosis," and Carl knew his eyes weren't the only ones that burned, but Danny wasn't done.

"Julia had a long talk with Josh's uncle the other day—and I'm aware that the four of you who were there left the room while they spoke—but some things were said then that I think you should hear."

"All the good shit happens when I leave," Chuck said, because he was always the smartass.

"That's my line," Hunter told him, smiling laconically.

"No, that's my line," Grace said. "I didn't even get to *see* him try to kill you all. It's so unfair."

"They bounced," Michael said, surprising Carl. "I mean, the plane bounced *hard* when he landed it. I'm surprised they didn't bite their tongues off."

Grace gave Michael a wholly genuine grin, and Carl's heart gave yet another aching throb. Grace, a young man known for being brilliant but not particularly stable or trustworthy, hadn't left Josh's side over the last few months unless Josh himself had ordered him to. Michael's little detail had made his day.

"It was terrifying," Carl reassured him. "Lucius and Michael were beside themselves."

"With laughter," Lucius added, winking.

Grace gave a sudden openmouthed feline smile, the type a cat gives when it's found the mouse of its dreams. To someone with Grace's perpetual FOMO, the details of that moment were a gift.

"Josh, they love me!"

"I can see that," Josh said, smiling back. "But let Danny speak. Cancer boy needs to go down for his nap in a few."

"Slacker," Stirling muttered.

Josh faked a yawn that turned into a real one. "Yup. That's me. You hosers have to do all the work this time."

"But we will need your fine mind," Felix said, his voice resonant and mild. Felix could call boardrooms to attention with a word. Only those who knew him well could hear the strain underneath it now. "As long as you could grace us with your presence."

Josh winked. "Sure, Dad."

Felix gave him a sweet smile, one without artifice or mastery, and Carl wished for the thousandth time that he could hate Felix fucking Salinger the same way Felix hated him.

At that moment, Phyllis and her acolytes of domestic divinity came in with serving trays, one for each end of the table, full of waffles, toppings, sausage, bacon, and fruit. For a moment, there was clatter and din as everybody served themselves and bacon-cheese biscuits were tossed around like beanbags. Carl caught one for him and one for Michael, thrown with unerring accuracy by Molly from halfway down the table, but Lucius and Chuck were on their own.

When the clatter had died and everybody was deep into their kibble, a sort of gentle hum went up—happy, contented people eating in company. Carl, who had spent an inordinate amount of time eating alone in the last fifteen years, never failed to get a little bit of a buzz when dining with the Salingers. It was pathetic and sad for a man his age, but his childhood had been spent eating with his vitriolic mother and his almost-silent father, and his adult dining seemed like never-ending takeout. Hearing Michael talk about his moments of finding himself via cooking with his ex-wife had been charming as fuck, actually, and it had made Carl acutely aware of the personal void his life had become.

He looked over at Michael, who was ecstatically swallowing a bite of waffle. When he was done, Michael grinned at him after wiping his mouth politely.

"There's not a waffle iron at the apartment," he said apologetically. "In fact, Danny had to help me order pots and pans when I moved in."

"Waffles are special-occasion food anyway," Carl noted, and took another bite of his, smothered in strawberries, bananas, and whipped cream. It was not lost on him that they were celebrating this hope for Josh's health.

"Here's to celebrating in six months," Michael said, glancing at the head of the table worriedly. "When that young man can eat more than fruit."

Carl had noticed that too. Josh was putting on a good show, but Carl suspected nausea from the chemo was making eating a bit of a chore.

"Here's to steak and red wine," Carl said, nodding. "I hear you."

It was almost a prayer.

# A Unique Set of Skills

BRUNCH WAS delicious, but what Michael was really waiting for was what would happen afterward.

In the past, there had been dinner, dessert, wine, and then he'd gone home, knowing that most of the people he was eating with would stay the night but not sure why.

This morning, he'd been there when an open admission had been made that there was something going on after the meal that was actually more important than the meal itself, and Michael wanted to be there.

In the past, he'd been okay with not being in the know. Being in the know was dangerous. The people going into the bank were in the know, and that had gotten him two years in prison that he didn't want to think about.

But this was different. Carl's caper had been all about securing medical help for Josh Salinger—that was a good thing. Chuck and Hunter weren't choirboys, but they had been right on board with that. And Lucius, he was on the up-and-up even if he couldn't tell powerful people just what *was* up.

It was only that suddenly, after some true human contact, after some warmth and hospitality, Michael was feeling the urge to *belong* to something again. He'd belonged to his family, to his brothers, all his life, and that had been toxic as hell. He'd belonged to his wife and his kids, and while those connections weren't severed—would never *be* severed—they weren't the steel bands that had held his life in place like they had before the bank job. Suddenly, as Danny said, he felt the need for a group, for friends. Carl, if nothing else, had been kind to him. A true friend, although Michael hoped for more. Chuck had been a good friend too, and surprisingly, so had Lucius and Hunter. This gathering of people around the table, this group who seemed to have a purpose together, could be a family without the suffocation, ties that bound without constricting, stability and grounding without rooting Michael to the earth and pulling him under.

He wanted in.

Breakfast was cleared; Phyllis's helpers were really efficient. Michael hardly noticed they were there until he turned to his plate and it was gone. He must have made a sound because Carl murmured, "There's almost always snacks downstairs if you're still hungry."

From the corner of his eye, Michael caught some of the workers carrying plates past the dining room and turning right at the stairs to the den.

"Do people really eat after all of that?"

Carl's eyes flickered to Grace, Stirling, and Molly, then to Hunter and Chuck. "There are some serious calorie burners here," he said dryly. "I personally try to avoid the pastry table because I'm getting to the love-handle age."

Michael felt like glowing. "I like love handles," he said, meaning it.

Carl's fair complexion washed bright red, and he was suddenly studiously interested in what Danny was saying.

"So, my darlings, how about if you stand and stretch a bit, maybe use the little thieves' room, and then we can meet downstairs in fifteen. Are we agreed?"

There was general assent, and Michael stood gratefully. As he did, Julia gave him a little wave to her side of the table as she, Danny, and Felix stood and stretched.

Josh stayed seated, and Danny's hand on the boy's shoulder held so much tenderness, Michael's heart gave a bruised throb.

"Hey, Michael," Josh said gruffly. "Sit with me, okay?"

Michael did as he asked, realizing that it had been Josh who'd wanted to speak with him.

"Look," Josh said. "We probably would have brought you in earlier. I've just been feeling like shit, and nobody wanted to make a decision like this without me. You know we're, uhm, sort of shady, right?"

Michael grinned reassuringly. "You mean like 'hiring an ex-convict to be your mechanic' shady or 'the insurance guy in a suit who can lift a wallet' shady?"

Josh gave a delighted if rusty laugh. "Both those kinds of shady," he said. "We don't want you to ever get into trouble on account of what we ask you to do. Everyone else here, they're here because this keeps them out of trouble. Except for Carl. I think he's here because he hasn't gotten into *enough*. But you've seen prison time, and we don't want to drag you kicking and screaming back into a situation that may expose you to that again."

Michael shrugged. "Look, I was in a bank with a gun. I get the feeling you people are a little subtler than that."

"We are," Danny said. "For one thing, we don't like guns."

"For another," Felix added, "our lawyers would never admit you were even in that bank."

Michael smiled at them, liking Felix's style. "Y'all have been real kind to me," he said. "And you pay me lots to keep up your cars. If you think I got something to bring to the table, as long as I'm not holding a gun and working with folks that're gonna try to kill me when they're done with me, I say shit's on the way up, you think?"

"We will try to keep you as free from culpability as possible," Julia said softly. "For one thing, Chuck would never forgive us if we promised you safety and got you thrown back in prison. For another, we would really, really like for this to succeed. But if things get too intense, nobody would hold it against you if you walked, do you understand? Just head on back to the apartment and be our mechanic, and you never have to admit you knew there was anything different going on."

Michael winked at her. "Yeah, but y'all would probably stop feeding me, right? Naw, you folks keep right on feeding me and I'll be happy to hang around after chow time if you think I got something to offer."

He was going to turn away then, but Josh stopped him with bony fingers on his arm.

"Michael?" he said softly, "we'll never stop feeding you. But I think you could have some very important things to offer."

Michael's entire body heated, and he mumbled something unintelligible as he broke away to find Carl and make his way downstairs.

"What's wrong?" Carl asked as they neared the carpeted stairs to the den.

Michael just shook his head, unable to put into words what that moment had meant. How to explain to this nice guy in a suit that Carmichael Carmody had grown up getting whooped on for not collecting enough eggs or shooting a deer out of season? That when he'd been attacked by the rooster while in his school clothes, he'd gone without dinner for a week because his jeans had gotten torn? And that even if he wasn't being punished, the odds of his brothers stealing the best food off his plate were very real, and while nobody would call them to account, he'd get in trouble for whining? Carl would never understand.

Michael and Beth had grown up vowing their children would never, ever have to go to bed hungry in the name of "punishment," because when they'd been in high school, she'd been the one to bring an extra sandwich, knowing the odds of him not having eaten the night before were considerable.

Josh couldn't have known that, couldn't have known any of it. But he'd looked Michael in the eye and told him that he could eat at the family table and not do a damned thing more than ingest food.

And now Michael would go to prison all over again—he'd do it twice—to help that kid cross the damned street.


HE'D NEVER seen the den, but the décor made him smile. Felix and Danny apparently had a thing for hometown sports teams, because the walls were painted red and blue, in honor of the Cubs and the Bulls, with silver and black in one corner for the White Sox and an orange and black stripe in another corner for the Bears—or, arguably, the Blackhawks. The exception was the blank wall adjacent to the wet bar, which had been outfitted with big viewing screens that were apparently connected to a small audiovisual table that sat next to a chair in the middle of the room. The rest of the room was furnished like an average sports den—squishy, comfortable couches, beanbag chairs, with soft throws and pillows stacked in open shelves in the corner.

"Looks like a good place for movie night," Michael said, thinking about how when Beth had bought the new house, she'd included a room like this for watching movies.

"It is, surprisingly," Carl said. "As well as sports." He gave a happy smile. "We watched basketball playoffs here in June. Sadly, the Bulls did not pull through."

Michael tsked. "I would've had to root for the Spurs anyway. You know that, don't you?"

"Well, whatever helps you sleep at night." Carl made it sound like an indictment, but then he winked.

"Shouldn't you be rooting for the Celtics anyway?" Chuck asked, passing them on his way to get to the cookies and pastries on platters in front of the couch.

"What makes you think I gave a crap about basketball when I lived on the coast?" Carl asked, rolling his eyes. "It's only really fun when you have people to cheer with."

"Huh," Chuck muttered. "I never really thought of that."

"That's because you've been sort of a solitary fish until now, Charles," Lucius murmured.

Grace's laugh was loud enough to echo off the low ceiling. "What kind of fish *are* you, Chuck? Are you a *Texas* fish?"

"Chuck ain't from Texas," Michael said, hoping he wasn't exposing any secrets. "His accent is almost right, but he's got some Ohio in there, I can tell."

He was suddenly the center of several sets of admiring eyes.

"Is he telling the truth, Chuck?" Molly asked, her purr almost predatory.

"He is indeed, Molly-girl," Chuck drawled, standing up and taking his cookies to the back corner of the room by the stairs. "I cannot tell a lie."

"You can too," Grace admonished. "But you apparently can't tell a Texas-sized lie."

Chuck's grin widened. "How big is a Texas-sized lie, little buddy?"

"As big as my—"

Hunter clapped a hand over Grace's mouth and pulled him over to the wall across from Chuck, and Michael realized they were positioned like sentinels to guard the room. Hunter let go of Grace, who kissed him briefly on the lips and wandered back toward the couches and the conversation pit.

Michael watched as Carl maneuvered himself back by the wet bar, accepting a glass of orange juice Danny poured him with gratitude. He turned and nodded, gesturing for Michael to go to the couch, and Michael looked at him questioningly, silently asking Carl if he was going to join him.

Carl was about to shake his head no—Michael could see that—but then Danny nodded him imperiously over, and Carl shrugged and went. He took the corner of the sofa, and Michael sat next to him, sliding down as the soft cushions gave under his weight.

Suddenly he was wedged up against Carl like a girl on her boyfriend's lap.

"Oh," Michael said, surprised.

"Yes, oh," Carl told him, wrapping his arm around Michael's shoulders, his lips pursed in humor. "The only people who usually sit on this end of the couch are Josh and Grace. Apparently they've lived in each other's back pockets for so long it doesn't bother them."

"But isn't Grace Hunter's boyfriend?"

Carl's chuckle rumbled against Michael's shoulder. "Yes. But we're not a make-out-in-public bunch."

Michael looked around again and realized it was true. "Why not?"

"People with secrets and pasts are private, I guess," Carl said. "But that doesn't mean we don't cuddle." He gestured with his chin to where Stirling was sitting in a beanbag chair, Molly was using him as a backrest, and Grace came to curl up at his feet.

"Friends since middle school," Michael said, having heard them say it before.

"Yup. And not afraid to show it."

Their conversation was interrupted when Felix walked to the console in the room's center and cleared his throat. "Julia and Josh asked that Danny and I take this, which seems unfair, because this is really their story. That said, I'll do the first part, Danny will do the rest, and our beloveds will tell us in private how many times we got the story wrong. We can bear any scolding they give us because we adore them." He blew a kiss for Julia, who smiled fondly back.

Danny moved then from the wet bar where he'd been busy pulling something up on a computer, to the center of the room where he connected the computer with an adaptor. The viewing screen came alive, but not with a basketball game.

Instead there was a candid photo of an almost-familiar-looking young man, smiling and waving at somebody off camera. Fine-boned, dark-haired, and dark-eyed, he had delicate features, and even in the still photo, there was a tremendous vulnerability in his eyes and jaw.

And an amazing potential for grace.

"This," Felix said, his tone low and sad, "is Matteo di Rossi, Leon di Rossi's younger brother. He is important to us because he was Josh's natural father."

The air in the room grew fantastically still, as though all the occupants had forgotten to breathe.

"Nicely chosen, Julia," Molly said, breaking the silence.

"Thank you," Julia murmured, a faint smile on her face. "I was impressed with him myself."

"As you should have been, dearest," Felix said. "By all reports—yours, Leon's, even the press—he was a very sweet boy. Matteo, sadly, had no idea that he'd fathered a child, and even if he had, he probably would not have claimed his son because his father was this man." The picture on the viewing screen changed. "Benito di Rossi, who was not, by all accounts, a particularly safe person to be around."

The man portrayed was several decades older than Matteo, his hair gray, his face wide and jowly. Matteo must have gotten his delicacy and grace from his mother, because the man in the photo had big square hands and the cold eyes of a fish. He also had a frame capable of great brutality; it emanated from the bulge of muscle in his arms and shoulders.

"Benito di Rossi worked his way up through the ranks to become one of the biggest smugglers in Italy. Of course 'smuggler' is a rather tame word, and it covers a variety of sins: drugs, women, guns, as well as art, rare plants, and endangered species. Benito di Rossi didn't care what people were buying and selling. He made his money off a network of spies and bureaucrats who got the goods through international security checks and across country."

"He looks like a bastard," Grace said. "He's dead, right?"

"Very," Felix replied, not a hitch in his voice. "Assassinated by a competitor, whom Leon, in turn, brought down with a bomb in his yacht, effectively ending that particular trade war."

"Yikes!" Chuck exclaimed. "These folks play for keepsies, don't they?"

"Since his father died, not quite as much," Felix told him. "Leon—pictured here—has in fact done a capital job of turning his business, which was like something out of *The Godfather* to a brand-new enterprise, like the *Millenium Falcon*." The picture of Leon di Rossi, shirtsleeves rolled up as he walked the property line of his villa in Corfu, certainly made him look rugged and dashing.

"He's kind of hot," Grace said, surprised. He glared at Hunter from across the room. "You never told me he's hot."

"Straight," Hunter said without blinking.

"So straight," Carl seconded.

"There is *no* bend in that penis," Chuck added in case anybody was confused.

"How lovely to hear *somebody* is," Julia inserted slyly, and Felix grinned at her before moving on.

"So Leon, who appears to be *very* straight, is still a smuggler, but with the death of the arms dealer who killed his father, the drug traffickers and other more unsavory types were willing to back away, hands up, when Leon declined to renew their business association with his company. I don't necessarily condone murder, but in this case, I think Leon was doing his best to not continue to roll around in blood, and that's admirable."

"Is he completely legit now?" Carl asked. He'd been the only person who had heard of Leon di Rossi before Felix and Julia had asked him to run point on making contact, and he'd known about Leon's illegitimate business enterprises from the get-go. He'd scanned di Rossi's records, but Felix and Danny would have more details to add as to whether the older scion was as good in real life as he'd made himself look on paper.

Felix, Danny, and Julia simultaneously held their hands parallel with the floor and made the universal sign for "maybe/maybe not." Danny was the one who cracked a smile and verbalized, "He lives and works in an environment in which his business couldn't succeed without some line-blurring. Is he enough of a good guy for your tastes, Carl?"

Carl grimaced. That had been a bone of contention between them during their brief liaison, one that Carl regretted now. "He is," he replied soberly. "I'm just hoping nothing we've done will trip him up in any way."

"No," Danny said. "But it's kind of you to worry. There is, however, something we can do for him. Felix?"

Felix nodded and continued. "Now, as you know, Matteo di Rossi passed away five years ago, a year after his father. What you may not know is that his death was under... mysterious circumstances."

"Did his yacht sink in a shallow bay with the coast guard less than twenty minutes away?" Molly asked.

Michael bumped him softly, aware of an undercurrent here, and Carl mouthed, "It's how their foster parents died."

Michael made a slight moue of surprise and then continued to listen, as though there would be a test on this later.

Well, there might be.

"No," Felix said in answer to Molly's question, "although now that we're getting good at this game, I think that may need checking out. You, Stirling, and I can do a little bit of homework, shall we?"

"Josh's father first," Stirling said, and Molly twisted in her seat to kiss her little brother's shoulder.

"'Course," she said. "That just bubbles up from my bitter depths sometimes."

"As it should," Felix acknowledged. "It has been too long unaddressed. As has Matteo's death." He let out a sigh. "We have much good to do, children. I hope you're ready."

"*So* ready," Grace said. "I have no idea why we're not out doing it yet. Go on!"

Some of the tiredness lifted from Felix's smile. "Of course. Matteo's mysterious circumstances were pretty much the exact opposite of a sinking yacht. He was killed in the middle of the Mojave Desert, along with thirty-six incubating eggs from a species of endangered bird."

There was a rather stunned silence.

"We'll get back to the birds later," Hunter said, although it was clear from his tone that the birds were very much on his mind. "How was he killed?"

"His car drove straight into a cliff."

Another stunned silence.

"Not *off* a cliff?" Chuck probed. "Because, you know, off a cliff would be a way to go."

"True. But this wasn't the Grand Canyon, where the roads are on top and the cliff was on the bottom. This was going through Nevada toward Arizona, in which the road was on the bottom and the cliff was just sort of there."

More silence, and then to Felix's obvious relief, an aerial shot came up of a long flat stretch of desert with a crossroad. To the southeast of the crossroads was the pointy pie end of what looked to be a long mesa, the striations of rock exposed by erosion splashed like paint along its sides. The mesa extended down the lower quarter of the picture and far beyond the scope of the camera, and everybody in the room gasped in comprehension.

"Ohh!"

"So instead of running him off the road," Chuck said, "somebody ran him into a cliff!"

"*Yes*," Felix cried, obviously excited for the concept to be understood. "That's exactly what happened. Two somebodies, we suspect. Matteo had planned a cross-country excursion, but a very peculiar one. He went from wine tasting in California before traveling through Nevada, and according to his brother, he was planning on continuing southward down Arizona to cross the border into Mexico and thence to the Gulf of Mexico to board a yacht about two weeks after his accident occurred."

"Why?" Molly asked, her eyes wide and horrified.

"Why what, dearest?" Julia asked.

"Why? Why? *Why* would you drive from California, through the desert, then go south through more desert, then cross the border through *more* desert, then catch a boat into the ocean and go sailing to—where was it, Felix?"

"It was to be a trip across the ocean," Felix said, eyebrows furrowed. "The yacht was fully outfitted to travel to the African coast. Why?"

"Because that's even *more desert*!" she protested. "Why would anyone do this? Why? Why?"

"Molly," Julia said delicately. "I do realize you, perhaps, might not have made that trip."

"She wouldn't have *survived* that trip," Stirling said dryly. "She blows up like a giant heat blister in the sun. She would have needed her own tent, fully formed, around her person."

Molly shuddered. "Heinous," she proclaimed.

There were some hidden smiles around the room, and then Chuck commented, "It's pretty country, Molly-girl. I know, I know. Hot. But the rock formations in Arizona and throughout the Sonoran Desert? There is some real beauty there. And the gulf is—" He grimaced. "—*was* a gorgeous place before mankind came along and fucked it up. If anyone wants to run a scam on the fuckers who did *that,* I am *all in*."

"Environmental polluters are third or fourth on the list," Felix said crossly. "We can only do so much."

"I hear you," Chuck said. "Did you hear that, Lucius? We'll get to your factory eventually."

"*I'm working on it*!" Lucius huffed, and Carl raised his eyebrows at Chuck because this had not come up during all of the soul-baring small talk of their little adventure.

Chuck mouthed, "Later," at him, and Carl nodded, content.

"And continuing on," Felix interrupted. "So Matteo was killed in a car accident that involved two other vehicles, according to crime scene photos." A picture came up—obviously from a helicopter—that showed a terrible twisted mass of metal mashed against the side of the cliff. The body was, thank heavens, not visible, but that this accident had been fatal for somebody was indisputable. Felix's voice dropped. "We were fortunate in this case that the scene was spotted by helicopter first, and the aerial shots were taken from far away. The tire tracks are very clear." They were, too, carved in the dust that coated the road like flour. The story was easily read; the crashed car had been going fast, tread marks straight and purposeful, when another car had pulled in front of it, sliding sideways to force it off the road. The car in the rear had driven parallel to the wrecked car just long enough to keep it from turning a complete 180, and the cliff face had been the only choice.

For a moment there was a horrified quiet in the room—not silence, because there were comments, clarifications, people making sure what they saw was what the others saw—but when the quiet was over, the silence was grim and resigned.

They weren't looking at an accident. At the very least, they were looking at a pursuit. At the worst, they were looking at a murder.

"Did the police find anything?" Josh asked. He sounded sharp—a little gruff, but sharp—and Carl wondered what a day like this would cost him.

Felix grunted, and the next words were thoughtful. "The problem," he said, "is that the first response when arriving at a scene like this one is to see if there's a chance of survival. By the time the police arrived, the crime scene was a giant dust storm, and several firemen and EMTs were attempting to cut the body out of the car. If it were not for the aerial shot from far enough away to not disturb the tire tracks, we'd have nothing."

"But we know he was driven into a cliff, probably going at high speed," Hunter said thoughtfully.

And it was Michael who asked the next question. "What was he driving? That wasn't no ordinary car, was it?"

"That, my friend, was an acid-lime-colored, up-to-the-minute Jaguar F-Pace. One of the fastest SUVs in the world. Matteo was something of a car aficionado. He even raced the European circuit for a number of years after he got married." Felix paused. "No children from the marriage, I'm afraid."

"Subtle, Dad," Josh said. "Real subtle."

"Well, we did look into all avenues," Felix replied modestly.

Michael stood up from Carl's side and got closer to the screen. "Danny, could you make that a little bigger?" he asked, pointing to the blob of iridescent green wreckage. "There's something here, to the side. Like it shot through the rear windshield and took out the whole thing. It's connected by wires…." He paced a little, muttering, giving everybody a look at something long and square, like a metal case. Then he spoke up again, turning toward Felix. "Felix, how fast did you say this thing was going?"

"The police report estimated 130, 140 mph. Why?"

Michael shook his head. "That's not fast enough," he said. "Those things top out at nearly 180. See these tracks here?" He pointed to the ones that ran parallel to the Jaguar long enough to make it hit the cliff face.

"Those are big," Chuck said. "Those are a truck or an SUV, something American made and clunky."

"How can you tell?" Lucius asked, skeptical.

"Lucius, what kind of suit was Felix wearing when he walked in the door the other night?"

"Desmond Merrion Supreme Bespoke," Lucius said immediately. "I've wanted one for years, but you have to make an appointment months in advance, and I keep forgetting."

"I have no idea how you knew that," Chuck said. "But I trust that you do. Trust Car—er, Michael and me on this, right, Michael?"

"Yessir," Michael said, nodding vigorously. "This car coming in from behind had big wheels and Positraction, which is great for a big muscle car. And it *can* go fast, but it shouldn't have been able to go Jaguar F-Pace fast. Something was slowing the F-Pace down."

"That thing plugged into the back, you think?" Felix asked, moving from his place near the side of the screen to the middle. "What is it?"

Carl frowned. "Bird eggs," he said.

"Birds again?" Grace asked. "What in the hell?"

"Felix mentioned them," Carl said. "And that thing had to be running off the car's electricity. See the wires Michael pointed out?"

"Yes," Danny muttered. "So you're saying it was a special compartment designed for eggs. That's sort of a stretch, isn't it?"

"What kind of eggs?" Carl asked.

Felix looked behind him and gave a helpless shrug. "I… some bird I've never heard of, to be honest. An African bustard?"

"Wait," Carl said. "An African *houbara* bustard?"

Felix sounded lost for the first time in their acquaintance. "Danny, could you check the notes?"

"Yes," Danny said, obviously scanning their notes quickly. "Carl had it right. Sometimes called the African houbara, and sometimes called the houbara bustard, this is a bird that is native to Pakistan and Saudi Arabia and is listed as vulnerable on the endangered species list. Why is this important, Carl?"

"The birds were hunted almost to extinction," Carl said in wonder. "But not how you think. The houbara bustard is a delicacy. It's considered an aphrodisiac."

A picture appeared in the corner of the screen of something that looked like a turkey but with a downy fuzz on its much smaller head. "That bird?" Danny asked. "That's… uhm… are you sure?"

Carl stood and joined Felix and Michael, moving to the side so everybody could see the bird itself. "Yes. I know it's not that imposing," Carl said. "But it's not that it's been traditionally hunted, or even that it's prized as a horny-bird on the wing. It's that it was hunted to the edge of extinction by *falcons*. For sport. If there's ever peace in the Middle East, it's going to be because this bird got a bunch of rich landowners together during a bustard migration, and they set their big predatory jungle-cat birds on his weird scrawny tail. So yes—if Matteo was found with however many bustard eggs destroyed by the car crash, I'd say that had something to do with his death."

Silence took over the room, and Carl turned and squinted against the projector to see what everybody was doing. "What?" he asked. "Why isn't anybody talking?"

"We're impressed, that's all," Danny said. "Felix and I had this entire presentation laid out to ask you to help us figure out who killed Josh's father. It was the only thing Leon di Rossi wanted in the world, and Julia…." He looked over to where Julia stood by the wet bar, one hand on Josh's shoulder as he sprawled in the overstuffed chair.

"I said I'd ask you all if you would want to look into it," Julia said clearly. "But I'll be honest, everyone." She let out a sigh. "I don't know what Leon will do with the information. He loved Matteo very much, and Matteo—well, the year after his father died, he divorced his arranged-marriage wife and got to live for himself. But it was only a year." Her voice grew a little wobbly. "He deserved more."

Felix picked up the thread. "And you two, Carl and Michael, just laid two very big pieces of the puzzle at our feet without prompting. I... like Danny said, we're impressed."

"We are," Grace said, sounding completely insincere. "But that doesn't change the fact that this guy was hauling these bird eggs through a completely different continent and we don't know why. And were they trying to kill him or just trying to kill those weird bald turkey birds? It had to be someone who'd followed him and someone who came to intercept. So experienced drivers? And we don't even know where he was coming from or where he was going to. Yes, I'm terribly impressed that we know about the weird turkey birds and the super fast car, but we're going to have to figure out who to con and what to steal or we're completely useless."

"Wow, Grace," Molly muttered in disgust. "Do you have any other buzzes you can kill? Is there a buzz bird you can take out with a cannon or something? We were very excited here!"

"Fine," Grace said. "You be excited. I'm itchy. There is something"—his voice dropped—"very dangerous...." He took a breath and finished after a moment. "There is something very dangerous here. And I don't mind dangerous, and I definitely want to do this, but you idiots might have to pull this job without me, and I don't like that."

"Let's wait and see what the job entails," Josh cautioned. "I'm stuck here, but you might get to travel." A sad smile flickered at the corners of his mouth. "You can't be my emotional support animal without *any* fun, Grace. What kind of shitty friend would that make me? Besides... it's like you said. We've got some questions to answer."

"I've got one," Chuck said. "I'd stand up, but the stage is full now." He glared, and Michael and Carl moved out of his way.

Carl glanced at Michael as they sank back into the corner of the couch. "Good job." He really was impressed.

"Thanks," Michael whispered back. "You too."

Chuck took center stage, where he was apparently comfortable. "Danny, pull up a world map—maybe one that tells us where the weird turkey-bird lives."

"Houbara bustard," Danny corrected dryly. "Not saying it won't make his name any less awkward."

"Sure. Oh, see!" Chuck pointed to the area indicated by the map Danny had just put up on the screen. "Look. The bird populates northern Africa and the Middle East. Now think about it. Matteo was driving like a bat out of hell from someplace in California? Is that right?"

"Napa," Felix said. "Famous for its wines and crafts, at least until half the state burned down in recent years. But it's trying to rebuild."

"So for whatever reason, Matteo was heading for the Gulf of Mexico, with a yacht waiting. A yacht big enough to brave the high seas?" he asked Felix.

"Yes, in fact," Felix answered. "It was a one-deck yacht, but it was nearly ninety feet long, and from what the skipper told Leon, it was fully outfitted for a months' long journey. Why?"

Carl had caught on, though. "He was taking the birds to Africa?" he asked. "Why would he be smuggling the birds to Africa? Don't they *originate* in Africa?"

"Wait," Danny said, doing some fast typing of his own. "I've got his financials. After his father died, he started giving a lot of money to conservation agencies. The environment was his thing, and endangered species in particular. So…." He paused, his voice growing far away. "What does that get us?"

"A place to start," Julia decided. "I think it's time to split up and do some investigating. Who wants to take what?"

"I'll take the birds," Carl said. "The bustard's primary appeal— besides being a weird-looking horny pill—is being falcon food. It looks like these eggs were being sent back to their native habitat to be what? Hunted? In the US, falcons aren't too pricey—maybe three thousand dollars fully trained. But in the Middle East, at a falconer festival? We're talking hundreds of thousands of dollars."

Grace stared at him over his shoulder. "How in the *hell* do you know that?"

"He likes birds," Michael said loyally, and Carl grimaced at him in apology.

"I do. But my company also *insures* birds, and I've had to make trips to Doha, in Qatar, before, with a fully trained veterinarian and falconry expert to verify that we could insure a hybrid falcon bred to hunt other birds."

"There's falcons in Qatar?" Grace asked, sounding interested and surprised.

"There's falcons *everywhere,* but the Souq in Doha is famous," Carl told him, remembering the giant room, almost like a livestock room at a county fair, with rows of stucco "benches" for the falcons to perch upon. Each bird had been hooded, the hoods brightly colored or decorated with bits of metal, and while their bodies had been at rest, there'd been a coiled tension in the air, as though every bird had just been waiting for its sight—and its freedom. "Falconry is a big part of their culture," he finished weakly and realized everybody was staring at him, waiting for more. "See, it's always been part of Middle Eastern culture, but for a while, all the birds were dying out because of pesticides. But in the sixties and seventies, we realized that we could reclaim endangered species by changing our own behavior. When we stopped using DDT, the falcons came back. So once the falcons returned, the Middle Easterners—the well-off ones, anyway—re-engaged in the sport. But by that time, the bustard, one of their principal game birds, was running out of land, and they were a favorite prey for falconers because of the horny-pill thing, so the birds were, like I said, nearly hunted to extinction. They're starting to come back now, but...."

"But they're still on the watchlist," Felix said. He nodded. "So, Carl, you've got a start and some contacts. How about you investigate the birds, like you said, and find out why someone might want to be hauling—how many was it, Danny?"

"Three dozen," Danny muttered, looking something else up on the computer as he spoke.

"Three dozen bustard eggs from California, where no bustards are usually found, to Qatar. Or wherever they were bound."

"I can do that," Carl said. "What else?"

"The car," Julia said. "Michael? Chuck? Cars are your specialty. We need to look into what kind of cars were involved in that accident. Not just Matteo's, but in particular the ones that drove him off the road. You may not be able to discover paint color, but something tells me that with some traffic photos to narrow down your options, you can get us an idea of what was used."

"I'll get the traffic photos," Stirling said. "I need dates and times and time of days—as many details as you can get me, and I'll see if I can narrow the rest down."

"I can work with you on that," Julia said.

"What do we do?" Grace asked.

"You and Hunter get to research Napa," Danny said. "We know that's where the bustard eggs came from, and bustards lead to falconry. Start looking up travel brochures to see what's mentioned, and call places to see what they have. It's not glamorous, but—"

"It's good detective work," Grace said, throwing his head back. "I can do that while I babysit Cancer Boy. Did you hear that, Josh? I said it."

Josh gave a rusty chuckle. "I heard it. Since we're speaking truth, can I call you Asshole? 'Cause that'll be fun too."

"Josh actually has his own job," Julia said, and Carl looked up to watch her lock eyes with her son. "Don't you?"

Josh looked away. "Only because we owe a debt," he said. "Because Leon di Rossi is doing this and we owe him."

Julia's mouth compressed, and she looked—for the first time in Carl's memory—displeased with her son.

Felix let out a sigh. "Josh, for whatever reason you're doing it, remember that Mr. di Rossi *is* putting himself out. Above everything, son, I hope we've raised you to be gracious."

Josh gave Felix a tortured look. "Of course, Dad."

And Carl understood.

"So," Julia said, "we'll have another family meeting in—what do you think, Felix? Seven days?"

"Four."

Everybody looked surprised, and Felix elaborated. "I got a call right before we came down. Mr. di Rossi moved heaven and earth, and that moved our timetable up. He'll be here tomorrow, and we can give him a good meal and some good conversation before his little trip to the hospital with Josh. And then Josh can come back with some more information that we need about his father."

"He was *not* my father," Josh said hotly, and everybody in the den took a breath. Ill, in pain, and emotionally overwrought, Josh was obviously having trouble dealing with the fact that the men he'd loved since he'd been born couldn't help him with this one damned thing.

"He's not your *dad*, son," Felix said gently. "And he's definitely not your Uncle Danny. But he was special to your mother, so please, for all of us, remember that we love you most for your heart."

They could all hear Josh's deep breath. "Yeah, Dad," he said after a moment. "I'm sorry, everybody."

And of course, Grace had to add, "I am so gonna be there when you grill Uncle Leon like a trout," he said with satisfaction. "It'll be great. I'll get to be the emotionally mature one in the room. Did you hear that, everybody? *I'm emotionally mature!*"

"Yeah, Grace," Stirling muttered. "We get it. You're getting laid, so you're less obnoxious. Go you."

"Go me," Grace said, nodding with finality. "I'm having popcorn for dinner in four days."

Molly sighed. "Great. So everybody's got something to do but me."

Julia cleared her throat. "Actually, uhm, Molly?"

Molly's eyes widened, and she sat up. "No," she said.

"But you said it yourself," her brother teased grimly. "I heard you. Nothing else to do."

"No," she pleaded.

"Please, Molly," Josh cajoled. "We were going to ask Michael or Chuck to drive you."

"Oh God," she muttered. "How many fucking days?"

"Three," Julia said. "If Felix is correct, the family will arrive tomorrow in the afternoon. Felix?"

Felix checked his phone. "Late midmorning."

"You heard him. Will they be staying here, dearest?"

Felix checked his phone again. "According to that phone call, yes, he's accepted our invitation."

"So," Julia continued, "tomorrow afternoon, and if the children are interested in sightseeing the next day while their father is in the hospital, and the day after while he's recovering, would you mind…?"

"Shit," she said. "I hate babysitting."

"Ooh," Grace murmured appreciatively. "I'll come sit on the babies. Think of all the things we can teach them, Molly! Picking pockets, lifting small objects from museums—"

"*No!*"

Everybody shouted it at the same time, and Molly glowered at Grace as though he was the only thief in the room. "No," she said. "No, Grace. We're just taking them sightseeing."

"Fine," he grumbled. "Get tickets to a sports game or something. I want one of those fuzzy blankets that says Chicago on it."

"Sure," she told him, obviously resigned. "I'll get you a fuzzy blanket. Any other merch you guys want?"

Michael leaned over and murmured into Carl's ear. "Can she get me a hat? I've never been to a game before. Any game. Hockey, football, baseball—I'm in."

Carl smiled at him, at the modest request, at the sweetness. He suddenly wanted to get the man a thousand hats.

"Molly," he said, his voice deep enough to cut through the multiple requests for the moon. "Michael's willing to accompany you. How about you talk to the kids about their interests, and we'll get you the tickets for where you need to go."

And bless the girl, she turned a beaming smile at Michael, one of pure relief. "Oh thank God. I *hate* driving in the city, and Chuck is going to be tied up at Lucius's place for part of that time. I'll buy you any merch you want if you'll help out."

Michael grinned at her. "A hat," he said cheerfully. "But only if we end up at a sports game."

"Deal!"

He sounded so excited Carl wished he could be there.

Their confab broke up not too much later—everybody had their tasks, and Carl had always marveled that the wonder of this thing he did with the Salinger family was that all Danny had to do was hand out jobs and people worked their asses off for him.

"You ready to go?" Michael asked as people stood and stretched and milled around. Josh and Grace were having an intense conversation that, if Carl had to guess, probably revolved around Josh sending Grace away from Chicago. Privately, he was hoping Grace won that argument. Josh had been so very, very strong about his illness, about people not stopping their lives to freak out over him, but it was obvious he was starting to fray a little at the edges. Carl thought that having a friend like Grace to help weave those edges back together was one of the perks of having a friend like Grace at all.

"I need to talk to Felix and Danny a moment," Carl said. "You, uh, don't mind having a roommate for a little while? I was going to go get my winter clothes so I don't have to keep flying to DC and back."

The smile that lit up Michael's face actually alarmed Carl a little.

"I was going to try to find an apartment here," Carl said. "I don't want to put you—"

That smile didn't lessen one bit.

"I have no idea why I'm that exciting to you," he finished hopelessly. And suddenly, Michael's smile became devious.

"Maybe not. But you just gave me a nice window to find out," he said, looking very pleased with himself.

Carl's ears were burning. He could *feel* them, and he cursed his vampire-pale complexion. "Felix?" he said. "Danny?"

But Danny was talking quietly to Grace, which was too bad, because when Carl was talking to Felix, he always felt like he'd trespassed enough.

"What's up?" Felix asked, and the smile on his face didn't seem as trite or forced as it had been in the past. Carl suddenly wondered if maybe worrying about Josh had made Felix reassess his need to put energy into a hopeless grudge.

"I… my company has a position open in Chicago. I travel a lot anyway, and I've got an apartment in DC. You guys have been nice enough to let me stay in the mansion when I'm in the area or helping on a job, but I was wondering, since there's another room in the city apartment, if I could—"

"Sublet it from us?" Felix asked, putting him out of his misery.

"Only if you don't have a problem with it," he said gratefully.

"Only the sublet part," Felix said. "Danny owns the place outright. You're welcome to move in and stay as long as you like."

"Felix, that's not necessary. I'm happy to—"

"You have no idea," Felix said, voice gruff. "None. How much it meant to the three of us that we didn't have to leave Josh to get this done. And you didn't hurt anybody or piss anybody off. Leon di Rossi was so impressed with us, and that's very much due in part to the first impression you left. If you and Carmichael can room together amicably, you are free to stay there as long as you like. I think Julia and Danny will be happy your base is a little closer to home."

Carl's chest was tight, and he hoped he wouldn't embarrass himself. Felix hadn't been his biggest fan at the very beginning, but Carl had kept getting called in to help. He was pretty sure that had been Danny's doing.

But now, maybe, he wasn't on Felix's shit list anymore.

He'd really like that.

Behind him, he heard Grace snicker and then say, "Ouch! You're stronger than you look, Cancer Boy."

"Leave them alone," Josh murmured. "They're new."

He turned to see what they were talking about, but Michael was at his shoulder, gazing at him expectantly. "I need to talk to Julia for a moment," he said. "You keep talking to Felix." He disappeared, that wiry body moving purposefully, and Carl turned back to Felix, the nice moment almost awkward now.

But Felix was smiling at him. His eyes were tired, and he still looked worried, but he was smiling.

"So, uhm, you and Carmichael?"

And Carl could feel his ears turn purple. "We get along," he said with dignity.

Felix's expression went soft. "He looks at you like you hung the moon."

"I don't know why!" And Carl could hear the panic in his own voice. Oh Lord. An ex-wife who had probably wished she could forget his name. A string of ex-lovers who'd probably forgotten they'd ever heard it. And Danny and Chuck, who thought he was a nice guy, but mostly an also-ran and therefore to be pitied.

And this one guy who had gone out of his way to know Carl better.

"Carl?"

"Yeah?"

"Danny spotted me running for my life away from a big bruiser of a man whose pocket I'd recently picked. He hotwired a Vespa, caught up to me, and asked if I needed a ride."

Carl blinked, enchanted. "And you did?"

"Most assuredly. I mean, I was trying to outrun the angry tourist, but I also thought Danny was the most amazing person I'd ever seen in my life. And I know that at one point so did you. Don't question when someone looks at you the way that young man is looking at you. Take it from someone with ten years of regret under his belt. Do *everything* you can to be the best person you can be, and try not to ever let that look slip away. Do you understand?"

Carl nodded, comforted as he'd never been as a child. "God, I hope so."

Felix chuckled and patted his shoulder. "When are you going to DC to pick up your clothes?"

"I was going to try to get a ticket tomorrow and be back in three days. I should have the information you need by the time we have dinner the day after that."

Felix tilted his head. "Is there something you're not telling me?" he hazarded.

Carl blew out a breath. "I have a contact who can get me to the Department of the Interior," he said quietly. This was what had made him decide to get his clothes *now* as opposed to after this caper was finished. "We're dealing with an endangered species here, and there's a whole subculture of crime that I'm not familiar with. I think sending out some feelers in that direction could really help. I don't want to make it a phone call—"

"Phone calls from across the country are far too official," Felix agreed. "You want to run into them, and say, 'Oh yes, I heard the strangest thing....'"

Carl touched his finger to his nose. Funny how *being* a con man and being someone who *investigated* thieves and fraudsters had so much of the same skill set.

"Very well. What are you and Michael doing for the rest of the day?" he inquired politely.

"Michael probably has work to do," Carl said with a shrug. "I was going to go to his little—" He frowned, remembering something he'd been planning to mention. "Did you know he's set up a sort of apartment in the hangar where you keep the plane and the cars?"

Felix blinked, surprised. "An apartment?"

"He used cubicle prefabs and got an old couch and a chair, a mini fridge, even a small dresser where he sets his drinks and probably keeps a change of clothes. I think sometimes, after shuttling vehicles all day, he doesn't want to drive back to the apartment."

"Fair," Felix acknowledged, "but that will get awfully cold in the winter, don't you think? They need space heaters there just to keep the oil from freezing in the cars."

Carl nodded meaningfully. "Yeah, uhm, I wasn't sure what we could do about that. But if you think of something...."

Felix's eyes widened appreciatively. "Ah. Yes. You're absolutely right." He glanced behind him to where Josh sat, making quiet jokes to Grace, Stirling, and Molly. "Maybe I'll put Josh and Stirling on it. If nothing else, they might know a friend who can figure out how to make a little apartment inside a hangar work."

Carl nodded, and then decided to spill the whole enchilada. "He also has a mews in the back where he's rehabbing an injured falcon. I think he stays there sometimes to feed the poor thing its weight in raw chicken or roadkill. Oh! And there's endangered birds in the field behind your airstrip. You don't need to report them to anybody. Right now they seem to be thriving. He's set out a bunch of plywood shelters on the ground so they can hide from the hawks—'cause there's a lot of them— and he's run some netting between the driveway and the grassy area."

Felix frowned. "Are the birds a hazard to aircraft?"

Carl had actually looked that up. "I don't think so," he said. "The landing strip is on the far side of the field from the lek—or the mating grounds. Airline regulations try to keep birds a certain distance away from the airstrip, and because the planes are taking off near the big gravel parking lot that used to be a fairground, I'm pretty sure there's enough yardage between the planes and the hangar to make it work without relocating the covey of grouse."

Felix shuddered. "Yes, but you hit the wrong bird at the wrong time and you might have to relocate your soul into another body. You do hear what I'm saying?"

"Yessir. I'll do more research and ask some people about sage grouse. If you can send me the stats on the airstrip, I can check with more accuracy."

"Of course." Felix let out a long breath. "I appreciate you telling me this. But I'm not going to worry about it until you get back to me with more information. How's that?"

"Thanks," Carl said, relieved. "I don't want to bother Michael with it, you know. He's working really hard to be indispensable. I just thought you should know."

"He is," Felix agreed. "So are you. By all means, get your things and move in. Let us know if you need anything else."

Carl nodded. "Thank you."

"Including a swift kick in the ass in the romance department," Felix finished dryly and then turned to speak to Josh.

For some reason, that final admonition, as snarky as it was, made Carl feel as if he'd been welcomed into the family.

# A Game and a Dog

"YOU SURE you don't mind coming with me?" Michael asked as he drove himself and Carl to the hangar, this time in Josh's natty little sportster, which hadn't been getting driven much anyway. They had the top down because the days were getting crisp and this would probably be the last time the car had a good run since it was going to live in the hangar until spring.

Michael had visions of a stronger, healthier Josh coming out of the mansion on a bright spring morning and hopping into this car like he belonged in the Italian leather seat.

He figured that vision would work as his prayer for the young man's recovery.

"Not at all," Carl said with a shrug. "I brought my laptop. You do what you need to, and I'll be using the tower Wi-Fi to...well, I actually have paperwork to fill out that should have been in my boss's inbox about a month ago."

Michael frowned. "Aren't you worried about losing your job?" he asked.

Carl *hmm*ed. "I did my job. I tracked down the buyer and seller of the lost piece of art, determined that the owner had nothing to do with the theft, told Interpol where the artifact could be found, and spent the rest of my allotted time doing the paperwork for Leon di Rossi's bone marrow donation and showing Lucius all the good tax shelters he could use to launder the money he's giving to his battered women's shelters. It's all totally legit, but this way it will be harder for another hacker to come along and figure out what he's hiding. It's a really important secret to keep."

Michael nodded. He'd gathered that defending the women's shelters was when Chuck and Lucius Broadstone had hooked up. He didn't begrudge either of them their happiness—Chuck had shaken his hand, gotten him a job with the Salingers, and treated him as a friend. He couldn't ask for more than that from a guy who'd saved his life and then given him the keys to change it.

"But you didn't do your paperwork for your real job," Michael clarified.

"My real job's sort of douchey," Carl told him. "They have lawyers that will wiggle through the eye of a needle just to stitch themselves into the right side of the law."

Michael was nonplussed. "Great metaphor, suit guy, but what does it mean?"

He heard Carl's sigh. "It means that insurance companies are like gambling with your life—or your life savings. The customer is obligated to pay into their policy, but the insurance company only makes money if they don't have to pay out. I work for a property insurance company, thank God, because if I worked for a health insurance company, I'd have to worry about all sorts of things that give me ulcers: drug prices, shitty customer care, giant deductibles, patient debt…. I couldn't do it. It would break my heart. See, I signed on because I had an art history degree and I was getting a degree in international law. I wanted to be an art broker, because it sounds great and I'd get to go to museums around the world."

"Wow," Michael breathed, impressed. "I bet your family is totally into art, right?"

"No," Carl replied bluntly. "My father was distant and seemed sort of consumed with his company job. And my mother's a chain-smoking nightmare who will forever be ashamed of me. But art is…."

He paused for a moment, and when Michael glanced at him, he was gazing off into space, not seeing the traffic on the freeway or the bright, crisp September day. "Art takes you places," he said after a moment. "It takes you to different times, to different people. If you're looking at a statue by John Flaxman, for example, you're not just looking at the art of Regency England. You're looking at the poetry of Homer and Dante and the drama of Aeschylus. You're looking at libraries and cathedrals and the process of making sculptures using relief methods. You're looking at Wedgewood, who was Flaxman's boss and one of his most famous contemporaries, and you're looking at all of the things Wedgewood had his name on that Flaxman had a finger in. You're looking at the most beautiful memorial sculptures you've ever seen and the way people look at grief and sadness and a belief in redemption. And you're looking at the art of Regency England, but you're also looking at the art of the

Renaissance and the Restoration. You're looking at the art of ancient Greece and Rome. Because it all went into the work of a small man with a big head who used to draw in his father's workshop, after being educated by his father's friends. That's one artist, and he's an entire solar system of humanity." He paused while Michael tried to catch his breath. "Think about how many galaxies a museum has."

Michael couldn't think. He couldn't talk. He couldn't *breathe.*

"What?" Carl asked, sounding a little grumpy.

"You have that—all of that—just floating around your head?" He remembered Carl's dreaminess when he'd been looking at the injured falcon, his fascination with the sage grouse. It was like he'd seen a teeny bit of the depths of this man in that moment, but he had no idea what an ocean there was underneath.

"You asked why art," Carl replied, because *naturally* an insurance investigator would love something with that sort of operatic intensity. "That's why art. And I got recruited by Serpentus, and I thought, 'Hey, I can be an investigator. That sounds sort of romantic. I can chase criminals, and that will make me a good guy!'"

"But that's not what happened." Obviously not if Carl was working with a crew of thieves and con men.

"It's not even that the thieves were more interesting than the insurance company," Carl said ruminatively. "It's that they were more *motivated.* They stole cars because they loved cars, and they loved to drive fast, and they loved the vehicle they rode in. They stole art to save their family business, which they'd put their entire lives into. They committed fraud to fund something that they needed—and sometimes it was heartbreaking things. Medical treatment because the health insurance company wouldn't pay. Stealing back a family heirloom because it had been repossessed forty years ago and their grandmother missed it. I mean, don't get me wrong. Most thieves aren't noble, and a lot of them are reckless and violent and don't care what happens to the people they encounter as they steal. And a lot of them are motivated by the same thing that motivates the company—pure, unadulterated greed. But there is always the chance that greed is the furthest thing from someone's mind." He sighed. "Sometimes the thieves are more human. That's all."

"It's hard to find a noble thing to do in this world," Michael said thoughtfully. "Being a police officer is supposed to be noble, but you see stories all the time about how the job has been corrupted. Being a lawyer is supposed to be good, but sometimes they're working for the bad guys, even if they're on the side of Johnny Law. Chuck got me a good lawyer—he got away with the money, but he put a lot of it aside for me, right?"

"I know the story," Carl said, probably because Chuck had told him. As much as Carl seemed to think he was extraneous, Michael had seen the way the other people in the crew respected him and seemed to think his opinion was important. Chuck may have come across as a good ol' boy, but he was careful about whom he trusted.

"What he didn't tell you was that he spent a fortune on a guy who got me two years instead of five, like my brothers are serving. And he got me sent to a different prison because my brothers probably would have killed me. Or shot their mouths off about me being a faggot and gotten me killed. And my lawyer was smart, and he was competent, and he worked real hard, but he was straight-up motivated by his fee. You could tell by the way he talked. Chuck's opinion was more important to him than mine at every juncture because Chuck was paying the money. I hold no grudges, but it hurt knowing I was just a paycheck. You... I mean, I know you got your problems with your company and all, but at least you weren't doing it because of a paycheck. I worry, that's all. That you'll get busted helping Felix and Danny and all and you won't even have that."

"I've got plenty saved," Carl said. "I made some good investments. Honestly, mostly by following what Felix did. I figured anybody who could do the things the Salingers did and not get caught would know a thing or two about making money, and they do. I'm not worried. If I get fired, my severance package alone would provide for me for a couple of years. And the company gives me good cover and good contacts. That's part of the reason I'm going to DC tomorrow—to talk to the people I know who can help us."

Michael let out a breath. "You really are their secret weapon as a man in a suit, aren't you?"

"I'm a small part of their operation, Michael," he said, like he was trying to let Michael down gently.

"Nope. You're exactly who they need you to be."

There was a silence then. Not a comfortable one because Michael could tell Carl wasn't good at taking a compliment.

"What?" Michael goaded after a minute.

"I don't know. I'm wondering, how did you end up robbing that bank?"

Michael let out a sigh. It was a fair question. "Desperation," he said after a moment. "My brothers—they're not nice people. My father died in prison, and Ma kept telling me that I'd never be half the man he was." Michael snorted, and he knew it was a bitter sound, but he couldn't seem to help it. "I didn't want to be half the man he was. I didn't want to be *any* of the man he was."

"What *did* you want?" Carl asked softly.

"I *wanted* a date with Dale Earnhardt Jr., but he's straight, so we can't always get what we want."

Carl's rich laughter was his reward, but he hadn't really earned it yet, had he?

"I wanted to be safe," he said after Carl's laughter faded. Carl had been honest with him, and he surely earned the favor. "Daddy beat on Angus and Scooter something awful, but I was too little to get beat, mostly, so they thought it was their job to beat on me. So did my ma. The safest place I had was my best friend in high school, Beth. So, you know, I got her pregnant by thinking of Dale Earnhardt Jr. and married her. And we did okay, really. I got a business loan for a car repair shop, and business was good. I could feed Beth and the kids. And even though I wasn't really *happy*, I felt *safe*."

"What happened?" Carl asked, and Michael was grateful because Chuck must not have told him this part.

"Angus and Scooter," he said in disgust. "The garage was making money. I was paying my bills, sort of. Then they broke in—I swear they broke in—and stole my cashbox. I reported it to the insurance company, but the cops figured out it was my brothers and…." He trailed off and winced. This had not occurred to him.

"And someone like me was the asshole," Carl muttered. "Fucking. Fabulous."

Michael gave a harsh laugh. "You know, until this moment right here, I always thought it was Angus and Scooter. Wait, no, still Angus and Scooter being the assholes. They broke a window, broke the lock, and no, the insurance didn't pay. That was bad enough. I started spiraling down the drain right then. But then they found out that the cops thought I was part of it and—" He shrugged. "—they kept stealing. Any night they needed a little cash. I-I stood up to them the second time. They broke my nose and my wrist, and then I couldn't work on cars, and—"

"It got worse," Carl murmured. "I'm so sorry."

"Yeah, I kept thinking it was a trap of my own making, but I couldn't figure out how I'd made it. Anyway, I was about to go bankrupt and had closed up the garage when my brothers told me they could make it all up to me. All I had to do was help them with one lousy fuckin' thing."

"Oh God," Carl whispered.

"To be honest, they'd gotten recruited by Wilbur and Klamath, the guys who didn't make it out of the bank. Chuck and I overheard them talking about the double-cross, but... you know, Angus and Scooter wouldn't have believed me." He gave a humorless laugh. "Which is sort of funny if you think about it. You know. *They* wouldn't have believed *me*."

"So you agreed to go to jail, basically." Carl sighed, the sound heavy and joyless. "Trapped was an understatement."

"It sucked." Michael didn't want to talk about how badly it had sucked. Nobody had asked him—not even Chuck. But then, nobody had to. He had "meat" written all over him, including a handy prison tattoo right next to his tender orifice that he was hoping nobody would see.

Carl made him feel safe, and boy, did he want the physical contact. He *craved* being held and touched with warmth, with tenderness, and Carl's kisses had led him to believe that all of that and more was waiting beneath the surface. But he didn't want pity. He didn't want somebody to look at him the way those men in prison had looked at him and then to use him like that. Not again. He didn't think Carl would do that, but he figured the less he told Carl about what had happened in those missing two years of his life, the more he wouldn't have to worry about it.

And then Carl asked, voice low and sad. "Are you going to make me ask the big question?"

Michael was almost at the airstrip, which was good. He was driving a small precision automobile at a relatively high speed, and his hands were suddenly sweaty and shaking. That was no good at all when they were on the freeway. He tightened his hold on the wheel, took the exit for the frontage road that led to the hangar, and tried to control his breathing.

"Why does everyone assume prison rape's a thing?" he asked, bitterness dripping from his voice.

"Because you turned pale," Carl said gently, "just thinking about it. And because you want someone who will keep you safe. And because you—you are so sweet. Such a good person. And you were in a place where that wasn't going to keep you from getting hurt."

"Do we have to talk about this?" he asked, but he sounded husky and distraught to his own ears.

"It's your choice," Carl said. "Always your choice. If you like, I can talk about the weather, which is gorgeous. Or I can talk about my trip tomorrow, which I sort of don't want to take. Or I can tell you the fun stuff to do with Leon di Rossi's teenagers, because you deserve a day out, and I sort of wish I was going."

"That last one," Michael decided miserably. "But why don't you want to take your trip?"

"Because." Carl very deliberately brushed Michael's knee with his hand. Not hard enough to distract him or fuck up his driving, but enough to let Michael know he was there and serious. "Because I liked waking up with you this morning. Even if we're still in our pajamas, I'd like to wake up with you again."

Michael swallowed hard. "We don't *have* to be in our pajamas," he ventured.

"Sure we do. Because if the time comes when we're *not* in our pajamas, I'd like very much to not have to leave you alone in the morning."

"When," Michael responded, like saying it would make it so. "*When* the time comes."

"Mm…," Carl hedged. "You might decide you deserve a hero."

"Yeah, well, you might realize you are one." He was. Michael could tell. But his faith was not contingent upon Carl's recognition of his own worthiness. Michael could do all that for him.


ONCE THEY got to the garage, Michael actually had some work to do. He changed into a set of coveralls and left Carl on the couch in the little "apartment," working on his laptop. After a couple of hours, he came to get some water and found Carl dozing, his head resting on the arm of the couch, his laptop sliding off his thighs.

Very carefully, Michael caught the laptop and set it on the seat of the couch. Then, because he was feeling brave, he bent over the side of the couch and brushed his lips against Carl's temple. When he pulled back, Carl was smiling a little in his sleep.

"Mm… whatcha doin'?" he mumbled.

"Was gonna go check on the falcon," Michael told him. "Hodges, the janitor kid, told me he found some fresh roadkill and put it in the fridge to feed him."

Carl grunted. "Mm…."

"Yeah, not attractive. I'll go do it. You stay and sleep."

Carl nodded a little. "'Kay." And then he was breathing evenly again, and Michael had to laugh. He'd obviously not recovered from his trip overseas yet.

Michael grabbed some of the steaks he'd gotten from Phyllis—they were a little past the expiration date but not spoiled yet—and hoped the roadkill in the refrigerator wasn't too bad. The bird had to eat 20 percent of its body weight in food almost daily, and it helped him remember the bird was wild if said food wasn't all carved up and only the meat remained. Falcons had digestive systems almost as tough as a vulture's—they ate bones, skin, the whole shebang.

When he got around to the back of the hangar, he found Hodges out there already, dropping the still floppy jackrabbit through the hole in the top of the mews to land at the falcon's feet. The bird was on it in a heartbeat, ripping, crunching, basically devouring, and Michael thought, not for the first time, it was a good thing his sensibilities had been hardened by hunting with his brothers when he was a kid or he wouldn't have been a good bet to raise birds. You couldn't be too squeamish when you were taking out rabbits and squirrels with a crossbow to get your own dinner.

"Man, that's gross," Hodges said with the visceral appreciation of a teenager working a part-time job. Craig Hodges was tall, rangy, and Black, with a handsome narrow face and velvet-brown eyes. Michael had gotten the feeling the kid may have had a crush on him, which, as far as Michael was concerned, didn't make no goddamned sense, and so he'd been kind but firm about maintaining boundaries. The father in him [wanted] to tell the kid to stay far away from bad men like Carmichael Carmody.

"[I]t is," Michael agreed, watching the bird pull out a nice elastic entrail and snap it in two. He admired the practicality of birds, and brother, could he appreciate the falcon's cold-eyed hatred of being cooped up.

"He seems to like the roadkill better than stuff that's been precut. How'd you know to do that?"

"My folks took us camping two years ago," Hodges said. "The place had a nature conservancy center that specialized in birds. Me and my brother visited every damned day, heard all the presentations, even got to let the birds land on our fists and take off again. I got lots of books to read after that. You want to borrow them?"

Michael thought about the meeting with the Salinger crew that morning. "Yeah," he said, thinking research couldn't hurt. "Did you know falconry used to be considered the sport of kings?"

"Yup." Hodges grinned. "Does that make you King Carmody and me King Hodges?"

Michael snorted. "Makes me a varlet or a valet or a butler or something. You're going to college, right?" All the Salingers were college educated, as far as he knew, and it depressed him. He'd read a lot in prison and had kept up the habit since, but he was only now beginning to understand why his ex had been so depressed about not getting to go away to school. He was starting to see that unlike birds, who could only stare at the wire of their cage and hate, humans had the ability to escape into a wider world by imagination alone.

Hodges stopped grinning. "Next year." His depression over this was obvious and palpable.

"You are a lucky bastard," Michael told him. "Your parents had to work hard to save up that money. The day I realized I had enough money to save for my kids' college was the happiest in my life."

"Not the day they were born?" Hodges asked.

"That too. But being happy because my wife did a great thing with a little bit of baby juice is one thing. Providing for my kids—that's a lot harder. Your parents provided the best future they possibly could for you. Don't take that for granted."

Hodges grunted. "You're not too old to go to school, you know."

Michael shrugged. "Was never any good at it. But I could fix cars. The fact that you thought to get all the books on birds? I didn't about that. You're going to be rich and famous and powerful someday. Be careful what you do with it. Use your powers for good."

Hodges gave him an odd look. "You mean, like feeding dead things to birds?"

It was Michael's turn to grin. "Yeah, but when you're smart and shit, you can use the word 'ornithologist.'"

Hodges laughed outright. "Who's asleep in your apartment, anyway?"

"A friend," Michael told him. "One of the people the Salingers work with."

Another laugh. "Do those people know any straight men?"

That made Michael giggle like a little kid himself, although he tried to hold it back. Finally, when he could talk, he said, "Let's say I'm glad this one's not."

"Ooh...." Hodges was teasing him, but Michael also detected some sugared-over hurt in the sound.

"You know, I'm ten years older than you," Michael said gently. "And I'm not a good catch. Go have a crush on someone not quite so beat-up, 'kay?"

Hodges grunted. "You mean you don't want to be the older man who seduces me?" he asked, and Michael could tell he had a whole scenario built up.

"No," Michael said. "But it's sweet that you think that would be fun. Kid, I've got kids of my own. Go find someone you can go to the movies with and hold hands with. Go away to college. Get a boyfriend."

"So you can go get it on with that businessman in there?" Hodges sulked.

Michael turned away from the bird, who was literally down to feet and ears at this point. "Craig," he said, his voice husky and hurting. "I... I've needed someone like that guy my entire life, but I didn't know how to look. The first time I saw him, looking super serious in his business suit and his glossy shoes, I thought, 'He wouldn't ever play at hearts. I need a guy like that.' You haven't been beaten up in the heart department yet. Find out what you need. I'm definitely not that guy."

Hodges grunted. "You, uh, still want those books on birds?"

"Yeah," Michael said, smiling. "That would be great. I think there's a lot more about birds than meets the eye." For one thing, they knew how to get what they wanted. For another, they knew how to fly.

"Michael?"

"Yeah?"

"You should be the guy *somebody* needs. I may be young, but I know that."

Michael thought about it and squared his shoulders a little. "You know, you're damned smart for a young guy."

Hodges grinned, and they watched the falcon finish off the feet. Yuck.

THE NEXT afternoon he was sitting right behind home plate at Wrigley Field, accepting armloads of merchandise from Molly, who had made a run down to the vendors with Leon di Rossi's daughter, Esme. Esme was a fourteen-year-old coltish girl with a thick braid of wild black hair and limpid brown eyes who spoke English with a brazen Italian accent but seemed more than happy to be in Chicago instead of Corfu for her holiday with her father.

"Corfu is lovely, you understand," she'd told Molly as Michael had driven them all into town. "But there is nothing to do! There is sun and there is beach and there is beach and there is sun, and there is shopping—but is nothing. Is all done. Chicago? Is not all done, no?"

"No," Molly had replied firmly. "Chicago even has a beach if you like. Not the ocean, but Lake Superior is nothing to sneeze at."

Esme had gasped in excitement. "You hear that, Bernardo? We can swim? Can we go swimming tomorrow? It is hot, yes?"

Molly grimaced and held out her hand. "It's September, so it'll be a little chilly. But then, it's still a beach. Bernardo, does that interest you?"

The boy—thin, intense, and obviously shy and displaced, gave her a nod and a shrug.

"I'm not sure what Corfu is like," Michael said, eyeing the boy in his rearview mirror, "but I gotta tell you, Texas is like an inferno nine months out of the year—at least my piece of it. Chicago will take some getting used to."

The boy gave him a slight smile in the rearview, and Michael counted it as a win. That had been the way of it as Michael had wrestled his way to the field to park in the W. Addison St. lot.

"You didn't want to park in the outfield lot?" Molly asked quietly after he'd bought his ticket.

Michael winced. "Sixty dollars!" he said, because the number had blown his mind.

She gave him a fond look. "Honey, I'm paying. Or actually, Julia's paying, but I'm paying 'cause I'm not going to invoice the woman. But don't you worry—you're doing us a favor. You get all the dogs, all the merch, and all the best parking on us."

Michael's cheeks warmed. "That's gonna take some getting used to, too," he muttered.

"Yeah, well, make Carl spoil you."

With that, she waited until he killed the engine before bailing out of the car, saying, "C'mon, kids, let me introduce you to world-class Chicago cuisine, and we can buy all the merch in the world!"

To both of their delight, the kids recognized Wrigley Field from movies, and even Bernardo perked up. While the women went to hit the merch tables—Molly had a list a mile long, and she made Esme her partner in consumerism—Michael sat next to the boy and ogled the big green wall and the fact that the fans, the players, even the ball looked bigger and larger than life compared to what he could see on TV.

"You ever been to a game?" he asked, mostly because his kids talked up a storm, and a silent child made him uneasy.

"Football," the boy said, and Michael had to remind himself that in Italy, that meant soccer. "There is always a game somewhere. There are, like, a thousand leagues in Europe."

Michael grinned at him. "Yeah? I ain't never been to a pro ball game. We had a minor league team in an adjoining town, though. I went to a lot of those. I'd take my kids 'cause you could picnic on the hillside for just five bucks a person. They had games and stuff for little kids, and we could bring lunch and snacks so it wasn't so expensive. We had a good time."

Those *had* been good times with him, Beth, and the kids. He'd have to tell Carl about them. He got the feeling Carl didn't know what happy families did in their spare time, with or without money.

Not that he and Carl would have any trouble filling their time, even if it was simple stuff. Michael had already learned Carl liked watching movies or television before he went to bed. Carl liked that Michael cooked, and he wanted to help. He liked talking about his job— not the paperwork or the politics, but the art or the valuables he was tracking down. He seemed to have a fascination for what people deemed important, and Michael thought that was a rather cool area of expertise.

Michael had thought Carl might like to fool around a little the night before, but that hadn't happened. There'd been kissing—kissing that had curled Michael's toes and probably a few chest hairs as well, if Michael had had any, which he didn't.

But in the end, Carl had pulled back, panting, and nuzzled Michael's neck.

"You want me, right?" Michael had said breathlessly.

"So much."

"Then why—"

"Because you want me too, and I don't want to waste that on a couple of quickies. Let it build. I don't get this a lot. I want to savor it." Then he'd bucked up against Michael's thigh and proven he wasn't bullshitting, and that was even better.

"I'm gonna expire from horniness," Michael had told him, grinding back, and Carl's low chuckle in his ear hadn't made things any less intense. But Michael had gotten it too. This wasn't a quick blowjob. This wasn't a drive-by. This wasn't anything Michael had to hide from his wife, whom he loved. This was a grown-up relationship, and it was apparently something Carl didn't get a lot of either. They *both* got to go slow. They *both* got to enjoy each other's company. That was nice.

But that didn't mean kissing Carl goodbye that morning as he'd run out the door to catch his cab to the airport hadn't sucked.

"You have children?" Bernardo asked shyly, breaking into Michael's musings.

"I do. They're with their mother now, in Ohio, but I get them over some of the holidays and part of next summer."

The boy nodded glumly. "My parents too. Does their mother hate you?"

Michael opened his mouth, stunned a little by the question. "No. No, sir. We're still real good friends. I just couldn't love her like she deserved. She needs someone who loves all the parts of her, and I couldn't. Breaking up worked for both of us."

The boy blinked slowly at him, his eyes as wide and luminously brown as his sister's. "Are you gay?" he asked suspiciously.

Michael had to smile. "Yessir, I am. Why do you ask?"

"My father. He said that many of the men we would meet would be gay, and we needed to be polite. I thought he was kidding."

Michael laughed a little at that. "Turns out, he wasn't far wrong. That a problem?"

Barnardo gave a shrug. "No. But you have children, and you like to take them places. That is nice."

"You betcha. Your father likes to take you places. Corfu sounds nice, right?"

Bernardo gave another shrug. "But instead, we are here for business. I don't understand why."

"Business? Is that what your father said?" Michael was surprised.

"Yes. Everything my father does is about business. At least that is what my mother complains about. But then she spends his money very well. Don't think Esme and I haven't noticed. When we are with him, though, he's usually very much with us." The boy grunted. "But not this time. Maybe my mother is right."

"She most certainly is not," Michael replied. "Your father is a hero!"

Nobody could have looked as surprised as this boy.

"What do you mean?"

"Well, my boss's son is real sick—like, so sick he might die. And your father only just found out the boy is his nephew, and that he's a compatible match to give his bone marrow so the boy can get better. That's why we're taking you and your sister out for the three days. Your father needs to have some blood tests done, and then the operation to donate, and then a day of recovery. He was worried, you see, that you and your sister would be bored and restless. And me and Molly—" He sighed. "—we were feeling sort of useless, you know? We want Josh to get better so bad, and we didn't have anything to do to help. But this? Taking you two out and showing you a good time? That makes us happy."

Bernardo blinked at him. "This Josh, he is my cousin?"

"Yeah, I guess he is. He's a little older than you, though. He's Molly's age."

Bernardo's eyes, already expressive, grew absolutely infinite with unshed tears. "He is Matteo's son?"

"Yessir. He was sort of a secret, for a lot of reasons. But his parents are so worried about him, they looked up your father to ask him to help."

"My Uncle Matteo, he was very kind to me and Esme," Bernardo whispered. "Why did nobody tell us about this? We get thrown on a plane and brought to that house. There were so many people there, and suddenly they said, 'Hey, you're going to a game,' and I don't understand the rules and—"

"Hey, hey." Michael squeezed the boy's shoulder awkwardly. "Hey. That was rough on you, I'm sure. I don't know why your father didn't tell you, but, you know, maybe he had his reasons. Maybe he was a little afraid of the procedure, or maybe he didn't want you to worry. Or maybe he was real busy, having to change his plans so suddenly. I don't know—you'll have to ask him. I'm just the car guy. My job was to take you and Esme out with Molly and show you a good time so your whole vacation didn't suck, and that was double the fun for me, you know? I get to spend some time with some good kids, and I get to help my friends so Josh gets better. So you just ask me the rules as we go, all right? This could be a real fun couple of days for you guys, and I know that's what your father wants. So you tell Molly and me what sounds like fun, and if we can't do it today, we can make plans to do it in the next three. How's that?"

"Was Molly lying?" Bernardo asked. "Is there a beach?"

Michael grinned. "There is indeed. But she was dead on about it not being warm enough to swim."

Bernardo shrugged. "We can see, right?"

"Absolutely."

At that moment, Molly and Esme returned, and Michael had his hands full stashing the bags of merchandise under their seats. When he was done, it was time for the national anthem, and then the game began.

And he and Molly found themselves serving as the world's foremost authorities on baseball and the rules of engagement.

But Bernardo's confusion stuck with Michael, and he remembered how clear, how candid, Carl had been the night before. Sometimes, someone needed the slow and steady guy, the explainer, the person to put into words the things that other people think you should understand.

Michael understood then that his attraction to Carl had more to it than just a deep-seated need to be safe. It had that respect, that admiration for the guy who took the time to explain, to look at reasons, to fill out the paperwork and take the steps to do things correctly.

# Accustomed Ways

THE SERPENTUS office suite was located about three blocks from the National Archives Museum that held the Declaration of Independence. Carl had to remind himself of that every time he went—somewhere in this cursed city was a place where people had put their good faith and good intentions in writing and had fucked up their job anyway.

It helped him not hate his bosses as the soulless sellouts they undoubtedly were.

"Mr. Cox, it's so good to see you!" Foster Aldrich said genially, catching Carl in the reception area for investigative services as Carl put a complete paper file into Aldrich's inbox, which hung from his door. Carl had already emailed the file to Aldrich's secretary as he'd endured the commercial flight from Chicago to DC that morning, but Aldrich did like his dead-tree-memorials to cases long buried.

"Hello, Foster," Carl said, refusing to call a man who was younger than he was by five years by his last name. "Got all your paperwork in under the wire." He had too. The deadline was the next day. Like he'd told Michael, he'd held on to it to give himself more time to do things for the family.

"Yes, yes. Are you ready for your next assignment?"

"Not for two weeks," Carl said without hesitation. "I need time to work on a matter for an independent client first."

Foster Aldrich—prematurely stout, prematurely humorless, and almost constantly red in the face over one indignation or another—started to flush. "Are you allowed to have independent interests?" he asked, blowing out his cheeks.

"I am," Carl said. "It's in my contract. It's how I've brought in a couple of very pricey clients for you, so it seems to work for the board." Besides Felix and Lucius, he'd worked enough independent cases for people who really *did* want their valuables back and were not merely satisfied with the insurance payout, to have claimed some autonomy in the matter. In fact, since his trip to Wales—and his memorable meetup with

Danny in rehab—he'd become something of an odd fish in his company, and while once upon a time he may have yearned for conventionality and respectability, now he sort of enjoyed being on the outside of this particular box.

"You may want to rethink that," Aldrich said, trying to sound threatening.

"Why?"

Foster opened and closed his mouth. "Because the shareholders might not always agree to it!" he said after an uncomfortable silence.

"Well, when they tell *me*, I'll deal with it," Carl said. "But I warn you, I've got a couple of whales that will go somewhere else if things change too drastically. Besides, it seems a shame to eliminate a practice which has only done this money pit some good."

Oop! There, it happened again—Foster's ears turned purple.

"That's borderline disrespectful!"

Carl took a breath and gave him a bland smile. "To the client, to pay our prices? Yes. Was there anything else I can do for you, Foster? I have a lunch meeting with Ginger Carson in fifteen minutes. It's at the station, and that's a bit of a trek." He was only partially lying. Ginger Carson, who was actually a member of the board and not the vice president of whatever it was Foster had just been put in charge of, really *was* meeting him for lunch, but she wouldn't be caught dead eating at Union Station. For one thing, she liked Carl. They were roughly the same age, and while she never did anything as crass as flirt with him, he'd been aware of an undercurrent between them—a possibility they'd both turned their backs on—on more than one occasion.

Carl had become increasingly discriminating about his lovers in the last nine years, and he enjoyed Ginger too much as a friend. Besides, she was arrow straight, with no room for equivalency or leaning, and he'd begun to realize he couldn't trust those people who served the higher god of law and order without looking to the lowly god of compassion first.

Ginger was actually waiting for him at Union Gold, which was less than a block away from the Serpentus building. But if Foster knew how close it was, he might ask to tag along, something Carl wanted to avoid at all costs. He wanted to pick her brain.

"Oh," Foster said, obviously disappointed that Ginger would choose Carl's company over his own. "If you could wait up for me, I'll call a cab—"

But Carl was already striding toward the door. "No time. I'm going to be late as it is!"

He practically flew down the stairs, outstripping the elevator, grateful he'd been working out more and more since May so he could keep up with Hunter and Chuck. He wasn't as fast—or as muscled—but he wasn't underweight with stooped shoulders or a potbelly like Foster, either.

God, he hated that guy.

Foster was a terrible, terrible suck-up, for one thing, and he was the kind of micromanaging executive who forced all the competent people in a department to quit, then congratulated himself on getting rid of dead weight. Right before being fired for destroying company productivity and forcing the executives to spend three years repopulating what had once been a perfectly functional department.

Carl had seen it happen several times at Serpentus. And he'd watched Foster Aldrich start the process all over again last May. Carl's independence bothered Aldrich—but as long as Carl's methods were sanctioned by the board, who had been really excited by Carl's propensity for bringing in clients, Foster didn't have a leg to stand on.

Carl just had to avoid the little bastard until Foster's own incompetence fucked him over, and for that reason, he kept up a ground-eating clip until he arrived at Union Gold and disappeared inside.

Ginger—petite, with hair to match her name, a little bit of padding in the hips and bust, and a pointed chin and upturned nose—always reminded him of a cheerleader. One of the modern ones with the athleticism and nerviness that should have terrified football players in every school in the country. She even had a nose covered in little bronze freckles, discreetly covered by makeup of course. They'd worked out together for a time, and he knew the only reason he could bench press more than she could was because God had given him the advantage of being six foot four with shoulders almost as wide as she was tall. Give the woman time and her determination would rectify that, he was sure.

But that didn't keep her from jumping to her feet in four-inch heels and greeting him at the table with a kiss on the cheek and a genuine smile.

"Carl! Honey, how're you doing?"

"Can't complain," he said, taking the seat across from her in the booth. "Club soda?" he asked, indicating the drink in his spot, and she nodded.

"With lime, just like you like it."

Ginger was drinking diet soda. As workout buddies a few years ago, they'd both confessed to being recently on the wagon, and it was one of the many things that had kept them from being lovers. Carl couldn't do that. Not again.

"Thank you," he said, giving her his best gracious smile. "But I have to warn you, I told Foster Aldrich that we were eating at Union Station before I left. You need to think of a reason to take a train after lunch. I'll pay for your cab!"

She grimaced. "Gah! What a reprehensible little toad. And boy is he interested in you. He's been looking up your contract, you know, to see what it says about your outside clients. He's got an ugly soul, Carl. Be aware."

Carl nodded, taking her warning seriously. "Watching my back," he reassured before scanning the menu and setting it down, ready for the approaching server.

"So," Ginger said when the server had taken their order and departed, "I'm so glad to see you actually here. How long are you staying?"

"Leaving the day after tomorrow," he told her, grimacing at her surprise. "I'm really only here to ship my winter clothes to a sublet in Chicago. That's going to be my home base for a while."

She cocked her head. "Not that you can't do that, Carl, but why now?"

He wondered how much to trust her. "For one thing, a friend of mine—the kid in a family I'm close to—is sick, and I just feel like I can do more for the family if I live in the same town and commute to the offices when I need to."

"And for another?" she wheedled.

He could not have helped the wildfire that swept up his cheeks if he tried.

"Oh really?" she asked, surprised. "A young woman this time, or…?"

"A man," he said simply. They were both bisexual, and having a friend with whom to freely discuss his love life was yet another reason Ginger had never been a part of that. "He… it's only starting, but it's got—" A vision of Michael's dark eyes after their kiss that morning flashed through Carl's mind. "—promise. So much promise."

Her look at him was kind. "That's lovely. I'm only jealous that it happened to you first."

Carl smiled gratefully. "Thank you."

"So, now that you've divulged all your secrets, are you going to tell me why you wanted to have lunch? Was that it? To flaunt your boyfriend and personal life because you have one and I don't?"

Carl chuckled. "No, no. I'm pretty sure I could have done that over the phone." He paused then and resisted the completely asinine urge to look around like a character in a spy movie. This was a perfectly innocuous question, after all. "Look, I've got a line on something odd going on, and I need to talk to your contacts in the DOI. Would that be a problem?"

Ginger frowned. "The Department of the Interior? Why? Is somebody smuggling alligators? Baby lions? Trespassing on tribal lands? Seriously, Carl, what do you need to talk to them about?"

"Endangered species," he said grimly. "And Saudi princes. You must remember, Ginger. I worked that case for your client."

Her eyes widened. "No," she whispered. "Falcons?" She'd been the one to authorize his trip to Doha in Qatar eight years ago. He'd brought back pictures of the Souk to show her because they'd both been fascinated by the idea.

"I'm thinking," he said. "But at the moment, all we have is someone smuggling bustard eggs."

She frowned. "Wait. Is this about the Italian national in the desert?"

Interesting that she knew about that. "Mm, yes. I had some dealings with his family recently. The situation caught my attention."

Her face hardened, and Carl was suddenly supremely aware that not only was she his superior, but she'd had a hand in some of the more hard-nosed decisions that he'd worked so studiously to circumvent.

"Leave it," she said sharply. "Tell the family you met a dead end. Mandy Jessup did that investigation, and…."

Carl's eyebrows went up. Mandy Jessup, the girl he'd flirted with back before Danny, had been on an investigation five years ago when she'd simply disappeared in Mexico. No body, no witnesses—nothing! She hadn't had a husband or boyfriend at the time because apparently Serpentus was the death of all relationships, and her bank account had been cleaned out immediately after her last contact with her sister. Carl had been in Europe at the time, running down car thieves, and had been unable to blow town unless he'd wanted to blow his cover too. After the near miss with Chuck, that had been his last chance to stop this particular ring, and their body count had been growing.

By the time he'd been able to return to the States and stick his nose into Mandy's investigation, the trail had gone cold. And given the investigator they *did* hire, a grizzled veteran with a lot of loudly voiced prejudices, anybody who would have helped them look for her had gone to ground.

"That's what Mandy was working on?" That didn't sound right, he thought. He'd been sure Mandy had been looking at property protection, not smuggled bustard eggs.

"Possibly." Ginger's cool expression remained, but something like a spasm of discomfort crossed her features.

"Uhm, Ginger—"

"Leave it," she said, her voice taking on an almost ugly timbre. "Was this the only reason you wanted me to bother Tamara Charter?"

"No," Carl lied, letting his voice rise in good-humored denial. "No. That was just sort of a curiosity thing. The real thing has to do with a lek of sage grouse near an airfield. It's a real lek—the birds mate and lay there—and the covey is doing fairly well. There are fences blocking them off from the strip, and a good stretch of the legs between the landing strip and the lek, but I wanted to double-check. Moving the airstrip would be a PITA for the insurance company, and offending the DOI would also not be a picnic."

Carl's heart was pumping in his chest as though he'd had a near miss, and he was thinking that he seriously had to thank Michael for the spot-on excuse for talking to Tamara Charter, who was apparently Ginger's contact at the DOI.

Ginger's expression had smoothed out as he'd spoken, and now she gave a charming smile, as though trying to be the same friend he'd always known. He did his best to pretend he hadn't seen some real fear there.

Something about Mandy Jessup's disappearance and smuggled bustard eggs had touched a real sore spot for Ginger Carson, and Carl made another note to have Stirling hack those files.

But first he had to talk to Tamara Charter.

"Of course I can set you up with her," Ginger said now, practically gushing. "Would this afternoon do? I know she plays squash at that gym outside of Georgetown. Isn't that by your apartment?"

Carl nodded. He'd given his tenants—three interns at Serpentus who split the outrageous rent among themselves, on the contingent that Carl got his bed back on the rare occasions he came to town—notice that he'd be returning that night after his brief dodge in to drop off his carry-on and would be freeing up some closet space before he left. A quick nip in to change into his workout clothes would hardly be a problem; most of them worked late hours on the best of nights anyway.

"What time?" he asked pleasantly. "I have some things to do at the office after lunch, but after that, I'm free."

"I'll text you," Ginger said happily, and then their food arrived and the rest of the lunch passed in pleasant conversation, almost as if those frightening moments when Ginger had become a dangerous, ugly person had never existed.

Carl laughed and chatted and told a highly edited version of his first "flying lesson" that was as much fiction as anything else, and then gave her a brief kiss on the cheek before they left.

But very quietly, in the back of his mind, he moved Ginger from the "friends to trust" column to the "business contacts to use" column he kept running in his head.

He knew what it was like to trust someone with his life now, and he wasn't going to make that mistake with Ginger, no matter how much water they had under the bridge.

HE HADN'T been planning to return to the office—once had been bad enough. But he knew that as good as Stirling was with computers, hacking into one the size and complexity of Serpentus's involved more than having a genius kid hunker over his laptop for a few minutes and announce "Done!" Most of the magic Stirling and Josh accomplished had hours of forethought and preparation put in beforehand.

In this case, they had maybe an hour before Foster Aldrich got back from his usually extended lunch.

"Stirling?" he said over Bluetooth as he strode toward the Serpentus building from the restaurant. "You busy?"

"It can wait," Stirling replied, his tones clipped per usual. Carl and Stirling had worked together quite a bit while figuring out who was trying to break into Lucius's women's shelter. They both understood that pleasantries and soft voices weren't necessary to do a job well.

"I need you to break into my company's website for information on Mandy Jessup. She disappeared around five years ago, about the time Matteo di Rossi was crashing into a cliff. She was a fledgling investigator then, had worked her way up from the reception desk, and I was out of the country. I didn't know the details of her disappearance, so I couldn't put it together, but…." He was striding down the street, looking determined and focused like most of the people in DC, but he was suddenly loath to go into the particulars of his lunch with Ginger.

It had been shocking and a little sad to realize that someone he'd considered a friend for so long could turn on him that suddenly.

"Complicated," Stirling said, breaking into his thoughts. "Elaborate later. Your company's damned near airtight. Can you get me in?"

"I was going to email you from someone's computer," Carl said, taking a right into an alleyway that would get him into Serpentus from the delivery entrance at the back of the building. "And I think I know where to find his passcodes. Will that do?"

Stirling let out a happy little hum. "You understand," he said, because Carl got that he was good but wasn't a magician. "Private address."

Meaning the email Stirling only answered on his triple-encrypted black-box computer, the one he surfed the dark web on, routed through thirty gajillion different servers with a plethora of spoofed ISP addresses.

"Roger. Gimme a few."

Carl saw that the service dock was open as the company took a delivery of office supplies and toilet paper, and he slid in silently, eyes scanning the large open area for the employee's entrance.

And there it was. Down a dark, hot hallway, on the left past restrooms he never wanted to visit, the hallway opened up into two rooms separated by a cinderblock barrier—women's on the right, men's on the left.

Inside were lockers and uniforms for custodians, plumbers, even the computer engineers who dealt with the actual towers of the server in the basement. Everybody who worked a blue-collar job in the white-collar building was stationed in this suite of offices with concrete floors and double-paned, wire-lined glass windows.

Carl hit the men's locker room without breaking stride, walking as though he had a mission to speak to one of the maintenance workers about a blocked toilet. Nobody looked twice at him, not even as he blew past the head maintenance worker's office and marched straight to the laundry where the clean jumpsuits were pressed and stacked in four cloth bins.

Carl snagged one of two gray suits from the XXL bin and stripped off his suit jacket and slacks, silently saying goodbye to his brown off-the-rack suit. It was old, he thought, and American cut, and after seeing Felix and Lucius dressed so nattily, he'd refused to buy another suit like it.

Besides, if Michael was going to look at him with those dark eyes because he was the "man in the suit," Carl wanted to be the man in the *well-cut* suit so he at least had that going for him.

Carl cleared out his wallet and phone and shoved them into the side pockets of the jumpsuit before he stuffed the old suit into the hamper. Then he hopped into the onesie, glad it was oversized so it covered his shiny leather shoes, and grabbed a company logoed baseball hat from the rack that ran above the lockers. This one looked new and clean and didn't have anyone's initials on the inside, and he used it to cover his noticeable blond hair.

There were toolkits against the far wall with a sign that said Don't Forget to Sign Your Kit Out! handwritten in black Sharpie above a clipboard with its own pen dangling from a purple piece of yarn. Carl signed Foster Aldrich on the clipboard, grabbed the toolkit, and strode toward the service elevator, practically running as he sensed the entire world coming back from its lunch break.

The entire world with the exception of Foster Aldrich, Carl knew.

Foster always had an extra martini at lunch, and he wasn't going to stop that habit today, not after Carl had so blatantly blown him off for Ginger.

And one of the things Foster didn't know was that Stirling had rekeyed Carl's access card the month before because Carl had wondered if it could be done. It could. As long as nobody had changed their passcodes to get into their offices, Carl had access to any room in the building.

As he walked, he stuck his hand in the freshly washed uniform, pulled out a lanyard, and attached the keycard to it like an ID.

He kept his head down, didn't make eye contact with the suits, and walked straight into Foster Aldrich's office without a single person questioning his presence.

God. Insurance companies. Great that they thought nobody would steal from *them*, wasn't it?

As soon as he shut all the blinds to the room, he called Stirling up on the Bluetooth.

"I'm in," he said. And then he pulled out Foster's middle drawer, where Foster wrote his computer and access passwords, and proceeded to break into his manager's computer and send Stirling sensitive material about his company. And he didn't feel a tiny bit bad about it either.

"Which files did you want?" Stirling asked.

"Mandy Jessup's," Carl said. "And anything related to peregrines or the houbara bustard. They might not be at this computer—"

"Do you have the email address of the person you think has them?"

Carl gave him Ginger's address, his back prickling with sweat.

"Is that everything?" he asked, standing up and peering behind the blinds. *Damn.*

"Yeah. You about to get pinched?"

Foster had stopped on the way through the reception room and was trying hard to flirt with one of the receptionists.

"Yeah. I've got to get while I can."

"Go," Stirling said. "I'll have the files ready for you when you get back."

"Thanks, man."

"Good work," Stirling told him, and from Stirling, who very rarely complimented anybody, that was high praise.

"You too," Carl said before grabbing the toolbox and slipping out the side door in Foster's office, which led to the foyer for the private elevators.

It was a risky move. If one of the CEOs or shareholders had been going from investigative services back to their own office, he would have run into them, and he was well known to all the executives. He'd done work for pretty much everybody in the building.

But he also knew their habits, much like he knew Foster Aldrich always had an extra martini at lunch.

These assholes—and with the exception of Ginger, they really were universally male—were out banging their mistresses, or in one case, their secret mister. Carl had made it a point to know all their vices, just in case, for instance, he ever got caught sneaking out of someone in middle-management's office dressed as a maintenance worker.

Nobody was in the elevator when he got in, and he could finally breathe. He took the car one floor down, then made his way to the service elevators. When he got to the maintenance entrance, a flood of workers were coming back from lunch.

Instead of venturing into the locker room and getting busted, he kept right on walking, leaving the toolkit at the loading dock entrance where it could be easily seen and not tripped over.

And then he just kept on walking.

He ordered a rideshare about six blocks from the building and gave a sigh of deep relief when he got into the back of the small Kia.

He scanned the rearview all the way to Georgetown, relieved—and sweaty—when he didn't see anybody following.

Risky. God, it had been risky. But clues like the one Ginger had practically poured into his lap didn't come that often. It would have been criminal if he hadn't tracked that down.

THE SWEAT served him well an hour later as he played racquetball with one of the toughest, most ruthless competitors he'd ever met.

Tamara Charter was an imposing woman.

Fit, wiry, in her midfifties, with tanned skin and a fierce crop of sun-spawned freckles, she wore her ginger hair cut short and attacked the ball with a sort of pixilated glee.

Kill that ball! Destroy it! All balls were fuckers!

Carl, still riding the adrenaline high of breaking into his own building, could get into that sort of thing.

He threw his shoulder into the swing and annihilated the little rubber ball, highly gratified when Tamara missed the return for match point.

He was dripping sweat and happy for the competition by the time they were done. Even if Tamara petered out as a source, getting the chance to play with her was an honor.

He stood and guzzled water at the side of the court and felt a little bit of satisfaction that she had to do the same.

"I've got to admit," Tamara said, panting slightly, "that when Ginger said she had a competitor for my afternoon match, I was pretty sure I was going to get a chubby executive who would be happier playing frisbee golf. I have to thank you for a really excellent match!"

Carl swallowed and wiped his face on his shoulder. It occurred to him belatedly that he hadn't tried to finesse this in any way, shape, or form. He'd arrived late, out of breath, still sweaty and disheveled from stripping out of the onesie and throwing on his workout clothes before jogging to the gym, his workout bag and racket slung over his shoulder.

"It's been a while since I played," he admitted. "And I ended up having an errand to run after lunch. I think the rush of being late gave me a boost. That was an anomaly."

Tamara laughed, the sound husky and genuine. "I'm quite pleased to be your anomaly. Let's hit the showers, and then I can buy you a smoothie and ask you what's on your mind. Ginger said something about sage grouse?"

Carl grinned. "Among other things, yes," he said before sticking out his hand. "And it's been a privilege. I'd be happy to have a smoothie with you."

She laughed, and they both headed off to hit the showers. It wasn't until he was getting dressed again that he realized that, somehow, as he'd been packing that morning, one of Michael's shirts must have gotten mixed up with his. Carl had brought jeans and a hooded sweatshirt to wear back to his apartment, but, absurdly, it touched him to squeeze his broad XL chest into that size M T-shirt. He had to rip the neck so he could breathe and then zip the hoodie up so nobody could see that the red T-shirt underneath was practically painted on. But every touch of Michael in his life felt like... like sweetness. Like a reward just waiting for Carl to claim it.

He couldn't remember the last time he'd felt like he had something good coming to him. But the thought of Michael, who'd be there to pick him up at the airport like he'd promised, made his chest swell.

Somebody—somebody nice and funny and important—was waiting for him to get home.

Damn.

He just had to keep that hoodie zipped!

Tamara Charter turned out to be good company. Funny, dry, and a good sport about losing to someone she didn't know. He explained the sage grouse thing to her, outlining the measures that Michael had taken to contain the covey and protect the lek, and how the presence of the sage grouse seemed to keep the predatory birds away from the concrete airstrip as a whole.

"Take pictures," she told him thoughtfully. "But if it looks like you've described, bird strikes shouldn't be more prevalent than they are usually." She grimaced. "And don't ask me how often they happen in real life. Everybody thinks they want to know the answer to that question, but they really don't want to know the answer to that question. Trust me."

He laughed uneasily at that, because she was right, and then went on to mention the houbara bustard and to ask why somebody would be transporting eggs to Africa.

His words seemed to hit her hard, and he watched her swallow several times before seeming to come to a decision. She squared her shoulders and nodded to herself as though she'd crossed an obstacle, but she didn't say anything immediately, instead gazing sorrowfully into space in a way that made Carl feel as though there was an infinite sadness just beneath the surface.

He didn't say anything, waiting for her to speak first, and they lingered over their smoothies for a bit. It wasn't until the gym cleared out a little that Carl realized how hard she'd been putting off their conversation.

"So," he said, drawing the syllable out. "Do you need a rideshare, or…?"

"I have my own car," she told him with a lift of her eyebrow that indicated he wasn't being subtle. "And no, that's not a come-on. I've got a perfectly wonderful boyfriend at home who doesn't agree with my politics but loves me for arguing with him. So that awkwardness is over. But…." She tossed back the rest of her smoothie and sighed. "This situation. It's complicated, and it sounds like something out of a sci-fi magazine. Do you know anything about hybrid birds?"

Carl grimaced. "I know that it happens in the wild, but it's not considered really successful unless the offspring are fertile. That's about it."

Charter nodded. "Birds aren't like Chihuahuas," she said. "Everybody wants to see that Great Dane/Chihuahua mix, because wouldn't it be a riot to see the little Chihuahua getting him a piece of Great Dane ass, right? But if you cross a predator bird with an indigenous prey bird, you can get an invasive species—one that could take out the prey bird, or worse."

Carl's eyes widened at the implications. "So instead of murder hornets, you get murder sparrows?"

"Scary, right?"

"Well, yeah." He frowned. "Is, uhm, somebody trying to *do* that?"

She tapped her freckled nose. "What do you know about falconry in Arab countries?"

"Sport of kings," he said promptly, thinking about the Souk at Doha. "One bird can make a family's reputation."

She nodded. "Indeed. And hybrid falcons are heavily ingrained in Middle Eastern falcon lore—kings with five hundred white gyrfalcons or falcons with color markings never seen in nature. A peregrine with legs like a harrier but the chest of an eagle. The list goes on. It's really only a little step—but a dangerous one—to think about hybridizing, say, a falcon's biggest prey bird."

Carl frowned. "But why? Why would you do that? It would put the falcons at risk. Hell, it would put the whole ecosystem at risk."

"And it would equalize families that could never afford a falcon, not in a million years. It would take away something that had only belonged to royalty and make it common, like a peasant, something easily exploited."

"But that's symbolic—the practical effect it could have! It could wipe out indigenous species. That's insane!"

She nodded. "And now you see where things get difficult. We're talking about using endangered species to start a war that would endanger more species. Things are really very delicate. We have no room for pity for a hybrid smuggler who lost control of his vehicle with three dozen falcon-slash-bustard eggs in the back."

Carl gasped, reeling, and the first thing he wanted to do was deny that Matteo di Rossi had lost control of *anything*. He'd seen the photos; that car had been run into a cliff at a high speed, and to say anything else was to deny the truth. While it was obvious that she knew *exactly* which case he was talking about, was it possible Tamara Charter was selling him sunshine and bullshit?

Or had someone sold it to her?

But he wasn't supposed to have seen those photos, and explaining how he'd seen them and who had analyzed them was not a place he wanted to go. After a shocked moment of opening and closing his mouth like goldfish, he remembered something even more important. "Matteo di Rossi was a big believer in preserving wildlife," he said. "He donated a significant part of his own money to wildlife rescue. He would not have been part of anything that put any species at risk."

Her eyes widened. "I did not know that," she said softly. She sucked in a breath. "That's... that is not information anybody ever gave me. Are you sure?"

Carl thought of Danny and Stirling, both of whom were some of the most skilled information gatherers he'd ever encountered. "My sources are impeccable," he said. "Whatever he was doing with those eggs.... Are you sure they were hybridized?"

"That was the information I had," she said. "Hybridized bustard eggs."

"But were they hybridized-with-falcon eggs? I know the gene pool has been getting awfully thin. Like cheetahs, their resistance to infection and birth defects is getting low. I mean, hybrid falcon/bustards would be a disaster, but cross a bustard with, say, a sage grouse, and you've got a whole different bird."

She tilted her head. "So... you think those bird eggs were for conservation?"

"Absolutely. Did you have a lab confirm the genetic material in the eggs?"

She grunted. "Of course. We had *your* lab confirm the genetic material in the eggs. Ginger Carson signed off on the report."

Oh holy hell. "Before or after Mandy Jessup disappeared?"

"After," Charter confirmed, looking at him quizzically. "But I don't think it was connected. I mean, I always assumed that Mandy had discovered a terrorist group that was working toward destabilization in Qatar, but her disappearance was five years ago, and there's been no follow-up incident. Hell, from what I've seen, there was barely an investigation!"

Carl suppressed a growl. "I was in Berlin," he yelped defensively. "It was not my fault!"

And that made her laugh. "Oh wow. Is somebody feeling guilty?"

He sighed. "I was tracking down car thieves, and I was undercover. If I blew my cover a second time, I was never going to get my hands on those assholes. I-I don't know. I thought they'd put their best people on it, but when I got back to the States, the trail was cold, and nobody could even give me a place to start investigating. I had no idea she was related to the egg smuggling thing until… well, her name came up." He did not want to talk about how Ginger had practically sprouted another head and fangs.

"Do you think it needs investigating?" Tamara asked, her brown eyes intense in her narrow, freckled face. "I could see how you would, but our agency is underfunded, and climate change is kicking our asses. I didn't have the resources to look into the Matteo di Rossi thing five years ago, and we don't have them now. If this thing is bigger and deeper than that, I need more to go on before I commit anything to the investigation."

Carl grunted and nodded. "I've got some resources of my own," he said, and then, risking a little, he added, "and they have nothing to do with my company. This is, in fact, for an independent job I'm doing. I will give you anything I can get, if you, perhaps…." Oh, how to ask this, how to ask this?

"Tell Ginger Carson you have a sage-grouse covey you need looked at but nothing more," Tamara said, her voice flat and no-nonsense. "I hear you. She's been texting me as we've talked. I haven't told her anything."

"You don't trust her?" Carl asked, surprised.

"We go way back—" Tamara let out a breath. "—so I don't want to burn that bridge. But…." She was fishing for words, and Carl got a very odd impression. It was as though she both did and didn't want to tell Carl everything she knew. Finally, she settled for what seemed to Carl to be a half-truth. "Ginger's the one who put that report on my desk about the falcon/bustard hybrid eggs. If you say the guy transporting the eggs was an avid environmentalist, and you trust your sources, then something hinky is going on. The only information I had was that he belonged to a famous family of smugglers."

"He did," Carl admitted. "But they were in the process of trying to go straight, which they've been, mostly, since their patriarch died. There was no reason—none—for him to be starting a war, not a trade one or otherwise. He was finally getting a chance to live without crime, which was something he'd wanted his entire life."

She grunted. "So it sounds like someone was using his reputation as a bad guy to hide something. That's interesting. Don't you think that's interesting?"

Carl thought about Josh Salinger, who probably would have loved to have met his father in spite of his resentment that Felix and Danny, whom he considered his family, couldn't give him their bone marrow. "I think that's *fascinating*," he said, a savage anger appearing from nowhere. Second chances. Everybody deserved them. Michael was living his to the best of his ability. Matteo di Rossi, finally free of the family entanglements that had defined and imprisoned him, was not going to get that chance.

The thought hurt him in ways he hadn't realized he *could* be hurt. The yearning to see Michael, to help make his second chance as magical as Michael deserved, was swelling in his chest.

Tamara nodded, as though she understood the things he wasn't saying, although she could not possibly. "I agree," she said. "Please, if you get any more information on this subject, don't go through Ginger." She reached into her wallet and pulled out two cards. One was her own, and the other was the cabinet chief in charge of the DOI herself. "Go through us," Tamara said grimly. "If my position stands for anything, it should be for the people trying to make a difference. That much I can guarantee."

CARL TOOK an Uber back to the apartment; it had been a busy day. The three roommates were playing Xbox, drinking beer, and eating pizza, but in spite of all the physical activity, Carl didn't join them. He grabbed a yogurt out of the fridge to supplement his smoothie, bid everybody a good-night, and retired to his room. He figured since he was kicking Ty, the official name on the lease, onto the couch for two nights, the least he could do now was retreat into the bedroom and spare everybody else the awkwardness of pretending they knew him.

He sat cross-legged on the bed, surrounded by Ty's garment racks because Carl's clothes were taking up the closet, and thought it was high time he found a real home. A part of his mind was already engaged in what he would ship to Chicago and what he would put in storage to ship later, while most of his brain was working on his laptop, taking care of some bullshit paperwork from the office. He'd get it off the table before it completely slipped his mind. When he was done, he checked his phone and saw a message from Stirling:

*Don't bother me. I'm working on it.*

He smiled. That figured. Stirling would get the job done and then report back, taking action if action was necessary. In nearly fifteen years on the job, Carl had never found a colleague as dependable as Stirling Christopher—or one he'd liked so much. It was true, Stirling wasn't a bolt of lightning around the table like the other young people at the Salinger mansion, but there was something deeply wicked and subversive in his eyes.

Carl put on a suit and grabbed his briefcase on the daily, but he spent his spare time helping the Salingers, and even before that, he'd been king of the workaround with Serpentus, helping people who'd committed crimes get the most out of their insurance dollar as often as possible.

He *liked* being the guy who looked legit but who fucked with the fuckers—he couldn't explain it. Maybe it all had its roots in those quiet hours in the vice principal's office, reading a book as punishment.

That had been the best time he'd had in the fourth grade.

Or maybe it had been that glorious month, just out of rehab, when he and Danny had rented a cottage off the Welsh coast in the winter. God, it had been cold. Not much to do but read by the fire and fuck like lemmings. And while the sex had been great, as he remembered it now, it had been the reading by the fire that had saved them both as they'd struggled with that first month out of the facility without a drink.

Still, Carl had sensed the restlessness inside Danny Lightfingers—yes, Carl had known his last name back then, though he was pretty sure Mitchell wasn't his real last name, even when Danny had guarded it so tightly. To Carl, he'd always been the elusive, charming thief who could sing the theme to *SpongeBob* to his adopted son in four languages. But then, Carl also knew Danny had hidden the darker, more hurt parts of himself even from Carl that month.

Only Felix got to see those. Carl had known it then, and he was even more certain of it now.

He hadn't been surprised when, one morning close to spring, he'd awakened to find a note on his pillow.

*I'll stay sober if you will—D.*

Not a word about the two of them, not even of regret. Carl had known, even as they'd fallen into bed, that he'd be nothing but a footnote in Danny's storied life. Danny had never given him false promises. For a con man and a thief, he'd been exquisitely honest about that, often talking about Felix in the present tense, as though he was going to go visit after his holiday in Wales.

But if staying sober was what he had with Danny, who had taught him about kindness and charm and a way to enjoy life even when it wasn't going his way, then staying sober was something he could do.

Something they both could do, he figured now.

But staying sober wasn't enough to build a life on.

He thought of Michael and his children, how he called nightly to keep track of his family. His ex-wife was a friend, and they shared their new experiences of being out in the world, far away from their hometown, with freedoms they'd never imagined and the money to make their modest dreams come true.

Michael, who didn't look at Carl like a bit player or an afterthought, but like a leading man.

Suddenly Carl needed to know how Michael was doing.

*How was your day?* he texted.

He got back a photo montage and spent a few minutes scrolling through pictures of Michael and two gorgeous teenagers, along with Molly, taking in the game at Wrigley Field, followed by shopping downtown and a dinner of deep-dish pizza. The kids smiled shyly, Molly blew kisses, and Michael, staring straight into the camera, biting his lip, looked so happy. Included. Like this had been something he'd wanted to do his whole life.

*Looks like a good day*, Carl typed. *Thanks for the pictures!*

*Missed you. Kept thinking of things I'd say.*

*Why didn't you text me?* God, a text from Michael right after he'd escaped from Foster Aldrich's office would have done so much to calm him down!

*Didn't want to be a bother. You were doing something important.*

Carl's chest ached.

*YOU are important*, he texted, not sure how it happened but not wanting to question it. Not a bit player. Not an afterthought. Not an almost-ran. Neither of them.

*Can we go to a game?* Michael texted back. *You and me? Can we take my kids? I want them to see a pro game now that I can afford one. We're doing the aquarium and the Art Institute tomorrow. I feel like I'm scouting future outings. Is that dumb?*

Carl chuckled at the string of sentence after sentence, as though Michael had broken a dam of sorts to flood Carl with information. Maybe he had. If Michael was important, then his dreams were important, and he was sharing them, as requested.

*That's fine. I'd love to do family things. I never actually did them as a family—only as an adult.* Chuck had dragged him to a game a couple of weeks ago when Lucius had been on a business trip. Hunter had come along, and they'd worn their hats and thrown popcorn at each other. In retrospect, maybe the "hazing" with landing the plane had been a long time coming.

*Me neither. Beth had a happy family—she told me how.*

*The Salingers are my best example. It looks like Molly knows a little too.*

*She's wonderful. Like the little sister I didn't know I needed. We had fun. I think the kids were okay with being stuck in Chicago for three days.*

*Any news on the home front?* He actually wanted all the news.

*Josh and his uncle met. I was across the room, of course, but it looked tense and sad.*

*Must be rough for both of them.*

*Di Rossi didn't tell his kids why he was here.*

Carl frowned. *Did you?*

*Yup.*

Uh-oh. *Uhm, did anybody say anything?*

*Why would they?*

Carl blew out a breath. *Sort of in the family, you know? As in, our family vs. the di Rossi family. Only a little bit of info at a time.*

The next text hurt him a little. *Did I do anything wrong?* God, poor Michael. Rules he didn't understand.

Carl thought about it before he texted. *No. No, I don't think so. Just remember—you're working with smugglers and thieves. Di Rossi is on the up-and-up, but his children's mother might not be. Kids get used as pawns all the time. That's why Josh's mother kept his father a secret for so long.*

*I'm sorry. Should I say something?*

Carl half laughed. *If they're kids, they'll say something on their own. Nobody gave you a briefing. How were you supposed to know?*

*You did.*

Carl sighed and hit Call.

"It's a game," he said as soon as Michael picked up. "A stupid one. The kids all know how to play because they've watched the adults play all their lives. It's a rich person's game—what the kids know, what people are allowed to know about their children. The Salingers sort of sucked at it. That's why their group is run by college students now, and why Danny and Felix never seem to grow up. The di Rossis were big-time criminals, the kind who played for keeps, and Leon may be working to go mostly legit, but he still knows there's danger out there for his children. So no, you didn't do anything wrong. You told the truth. That's what you do. Julia, Danny, and Felix wouldn't have expected any less from you. Leon di Rossi is going to have to deal with the fact that we don't keep secrets like that, and that's all there is to it."

He blew out a breath, having run out of things to say to reassure Michael, and was greeted by a soft chuckle.

"What?"

"You called me up to say all that?"

Carl gave a half smile, and realizing nobody was there to see it, allowed it to grow into a full one. "And to hear your voice," he said with dignity. God, his voice was sweet. That Texas twang that Chuck seemed to turn into a come-on without trying sounded more like a come-hither when Michael spoke. Carl liked it. Michael's voice, his big brown eyes, and a simple touch of his hand could bring a wandering spirit like Carl home.

"Good to hear your voice too. Anything big happen today you didn't text?"

"Won a game of racquetball," he said blandly. "Found out some good shit to tell the family."

"Stirling said you were doing some *Mission Impossible* shit this afternoon," Michael said chirpily. "I wanted to hear about *that.*"

"Stirling wasn't even there," Carl teased. "For all you know, *Mission Impossible* shit to him is like dusting the blinds for me." He chuckled softly, because that hadn't been far from the truth.

"You can't tell me just a little," Michael wheedled. "Just a little bit?"

"You don't want to hear," Carl baited, liking this game. "Boring. So boring. Wasn't even—"

"*Please!*"

Carl laughed outright. "Since you asked…." He launched into a soft telling of his trip to Foster Aldrich's office, leaving out the fact that the company could and would have pressed charges if he'd been caught.

"All that!" Michael said, sounding so impressed. "That thing with the onesie was so smart! But you left your suit there?"

Carl had thought of this. "I've made it very clear I'm here to clean house and move my base of operations to Chicago. If the suit is ever tracked back to me, I'm giving a lot of stuff to thrift stores over the next couple days. Who knows how that happened?"

Michael chuckled. "You're bad. You're gonna get caught, you know."

Carl shrugged. "And then I become an 'Independent Security Consultant,' which is what I do for most of Felix's friends anyway. They pay me pretty well. Like I said, not a hardship."

"Would you miss it?"

Ooh. Good question. "Not as long as I had something to take its place," he said. "What I'm doing with the Salingers works fine."

"Well, I don't want you to get caught anyway. I want you to be able to tell everyone to take the job and shove it."

Carl laughed outright. "If it ever comes to that, I'll be sure to film it. You can watch it on loop."

Michael's open guffaw was like music to his ears. "You're *so* bad," he said, but it sounded like he thought that was fine, just fine.

"I talk big now," Carl said softly, suddenly feeling vulnerable. "But if I hadn't run into Danny and Felix in March, I might not have been this brave. Just, you know, in case you think you're getting a hero."

"But Chuck's got stories about you," Michael protested. "You learning how to be a getaway driver to track down thieves—tell me that was you."

Carl grunted. "Well, yeah."

"You working with the police when a bunch of gangsters got shot looking for the information *you* guys gave to Interpol."

"Grace and Josh did most of the groundwork on that."

"You beating the shit out of a wife-beater in an epic takedown!"

"How long did you talk to Chuck?" Carl asked, feeling a little violated.

"That last one was Lucius," Michael said smugly. "He said they watched you take a couple of hits and were like, 'Oh shit! Somebody go help Carl!' and then you turned around and whaled on the guy!"

Carl shook his head. "I'd forgotten there were cameras," he muttered, partly to himself.

"Lucius wanted to know if you boxed during college. Josh was listening in, and he looked it up, but your school didn't have a team."

"The only gym for miles was a boxing gym," Carl explained, feeling dumb. "I had a lot of anger to take out. The guys in the gym gave me pointers."

"The guys are really impressed." Michael let out a happy little hum. "So am I."

"Did you really spend the entire day entertaining two surly teenagers?" he asked, not wanting to explain that, like most executives, he looked good on paper.

"They were sweet," Michael defended, and for a brief, blissful time, Michael told him about the kids and how Bernardo had opened up about his father and how exciting it was to have a new cousin and how Molly had looked at the weather the next day and convinced the kids that the Art Institute would be better than the beach. Carl listened to his voice—and his adventures—and smiled.

"I'm sorry. I'm boring you," Michael said, finishing up.

"No," Carl said, stifling a yawn. "It's been sort of a day, but I'm not bored."

"Then what?"

"You're just easy to talk to. Kind. You keep talking about me being safe, but you're not mean or catty. You're safe too. You've got a good heart. It makes me want to listen to you talk about anything—cars, engines, birds, kids. You make it good."

"Coming from a superhero, that makes me feel pretty awesome," Michael said, and then, "Oh, shoot. Sorry, Stirling. You been waiting there all this time?"

Carl's eyes popped open. "You're at the Salinger house?"

"Oh yeah. Molly had me get some clothes so I could sleep over since we're leaving with the kids early in the morning. Stirling came in about halfway through me boring you shitless. He wants to chat."

Carl grunted. "It's a good thing we're not into sex talk." God, how embarrassing.

"Yeah, well, you're dealing with someone who came out of the closet *months* ago," Michael said frankly. "Calling someone a dick right now is like watching a porno for me. It's about as sexy as I'm gonna get. Here's Stirling."

There was a shocked silence on both ends before Stirling cleared his throat. "Uhm, I don't know what to say to that."

"I too am at a loss," Carl responded, completely bemused. "How about we pretend he never said it and you tell me what you got from Foster's computer."

"Oh thank God. You're a good guy, Carl. Also, Foster Aldrich is crooked as fuck, but not in anything we're worried about. I mean, he's siphoning funds from the company. Would you like proof of that?"

"Yes," Carl said. "Dear God, yes. When's your birthday, Stirling? I feel as though you're not celebrated enough."

"In November," Stirling said. "And having people in the room for dinner is pretty much my best present. Be there. I'm not kidding."

"I won't miss it," Carl promised, liking this kid more and more.

"I'm sending you an entire file on why Foster Aldrich is a terrible human being. But that's not the important part."

"What is the important part?" Carl asked, truly curious now.

"Ginger Carson has her own file of stuff that we are going to need to study like an ancient text. A lot of it is about Mandy Jessup's disappearance, and out of curiosity, I made a copy in my own computer and ran a search on it using the weird shit that we're looking into. Falcons, houbara bustards, Matteo di Rossi...."

"And?" Carl's stomach was tight and his skin very, very tingly at this point. His instincts had been on point—*so* on point—and Stirling was confirming every screaming nerve ending.

"And all of them are in this file. All of them. Whatever happened with Matteo di Rossi involved Mandy Jessup completely and Serpentus to the nines. Or at least Ginger Carson, who knew about it. Your hunch and a little B and E gave us some serious shit to work with."

Carl was about to let out a whoop of pure exhilaration when Stirling stated the obvious.

"And it put you in a really shitty position with work."

Carl's whoop deflated, but his resolve stayed strong. "Oh, Stirling. My dear, sweet, innocent boy. Who do I work for, *really*?"

Stirling paused as though thinking this through, which was fine. He tended to take things literally.

"Us," he said after a moment. "You may get a paycheck from Serpentus, but you're loyal to us."

"You bet your ass I am," Carl told him. "Is there anything else?"

"My sister says Michael is wonderful, and you need to treat him like a prince."

Carl grinned. "I'm gonna do my best. I'm spending tomorrow packing shit up and sending it to Chicago, and I should be in town after dinner the day after that. That's when we're meeting, right?"

"Next day," Stirling said, voice dropping. "Josh is going to need two transplants. One now so he can get through the rest of chemo, and one at the end of chemo. He's going to need an extra day to recover."

"Shit."

"Yes, well, you need to come in the day you planned to anyway."

"Why?"

Stirling's voice never rose. "Because Michael's listening to me, and he's got the *saddest* expression thinking you're going to be gone longer."

"Oh." Carl had to smile at that. He had someone who would miss him. "Put him on and I'll tell him when he can pick me up from the airport if he likes."

"Good deal. I'm going to take all this data to Danny and Felix, who are trying hard to stay out of Josh and Leon's way."

"They'll appreciate it," Carl said gently. "That's a kind idea."

"I'm the computer guy. It's all I do."

And for a moment, Carl got a glimpse into why people got mad at *him* for trying to make himself look small. "Stirling, you're indispensable. And more than that, you're loved. Fifteen years I've investigated crimes, and I wish I'd had someone like you with me that entire time. We could have had so much fun."

Stirling let out a blocky sound, a snort and a guffaw mixed into one, and Carl realized he'd never heard the young man laugh.

"We can have fun now," he said. "Thanks, Carl. Here's Michael. Remember, Molly said—"

"Like a prince. I hear you."

And then Michael came on the line.

"So, day after tomorrow, right?"

"Yup. And warn the super that cases and luggage are going to arrive and need to be brought up to the apartment."

"He'll do that?"

"Yeah, Michael, he'll do that. But it's nice to tip him when he does, in case I'm not there."

"Yeah, okay. How much?"

"Five bucks a bag is good, round it up to a twenty."

"I sort of forget I've got money now. You should have heard Molly nag at me about parking too far away from things."

Carl would have said Molly was spoiled, but the truth was, Molly and Stirling had lived in foster care before they'd been adopted, and they'd loved their adopted parents fiercely before the two of them had been killed. If Molly wanted to use her trust fund to park close to a ball game, Carl figured she had that right. Everybody knew the two of them would rather have their parents back than all the trust fund money in the world.

"If anyone can teach you how to spend money, I'd say it's Molly Christopher."

"Yeah, I'm planning to drag her with me when it's time to go shopping for Christmas presents." Suddenly his voice rose with wonder. "Hey. *Hey!*"

"What?"

"I-I can go shopping for my kids for Christmas without worrying about money! I mean, I'll talk to Beth and we can figure out what's best, but... oh my God, Carl. You don't understand. I once worked double shifts at a 7-Eleven so we could give our oldest a toy truck and a pair of pajamas when he was a baby. We can buy our kids presents and not worry about what we're gonna eat for two months. Wow. Oh my God!"

Carl's eyes were burning. This was so important to Michael—and such an awesome thing to be excited about. All the people Carl knew at Serpentus were absolutely evil over their seven-figure incomes, and Michael's biggest joy in the money he'd spent two years in prison to acquire was that he got to spend money on his children.

"You'll have so much fun looking," he said softly. "I bet Molly will help you shop for them too."

"Will you?" Michael asked wistfully.

"I'll suck at it, but yeah. I'll hang out behind you and Molly and watch you get excited. It'll be like Christmas for me."

"Having a boyfriend would be my best Christmas present ever," Michael said bashfully.

"No wonder you all think I'm such a superhero," Carl laughed. "You people set such a low bar. Right now, that seems like the easiest thing in the world."

"Really?" Michael's voice throbbed with promise.

"Really."

"We're gonna have a whole night and most of a day when you get back. You know that, right?"

Carl smiled dreamily. "It's been a long time since I had that sort of promise. Are you taking the day off?"

"Julia wants us all at the house in the afternoon. Not formally. I think she just wants to count her chickens." Michael yawned, and the sound of it made the yawn spread to Carl.

"We can do that." Carl made a happy hum. "Text me tomorrow, okay? Even if I don't answer, I want to know how your day goes."

"I want to know if you go all badass superhero," Michael told him.

"It doesn't happen often. I promise nothing. But I'm heading toward the capitol in the evening. I'll send you some tourist pics. Promise."

"Wow. That's something else I'd like to see," he said wistfully.

"Someday, you and me," Carl promised rashly. But then, they were just starting out. Wasn't that the time for rash promises? He couldn't remember ever wanting to please someone so much before. He made the trip from Chicago to DC three, four times a month. How hard would it be to bring someone with him? "I'd get us a hotel," he said. "A nice one. We could eat out."

"You might have to introduce me to your friends," Michael said practically. "That'd be no good. We'll get room service."

Carl thought about Ginger, who had seemed so warm and sweet he'd almost thought he could trust her, but it turned out she was just as crooked as Foster Aldrich. "You're better than all of them," he said thickly. "We'll eat out. We'll see a show. We'll go on all the tours. You could see all the places. It would be an honor."

"Even if you can't make it happen," Michael said indulgently, "it's real nice that you'd try."

Carl's heart clutched. Trapped, both of them, for so long it was as though they stood in front of a great open gate and neither of them knew how to go through.

"Yeah," Carl vowed. "I can make that happen. I might not be a superhero in all the other ways, but a trip to DC? A good one? If I can't manage that, you should dump me."

"Dump you? I ain't even tasted you yet!" Michael cackled, and Carl laughed too. But he didn't forget his promise.

They talked a little more after that, sleepily, and Carl wondered if Michael was in his pj's, probably in Carl's usual room since Felix and Julia had a mansion full. He didn't remember to ask, though, because before he knew it, he and Michael were signing off. Carl pulled off his hooded sweatshirt and slid into bed, wishing for his own sheets and comforter that were tucked in the closet.

Tomorrow. Tomorrow he'd start packing up his belongings and get them ready to send to the apartment in Chicago, where his real life waited.

Tomorrow he'd start fixing his life so when he went to sleep, he was somewhere he belonged.

# Magic Carpet Rides

GRACE, HUNTER, Chuck, and Lucius were gone the night Michael was supposed to pick Carl up from the airport, so dinner at the Salinger house was mostly for their guests.

Stirling and Molly were there, as were Danny, Felix, and Julia, but besides Michael, the purpose of the meal seemed to be about making Leon, Bernardo, and Esme comfortable knowing their cousin, Josh.

Michael, sensing impending awkwardness, had tried to get out of it.

"I'm not even secondary family," he'd complained to Molly. "You know that, right? I'm like third tier, or fourth. I'm some guy Chuck dragged home because he felt like it."

"You just spent three days hauling this man's children hither and yon while he did important emotional and medical things for Josh, and he'd like to say thank you," Molly retorted. "Look, I'm putting on a pretty grown-up dress and my mother's diamond earrings, and I'm dressing to make Julia proud. The least you could do is put on that nice suit Julia had made for you and smile quietly and say 'It warn't no big deal, Mr. di Rossi. We had fun.'"

"I don't sound like that." Michael scowled, trying not to be charmed by her.

"You do too. I thought Chuck had an accent, but my God, Chuck has a tickle in his throat compared to you. As far as those kids are concerned, you're what a real American sounds like, so, you know. Play it up."

"I had no idea you were measuring me for a suit!" The day before, when Molly had talked Bernardo and Esme into more shopping instead of going to the beach when it was cold and windy, she'd apparently used getting Michael fitted for some nice clothes as bait. It was supposed to be some sort of thank-you for showing the kids around during the week, but when Michael had been presented with the clothes after a quick trip to Navy Pier that morning, he'd been aghast.

"That's real nice of you, Miss Julia, but you know, I'm the mechanic. I don't know when I'll dress fancier than jeans!"

"Tonight at dinner, if you please," Julia had replied, smiling kindly. "And that way you'll already look slick when you go to pick up Mr. Soderburgh—I mean, Cox."

Michael squinted at her. "I still don't know why you call him that," he said.

"It has to do with a movie director," Julia replied airily. "And Carl's rather fortunate resemblance to a couple of movie stars. Anyway, you'll look very nice when you go to pick him up, won't you?"

Michael grimaced. "My hair's a bit long," he said. "And I probably need to shave."

Julia waved her hand again. "Molly, love?"

"Yes, Julia," Molly said sweetly.

"Can you direct our young mechanic to my stylist while the children are resting after lunch? I'll phone him when you're on the way over. While you're quite presentable as you are, Mr. Carmody, a haircut never fails to boost the confidence."

"Ooh, yes!" Molly gushed, grabbing Michael's arm. "And Stefan's the greatest! He loves baseball. You guys can talk about the game and how the team's doing. It'll be great."

"I'll have your clothes brought up to Carl's room, where you spent last night," Julia told him as Molly tugged him out the door.

Less than two hours later, he was back at the Salinger place, putting on a pair of black slacks with a slick red western-cut shirt and a handsome gray blazer to go over it. Molly burst in on him, showing exactly the same amount of respect for his personal space now that she'd shown over the last three days, which was none.

"Julia forgot a tie," Molly said. "Grace stole this from Josh and said you should keep it."

With that, her fingers made quick work of a bolo tie with a polished teardrop-shaped blue opal in the middle. She tucked the leather thong under his collar and straightened the stone, smiling happily.

"There, that's much better."

Michael gaped at her, stunned. "But... but... this is Josh's!"

"No, no—it was never really his. His ex gave it to him, and Josh has been over that guy for months. Besides, Josh? In a bolo? This is just proof that Sean didn't know who Josh Salinger was. But it looks very nice on you."

"Josh dated a guy named Sean?" Michael asked, muddled.

"He dated a *douche* named Sean, and I think the whole reason he dated a douche named Sean was because he was in love with a married guy named Nick, but he didn't want to be, so he settled. It was all very angsty and tragic, and Josh told nobody about it, not even Grace, which means that Grace had to steal all the artifacts from Josh's room and disperse them among the rest of us so they weren't just hanging out catching bad juju."

"Was Josh aware of this?" Michael asked suspiciously.

"No. No, he was not. And he still isn't. And the test of whether or not Grace was being a good friend or a misguided asshole will be if Josh recognizes this thing on your neck. Now come on. The kids are here, and if we don't go talk to them, all they'll have to do is smile at Felix and Julia, who seem to scare the crap out of them."

"Where's Danny?" Michael asked helplessly.

"Getting dressed. I think he was going to try to have this dinner wearing black yoga pants and a black turtleneck, but Felix put his foot down."

Michael didn't have a chance to say anything before she dragged him down to the little-used sitting room, but it was sort of a relief that he wasn't the only one who was being gussied up and turned out to have dinner with Josh's uncle.

But the kids were happy to see him and Molly, and given that both of them had changed for dinner, that made Michael feel better about dressing too. After they greeted each other with relief at knowing someone else in the room, Esme, the oldest, took Molly's hand and led her and Michael to Leon, who was still standing by the couch.

"Papa," she said, before launching into a brief spate of Italian that made Michael catch his breath. He knew quite a bit of Spanish because he'd lived in Texas and there was a big Mexican population in his town, but that kind of fluency always impressed him.

"Yes, Esme," Leon di Rossi said, smiling kindly under his beard. "You've told me about them for three days now. I almost expected Mr. Carmody and Ms. Christopher to be able to fly."

"No flying," Michael said apologetically, sticking out his hand. "Just driving. Your youngsters have been a joy to tour the city with."

Leon shook with a warm, firm grip as Bernardo said, "Papa, he was new to all the things too. Molly would tell him where to go, and he'd be like us! 'Ooh, wow, that's amazing!' He was so much fun."

"Are you new to the area?" di Rossi asked politely as Bernardo, Esme, and Molly deserted them to go talk to Josh and Stirling.

"Yeah. Uhm, I lived in Texas until just this summer." He didn't want to mention prison or bank robberies or any of the things that had kept him someplace else. This tall man with the beard and the imposing presence was scary enough without knowing all of Michael's history. Suddenly he knew why Julia had taken such pains to make sure he was all gussied up and pretty. It had nothing to do with her comfort and everything to do with his own.

"I'm grateful. My children have been full of news about you and Ms. Christopher and your kindness."

And Michael felt like it was his turn to say what the rest of the crew had been thinking. "Well, we're grateful for what you did for Josh. I know you've been at the hospital for the last couple days, and that's no way to spend a vacation. Anything we could do to make that easier for you, that's no trouble at all."

Leon looked across the room to where Josh, pale but composed, was sitting in a corner of the couch with Stirling next to him as they talked quietly to his cousins. Molly stood with them to help fill in any conversational gaps. He looked exhausted but also interested, as though discovering he had family he'd never known before was surprisingly exciting.

"We had a chance to talk over the last two days," Leon said, his eyes growing sad. "I'm sorry my brother didn't live to see him. He's quite a fine young man."

"The whole family is wonderful," Michael said, keeping Carl's words about things people didn't know firmly in place in his mind. "Danny and Felix and Julia—they're the best people. I'm… I mean, you know I'm their mechanic, right?"

Leon gave him a sudden, surprised smile. "No, I did not."

"Well, yeah. I came out of a bad spot in my life, and my friend introduced me here, and they gave me a job. It's like the best thing they could have done. Your kids are great. I got kids of my own, and I hope they're half as kind to strangers when they hit the teen years. But

I would have done it if they'd been monsters, because you don't find the Salingers' kindness everywhere, you know?"

Leon's eyes went shiny. "I did not know, but I'm beginning to fathom. They seem to have surrounded themselves with interesting—and eclectic—people."

Michael nodded. "Yeah. But good folks."

"The man—men, really—but the lawyer who introduced the family to me seemed to be both kind and clever. I assure you, getting in to see me when I had no idea of the reason was not easy. And aside from a few bruises to my security, nobody was hurt." He gave a brief chuckle. "They were most complimentary, by the way, when I revealed the reasons the group of intruders had come to see me. They assured me the operation had been slick and smart and, fortunately, mostly violence free. I got the feeling the lawyer was the reason it went so smoothly. Is he not here?"

"Mm, I think most of the guys are out and about," Michael replied. He was fully aware of the fact that Grace wasn't there on purpose to force Josh to talk to his family, and Hunter was off with Grace to take advantage of the alone time. Chuck split his time between Chicago and Lucius's business in Springfield, but that all seemed like too much information. Then the full import of "lawyer" hit him. "Oh! Yeah. Carl is coming back tonight. I'm getting him from the airport."

Leon smiled, clearly relaxing a smidge. "Where did he go?"

"His day job is in Washington, DC. He does stuff for Felix and Julia because he likes them, mostly. He's making his home base in Chicago, so he wanted to ship some of his stuff to an apartment in the city." He smiled prettily and tried to make this sound as platonic as possible. "It's Danny's old place. I stay there too."

"He's a good man," Leon said, clearly not suspicious at all. "I would not have given one of the others a chance to speak." He rolled his eyes. "One of them was police, one was a mercenary, and the other—I don't know what he was, but he wasn't someone I'd trust."

Michael gave half a laugh. "Chuck? He's munitions and transport. He's seriously the world's most trustworthy guy. Wouldn't leave a friend hanging, not even if it was easier."

Leon regarded him with some surprise. "And the others?"

"I don't know the Interpol guy—never met him—but Hunter's the muscle. Smart muscle, but he's got his strengths. But you gotta know, if they're here with Felix, Danny, and Julia, they're good folks." Michael paused and remembered that talking thing again. "But tell me about yourself," he added weakly.

"I'm a man very curious as to how my nephew has such interesting friends," Leon purred.

And suddenly Michael was on firm ground. "Look at him," he said, nodding at Josh, who was currently regaling the kids with a story about his best friend. He had no idea if the story was mostly true or mostly bullshit, but he was being charming and funny and obviously working to put his new cousins at ease. "I mean, wouldn't *you* want to know him if he wasn't in your family?"

Leon chuckled. "Yes," he agreed, before his smile faded. "He... he's been very guarded with me."

"He thinks you're here to replace his fathers," Michael said baldly, remembering Josh's painfully revealed insecurities four days ago. "I know it sounds silly, but, you know, he's been sort of raised on this legend of family. He's built his identity on it, really. And to find out something about his real father—or his real father's family—that would hurt the idea he has of who he is. That's hard, you think?"

"How would you know all this?"

Oh, this was embarrassing. But Michael figured if he was thrown in a room with grenades, he should probably throw himself on one for general good will.

"See, I went to prison for robbing a bank," he said and tried not to melt into the floor when Leon di Rossi's eyes got really large. "And I shouldn't've have been anywhere near a bank—or a semiauto for that matter—but my brothers kept stealing from my business, and they figured the bank job was the best way to pay me back. Now my oldest boy, he adored my brothers. They took him bow hunting when he was supposed to be in school, and they taught him bad words. He's nine, right? Well, back when he was seven, they gave him beer when he was supposed to be home with his mom. We had to take him to the hospital. They were bad people, and hell—it was Texas. We couldn't find a lawman in the county that would keep those two assholes from my kids. Something about their right to know their kinfolk or something dumb like that. But trying to tell Jakey that his uncles were bad? That was hard. They were adults, and they were paying special attention to him. Who wanted to hear that bad news, right? But then... then things got worse. And I got sent away. And apparently Beth, my ex, she sat down with that kid and told him the truth—that his uncles were bad people. They stole from his dad, and the only way Dad was going to keep his house and feed his kids was to do something desperate, and now he was paying. You want to know what happened next?"

Leon was staring at him, absolutely fascinated, and Michael tugged at his collar. "I do," Leon said. "I really do."

"That kid stopped talking to his *mama*. Because as bad as those assholes made my life—his life too—she'd broken this idea he had, about how they loved him special."

"Why do you think they paid all that attention to him?"

Michael let out a bitter laugh. "Same reason they stole from my business and put a gun in my hand. I never had a damned thing—chicken leg, piece of licorice, wife, or great kids—that those fuckers didn't want. They wanted to make him theirs."

"That's reprehensible," Leon said, his accent making the word sound almost like it wasn't English.

"Well, I may have mentioned they were fuckers."

"How did you fix things? Or how did your wife fix things? Between your son and his mother?"

"We both did it," Michael said. "I wrote him, wrote them all, letters from prison. Every day if I could. Beth had the kids—even the littlest, who could only hold crayons—send me something as often as possible. And I never told them that their uncles were horrible people, but boy, you can bet I told them that their mother was the kindest, strongest, best woman they would ever meet. That my brothers, Angus and Scooter, couldn't get a woman as good as Beth to even talk to them or look at them twice, because no good woman would touch them. And by the time I got home, Jakey and his mama were close again."

"You said she's your ex-wife? You don't live with them anymore?"

Michael shrugged. "That's a whole other story, and I have bored you enough with my personal life. I just wanted to say—"

"That the way to Josh's heart is through the people he already loves," Leon said, nodding wisely. "It's a very good point. And one you didn't have to bare your soul to make, and yet you did." He arched his eyebrows at Michael's red-faced, sweaty-pitted discomfort. "Anyone can see you weren't comfortable doing so. Why?"

"'Cause these people?" He nodded at everyone in the sitting room. "And the people that are missing, even? They'd all do the same thing to make you comfortable here. They've done the same thing for me, and I'm an ex-convict with no pedigree. When someone's good to you like that, you do your best to pay it forward."

Leon's expression grew sober, and he knocked back the drink he'd been holding even as it sweated in his fingers. "You, sir, are more than an ex-convict with no pedigree. And you've given me a very important lesson in remembering my place here."

Michael didn't know what he meant by that. "Well, in a few minutes, it's going to be at the table, because these folks don't let anybody go hungry."

And at that moment, Phyllis came in, dressed in a white shirt with black pants, looking so miserably uncomfortable that Michael wanted to hug her. He'd never seen her in anything but snarky T-shirts and jeans.

"Dinner's served," she said brightly, and they all migrated to the table.

As they took their places, he held the seat for Molly, who grinned at him as she sat down.

"Did you see that, Stirling?" she asked, prodding her brother. "Did you see that? Those are moves. Would you like some moves, little brother? Because I'm not getting any action, so I need you to get some to show me what it's like."

Stirling regarded her with the narrow-eyed disgust that only siblings could show for one another. "My moves on a potential mate would be very different from Michael's for a friend."

"Still a move," Molly told Michael. "A good one. Remember it for Carl. When are you going to pick him up, by the way?"

"Probably before we're done with dessert," he said, keeping an eye on the Picasso clock over the back wall of the dining room. He'd learned at the Art Institute that Chicagoans had a big ol' crush on Pablo Picasso, and Michael finally understood why the blue clock with the weird-looking guy and the guitar had seemed like such a good idea to someone who looked as good as Julia Dormer-Salinger.

Phyllis overheard him as she was setting out a family-style salad bowl on their end of the table. "We're having brownies and ice cream," she said. "I'll have Patty make you a care package—ice chest for the ice cream, Tupperware for the dinner, and a warm brownie. Carl will probably be starving. Nobody eats well when they travel."

Michael grinned at her. "You are the nicest woman," he said in complete admiration. "I would not have thought of that."

"Of course you would have," she said fondly. "You just wouldn't have thought to ask." With that she trotted back to the kitchen, probably to bring out a platter of something delicious, leaving Molly to laugh.

"What?" he asked defensively.

"She's right, you know."

"About what?"

"You wouldn't ask for anything for yourself."

Michael thought about that carefully as he took the salad bowl from Molly and dished himself up some on his own plate. "One thing," he said, because his single-minded quest to get closer to Carl hadn't gotten one bit less intense.

"Oh," she said, winking. "As long as it's important."

Oh, it was.

JULIA INSISTED he drive one of the SUVs, so negotiating traffic at O'Hare was still horrible, but at least he felt like he had some power behind him as he wrestled with people who wanted to go one way when he had the right to go the other. He wasn't Chuck Calder. He didn't go Mach 5 with his hair on fire, and maybe part of that was that he'd had kids about three years after he'd learned to drive. It wasn't his own mortality he worried about so much as it was the welfare of the people in the car with him.

But another part of it was confidence. Chuck had the confidence to stand on the accelerator and know the car was going where he wanted it to go as fast as he wanted it to.

But tonight, as Michael fought his oppressors… erm, battled the other drivers for spots and emerged victorious, he found that his desire to see Carl again gave him some ambition when it came to driving. He'd started out running about ten minutes behind, but he arrived at passenger pickup just as Carl emerged, a luggage cart in tow. Michael found a spot against the curb, put the SUV in park, and set the brake, and then he hopped out, hurrying to help Carl with his bags.

"Wow!" he said, grinning as he unlatched the back. "You weren't kidding about moving in!"

Carl shrugged. "I mean, since I *had* the luggage, it made sense to fly it back full, right?"

"And there's more to come?"

"I let the tenants keep the furniture," he said. "I make a tidy little sum leasing the place to them. But my clothes and bedding and personal stuff I sent here. We should get some packing crates next week."

As they spoke, they were hefting suitcases—a nice matching leather set—and stacking them in the back of the SUV. When they were done, Carl returned the luggage rack, and Michael slammed the hatch shut, shivering a little in the wind off the lake. It sure did get cold fast here.

Michael hopped back into the SUV at the same time Carl did but paused in the act of putting his seat belt on when Carl's hand landed on his knee.

"Michael?"

"Yeah?" He turned, and for the first time really took Carl in—the dark blond hair, the sober green eyes, the square chin. He was wearing a hooded sweatshirt and jeans, and as it had before, the casual clothes touched something in Michael's stomach, something warm, as though he was one of the few allowed to see under the armor of the suit. Carl's lean mouth was curved softly up in a smile.

"You look really fantastic. It's so good to see you."

Oh! That was unexpected. He bit his lip. "I was gonna say the same," he admitted shyly. "I-I mean, yeah, I'm gussied up. We had dinner with Leon, and Julia bought me some new clothes and all. But you... you look good even in blue jeans. It's good to see you."

Carl leaned forward, but Michael met him halfway, and the kiss, restrained as it was for the time and place, held such warmth, such promise, Michael's eyes burned as they pulled away.

"Nice?" Carl asked, sounding uncertain.

"Fantastic," Michael reassured. He straightened then and remembered his seat belt, making sure Carl got his on too. He pulled away from the airport, driving carefully and making his way through the light rain that had begun after darkness had fallen.

He had to be careful; he had something important in the car with him.

They spoke easily on the way to the city and the apartment. The habit they'd started the first night Carl had been away had served them well, and they'd fallen into a nice pattern of chatting about their day.

Michael, who remembered this from being married, was reassured. He and Beth may not have had a complete marriage, but they'd cared about each other and had built a family together. The talking, even about small things, like the woman who'd sat next to Carl on the airplane and talked his ear off about her cats, was one of those things that made a relationship so much easier to sustain.

When they got to the building, Carl had Michael drop him off at the front door with the luggage so he could have the bellman get him a luggage cart. Then they met up at the apartment and continued their conversation as though they'd never stopped. They put together the care package from Phyllis, because she'd been right and Carl was starving, but Carl suggested they put the ice cream in the freezer and leave the brownie wrapped on the counter for later.

"What later?" Michael asked, doing as he'd suggested while Carl sat down with a plate of salad and lemon chicken.

Carl said nothing, shook his head and tucked in, and Michael suddenly felt foolish.

"Really?" he said, excited.

"I wanted to shower first," Carl admitted. "And I wasn't on a schedule. I just thought, you know, cuddling and dessert go together. He looked a little sad. "If memory serves."

"No, you're right," Michael told him. Those had been some of the best parts of marriage. The sex had been… well, he didn't want to think about the sex, because it had seemed so wrong lying to his friend like that. But the cuddling? He swallowed. "I've missed that," he said, his voice naked. "Touching, making it sweet. After I told Beth about me, she couldn't. It wasn't fair. We had to think of ourselves differently, and she couldn't do it if we were cuddling."

And for nearly two years before that, it had been prison, where no touch was a good touch. But he didn't want to talk about that either.

"Have I told you how much I admire you?" Carl said between mouthfuls of food and washing it down with a glass of milk from the fridge.

"For what?" Michael finished with the cleanup and did what he'd been longing to do, which was sit next to Carl at the counter.

"For taking care of your kids. For not being shitty about your ex-wife. For staying friends with her. For doing your damnedest to leave absolutely everything in your life in a better place than it was when you found it. I think it's really special," he said. And then, like he hadn't just rocked Michael's world, he took another bite.

Michael couldn't stop looking at him until Carl stopped chewing, swallowed, and stared back.

"What?"

"You think I'm special?" he asked, his heart absolutely on his sleeve, but he couldn't help it.

"Yeah," Carl responded, gazing into his eyes. "Yeah. I... I'm not easy with people. I'm awkward and reserved and quiet. But you I can talk to. And the more I talk to you, the more I want to be close to you. When I first realized you were crushing on me, I kept looking behind me. I was like, 'Me?' and then the more you looked at me—sort of like you're looking now—the more I wanted to be that guy. The guy you seem to see. And the more I get to know you, the more I think being someone you think is awesome could be the greatest thing I ever get to do in my life."

Michael couldn't help it. He wiped his eyes on the shoulder of his new blazer, and he was going to do it again when Carl took the napkin by his plate and held him still, strong fingers underneath his chin while he mopped up the tears.

"Why's that make you cry?" he asked softly.

"I've never been much," he managed to say, voice creaking. "But you make me feel like I'm everything."

Carl's mouth on his was tender, and the kiss was probably a mess. Briny tears and traces of lemon chicken and all the things romance books said were bad were probably wrapped up in their lips and teeth and tongue.

But Michael didn't register any of those things.

What hit him was Carl's kindness and his strength. He gave a little moan and returned the kiss, harder, with interest. He needed that, all of it, kindness and strength, wrapped around his body. Wrapped around his heart.

Carl slid off the stool and cupped Michael's face, holding him gently while he took over the kiss, mastered it, which was probably a good idea because Michael wasn't an expert in that department. He followed Carl's lead, though, opening his mouth, allowing Carl to taste, tangling their tongues and giving general enthusiastic encouragement. Carl pulled closer, stepping into the vee of Michael's legs, shoving his hands under the back of Michael's blazer and palming the small of his back under his shirt. Michael gasped and wrapped his legs around Carl's waist, his body a live wire as his skin let out a primal roar of hunger, of yearning to be touched.

Carl pulled back, panting and burying his face against Michael's neck. "This is not… going to plan…," he breathed. "There was going to be a shower and the brushing of teeth and—"

Michael wasn't proud of the sound he made right then, but he couldn't help it. Every molecule in his body was crying out for touch, for the mix of tenderness and steel that Carl's hands, his mouth, even his low, gruff voice promised.

"Please?" he mewled, out of words or complicated ideas right then. All he wanted was to be held.

And Carl gave him even more than what he wanted.

Carl took his mouth again and hefted him up by his thighs. Michael took the hint and wrapped his legs around Carl's hips, holding on as Carl carried him into Michael's bedroom and very carefully released his legs so his feet could hit the ground.

"We got condoms in the end table," he said as Carl pulled back, but Carl shook his head.

"Won't need them yet," he said roughly, sliding the new blazer off Michael's shoulders and kissing his neck. "There's so much more touching to do."

Michael didn't protest, although he wanted to. He wanted to argue that he had bad memories to lose and needed good ones to replace them, but he hadn't talked about the bad ones yet, so maybe he should let Carl…. Ah! Carl was kissing his way down Michael's chest now, unbuttoning that pretty red shirt and laughing slightly at the white tank underneath.

"What's funny?" Michael gasped.

"You're just so, so sweet," Carl gasped, nibbling on his collarbone as Michael shed the shirt. "I want to kiss every part of you."

Michael was going to be very blunt and very rude then about the one part of himself he'd really like to have kissed, but right then, Carl rucked up his undershirt and brushed his nipples with rough thumbs.

Michael made another one of those sounds, the needy kind that made him wish nobody could hear him.

Carl all but yanked the undershirt over Michael's head and bent to suck a sensitized nipple into his mouth.

Nobody had ever done that for him. Michael whimpered, aroused and shaking, tunneling his fingers through Carl's thick blond hair.

"Augh! So good!" He had to work to get the words out because he was afraid Carl would stop if he didn't. His hips started little minithrusts all on their own as his body sought to rut.

Carl moved away from his nipple and took his mouth again, calming him, leaving him clutching Carl's sweatshirt with shaking fingers.

"Slow it down," Carl whispered. "Here." With that he stepped back and pulled off his sweatshirt and T-shirt, leaving his body—wide-shouldered, heavy-muscled, well-defined, pale-skinned—gleaming softly in the overhead light.

Michael made another little sound and stepped forward to stroke the patch of wiry blond hair between Carl's pecs. "Soft," he said, surprised. His chest had maybe three hairs on it, and he'd never really explored a man before. Even his doomed relationship with Chuck had been a series of stolen blowjobs, snuck in during corners of time when nobody would even know they were together.

"Touch me too," Carl told him, and he rubbed his palms over Carl's chest in response. "Good. More nipple."

"I like nipples," Michael said sincerely, and then he stepped forward into Carl's warmth and licked the salt off one with his tongue.

"Harder," Carl whispered.

Michael suckled it, enjoying the tug of Carl's fingers in his hair as Carl tilted his head back, enjoying himself.

Oh, this was nice. This was permission to play. Michael moved to the other nipple, suckling while he pinched the still-wet nipple cooling in the air.

Carl let out a sound of arousal—of desire—and pulled away to take Michael's mouth in his, his hands working Michael's belt. He shoved at the pants and briefs as soon as he could, and Michael worked hard to keep up the kiss and kick off his cowboy boots, which he'd worn because they were his best dress shoes.

After a moment he stumbled back onto the bed, still struggling with the boots, and Carl grinned at him from a seemingly impossible height, haloed by the light behind his head.

"Here, let me get those," he said, and Michael leaned back on his elbows, bemused by the sight of it, this amazing golden man sliding Michael's boots off, palming his calves, then shucking his pants off, seeing Michael in the light.

Oh shit.

Carl straightened and started working on his own belt, jeans, and shoes, and Michael struggled to get under the covers. Carl straightened, naked as the day he was born, and Michael's desperate attempt to roll himself into a burrito stalled out completely.

He knew his mouth made a little "oooh…" sound, but he couldn't help it. "God, you're pretty," he muttered, tangled in the comforter.

"You are too," Carl said, frowning. "At least I'm pretty sure you are. What in the hell are you doing?"

Michael covered his eyes. "Can you turn off the lights? I'm… there's something I don't want you to see."

Carl sighed and sat down next to him, capturing his mouth and kissing him softly. About the time Michael's common sense deserted him, Carl's hands untangled the comforter, smoothing it down across the bed and leaving him, naked and vulnerable, on top.

He opened his mouth to protest, but Carl kissed him some more, and because he was weak and had no spine, he melted into the pillows like chocolate. When Carl covered his body with his own massive, naked one, Michael almost wept at the feeling of all that hairy male skin-on-skin contact. He wrapped his legs around Carl's hips again, and their groins rubbed together, erections bobbing and weaving, and Carl didn't stop the kiss, the marvelous, gorgeous, amazing kiss that destroyed Michael's brain like a fried electrical system and replaced it with candy floss.

Michael's movements were getting more urgent, and he couldn't seem to stop his hips. "Not yet," he begged, but he couldn't seem to stop.

"Shh…." Carl bumped his nose along Michael's cheek, pausing to whisper in his ear. "Let go. It's okay. We have all night." He finished his words by sucking on Michael's earlobe, and who knew that was a real thing?

Michael's fingers seemed to clench on Carl's biceps all on their own, hard enough to hurt, but he couldn't stop them, couldn't stop his hips, couldn't stop his cock from—oh God—from rubbing, from bumping….

Carl leaned on one elbow and reached between them, grabbing Michael's erection in his wide-palmed hand and squeezing from bottom to top, stroking solidly, slowly, his thumb and forefinger tightening around the head.

Michael cried out and came so hard he couldn't see, his entire body bucking, ejaculate pumping from his cock in what felt like a never-ending stream.

Finally the orgasm subsided, and he fell back limply against the mattress, lost and dazed, not sure if the night was over or what would happen next.

Carl's mouth on his was a surprise—a good one—and he returned the kisses, small ones this time, teasing, sweet, hints of tongue, of play, not unhappy in the least. Carl slipped away from him after a few of those, scooting down along Michael's body, pausing to lick his nipples, to suck, and then to move down some more.

A tongue dragged across the puddle on Michael's abdomen, tasting his come, and then licked down to his cock, which was still hard, still twitching. Gently, seeming mindful that he might be tender, Carl engulfed his erection with his mouth, cleaning him, licking him, sucking him until he was hard and gasping again.

Carl shifted on the bed until he was between Michael's legs. One hand still stroked his cock, but his mouth, oh God, his mouth was still exploring, His tongue hit that place at the base of Michael's cock that drove him wild, and then he took first one testicle and then the other gently into his mouth. Michael moaned, eyes closed against the pleasure, his thighs spread as wide as they could go. That feeling of safety, of trust with this man, had never left him, and the doubts, the worries about that one thing he was afraid Carl would see, all of that fled.

He was starting to shake with need again, but he had no words for what he wanted. Penetration had only ever been painful, violent, but he didn't know where else this could go. When Carl shoved up at his thighs, he was almost relieved. This would hurt, it would be invasive, but finally, finally, he would know what to do, how to quantify the sex act as he knew it.

And then he felt Carl's tongue dragging along his hole and even that went away. He moaned, unmanned, completely lost as Carl rimmed him, and he lost track of what to do with his hands.

Carl's voice, muffled, drifted toward him. "Your cock, your nipples, anything that feels good—stroke them!" And Michael grabbed on to that idea and to his cock, taking over from Carl and stroking with one hand while the other hand plucked at his nipple. And Carl's tongue… oh God.

"Gonna come!" he almost screamed, his entire body flailing about on top of the covers, under the light. Jizz scalded his fist, creaming down his forearm, but that was incidental to the rockets launching through his bloodstream and igniting all his nerve endings, blowing everything he thought he knew about sex out of the water.

When he came to, Carl had scooted up, wrapped his arms around Michael's shoulders, and thrown his leg around his hips, tangling them together, surrounding Michael with that glorious heat, that beautiful feeling of skin on skin.

Michael's shoulders were shaking, and he couldn't quite find his center. He buried his face against that broad chest and realized his cheeks were wet, and Carl's breath was coming hard and fast.

"I don't know what's next," he confessed, wanting to pleasure Carl like he'd been pleasured but not even sure he could move to get under the covers right now.

"This is good," Carl whispered, dropping a kiss on his temple.

"But you didn't…. You haven't…." Carl's erection was still there, pulsing against his stomach.

"Later." Carl tilted his face up and kissed him, and Michael tasted himself, the salty, bitter mess of him, on his lover's lips. Michael fell into the kiss, the earthiness of it and the feeling of Carl's big hands drifting along his back, palming his backside, keeping him safe and pleasured and calm.

"Mm…." The kiss faded, and Michael was content just to lie there, being touched, filling up on the tenderness of a man he'd wanted from the very beginning.

Then it sank in that he wasn't the only one with wet cheeks and the brine in their kiss hadn't been his alone.

"Carl?" he asked, struggling again to put words to emotions. Oh God. He suddenly remembered the thing he'd tried so hard to hide—so hard to forget, to overcome, to ignore. His body had been spread out, the scars of violation, the prison tattoo that had made him scream and weep, all there for Carl to see. He tightened his knees together, attempting to curl up into a ball, to hide himself, but he couldn't, not and remain plastered against Carl, wrapped in his arms and legs, safe and secure at the same time.

"You," Carl said thickly, not stopping any of the things that were pulling Michael into a happy, dreamy haze, "are not meat."

Michael's breath caught.

"Carl?"

"You're Michael," Carl told him huskily. "You're wonderful. You're kind. You're generous. Your soul is so fucking shiny, I could still see all of you if we turned out the lights. And I don't care what people tried to make you into, you are not meat. You're Michael. And I never knew I needed you in my life, but I do."

"Okay," Michael said, not sure he had any other words.

"Nothing about you needs to hide," he said, his shoulders shaking. "Every part of you is beautiful."

Oh.

"Okay," he said again. He was weeping against Carl's chest now, but he was also falling asleep. Tired. So tired. So many years hiding, and two brutal years unable to hide anywhere but inside his own head. He'd spent his entire life wanting a place where he'd be safe, be protected, be cared for.

Now that he'd found it, here in Carl's arms, all his body could do was rest, replete. And finally, *finally,* he was no longer afraid.

# A Shift in Expectations

CARL STARTED to get cold, lying on top of the covers without any clothes, but Michael was sleeping.

It seemed imperative that, for this moment, Carl let him sleep.

Finally when he was not only cold but also had to pee, he worked carefully to situate Michael under the covers before sliding off the bed and into his briefs and T-shirt before using the facilities.

He stayed in the bathroom for a moment after washing his hands and splashing some water on his face to see if anything about him was different. Same guy, he thought. Starkly handsome in a broad-shouldered, Viking sort of way. Green-eyed, a nose that was short a millimeter from being described as "Roman," and an almost perpetually quizzical expression, as though he was used to watching the world behave in absurd and strange patterns around him.

*I can't be that guy anymore.* The guy who fell into things, like he'd fallen into his job or fallen into his attachment to the Salingers, no matter how satisfying that was. Michael hadn't just fallen into his bed—Michael had *chosen* him, after a whole lot of heartbreak and a whole lot of violence and pain and fear. The violence and pain and fear had been written on his skin, and the thought of that made Carl's hands shake.

Michael had walked through fire, and apparently he thought Carl was one of the good things that had been waiting for him on the other side. Carl needed to do better, *be* better, to be that sort of reward. Michael deserved better than an also-ran. He deserved a hero.

But not a hero like Chuck or Hunter, who, though pretty damned heroic, didn't really fit the mold Michael had in mind. Carl had seen the signs in him from the very beginning: making an apartment out of an airplane hangar, learning to cook with his ex-wife, thinking about how to integrate his children into the life he was building in this new city.

Michael needed a hero who could be proactive. Not about the adventures that might befall them all, but about their personal life. Carl's ex-wife had done the wrangling, the proposing, the "Where's this relationship going, Carl?" and that had been fine with him. He'd assumed he'd get married, assumed he'd be unhappy in that relationship—or absent—and had then fulfilled both prophecies nicely.

Carl had known his relationship with Danny had been doomed from the start. You didn't fall in love with someone in rehab when they said right up front that they could kick the whiskey, but they couldn't quit their addiction to their one true love.

This was different. It wasn't a hookup like Chuck had been. It wasn't a one-off or a "hey, let's see where this goes," only to have it go nowhere. It wasn't a "wait-and-see" like Ginger had been, which he was glad hadn't gone anywhere because apparently she was as corrupt as most of Serpentus.

This was someone Carl liked, admired, and cared for, and he'd made Carl his holy grail.

Carl needed to pony up. That didn't mean "Hey, we like each other, we're probably going to sleep together—let's share a free apartment because it's easy!" That meant intent. It meant commitment.

It meant making Michael's thoughts, his feelings, his plans for the future, all of it, a priority.

Carl hadn't done that with any other person in his life. Not once. But he really, really wanted to now.

*So what? Churches? Wedding bells? A house in the suburbs? All after one night together?*

Well, no. But they were living together, by accident or not. Maybe it was time to begin as they meant to go on.

To that end Carl walked into the kitchen and cleaned up what was left of dinner, making sure his dishes were rinsed and put in the dishwasher and his place mat wiped off and put away. And then, feeling a bit peckish, he cut the enormous portion of brownie Phyllis had sent for him in half and put it in the microwave for about thirty seconds. Just enough to heat it up. He put that in a bowl and added two scoops of ice cream—and two spoons—before grabbing a towel and a glass of milk. He made his way into the bedroom and set everything on the end table before sliding into bed, clicking on the lamp, and turning on the television.

Michael grunted and stretched, then rolled over to glare at him in confusion. "You let me fall asleep!"

"Yeah, you seemed to need a nap. Here, lean forward and I'll shove some pillows behind your back. Are you up for stupid TV?"

Michael did as he asked, and Carl could see him processing.

"But aren't we going to…? I mean…. Oh." His disappointment was more than Carl could bear.

"Don't think that," Carl said softly, squeezing their bodies together so their sides, thighs, and shoulders were touching. "Of course we're gonna."

Michael gave him a suspicious look, and Carl sighed, figuring he was going to have to be more explicit than that.

"Yes, Michael Carmody, I want to make love with you some more. A lot, actually. But this first time—that was special and hard on you. I love touching your body. Don't ever think I don't." He draped a deliberate arm around Michael's shoulders and pulled him even tighter. "But I think you need more than a fuck and a suck. And I think you've needed more than that for pretty much your entire adult life. So if I'm going to give you what you need, we're going to start with the idea that making love doesn't ever have to be penetrative. It doesn't ever have to scare you. And it doesn't ever have to be transactional. That means you don't have to repay me because I pleasured you. It means we made love, and we're done for the moment, and it's time for ice cream and a brownie."

He pulled away long enough to set the dessert bowl between them. "Two spoons, see?"

"That's a big brownie," Michael said, his voice thick.

"Yeah." Carl brushed his knuckle against Michael's wet cheek so he'd know Carl wasn't fooled at all and that Carl knew how much this meant to him. "So it's got to be both of us working on it."

"I…. It wouldn't be a hardship, you know. Making you feel good." Michael searched Carl's face, and Carl dropped a kiss on his lips.

"You just did," he murmured. "But I think you need more than the sex right now. I think you need dessert and a snuggle and to feel comfortable in your own home, in your own bed, in your own skin. So that's what we're going to do."

"Okay," he said softly. Then he gave a little smile. "Can I pick the show?"

"Is it mindless and funny?" Carl craved it like he craved his next bite of brownie.

"Oh yeah."

"Bring it on."


THEY WATCHED TV companionably for an hour, and then Carl took the dishes to the kitchen again, shivering a little in his underwear. Since Michael was putting on pj's, he spotted the suitcase with his leisure clothes in it and unzipped the thing enough to pull out a pair of sweats and an extra pair of underwear. If he didn't have to be anywhere until the family meeting the next evening, he was going to spend the day hanging in his sweats and getting his stuff unpacked.

And touching Michael as often and as tenderly as possible.

He brought his clothes back into the bedroom and set them on the chair he'd fallen asleep in that first night before climbing back into bed and waiting as Michael made a neat and tidy circle of the apartment, making sure all the things were shut off or locked, accordingly.

When Michael came back to bed, he turned off the light and slid under the covers, wearing pajama bottoms and a T-shirt. Carl slid to his side, the way he'd been lying that first morning, and waited until Michael rolled enough to look at him in the dark.

"What?" Michael whispered.

"You want to tell me about it?" Carl asked.

Michael closed his eyes and shook his head. "Every bad thing you can think of," he said, voice flat. "I went to the infirmary six times. They… I mean, they said it was time off for good behavior, but I think the guards talked to my lawyer and made him apply to get me out of there. I-I wasn't gonna make it much longer."

Carl sighed and pushed Michael's hair back from his eyes. He liked Michael's hair: long, dark, silky, down past his collar in spite of the recent trim. "You are so sweet," he said softly. "So kind. How did that make it through such a terrible, terrible place?"

Michael lifted a shoulder. "Beth," he said, and Carl would never, ever resent or be jealous of that woman just hearing Michael say something like that. "My kids. Mostly my kids. Writing letters to them, trying to tell them to mind their mama, to do good in school, telling them they didn't want to be like me." He smiled a little. "Beth made me stop doing that. I guess being polite and saying please and thank you was being like Daddy too, and she didn't want them to lose that because I'd made a mistake."

Carl let out a sigh. "The world is such a hard place," he said after a moment. "When you are with me, I want it to be easy. Don't be afraid to ask me for something in this relationship, okay? I will do my best to be considerate, but I'm sort of a bastard. You've had practice living with someone, remembering to fend for your kids when they couldn't do it for themselves. I don't know any of these things. I'll try to learn but—" His voice was trying to crack and he wouldn't let it. "—don't do anything in bed with me you don't want to because you think I want it. That's all I ask. Do it because you want it too."

"You're not a bastard," Michael said staunchly. "You…. What we just did? I never, not in a million years, knew a man could touch me like that. Not just the"—his face went pink; Carl could even see it in the dark—"not just the licking. But the sweetness. You touched me like I was important. You keep touching me like I'm important and I'll probably find pleasure in anything we do."

"I can do that," Carl said gravely. "It's so easy to touch you like you're important."

Michael's smile glinted in the light from the city that glowed through the drapes on the window. "I… I'd like to touch you too. To be honest, I don't think I've ever been with a man in a bed with, you know, time and privacy." He bit his lip and touched Carl's chest, fingertips stroking through the shirt. "It would be fine to touch all of you."

"I'd like that," Carl said and then caught a yawn Michael was trying to suppress. "Tomorrow," he said, capturing Michael's fingers with his own and placing a gentle kiss on the knuckles. "All we have to do tomorrow is move my clothes in and make love. And maybe eat."

Michael grinned. "I'll get donuts—"

"And I'll glaze yours," he said with a straight face, mostly to watch Michael break into the naughty laughter of a little kid.

"You're bad," he said, almost gleefully.

"I try." Carl sobered. "But I have to ask you about the clothes." He looked around the bedroom, at the rustic furnishings that didn't quite match the tone of the upscale urban apartment. "This is your place. You worked hard to make it your place, even though you're probably thinking of a more kid-friendly place by next year, am I right?"

Michael nodded. "Yeah. I like living in the city, but I promised Beth that I'd have them for the summer, and this place, it's nice and all but—"

"It's not meant for three active children," Carl said. "I get it. And I've got some plans that might help. But right now, I'm asking for me. I can move all my stuff into the guest room and spend as many nights as you can stand me here in this bed that you picked out. But it's your space, and you haven't had much of your own in that way, and I'm going to need your guidance to tell me how you want me in your space."

Michael glanced around the large, comfortable room too.

"It's almost too big," he whispered, looking nervous. "You don't understand. My cell was eight by ten, and this—this could fit six of 'em. This room alone could fit half the house we rented before I went to prison. We had two bedrooms. The kids had two bunk beds, so we could store stuff on the spare top bunk. I think that's where Sarah's—she's the youngest—I think that's where we kept her clothes and toys. I don't mind if you put your clothes in this closet or sleep in this bed with me. I'll be honest. That morning we woke up together? That was the first time in my life I don't remember feeling lonely."

"Well, then," Carl said, wondering if he could breathe past the lump in his throat. "We'll try not to ever let you feel lonely again."

Michael nodded happily and yawned outright this time. "I'm sorry," he said wretchedly. "The last three days, chasing the teenagers around the city—I think it tuckered me out."

"Yeah. I was moving, so I hear you." Carl covered his own yawn and then gestured with his chin. "Roll over and I'll be the big spoon."

"Sure." But for a moment Michael didn't move. He stared at Carl and then kissed him, a quietly needing sort of kiss, one that banked passion for later. He pulled away and said, "I spent my whole life waiting for a moment, for a lover, just like this. It was a long-assed wait, but I gotta tell you. Worth it. So worth it."

And then he rolled over, letting Carl drape his arm over his waist and pull them close. Carl buried his nose in Michael's hair and breathed in, thinking now that he knew what to look for in a lover, he'd never settle for anything less than this moment right here.

CARL WOKE up as Michael sat on his side of the bed, looking freshly showered and bright-eyed and bushy-tailed.

He had a pastry box with him.

"You've been up for a while!" Carl yawned. "I'm such a slacker."

Michael grinned. "It's been a while since I slept that well." He looked away, biting his lip. "Thanks."

"Completely my pleasure," Carl replied, curling over on his side so he could palm Michael's back under his sweatshirt. He fought a yawn. "So give me a few to shower and shave, and then it will be donuts and unpacking. How's that?"

Michael gave him a sideways look. "And... uhm...."

Impulsively Carl tugged him back onto the bed and into his arms to kiss his temple even as he tickled his ribs. "Uhm?" he asked. "Uhm? Uhm...?"

"Oh my God! You're so bad. Stop it!"

"Uhm?" Carl prompted, turning the tickling to something softer, with more sensual promise.

"Uhm naked?" Michael almost begged. "You promised!"

"Yeah, but I'm not keeping that promise until I've scrubbed under my balls," Carl told him. "You only get the privates that are sparkly clean. It's a moral imperative."

Michael grinned at him, turning to kiss him on the mouth. "You're good to me," he said solemnly.

"It's the least I can do for a man who brought me donuts in bed," Carl told him before giving him a gentle shove. "Now let me up so I can carbo-load and get busy."

The other boxes Carl had shipped came while they were eating, and Michael watched with solemn eyes as Carl tipped the doorman before he wheeled the now-empty luggage rack out.

"How do you know to do that?" he asked when Carl had shut the door.

"Tip the doorman?" Carl laughed a little. "Well, I didn't the first time something like that happened. He was an old guy, crusty, not afraid to talk back. He stood there looking at me as I looked blankly back at him, and he finally said, 'I'll give you a pass because you're practically an infant, but you need to give me money, junior, or I'm not doing shit for you from this moment forward.'" Carl chuckled at the memory. "And it occurred to me how nice it had been to have help and how handy the luggage rack had been and how miserable it would be if that service was never available again. So I said, 'I'm sorry, sir. How much is customary, sir? Can I double that, sir?' and he told me he'd let me off with a twenty, and I've been rounding up ever since."

Michael grinned. "And that was it? Suddenly you're Mr. Smooth?"

Carl shrugged. "There's caveats too. Like, if you give a dollar to everyone you meet in New York, your trip's gonna go a lot better. And—and this was from an ex-girlfriend—if a bellman ever does the equivalent of walking two blocks in the snow to get you M&M's when you're on your period, you had better give that man all the twenties in your wallet."

Michael snickered, all little boy again. "I'll be sure to tell Beth," he said solemnly. "It sounds like good advice."

"Anything I can do to help," Carl said with a bow and a flourish. Then he looked around at the luggage and boxes and sighed. "Clothes first," he said after a moment. "There's a desk in the guest room, and I'll set my electronics up on that later. Everything else we can stow in the guest closet. How's that?"

"Sounds like a plan," Michael said, clapping his hands and rubbing them together. "Let's get crackin'!"

They made short work of the boxes, calling out to each other as they pulled out summer clothes, then winter clothes, and made decisions on the fly. Carl's first major fight with his ex-wife had been over unpacking dishes in their apartment, and he'd always figured that a good acid test of a relationship came when two people merged possessions and personal space.

After about an hour and a half, Carl called a halt, packing his smaller suitcases inside his trunk-sized one like nesting dolls and setting them upright against the back wall of the guest room.

"There's a storage space in the basement we can put those in," Michael said, standing in the doorway and nodding.

"Tomorrow," Carl told him, looking around happily. The boxes had been broken down flat and stowed behind the suitcases, and the clothes and shoes were all hanging up or folded neatly in one of the two dressers in Michael's room. He'd put his own sheets and comforter on the guest bed, folding the unused all-white set and putting them in the closet. He liked his comforter—deeply colored in burgundy, indigo, and forest green, it had old Nordic runes printed on the fabric in gold. It reminded him of the bronze artifacts found at Sutton Hoo, and seeing it actually *on a bed* made him feel like this could be his home too, for a while. "That gives us a couple hours of downtime before we have to leave for dinner."

He was going to say something suggestive then, make an innuendo, but Michael had moved into the room and picked up one of the few pictures he'd set out on the desk.

"You, Hunter, and Chuck," Michael said, chuckling a little.

"Yeah. They took me to a baseball game. Chuck insisted on a selfie. I wasn't expecting him to make a print, but—" He bit his lip, still pleased. "—it was nice."

"Nothing from work?" Michael asked, and Carl shrugged.

"There's a box of awards and certificates—my diplomas, I guess. They're up in the closet with the original comforter."

"Not important?" Michael wrinkled his nose.

Carl shrugged again, and Michael moved to another picture, this one of him and Stirling working side by side at Lucius Broadstone's company when they'd been fixing a security breach that summer.

"He's a good kid," Carl said, in case Michael got ideas. "We worked together really well. That doesn't happen a lot for me."

"But not a person from your other work?" Michael asked.

"I've got some shots accepting awards at dinners and stuff," Carl said. But after a moment of silence, he was forced to concede, "I don't really like those people."

"Is this your mom?"

Carl grimaced. She was on the smoking deck of a cruise ship with his Aunt Bessie, her platinum hair floofed and sprayed, wearing a tight shirt that showed off lots of leathery bosom. Bessie's hair was strawberry blond, and her bosom was smaller but just as leathery.

"Yeah," he said. "She's, uhm, sort of toxic."

Michael gave him a grave look. "I've got one of those. You don't need to apologize. One of the happiest days of my life was when Beth told me my mom wouldn't speak to her if she moved to Ohio. I was like, 'Then by all means move!'"

Carl grinned. "Why Ohio?" he asked.

"Beth was accepted to Ohio State after we graduated from high school. Her folks didn't have the money to send her, but we both figured that since we had money now, she could go to school. I mean, I guess she could have applied anywhere, but she'd been all excited about Ohio State when we were kids, so, you know. Her dream, right?"

Carl moved behind him so he could wrap his arms around that slender body and pull that optimism into his soul.

"You are the only person who could make a wife and three kids sound like a bonus in a relationship, do you know that? I want to meet them. I want to see you with them. I want to see them be a part of your life."

Michael turned a shining smile toward him. "Really? 'Cause that was one of my biggest fears, I gotta admit. That I'd find a guy I really liked, and he'd be like, 'Ex-wife and three kids? See ya!'"

Carl started kissing along his jaw, liking all the tastes. A little bit of shower still lingered, plus a bit of brisk wind from his trip to get donuts, plus some sweat from hauling clothes throughout the apartment. "Every good thing you say about them tells me what a good person you are," he murmured, and then, because it seemed to really do it for him, he bit Michael's earlobe precisely and listened to the delicious sounds he made. Feeling a sense of pride that someone like Michael Carmody wanted him, he slid his hands under Michael's shirts and spanned his rib cage, liking the stringy strength, the slenderness, the concave stomach and smooth skin of him.

Michael groaned and leaned back against his chest. "Bed?" he begged. "Now? Naked?"

"Yeah."

He spun Michael around and kissed him, stripped his shirts above his head and then started the kiss up again. Michael shoved at his own clothes, and together they kissed, stumbled, and laughed their way to the other bedroom, leaving a trail of clothes behind them.

When they got there, Michael remembered to pull the covers down, and then he looked up into Carl's eyes with all seriousness.

"Can I play?" he asked. "With your body? Can I play?"

Carl grinned. "It's like I've waited my *entire life* to hear somebody ask me that," he said, and the next time Michael shoved gently on his chest, he went down, splaying himself out in broad daylight, biting his lip a little in embarrassment.

Michael rolled his eyes before lying down next to him and starting a tentative exploration of his chest. "I don't know why you're embarrassed. You must work out a *lot*!"

"Human nature," Carl murmured. "Mm… that. That thing you did with my nipple." Michael pinched it, and Carl gasped. "Yes, *that*. More of *that*!"

"Want me to suck it?" Michael asked, but he was already scooting down the bed, getting ready to suckle, and Carl moaned softly as his mouth took hold.

"Yes!" he hissed. "Now the other one!"

Michael moved like he asked, and his body, naked and sprawled over Carl's, was almost as erotic as his mouth. Then he started to move, kiss by suck by taste, down Carl's stomach, down to his cock, and he looked up along Carl's body to smile.

"This is really nice," he said, gripping the thing to indicate what he was talking about.

"What makes it—ah!" Because Michael had begun to squeeze it and stroke it, and Carl was enjoying every sensation. "Nice?" he finished weakly, panting with desire.

"It's big," Michael said, sticking his tongue out to taste. The flutter of tongue against the tip brought an honest-to-God whimper from Carl's throat, and Carl was wondering if Michael didn't have a little bit of sadist in him after all.

"Ye—ah?" Flutter, flutter, flutter.

"But not so big it's scary."

"Goo—ah!"

Michael engulfed the cap with his mouth, and Carl was suddenly past flirting.

"Suck it, please!" he begged. "Stroke it, suck it. Oh!"

Michael was good at this. Not expert, but he obviously enjoyed it, and Carl moaned softly in encouragement, spreading his thighs as wide as he could get them, mapping his own chest with his fingers as he lay back and appreciated the attention.

Michael's mouth popped off the end, but Michael kept up a long, delirious stroke with his fist.

"Carl?" he asked, his voice a little tentative.

"Yeah?" He tried desperately to keep his hips down.

"Can I—uhm, if I use lube and all, can I, uhm… you know. See what's what down below?"

Carl made a sound like a winded bull and struggled with the end table so he could root around in the drawer. "Seriously?" he muttered. "God yes. Thank you for asking. I'd love my ass played with if you wouldn't mind."

Michael remembered what he'd been doing with Carl's cock and sucked deeply again before Carl managed to locate the bottle of lube.

"Ah! Here. Take it. Play. But I'm going to come very quickly once you do, just so you know!"

Michael paused again and took the lube from Carl's shaking fingers.

"Really? It… you like it that much?"

"Yes, yes I do." Carl couldn't believe this conversation, right at this exact moment. Michael lowered his head again and Carl fell back against the pillows, his entire body trembling with need.

For a few moments he lay there and took it, enjoying everything from Michael's stroke with his fist to his fluttering tongue. Then he felt it, the tentative foray of a bold, slickened finger down under his balls and along his taint. For a moment, his entire body froze in breathless anticipation as that finger slid and searched and searched and… ah… ah… ah….

"Yes!" he cried as the finger penetrated and Michael sucked him in hard and deeply, bottoming out in his throat, where he swallowed, milking Carl until he came.

For a few moments, everything in his life was stars and the lightning-strike nerve endings of orgasm as he clawed at the sheets, crying out, and shot until he was dry.

Finally he came down to earth to find Michael, up near his shoulder, wiping his mouth on his own upper arm. He looked up, and his face was still glazed with spit and come, and Carl needed to kiss him so bad his stomach cramped with it. He practically roared with want as he took over the kiss, and he didn't stop until Michael went limp with submission and collapsed against him, moaning softly.

"What?" Carl asked, hoping he hadn't scared him off.

"Now I've got a hard-on," Michael whimpered. "And I want you to do what I just did!"

Carl chuckled and wrapped his arm securely around his shoulders. "Give me a minute," he murmured. "A man has to recover from a blowjob like that."

Michael chuckled too. "Did you really like it? The, uhm, finger in the, uh, you know. Place?"

"Yeah," Carl said softly. "There's lots of nerve endings there. Which is why, when it's bad, it's so very, very bad. And when it's good, it's fantastic."

"Mm…," Michael murmured. "Maybe, you know, if you're sweet, like you were last night, you could do that thing a lot?"

"You'd like that?" Carl asked, his nerve endings beginning to awaken again at the thought.

Michael looked up at him, his eyes heavy-lidded and sensual and his smile excited. "I'd like to try. Lots of shouting about that. Would like to see what it's all about."

"Five more minutes," Carl teased.

"Is that all?" Michael teased back.

"And maybe another kiss."

His mouth on Carl's was bold this time, confident in a way that had been missing in the beginning. Carl drank him in, the confidence like an aphrodisiac when Carl had already been humming with sex and pleasure.

This, he thought, was gonna be good.

# New Adventures

MICHAEL COULD hardly sit still on the trip to Glencoe.

Part of it was excitement and butterflies because in his entire life, he could never remember feeling like his body was flying before. And part of it was that his bottom tingled.

Carl had just left the freeway when he startled Michael by putting a hand on his knee.

"You're going to need to sit still," he said softly into the comfortable silence. "Everybody's going to know anyway, but you're wriggling like a puppy."

"I can't help it," Michael almost crowed. "I feel *amazing*!"

Carl's deep chuckle soothed something inside him, grounded all the tingles and the butterflies, suffused his body with peace.

God, what a rush.

He'd known, sort of, how good things could get from the night before. But that had been a surprise, and he hadn't been very proactive about it. Carl had taken over and shown him the light. But that afternoon, he'd not only gotten to hold the reins himself, but Carl had picked him off the kid's pony and put him on a racing stallion, and now sex was suddenly a whole new animal.

It hadn't just been the gentle licking, then the one finger and the stretching, and the two fingers, coupled with Carl's mouth on his cock— but Lord, that had been amazing. It had been the control, the way Carl had told him to say faster, or more, or wait a second, and then Carl had done exactly what he'd asked.

Right up until the moment when Michael had begged, "Please, more, anything, more, now!"

And Carl had slid the third finger in and sucked him down hard, and Michael had flown forever and ever and ever, and when he'd come down to earth, he'd floated and not fallen.

He'd had a hard time putting his brain together after that.

Carl had held him and told him sweet things, and when he'd asked why he was so floaty still, Carl had explained a thing called "subspace," which meant that when you turned yourself over to someone the way Michael had just done, when you opened your body up for invasion and trusted that it wouldn't turn into pain, your mind went to a special place that gave your body permission to turn over the controls, so to speak.

"This didn't happen to you," Michael had complained almost tearily.

Carl had *hmm*ed. "I think," he said slowly, "you're used to going to this place. Only nothing good ever happened to you when you went there."

And Michael had remembered those vague, numb moments of aftermath in prison, when his body had picked itself up and kept on going, whether he'd been bleeding through his jumper or not. "But this feels so good," he'd said, wondering.

"Because something good finally happened to you when you went to that place in your head."

Michael had nodded, and then to his horror—because the night before had been such an anomaly, he never did this, not even that first night in prison when everybody did it—he cried quietly, waiting for his body to come down.

His brain finally started responding to commands, but his body?

Apparently it was flooded with endorphins—at least that's what Carl said. Michael told him that if this was what endorphins felt like, he *liked* them, and Carl agreed and kept snuggling with him, grounding him, touching him sweetly, kissing him, until he came down enough to get ready to leave for Glencoe.

He'd managed to function, but he hadn't been particularly talkative, and it occurred to him now that Carl had been thoughtful and quiet the whole time too.

"Is anything wrong?" he asked as the pretty, ordered streets of the wealthy suburb passed them by on either side.

"No," Carl said immediately. "I'm... well, part of me is going over what I need to tell everybody tonight, because it's a lot, but part of it is—" He bit his bottom lip. "—I'm curious about something that's none of my fucking business, and I don't know how to ask you."

"Ask me," Michael said, chuckling slightly. "I don't think I can take offense right now anyway."

"Okay, then. Feel free to tell me to fuck off if it's too intrusive. You and Beth got together in high school," he said.

"Right after. We graduated, she took me out to a camping spot in her backyard, and I closed my eyes and thought of NASCAR. Nine months later...."

"Baby," Carl said, his lips twitching. "Jakey? Didn't you say it was Jake?"

"Yeah. Jakey, Liz, and Sarah, the baby." It pleased him that Carl had been listening.

"And the baby's three. She was only a few months old when you went in."

"Yeah." That had hurt. Beth had sent pictures once a month, and he'd watched his daughter grow. Now Beth texted him almost every day. His phone was filling up, but he didn't care.

"Did you have many... uhm, hookups, like you had with Chuck, while you were married?"

Michael grimaced. He wasn't proud of what he'd been doing with Chuck, but God, he'd been so damned lonely. "No. I didn't tell Chuck, but he was the first guy who ever just took me aside and sort of touched me. You know? I guess I was lucky he was sweet."

"You were," Carl said, his voice getting odd, scratchy and swollen somehow. "I think Chuck really was good luck for you. If he hadn't shown up, you probably would have gotten killed in that bank robbery."

There was an "and" hanging on at the end there.

"And what?" Michael's focus was returning, brought on by the raw emotion in Carl's voice.

"And you might never have been touched by someone who knew who you were," Carl whispered roughly. "I'm overwhelmed, Michael. You picked me? You've been waiting your whole life to be touched by someone who knew you, and you picked me?"

Michael thought about that. "I was right, wasn't I?"

"God, I hope so, baby. I hope in a million years you never regret picking me."

Carl sounded sort of upset about the idea, but Michael didn't have it in him to be anything but Zen. "Yeah," he said, images of that afternoon floating into his head with delicious clarity. "But I think I'm pretty lucky. You'll do fine."

MICHAEL DID pretty fine too, all the way through dinner and dessert, even though the verbal roughhousing seemed to be circling the table without him. Carl was part of it, though, giving as good as he got, telling the story of how he'd snuck into Serpentus like Stirling was exaggerating.

"So you just put on a onesie, walked into your boss's office, set the computers up to hack, and left?" Danny asked, eyes bright. "That's impressive. What if someone had caught you?"

Carl gave a wicked smile. "Well, I went out through the executive's elevator," he said. "You need a passkey to go up but not down. I know which closets to look in to find the mistresses, I mean skeletons—"

"Which gardens to dig in?" Molly quipped.

"Which hats to look under?" Grace added.

"Which vests to remove?" Chuck put in.

"Which assholes don't want me talking," Carl said, his mouth stern but his eyes dancing. "So I figured if I got caught there, no big deal. Anyway, I got back down to the service entrance, walked out the front, and kept going. Somewhere in the bottom of the laundry is my brown wool suit. Once it goes through the permanent-press cycle, it will no longer be brown, and it will no longer fit anybody nearly my size, so I think I'm safe."

There was a scattering of applause, and Carl gave a sitting bow.

"Was it worth it?" Danny asked Stirling.

Stirling was chewing on a piece of meat, but he nodded enthusiastically. "*So* worth it," he said after a hard swallow. "Fucking *gold*!"

"Nice!" Felix commended. "Did you get anything else while you were there?"

"Yeah." Carl looked around and made sure everybody was listening. "If we can prove something illegal and potentially environmentally dangerous, I've got some big guns to back us up. The DOI does *not* like it when people fuck around with endangered species or potentially invasive species. Bad, bad magic in that. So if things get dicey—"

"You've got someone to call," Felix said, nodding. "Excellent."

When they'd been keeping the women safe in Lucius's shelter, they'd needed Hunter's contacts in the FBI because many of their bad guys had been law enforcement. This was much the same; they could con, grift, and steal, but sometimes they needed someone who could prosecute or imprison. Conning people into the legal net was also a fun game.

"Did you have to do something cool to get that?" Grace asked, his grin impudent.

"I had to slaughter a fifty-year-old woman in squash," Carl replied, his eyes twinkling. "It was *brutal!*"

Michael laughed like the rest of the table, but he remembered the longer version of the story, how much Carl had liked Tamara Charter, and how much his friend Ginger had *not* wanted Carl to tell her the truth. He hoped the whole story would come out after dinner. He had the feeling that both women were dangerous, and only one was their friend.

BY THE time dinner and dessert were over, Michael had overcome some of the dreaminess that had ridden him since that afternoon. Part of it was probably the food, since they'd skipped lunch to play around in bed, but a lot of it was definitely the company. A person didn't bring their space game to the Salinger dinner table—they brought their *A* game.

He was sharp enough to notice that Josh, while looking a little better, was also looking introspective and thoughtful throughout dinner.

As they were gathering to go downstairs, he was surprised when the young man nodded him over so they could walk together.

"'Sup?" he asked.

Josh gave him a quiet smile. "After you left last night to go pick up Soderburgh there, I had a chance to talk to my uncle some more."

"Seems like a decent guy," Michael said carefully.

"He is." Josh sighed. "He started talking about my father and telling me what a sweet man he was and how he hadn't deserved the life that got forced on him. At first I thought he was dumping on my parents. I got super defensive, and he tried to tell me how much I looked like my father and how I'd make pretty babies, and I told him I was gay and asked if that was a cheap shot."

"Oh no," Michael said, genuinely appalled. He'd tried to give advice—he had! And Leon di Rossi had walked into it like a big trap.

"And just when I thought my uncle Leon couldn't be more of an asshole, he almost broke into tears and told me about you writing to your children to mind their mother from prison and how he just wanted me to know that he wanted to be part of my life."

"Oh God." Michael felt faint.

"And I was so surprised, I asked him to tell me the entire story, and because fuck my life and fuck cancer, I started to cry."

"I'm so sorry." Michael wanted to fall through the floor and out the other side of the world.

"Don't be." They were at the top of the stairs at this point, and Josh turned toward him, thin pale face earnest and almost transcendent with a quiet joy. "Because I started to cry, and Uncle Leon started to cry, and we both said, 'That guy is the *best* guy on the planet!' And we talked about how brave you were to give him that story when it couldn't have been easy for you. You didn't know him, and you were put in a situation where you must not have been comfortable, but you went out of your way to do something nice for Leon *and* for me. And I wanted you to know that it worked. We had something to talk about that we agreed on. And then we both agreed that kindness needed to be paid forward, which is a big thing with us, you might have noticed. And then we both agreed that my father got cheated, and I finally had to admit that I might have liked to meet him, after it was safe to do so. And then we both agreed to stay in contact after he had to go back to Italy, and then I cried a little more, because I guess it was that kind of night, and he asked me if he could hug me, and he sobbed like a baby. He thought his brother had been lost to him, and he just wanted a little piece of Matteo to hold on to."

"Oh wow," Michael said, completely at a loss. "I don't know what to say."

Josh hugged him, surprisingly strong for all that he looked like a stiff wind might blow him away. "Don't worry about fitting in here, Michael," he said softly. "I know it probably feels weird, because you've got an ex-wife and kids and prison and all the stuff that we don't. But you are special. And awesome. And I want you here in my home. Thank you for giving me and Leon a place where we could connect. You'll never know how important it was."

And with that, Josh broke off the hug, probably because Grace was down at the bottom of the stairs calling up, "I think if you want to make out with him, Carl's gonna beat your fragile bones to powder. Maybe let him go now?"

And with that, Josh winked and went down the stairs, leaving Michael to trail after him, thinking the world was the damnedest place.

"So," DANNY said, after setting up at the computer again. "Here's where we stand. Chuck, you were supposed to find out about—"

"Why Napa," Grace said as though he hadn't spoken.

Danny stared at him, and then looked at Hunter, who shrugged. "He's really excited about it," Hunter said. "Let him go first and he'll probably shut up for the rest of the presentation."

"You know me." Grace grinned at his boyfriend, all teeth, before going on. "So why Napa? Well, what's the bald-turkey bird-boner pill called again?"

"The houbara bustard," Danny said, as though he couldn't believe this was his life.

"Yes, whose big claim to fame is being falcon food, right?"

"Right," Danny agreed.

"So Napa has falcons. Lots and lots of falcons. Apparently it's, like, a tiny-house business—"

"Cottage industry," Josh supplied.

"Whatever. It's a tiny-house business to supply falcons to the wineries so the falcons can keep the crows away from the grapes. It's billed as very eco-friendly, because, you know, if a falcon catches a crow, it eats it, and the other crows get very afraid. So many of the wineries employ falconers to keep their stock from getting eaten, but some actually have falconers in-house. There are even a couple that have falcon tours, and it's all very *Wild Kingdom*, where the falconer comes out and lets the falcon land on someone's hand and people get excited because a bird that's one-hundred-percent predator isn't eating their eyeballs. So if the bald-turkey boner bird is the focus of all this, odds are good so are falcons, and the wineries in Napa are where you find people who want falcons, so there you go."

There was silence, followed by reluctant applause.

Grace spread his arms, stood on the back of the couch, and took a bow. "Thank you. I am not just decoration."

Then he did a backflip off the back of the couch and probably would have stumbled into the wet bar, but Hunter caught him.

"But you are an attention sponge," Hunter said, teasing. "Well done."

Grace gave him a dazzling smile and then apparently got lost in his eyes while Danny called the group to attention.

"So, wineries in Napa," Danny said, sounding surprised and impressed. "Good. Hopefully that, with our other information, can help narrow things down a—"

"I can help us find *which* winery," Chuck said, sounding surprised himself.

"Holy God." Danny indicated the rest of the room and sat back, folding his arms over his chest in a classic listening pose.

"I *couldn't* have until Grace went," Chuck said. "Danny, could you flash the slides I sent?"

"Sure, sure. AV geek is my calling," Danny muttered, putting up pictures of an oversized F-350 on the screen.

"It's a good one," Chuck said with a wink. "Unlike this vehicle, which is a waste of gas, a waste of space, and a waste of good metal."

"Monster trucks aren't your thing?" Lucius asked dryly.

"No. No, they're not," Chuck said. "Michael, tell them why we don't like monster trucks."

"For one thing, they suck for the environment," Michael said. "And you can smell the ozone they emit. In a closed venue, it can seriously affect your lungs. But worse than that, they're inefficient. They're supposed to be all about the torque and the power, but I can get more torque out of a basic F-150, because by the time you put the tires and all that chrome on them, it cancels out most of the power. All they're good for is crushing other cars and sort of bouncing along on top of them. It's entertaining, but it's also loud and wasteful, and I am not a fan."

"You do Texas proud, little buddy," Chuck said, nodding. "There were two sets of tire tracks in addition to Matteo's Jaguar. We figured one to herd him and one to stop him and force him into the cliff. The one that was supposed to stop him did not have standard tires—the treads were far too wide, and it seemed to skid an awful lot for a hot road, even if there was sand. I figured with the width of the wheelbase, it would be a specially modified chassis, and with the type of tire, one of these eyesores. Thanks to Lucius and his guy Linus, who helped me hack the satellite feed in the area since Stirling was busy, we narrowed it down to a couple of monster trucks. There are a number of events out in Napa, so there were more modified chassis and oversized wheelbases than you might think, *but* there are a couple of wineries that sponsor some of the events out there, and many of *them* have their own monster trucks."

"Do they have their own falconers?" Felix asked, sounding excited by the possibility.

"That would be your job," Chuck said, touching the point of his finger to his nose. "But I'm telling you, we've got that as a lead."

"Well done!" Danny said. "I'll start looking—"

"On it," Stirling told him without looking up.

"Of course, my boy, but you have other information to share with us, don't you?"

Stirling *did* look up at that. "Yes," he said, "I do. But I think Carl needs to tell us what happened, 'cause I'm telling you, he did some James Bond class shit to get this info."

All eyes focused on Carl. "You all heard that at the dinner table," he said modestly. "But I think there were a couple of things you missed in all the excitement over a change of clothes and a toolbox."

"Do tell," Danny said, cocking his head curiously.

So Carl went on to talk about how Ginger Carlson had turned into Satan incarnate when he'd mentioned the case—and the houbara bustard—during their conversation and had dropped enough information about Mandy Jessup to make Carl want more. He talked briefly about getting the file, laughing when Stirling asked, "So, would you like me to trace this leak back to that Foster guy so your firm can nail him to the wall for embezzlement?"

"Absolutely," Carl said. "I think that's poetic and perfect. But I need to give you all some background on Mandy Jessup, the investigator who disappeared in Mexico around the same time Matteo di Rossi was killed."

"What was she like?" Michael asked curiously.

Carl gave a sad shrug. "Sweet kid, actually. We flirted. She was originally in reception, then she worked her way into research, and then she took a very fine mind and went into investigations. She was… earnest," he said after some thought. "She really did want to do the right thing. I remember after I came back from Wales…." He and Danny met eyes, and Danny gave a crooked smile. "Anyway, I came back, and she was the only person at the firm who knew I'd taken the time off to clean up. She was really the only kind word I had here in the States. When I went back to Europe to get that car-smuggling ring, she provided all of my intel, both tries, and she was sort of a one-person cheerleading squad. I told her I'd be the one to help her for *her* next assignment, and she said it was a deal. Then she disappeared when I was undercover. By the time I got back, her trail was stone cold. I was furious, but it was done. She was lost."

Stirling made a soft noise, and Danny pulled up a picture of her from six years ago. She'd been in her twenties then, with a sweet heart-shaped face, round cheeks, and curly hair pulled back into a ponytail.

"That's her last ID picture," he said.

"But not her last picture period," Stirling told him. "This was in Ginger Carson's files from three years ago. I think, if you look at the mountains in the background, it was taken slightly north of San Diego."

"Three years?" Carl asked, obviously startled. "So she could still be alive?"

"It's very possible. Look at her."

The picture was blown up, so it was grainy and slightly pixilated, but the woman in it was very different. Her face was lean, and the bouncy curves that had made her a temptation six years ago had been replaced by a lean toughness that was very differently sexy. Her hair was hidden by a scarf, although she was wearing a khaki shirt and pants, and over her arm, she wore a worn leather gauntlet.

On top of the gauntlet sat one of the biggest falcons Carl had seen in his life.

"What in the fuck is that?" Chuck asked, which was fine because Carl was still fumbling for words.

"That," Carl said finally, squinting at his screen, "is a bird that should not technically exist."

"Is that a cross between an eagle and a falcon?" Julia asked, obviously fascinated.

"I think so," Carl said, taking in the wingspan and the size of the bird from beak to lethal talon. "With a little condor thrown in." Because the face was bald and red and long, like a condor's, while the beak was lethally sharp and curved like an eagle's or a hawk's.

"That shouldn't happen," Michael said, finally comfortable enough to speak about something besides cars. "That—see, most birds, when they crossbreed, they're only a species away. Like ducks mating with other ducks. They're different species, but they're species of ducks, right?"

"So falcons can breed with other falcons?" Josh said, as though making sure.

"Yup." Michael nodded. "It happens in the wild. Not all the time, but enough for people to go, 'Oh, this black-shouldered hawk got lonely and there was a red-tail nearby, and voila, we've got a real colorful baby hawk.' But eagles, hawks, and condors are a different—" He flailed for the word for a moment. He'd done the reading, but he had no degree in anything close to Latin.

"Genus?" Josh supplied.

"Yes! They're a different genus. And nobody wants them to mate because… look at that thing."

It was a monster. Even bigger than an African Martial eagle, which was not a small bird, it had the sleekness and the speed of a falcon and— judging by Mandy's grip on the jesses and another handler's grip on the hood—a whole lot of pent-up aggression. Its wings were only partially extended, but Carl got the impression its wingspan was wider than a lot of apartments.

"That thing could wipe out the bustard population all by itself," Carl said blankly. "Who in the hell would breed something like that?"

"According to this," Stirling said grimly, "Serpentus. Your insurance company would."

Carl turned toward him looking very much like a man lost in a dream. "They'd what?"

"Not them exactly. But your erstwhile friend, Ginger Carson. She gave the okay to try a crossbreeding program in Mexico in order to breed predators that could help protect Serpentus's assets, such as—"

"Wineries," Carl said flatly.

"Also poultry farms in the Midwest and a chinchilla farm in France."

"Oh dear God," Carl said, his eyes wide with horror. "This—this is monstrous. These animals could wipe out entire populations. There are *laws* against crossbreeding predatory species. One of these could wipe out ten coveys of sage grouse in a month. This is horrific! Mandy wouldn't want any part of this!"

"Well," Danny said, meeting eyes with Stirling and getting a go-ahead nod. "According to the information Stirling mined from those files you sent, she absolutely would not. In fact, the reason she disappeared into Mexico was because she'd gotten information that the crossbreeding was happening there. In fact, besides the last picture, which looks like it was mined from facial recognition software, that was the last entry on the hybrid birds."

"They've been released into the wild?" Felix asked, obviously as horrified as the rest of them.

"Yes," Stirling said, because Danny seemed to be skimming as fast as he could. "Apparently they first appeared in the wild in Qatar, and one of the first things they did was—"

"Attack the bustard population," Carl said grimly.

"Exactly," Stirling said, putting his finger on his nose. "So, if there were illegal breeding programs for predatory birds, maybe there were...."" He bit his lip, obviously trying to make the connection.

"Maybe there were some programs for birds that fed the predators," Hunter said, stepping out. "If you're trying to keep a population of falcons healthy and breeding while you're teaching them to hunt, maybe what you do is breed their favorite food."

"Three dozen viable eggs," Julia murmured. "Three dozen viable eggs, whether they were going to Africa to help replenish the population or going to Mexico to help keep these monstrous predators under control. Either way, that was an amazing windfall Matteo was transporting. That was a very worthy cause."

The last slide Danny had brought up was the awkward-looking bustard, and almost in a trance, everybody in the basement stared at it.

"And given how many laws were broken," Carl said, "and how much was at stake for Serpentus and for the people behind funding this potential environmental disaster, it was a cause worth killing for."

There was a heavy silence, and into it a new voice spoke, one that was a little familiar but not quite family yet.

"So what do we plan to do about it?"

Everyone turned to look at the base of the stairs as Chuck said, "Dammit, Hunter, how did you not see that guy?"

"I saw him," Hunter said. "But we're talking about his brother. I think he gets to be in the party room."

"He does indeed," Felix said, striding forward to shake Leon di Rossi's hand. "So glad you could make it, Leon. How are the children?"

"Exhausted," di Rossi said. He smiled at Molly and then directly at Michael. "I understand Mr. Carmody was busy today, and they missed him, but Miss Christopher apparently has the world's most tremendous job, and they enjoyed going backstage with her and her brother very much today."

Michael hadn't known that was happening, and for a moment he was jealous. Then he remembered what he'd actually been doing, and he had to concede it was okay to take a day off.

"The theater is starting a new production in a couple of weeks," Molly said. "Which makes this the exciting part. Everybody's practicing and building sets, and today was Stirling's setup day. It was fun."

"I confess, I needed the time to sleep," Leon said, nodding his head. "But it was lovely to take them out to dinner tonight and hear all about their last week here. I can't thank you enough, all of you, for making this week easier on us. I would have come anyway, but you've all made me feel like I came to visit friends."

Felix said something suave and gracious, which Michael didn't hear because he had a thought and turned to Stirling. "Do you ever sleep?"

His reward was a bright smile from a young man who didn't smile enough. "I do," he said. "I hang upside down like a bat with my computer connected to my brain."

Michael snickered at such an outrageous image, and Stirling smiled to himself. Michael could see why Carl liked the young man so much.

"Come sit," Felix was saying as he stood from his stool at the wet bar next to Julia. "Are the children upstairs?"

"Enjoying dessert with your housekeeper. And your cats. They appear to have what Esme calls 'the zoomies,' and everybody was highly entertained."

Michael had noticed the cats, both of them black, ghosting in and out as he'd been in the house. The idea of cats—or dogs for that matter—suddenly made him want to have a house here for his kids too. And a dog sure would fill the time when the kids were with their mother.

He was, after all, going to have to set the falcon behind the hangar free soon, wasn't he?

"Definitely come sit," Julia said. She indicated the seat nearest her and Felix.

"Thank you," di Rossi said graciously, sitting. He cast a surprisingly diffident smile at Julia, who returned it with a carefully polite smile of her own. The hair on the back of Michael's neck went up as he had a thought. "I'm sorry to interrupt," di Rossi was saying, "and to ask such an awkward question. It is just that in five years, the lot of you have gotten closer to learning what happened to Matteo than anyone I've hired or any of the authorities I asked to help. What can we do to find out who was responsible?"

"We've got a couple of places to start," Danny said. He looked up at di Rossi, and Michael saw his eyebrows raise infinitesimally as he took in the distance between the broad-shouldered man and Julia Dormer-Salinger. Michael was relieved to know he wasn't the only one who sensed something. "In fact, let me see what Stirling just sent me and...."

Danny's fingers flew to a background of quiet murmurings as he pulled together the information. Michael took the opportunity to lean close to Carl and say, "D'you see that?"

"See that di Rossi's crushing on Julia like a sweaty teenager?" Carl returned, practically in his ear. "Yes. Yes, I see that."

Michael hid a snicker behind his hand. "Don't know if he wants us to know."

"He picked the wrong crew to blush in front of," Hunter said, leaning down to talk to both of them. "Chuck called it the minute his foot hit the floor."

"Money on how long it takes Grace to see it," Carl said.

Hunter's low laugh told them both it was no bet. "Sometime after the first fight and before the wedding," he predicted, and then he moved back to his spot, making sure nobody *besides* Leon di Rossi came down to the basement den.

"So we've got it," Danny said, and three different pictures appeared side by side on the screen in front of him. Each picture featured the hotel and tasting rooms of three different wineries. The one on the left, which read The Aerie, looked intentionally rustic, with the tasting taking place in a converted barn and the hotel being bigger than necessary for an exclusive vacation spot, as well as looking commercial and out of place for the rugged surroundings of the vineyard and the nearby mountains that barred the view of the coast.

The one in the middle was also intentionally rustic—the tasting room was done with bare rock walls and a rough-hewn plank floor—but the attached bed-and-breakfast was a colonial style house that had obviously been built to be lovely and converted to host perhaps six different guests. A sign made from flowers at the entrance to the drive read Jesses and Jewels, and there were no fewer than three falcon-shaped weather vanes on the various location photos.

The one on the far right was nestled in the coastal mountains, with the grapes and planting lands extending out toward the plains of Napa, and it was, for lack of a better word, exquisite. Michael hadn't seen such a building in real life; built with polished stones, it looked like a chateau or a castle, and the pictures of the interior were of champagne-colored carpets and chandeliers. The sign on the drive read Pensive, and while Michael couldn't see a single reference to falcons there, he had to admit he'd still like to tour it.

"So," Danny explained, "we cross-referenced falconry and monster trucks and wineries, and you know, that's not a search I think anybody's done before, so go us."

"Those are our options?" Julia asked. "Oh my. I like the one on the right."

"You should, darling," Danny said. "It's one of the premiere vacation spots in California, known for its dazzling views, its superb dining, and its sophisticated wines. It's a short bit of driving to the Pacific Ocean, and you can rent equipment and even a vehicle and wet suits to take you surfing or sailing or sightseeing. A little more driving and you're in San Francisco, which is one of my favorite cities in the entire world, and I've seen a few. Pensive—the winery's name—is well worth the ticket."

"I should like to visit myself," di Rossi joked, and Michael wasn't the only one in the room who caught his breath when Danny muttered, "Done!" to himself and then looked up.

"Excellent. I've booked a room. The one in the middle, the Aerie, is known for its falcons. Almost exclusively. It has wine, but nobody in Europe is drinking it, and it has monster trucks, but they're not winning any races. What it does have is a breeding and training program of birds as pest control that the other wineries have either hired from or copied. This—" The photo of the wineries disappeared, and a picture of two tough, weathered people in their forties or fifties appeared, each one of them with a bird of prey sitting on the well-worn gauntlet on their arms. "—is a picture of the Bartletts. Abel and Maisy Bartlett have spent their lives training falcons, and they're one of the principal attractions of the Aerie. The birds give demonstrations almost daily, and people are invited to come to falcon camp, which runs once every month. The idea is that people bring their own animals to train, and there appears to be a camp running… hmm. Next week. Perfect. Rooms booked. Anyway, the Bartletts don't own or run the place, though. That honor goes to this family here, the Meyers. Yes, there's a dozen of them, but you can see the matriarch and patriarch, Deanne and Calvin. They run the joint. Whereas Pensive goes for quality and ambiance, the Aerie goes for family coziness, fun birds, and a monster-truck rally once a week on a stretch of land that can't even grow cacti."

"How do the birds like that?" Michael asked, thinking that much noise would make birds nervous.

"You know," Danny said, sounding surprised, "I doubt anybody has asked them. Anyway, that's the Aerie."

"Which leaves…. What's the other one?" Chuck asked.

"Jesses and Jewels," Danny told him. "Run by Jesse and Jewel Comstock, pictured here." The couple in the publicity shot was young, blond, and—in Jewel's case—busty. They were fringed and bedazzled in flashy western gear, and the shots of the winery were Western in flavor: dark oak furnishings with interior shots of rustic bars, a dance floor, even a mechanical bull. The hotel was built like a great two-story ranch house, something right out of *Dallas*, and the winery was in a great valley, with the coastal mountains only a hint on the horizon.

They had a falconry program that was "descended from the famed Bartletts," and while they offered horseback riding far more prominently, their Mr. and Mrs. Monster Trucks were featured at the Aerie as regular guests as they boasted of their proximity to the Aerie's rallies.

"Don't they seem cozy," Carl said, and Michael's head was reeling with the number of possible suspects. Something was bothering him… something important. Then Carl said, "Danny, can we see that mass photo of the whatsit? All those freckled faces with the red or blond hair."

"The Meyers?" The picture came back up, and Carl searched the picture, apparently looking for somebody—somebody he knew.

"What do you see?" Felix asked, and Carl shook his head and grimaced.

"I'm sorry, Felix. I don't know anybody here, but I feel like I should." He met Michael's eyes apologetically. "I feel like I know somebody in their family. I can't put my finger on it."

"Mm...." Danny tapped his upper lip with his finger. "Are you out at work? I know it's a personal question, but it's relevant."

"Yes, why?" That Carl's eyebrows didn't even go up told Michael he wasn't offended in the least.

"Because if I put you there, I need to know what to do about your cover. If you *do* end up knowing somebody there, it's best I send you under your own name. If you're out, you and Mr. Carmody will do fine. If you're not, it's either Molly, Julia, or I imagine we could persuade the lovely Miss Talia, since Wimbledon is quite over."

"Me!" Michael said without even knowing he was going to say it. He knew the tennis star they were talking about, and he was not going to see her cozying up to Carl like he was catnip. "He's not going on a romantic getaway with anybody but me!"

Then he clapped his hand over his mouth and reminded himself he didn't really get a say here.

Except he apparently did.

"Done," Danny said mildly. "Don't you have a falcon you can train? If we can get you into this camp on an organic level, it will give you a good chance to poke around under the guise of curiosity."

"I was going to let it go once its wing healed," Michael said, now thoroughly confused again. "But I guess they don't have to know that."

"How do you let a falcon go?" Hunter asked, sounding legitimately curious.

"You feed it on a series of feeding platforms," Michael told him. "Each one higher and harder to get to than the last. You figure that by the time he can get the food off the highest platform, he can hunt again, but you keep putting food up there anyway. You just stretch out the intervals. If he gets hungry and wants to hunt, he'll hunt. If he doesn't, you haven't left him out there to starve, 'cause that's cruel. Eventually he'll either eat or get sickly, and if he gets sickly, you start the process over again." He sighed. "Some of them do like being fed all the time, but most of them take the hint and go get their own prey."

"You're a natural," Danny said, sounding proud of himself. "You and Carl get one room in the Aerie. Hunter and Grace get the other. Chuck and Lucius get Jesses and Jewels, and Julia, you and Leon get Pensive, if that's all right with you, Mr. di Rossi?"

"It is, of course," Leon said, but he glanced around the room, surprised. "Not that I object, but there is nobody else who can take this room?"

Danny and Felix made eye contact. "I've got Molly a job working for the monster-truck rally company—only a couple of hours a day except for the rally day itself. Molly, love, I hope you don't mind going in a week early? We've got your lodgings, but they're fairly cheap. And you can room with your brother, who's going to do groundwork once he's there. Is that all right?"

"Except for rooming with my brother," she said, giving Stirling the stink-eye. "But that's fine." She paused then and asked the question they were all asking. "Aren't you—you and Felix—coming along?"

"No," Danny said, looking at Josh. "During our last little adventure, Josh promised he'd stay home until he was better, and we're holding him to that. Felix and I will stay here with him."

"Wait a minute!" Grace said, and for all he had an IQ exponentially bigger than anybody else in the room, Michael felt for him as it occurred that he was going off without his other half. "You said Hunter and I are investigating one of the wineries!"

"You are indeed," Danny said gently.

"No," Grace said, sounding lost and adamant. He and Josh were sitting together on the couch, and for the first time, they all realized Josh had fallen asleep, his head against Grace's shoulder. "Look at him." Grace's voice was breaking. "He needs me."

"He does," Danny said, his voice so gentle Michael thought his own heart would break. "He needs you so badly. But he needs you whole. His doctors told him he's going to be turning the corner this month, but a lot of that turning is going to be sleep. He's bored, Dylan Li. And restless. And cranky. He asked me earlier if he could send you and Hunter off together so you could have time to heal too."

"But who's going to be his Grace?" Grace's voice was cracked and sad, but Michael still wasn't expecting Julia to lean over the couch and wrap her arms around his shoulders.

"I suspect," she said, her voice thick, "that I'm being sent away for the same reason. Is that right, Danny?"

"It is indeed," Felix answered for him. He'd moved too, so he was next to her, his arm around her shoulders. "You've had the hardest parts of it, darling. Danny and I thought we'd stay home and do our bit, and you could go drink wine and remember you're a very young woman with a lot of money. Is that okay?"

"No," she replied, but she was weeping softly as she said it and allowing Felix to hold her close. "It's not. But I find I can't fight you."

He dropped a kiss in her hair. "Which means you're very much in need." He cleared his throat and pitched his voice for everybody in the room. "Any other questions on room assignments? Lucius, Chuck, you're at Jesses and Jewels alone because they don't have that many rooms. I realize we're pulling you away from legitimate work—"

"It's nothing," Lucius Broadstone said, his voice absolutely casual and yet unyielding. "I have no problems at all taking a vacation next week. You, Charles?"

"As long as you're with me, Scotty Brice," Chuck said gamely, and Michael wondered about nicknames again, because it seemed everybody had one.

"So it's settled." Danny let out a long breath, and Michael realized how intense the meeting had gotten. Abstractly, it occurred to him that this was what he'd signed on for—this was one of the reasons everybody had wanted to make sure he wanted to be there.

He wanted more than anything to be there.

"I think we're done for the night," Felix said, taking over the suddenly personal, painful meeting of the minds the way he probably took over boardrooms. "Dearest, allow me to take Josh up to his room. Hunter, could you...?"

Felix strode around the couch and lifted his son into his arms with the same strength and ease he'd probably used when Josh was a child. Hunter bent to put his hand on Grace's shoulder, and Grace leaped into his arms, wrapping his legs around Hunter's waist and crying softly into his neck in a way Michael suspected the young man would do with nobody else.

Together the two men made their way up the stairs, and Danny folded his laptop quickly and moved to take Julia into his arms. She held him, her own tears silent, and the rest of the party ghosted away.

# Jet Plane Dreams

CHUCK'S NONE-TOO-SUBTLE shoulder bump on the way up the stairs told Carl that there was gossiping to be done. By unspoken accord, they both made their way toward the tiny sitting room off the foyer. It wasn't the entertaining living room, but it held six people and a television comfortably in the same way Carl's apartment in DC was comfortable. Two parts cozy, one part cramped, but very conducive to intimate conversation.

Carl wasn't surprised to find Michael at his heels, but he was pleased to see Stirling and Molly joining them as they sat. Molly had brought Phyllis with her, as well as a tray of sodas and soda waters.

"What happened?" Phyllis asked bluntly, sitting on the arm of the couch next to Carl.

"Danny and Felix are sending us all to Napa and told everybody they're staying here with Josh to give people a break from worrying themselves sick," Stirling summarized neatly. "There were feelings."

Phyllis pushed her hand to her mouth and took a quick breath before getting herself under control. "I imagine," she said. "Julia agreed to it?"

"Apparently so," Lucius said dryly. "And she didn't object one bit to being put in close proximity with Josh's Uncle Leon. Did you notice that? I noticed that."

"So did I," said Leon, coming into the foyer and scaring them all to death. "No, no, don't get up," he said, when it was apparent they all might. "Please. I'll leave if you'd rather, but...." He gave a very European, very casual shrug that told Carl everything he wanted to know about being in a strange country and the odd man out in a well-established family.

"Sit," Phyllis said, standing.

"No, no." Molly left her spot on the big stuffed chair to sit on the floor and wriggle her way in between Stirling's knees. He let her, balancing his laptop on her head playfully, and Carl was struck again with how much the two of them seemed to need each other, even as adults. "Phyllis, you stay," she added, "but Leon, join the secret club. We'll give you the handshake and password later."

"Understood," Leon said, his mouth quirking up as he took her spot. "Is there a whistle? I've never learned to whistle."

"Someone will teach you," she said complacently before putting her finger on her nose and saying, "Not it."

Everybody else in the room followed suit except Lucius, who stared at them all blankly until he realized he was the only one left besides Leon.

His eyes narrowed. "You all suck, and I don't know how to whistle."

And that broke them all up a little. There was some chuckling before Chuck said, "Okay, so we all know our assignments. Whatever we talk about here, me or Carl will pass on to Hunter, so no worries. We're obviously going to investigate the connection between one of the three wineries and Matteo—" He nodded at Leon. "—or Mandy and Serpentus." He nodded to Carl. "Is there any information we missed in our mass exodus to avoid all the feelings?"

"Two wineries," Stirling said.

"The Aerie, Jesses and Jewels, and—" Chuck repeated, blinking when Stirling cut him off.

"Pensive doesn't have a thing to do with any of it," he said, looking at Leon apologetically. "I was looking up wineries and cross-referencing, remember? I think that was a lie. No, a *ruse* to keep Leon safe and give Julia a chance to... you know. Recharge. Rest. Leon, so you know, I think that makes it your job to keep her occupied and make sure she rides horses and drinks champagne and shit."

"Do you people have a thing against alcohol here?" Leon asked, frowning. "I noticed I seem to be the only one getting wine at dinner."

"Danny and I are recovering alcoholics," Carl said, feeling safe to talk about Danny because Danny himself wasn't shy about voicing it. "That's mostly in deference to us, and Julia is the biggest advocate for orange juice and sparkling water. But I'd say if anyone deserves a real fucking mimosa right now, it's Julia Dormer-Salinger."

Leon nodded. "Oh," he said softly. "You people once again humble me. If I'm to play her escorting knight, it's the least I can do, given what all of you signed on to do for... for what? For me? For Josh?"

"For Africa," Chuck said. "And the houbara bustard."

Carl grinned a little. "For the environment and endangered species everywhere."

"For Carl's ex-girlfriend," Michael said, surprising Carl very much. "Even if they never did the thing."

"We flirted," Carl reiterated.

"Whatever. Doesn't bother me none."

Carl and Chuck both snickered a little, because from the tone of Michael's voice, it was clear it bothered him at least a little.

"Fine," Carl said, and he found his voice dropping. "For a sweet girl I flirted with who thought my job was exciting."

There was a collective sigh then because it was clear that, whatever had happened to Mandy Jessup after she disappeared, the woman in that picture had very little sweetness left.

"For Matteo," Molly said, firmly snuggled against Stirling's shin. "Because nobody fucks with our little brothers but us. Right, Stirling?"

"I count on it," Stirling said serenely.

"And for Josh," Lucius said softly. "Because I lost one little brother to cancer, and I'm so glad it looks like I might not have to lose another."

Leon did the manly thing then and wiped his eyes with one palm, first one eye, then the other. "You all humble me."

"Take care of Julia," Carl said, although this was probably something Leon knew. "Make sure she has some happy moments. I don't think I have to tell you what a valuable job you're doing here, even if you're not really investigating the case."

"I'm guarding one of your greatest treasures," Leon said, inclining his head soberly. "I just wish I knew what to do with my children."

"They can stay here," Phyllis said. "In fact, Grace's young friend Tabitha, from the conservatory, called the other day, asking if she could do anything to help Josh out. I think having her come stay would be just the thing. She's delightful."

"Oh!" Molly said brightly. "Talia Clark can come help as well!"

"The tennis player?" Leon asked in surprise.

"I'm sure she'd love to help," Molly said. "She's like Tabby, wanting to do something for the family but not knowing where to start. This is perfect."

"You're not gonna invite Torrance Grayson to babysit, are you?" Chuck drawled. Torrance, a YouTube reporter with a following in the hundreds of thousands, had been in on some of their more outrageous adventures.

"No," Carl said, "but that doesn't mean we shouldn't fly him to Napa."

There was a collective intake of breath. "Ooh…," Stirling said. "Danny and Felix *are* off their game if they didn't think they'd need someone to make parts of this public."

"That's what they trust us for," Chuck said, nodding. "Stirling, wherever you and Molly are staying, make another reservation for Torrance. I'll call him tonight and set things up." He paused and grimaced. "And not to sound too bougie for words, but do we really have to take three goddamned jets to Napa? 'Cause seriously—one is necessary, but three is overkill."

Leon gave a feline grin. "It's only overkill if the lovely Ms. Dormer-Salinger and I have to share mine."

"We could all fit in one," Lucius said thoughtfully, "but I don't think that would be a good idea. People talk. Three jets, three different independent airfields, three different cars set to bring us where we need to go."

"Mm… maybe not. Book Hunter and Grace a room at the cheap hotel too," Chuck said. "Just for a couple of days before their expensive hotel reservations kick in. Hunter can fly the four of you down and do some more poking around. I just might go with him. I have the feeling that if we find this nest of snakes, it's gonna be rattlers."

"Fly me down with you," Carl said. "Michael, you should meet us in Napa. That should give you time to figure out the best way to crate the bird. I may need to drive to Mexico for a bit, or maybe somewhere else in the state. I'd like to see if Ginger's files have any more information on where we can find Mandy. I have the feeling she's the key to all of this."

"But I want to come with you," Michael said indignantly. "You're leaving me behind?"

Carl grimaced unhappily. "Baby, if Mandy is running around Mexico with big old velociraptor birds, there are probably some really dangerous people down there. I want you out of harm's way."

"Calling me baby is not going to make me forget that you're trying to ditch me," Michael retorted, eyebrows knitted together.

"Some of us need to stay here and keep things running," Carl reasoned. "You're sort of necessary to the whole household—hell, you're necessary to the rest of us flying off into the wild blue yonder. And you've got a family, kids. Wouldn't you rather…?"

"Mm, I think Saoirse can take over for Michael here," Lucius said smoothly, referring to his own mechanic. "Particularly if I'm joining Chuck in Napa."

Carl glared at him. "Mexico," he said, hoping everybody in the room would understand the depths of his worry.

"Texas Delta Prison," Michael responded, like that was the same thing. "And I speak Mexican Spanish, which is real different than Spain Spanish. You know that, right?"

Carl blew out a breath. He did speak Castilian Spanish, and he knew Michael was absolutely correct about that. "Look, we're already taking Danny's plan and tweaking it—"

"We're tweaking it because Danny, Felix, and Julia are exhausted and sad and doing too much," Chuck said flatly. "Michael, we'll leave in three days. That should give you time to catch up with work and crate the bird. Lucius will have Saoirse fly in after you leave. I'll give her permission to insulate your little hangar apartment. It might even be better when you get back. Carl, you were right earlier, but not now. He's a big boy with big boy underpants, and he gets to come with the big boy expedition. Is there anything else?"

"Wow, Chuck," Molly said with big eyes. "You sounded like Felix just then. Didn't he sound like Felix, everybody?"

There were general nods of the head, and Lucius gave a sweet grin. "Sexy, right?" he asked.

"Oh, definitely," Molly replied, her face completely straight.

"You people keep trying to get me to agree when you say things like that," Stirling said, "and I'm still twenty years old."

"Carl?" Chuck said, and Carl felt misgivings deep in his bowels, but Michael was still looking at him like he could spin moonshine into gold.

"Fine. You tell Hunter, I'll tell Torrance Grayson. Stirling, text us the exact dates of the reservations and we'll all go." He looked at Phyllis apologetically. "You're going to have an empty mansion for a bit, sweetheart."

Phyllis shook her head and wiped her eyes on her shoulder. "As long as you all come back to fill it," she said thickly before looking at Leon. "You and your children are welcome to stay as long as you need to. We can coordinate in the next few days."

Leon nodded. "I am… honored," he said after a moment. "For lack of a better word. I am honored to be part of your conspiracy."

"Well, it's clear Josh got his bentness from both sides of the family," Chuck said, raising his glass of sparkling water. "That's a compliment, son."

Leon raised his own glass of sparkling water. "Again, an honor."

They spent the next hour hammering out their plans, talking about approaches to use and giving each other shit. Carl was aware the entire time that Michael was sitting close enough for their thighs to touch, with his hand in the small of Carl's back.

Carl's sense of responsibility for the man was almost overwhelming.


THREE DAYS later, Carl closed his laptop, leaned back, and closed his eyes wearily. Thanks to some information Stirling had gleaned from the stolen files that pinpointed Mandy Jessup's base of operations in coastal California—not far from the wineries in fact—instead of Mexico they were on their way to Napa, but he wasn't any less worried now than he had been three nights before while staying up late and making plans.

As if hearing his thoughts, Michael, who was sitting next to him in Lucius Broadstone's jet, yawned, snuggling his head a little tighter on Carl's chest as they made use of the bench-style seat near the window.

They'd had three late nights, making love, talking, planning, cementing their lives together more tightly than Carl had ever dreamed possible, and Carl had come to an inevitable conclusion.

It hadn't been responsibility he'd felt that night in Glencoe. It had been love.

He hadn't known it then. He'd known he cared for the young man, known how lucky he was to have caught Michael's attention, but he'd always been emotionally dense, and falling in love with Michael Carmody hadn't fixed that.

That sense of well-being a person got when he woke up in the morning and saw his lover in bed next to him? That was love.

The hopes for the future, the subtle moments of planning, of thinking, "When we have a house, we'll have to make sure it has two bathrooms," or, "Wouldn't a dog be nice?" That was love.

The unbearable moments of empathy, when a person realized how much his lover had suffered, and he wished, heartily wished, that it had been him instead? God, that was love too.

The moments of panic, the waking up with a pounding heart and terrible fears of an uncertain tomorrow? That was love as well.

Love wasn't always happy. Sometimes it was terrifying or painful.

But the last four days had taught Carl that once it had happened, *really* happened, once the fall to Neverland had occurred, there was no flying out of that well. He was stuck, and his heart would only survive if Michael reached down to get him, day after day after day.

He had to absolutely make sure Michael was there to do that.

"Stop worrying," Michael mumbled against his chest. "You keep telling me there's no danger."

"It doesn't seem that bad when it's just me." Carl nuzzled his temple. Suddenly he didn't care that Lucius and Chuck were sitting on the opposite side of the cabin, or that Grace was stretched out along a bench near the tail, napping. It didn't matter who saw them. It didn't matter that all their friends knew. This way people would know that Michael Carmody was important to him—important to a number of people, actually.

Someone like Michael was far too important to be allowed to rot in jail or to get hurt doing something foolhardy. It couldn't be allowed.

"Well, it *is* bad when it's just you," Michael mumbled. "You're making my head hurt. Catch some z's."

Carl looked around and saw that was the consensus. He thought sadly of Grace, who, Hunter confided, fell asleep almost as soon as he left Josh's side these days, as though exhausted by sadness. Sending him away for a while had been a kindness—anybody could see that—but Grace's parting words to Josh had been, "Don't plan on napping in hell if you get there first, asshole."

"Feel free to get all the sleep you want if you beat me!" Josh had replied. "I'll be here in Glencoe when you get back."

And then Grace had given Josh a brief kiss on the forehead before he'd turned and left for the car, leaving Hunter to get his luggage.

By the time the rest of them had wrestled their bags out too, the young man had fallen asleep.

Carl had been the one responsible for posing the change in plans to Danny and Felix, in a quiet meeting the morning after the big dinner at the house. He'd gone alone, begging a ride from Chuck, and had plotted with Molly to have Julia take her and Esme shopping again while Leon and Bernardo watched a soccer match nearby.

He'd intruded on Danny and Felix's private brunch and felt bad. After their ten-year separation, they deserved more time to themselves, but like any vehicle Chuck drove, life had a way of taking off whether you were holding on to the chicken stick or not.

"Sit down!" Felix said pleasantly, looking natty, if exhausted, in an ivory turtleneck and casual slacks. "Can Phyllis get you anything?"

"Waffles on the way!" Phyllis called from the kitchen, and Carl practically groaned.

"I'm getting fat," he said helplessly.

"If only," Felix said, but he had a twinkle in his red-rimmed eye that said he knew Carl wasn't a threat to him and Danny and probably never had been.

"What can we do for you?" Danny asked from behind a yawn. He was wearing his thief's clothes—black yoga pants and a black turtleneck, which both looked rumpled.

Almost as if he'd slept in them after a long night and had barely made it down for breakfast.

That, ultimately, was what gave Carl the courage to speak.

He sat down, laced his fingers together, and said, "Gentlemen, I'm here to let you know that we've taken the wheel."

Felix frowned, and Danny's eyebrows shot up.

"I beg your pardon?" Felix said, and in spite of the shadows under their eyes and the general feeling of exhaustion, Carl knew he had their complete attention.

"You're tired," Carl said, making his voice as kind as he could. "And you've given us a great adventure to have. But you missed a couple steps last night. Don't worry about it—we've fixed the plan a little. We've got some ideas. We'll keep you involved. Stirling is emailing all our travel plans and itineraries, and the invoices if you want them, but I'm telling you right now, you may have to fight Leon and Lucius for them." They'd already been engaged in a subtle campaign to get Stirling to send them the charges, but privately Carl thought Stirling and Molly—who had their own fortunes for all they loved living at the mansion with the Salingers—were going to beat the two billionaires to the check. "But the fact is, you pointed us all in the right direction and said 'go.' You two and Josh—you've got better things to do right now, even if it's merely sleep."

Danny scowled at him. "Rude," he said, one icy syllable somehow morphing into two.

"Is he saying we're old? Old is what tired really means, Danny. You know that, right?" Felix sounded distressed in the extreme.

"I'm saying," Carl clarified with patience, "that the three of you have hired no nurses. You've hired no special transport. All those things that rich people can afford when their families are sick, you've all pretty much kicked them to the curb because he's *your* kid, and nobody takes care of *your* kid but you. And we get that. And we are completely on board with it. We'll help until he's jumping off buildings again, although, you know, we all really wish he wouldn't do that."

"God," Danny muttered. "We really do."

"But besides hiring a nurse, which I think you should do, and maybe a temporary chauffeur, since Chuck, Hunter, and Michael are all going to be gone, I think you all should take this opportunity to sleep, catch up on work, give yourselves a break. Did you think you were sly when you sent Julia and Leon to a winery with absolutely no connection to falcons or monster trucks or this case at all? The only reason Julia didn't see it is because she's as off her game as you are, which is good because it's a good move, and Leon's on board."

"This is embarrassing," Danny muttered, cupping his elbow in one hand and chewing on his thumbnail.

"I seriously have no words," Felix agreed, lacing his fingers behind his neck.

"So your house is about to empty out, and we'll be on the plane in three days, not a week. We'll stay at the Residence Inn where Molly and Stirling will be, and when you get a chance, you can laugh to yourselves at the fact that neither of them made a move to book another room. Bitch about each other in proximity, yes. Actually separate to give the world the impression they're not conjoined twins? Hell no."

"Much like Julia," Danny said, his mouth twitching a little. "I never want her to leave."

"She probably doesn't want to go, if that helps," Carl said, smiling a little. He hadn't understood that nine years ago, but he did now. "And like I said, we'll keep you in the loop. But we need your involvement to be like checking your social media feed. You do it every now and then to comfort yourself if you have to, but you can't obsess over it. We will ask for help if we need it, but until then, assume we'll be fine."

Danny kept worrying his thumbnail until Felix captured his hand and pulled it to his own lips.

"They're children," Danny said thickly to Felix. "I don't know what makes them think they can have adventures without us."

"Because," Felix murmured, "if we're supposed to be the adults, we need to know when we're off our game and sit this one out."

Danny nodded and palmed under his eyes just as Phyllis brought Carl's chocolate-chip/banana/strawberry waffles out.

"Oh my God," he said, looking at the stack of all the good things at once. "Are you trying to kill me?"

"You told them?" she said, ignoring him and pouring a glass of orange juice.

"Yeah."

"Good. You finish that and I'll drive you back into the city. I've got a friend who works in-home nursing. She said she could work here for a month or so, keep an eye on Josh, read some newspapers in between. Let these two catch up on their day jobs. I was going to pick her up."

Carl felt a sort of transcendent lightness suffuse his being. "You mean I don't have to ride back with Chuck?" he asked, since Chuck had been dropping Lucius off at the airstrip before returning to their city apartment.

"No, my boy. You're going to have to settle for getting there today instead of last week."

"Thank God," Carl said fervently. "Seriously, Lucius looks like a very conservative guy until you realize he lets Chuck drive him around and he never once screams, 'We're all gonna die!'"

Danny and Felix laughed a little, sputtering teardrops across the table.

"Eat," Danny told him, his voice completely out of his control now. "I need to go—"

"Stay right here," Felix rumbled, wrapping an arm around Danny's unresisting shoulders and pulling him close while, like Julia the night before, he cried quietly.

Carl took his plate and his fork and stood up. "I'll just go to the kitchen," he said, beating a hasty retreat. Phyllis followed him with the orange juice.

The time after that had been busy, frantically busy, and he'd worked hard with Stirling, Chuck, Hunter, and Lucius to make sure they would be making the best use of their time.

But that hadn't kept him and Michael from stealing their own moments together.

Carl had forgotten what it was like to wake up every morning with a companion in his bed, somebody he could laugh and be tender with. And he remembered that moment between Danny and Felix eating breakfast in the dining room, and thought, *It was like a moment captured in time, like art. I'm working toward that. I might have it already in my arms. How did my life—my life—become art?*

And of course, the answer was simple. Obvious. And happily snuggled against his chest.

LUCIUS AND Chuck had an extra week booked at Jesses and Jewels, which was outside the small, elegant town of Napa and lovely, because Lucius was just that guy. The rest of them took a rental SUV to the Residence Inn on the other side of town so they could have a hub of activity and information, which comforted them all.

Their first order of business was to unload their luggage and change clothes. Hunter and Grace were going to scope out the falconry program at Jesses and Jewels, so they were driving Lucius and Chuck there and acting as staff. Meanwhile, Carl and Michael checked out a place that had continually popped up on Stirling's searches in an odd way, both in Ginger Carson's files and on the internet. It was nonprofit and dedicated to the environment without a single nongeneric photo to be found. And while it had existed for over ten years, it had only really picked up in donations over the last five.

Mandolin Bird Conservancy lay almost dead east from Napa in the Napa Valley—but nothing about getting there was a straight line. After winding about the picturesque wineries under a brilliant blue September sky, they found themselves in the mountains, where their GPS gave them a surprise coordinate. It was, in essence, a badly marked left turn onto a road that might let two SUV's pass each other if one of them was off-roading and the other one could suck in its gut.

The country was still ruggedly pretty, but the groomed wineries had given way to scrub brush and decomposed granite, and the blacktop they were depending on sported cracks and potholes that revealed it hadn't been laid on firm soil. It wasn't until they'd gone a good ten miles, the slope of the hill the road was carved into getting closer and closer to the blacktop of the road itself, that Carl realized the entire road was a trap from a horror movie.

After ten miles, they couldn't back up, they couldn't turn around, and the only way to go was forward—maybe.

"How far do you reckon it is to the bottom?" Michael asked, his voice barely shaking the third time the back wheels of their rental Jeep Cherokee lost traction on the sketchy pavement and fought for purchase on the disintegrating soil on the side of the hill. They'd been on the road for about forty-five minutes, and he'd spent the entire time looking straight down from the passenger window and trying not to hyperventilate.

"That depends," Carl muttered, hugging the cliffside as tightly as possible without scraping the side of the vehicle.

"On what?"

"On whether we drive, tumble, fly, or parachute," Carl ground out. He looked ahead of them, and his heart stuttered as he realized the road had been washed out for about two car lengths. If the SUV didn't make it across what looked to be a dried mudslide, they would know for certain how far it was to the bottom. "Hang on," he ordered, then girded his figurative loins and stood on the accelerator.

His heart actually stopped stuttering and stood still as the wheels spun in the dried mud for a moment before he downshifted and punched the gas again. The Cherokee lurched forward, jouncing like an aging roller coaster, and kept jouncing until the front wheels found the pavement. Behind them, the rear wheels spun on empty air before the weight of the front—and the engine in the front—pulled them forward enough for the back wheels to catch. Carl kept going until the vehicle was safely on the pavement, his heart hammering in his ears. He didn't dare take his eyes off the narrow, winding road, but next to him, Michael caught his breath.

"Carl?" he said, his voice thin and reedy.

"Yes?"

"Don't look back and don't stop, okay?"

"Yeah, sure," Carl told him, keeping their pace steady. Behind him he heard the thunder of another rockslide, this one probably taking out the rest of the road as they knew it. Carl kept his eyes front, his heart giving some tentative hammers in his throat when he realized they were actually heading down into a secluded valley.

As soon as the road leveled, the blacktop gave out, and they were four-wheeling it again. Carl gave a wince as what sounded like a particularly nasty granite boulder hit the oil pan.

"Still got no cell service?" he asked, because Michael had been monitoring it steadily as they drove in.

"Nope."

"Good thing we've got water and food," Carl muttered, although both those things were a lucky coincidence. They'd bought flats of water on general principles before they'd checked into the hotel, and protein bars and jerky because hotels and restaurants were unreliable things at best. If they had to rely on water and protein bars, it was because they hadn't bothered to unload what was in the car to the hotel.

"Does it get cold here at night?" Michael asked.

"Not so much," Carl said. "Not as cold as Chicago, at any rate. It'll be a long, shitty walk back, but we'll make it."

And just as they decided that, the road became paved again, level, and well maintained.

"Wow," Michael muttered. He half sat up in his seat and turned around.

"What're you looking for?"

"An oil trail. So far, so good—we're not leaving one." He turned back around and patted the Cherokee's dashboard. "Good car. Go-oo-ood car!"

They both blew out a sigh of relief and then rounded a corner and came to an opening into a small valley with a large ranch-style house to the left and what looked like several aviaries and mews to the right.

At least three of the mews held giant predatory birds. They had mottled plumage—brown to gray to black and irregular from bird to bird. Instead of the clean, sharp faces of falcons, they had the craggy, bald faces of condors or vultures, made grotesque by the bloodred skin. The tallest stood nearly four feet from toes to nose, which was scary enough, but they sat in mews that were larger than most prison cells. One of them ruffled his feathers and stretched out his wings, and Carl caught his breath. Ten feet? Twelve feet? Fourteen maybe? That was a twelve-foot wingspan or Carl had never seen a California condor. Those birds shouldn't exist. The fact that they did was terrifying.

"Think this is the right place?" he asked, and at that moment, three people emerged, two from behind the bird outbuildings and one from the front porch of the house.

All three held shotguns up, aimed and ready.

"Yup," Michael said. "I'm betting so."

Together, they raised their hands over their heads.

# Allies and Aviaries

"OPEN THE door," shouted the woman coming from the house. She was dressed simply in khaki cargo shorts and a frayed denim shirt, but the tone in her voice said, "No bullshit."

"Sure," Carl replied. "Moving my hands now to open the door and unbuckle the belt. Please don't shoot. We are not with anybody who can hurt you."

The door was flung open, and while Michael stayed inside the Cherokee—which was making cool-down noises they could hear now that the door was open—Carl was hauled unceremoniously from the driver's seat and whirled against the side of the vehicle and frisked. The woman took his cell phone and his wallet and nodded to her companion, a young woman on Michael's side of the Cherokee.

"Be gentle with him," Carl said, not combatively but with authority. "He's done nothing wrong here. Please, no bruises."

Michael tried not to recoil when his door was pulled open, but the woman lowered her gun and gestured for Michael to unbuckle his seat belt. Michael was given room to slide out of the vehicle and turn to put his hands on the window while firm, impersonal hands groped him through his jeans for weapons.

From the driver's side of the car, he heard the woman say, "Carl? Carl Cox?"

Michael looked up to see the woman holding the wallet out, Carl's ID front and center, while she lowered her gun. Now that he could see her face, Michael could see a leaner, sharper version of the girl with the apple cheeks and bouncy curls from the Serpentus ID.

"Hello, Mandy," Carl said apologetically. "I, uh, hate to bother you, but we've got some questions."

Mandy Jessup looked at him unhappily with eyes like obsidian. "Questions for Serpentus?"

"No." Carl shook his head. "They're not who I'm working for on this. Not that they know that, but that's not my company phone, and my company laptop is in Chicago, and my personal laptop was last opened somewhere over Colorado, during a noncommercial flight. We've got friends who know where to look for us, yes—but they're not Serpentus friends."

The woman who scowled at Carl did not look impressed. "How do I know that's true?"

And then Carl took a gamble, and a leap of faith Michael might not have.

"Matteo di Rossi," he said softly. "Does his name mean anything to you?"

She swallowed rapidly, and her hard, dark eyes grew softer, shiny, and red-rimmed. "Yes," she whispered. "Yeah. Matteo. He was—"

"A friend," Carl murmured. "And a good guy. I know. I know his brother. Can we come in and talk?"

She nodded then and gestured with her chin to her two companions. "He armed?"

"No," said the young woman—tall, thin, gangly, with pale brown skin, straight brown hair, and round brown eyes. "His license is different. He's sweating."

Michael was still wearing the jeans and the hooded sweater he hadn't taken off since they'd landed. It had been about fifteen degrees cooler then, he thought now, sweat trickling uncomfortably down his back. The young man behind the young woman looked just like her, but without the hair pulled back into a ponytail. Other than that, they were probably twins.

"Ex-convict," Michael said weakly. "It's on our license."

Mandy stared at him in confusion. "Carl, who's this?"

Carl gave a serene smile. "Michael. My boyfriend. He's here investigating with me."

Michael nodded. "I fix cars," he said.

Mandy didn't look any less confused, but she did lead them through the long swath of field from the bird enclosures to the house. As Michael looked around the dwelling, he saw what looked to be pastureland stretching into the distance, kept marginally green by industrial sprinklers. He also saw tiny specks of some sort of livestock on the face of a neighboring hill. Sheep? Goats? Something. The grasses under their feet had been cropped short in irregular clumps, which usually meant grazing.

Eventually they crossed a rickety porch into the house. Mandy flung open the door, and the blast of cold air hit Michael before he heard the hum of the air conditioner, which stayed brisk and lovely as Mandy led the way through a short hallway. He saw a door opening to an old-fashioned living room on the right, but the hallway itself opened into a midsized kitchen, complete with flowered wallpaper and peach-colored appliances, with a table in the middle.

And still that lovely cool air.

"Thank *you*," Michael murmured. He'd been starting to think that central California had more in common with Texas in September than he'd ever imagined.

"You're welcome," the young woman said without irony. Now that she'd spoken, Michael detected an odd note in her speech. Some sort of speech difficulty? A developmental one? He smiled at her, trying to catch her eyes.

She wouldn't meet his and instead leaned up against the corner of the back wall and the counter, then slid into a sitting position and wrapped her arms around her knees.

"Sunny doesn't take kindly to strangers," Mandy said. "Harry, would you like to get us some iced tea?" She looked at Harry, who stood awkwardly in the hallway still, and he nodded and set his shotgun in the corner, next to Sunny's. Without saying a word, he started to move about the kitchen, getting glasses, ice, and a pitcher. Mandy turned toward Carl and Michael. "Would you like to sit down?"

"Yes, thank you." Carl looked at him and nodded, and Michael hadn't realized how much his knees felt like water until he sank onto the cushioned chair.

The young man came to the table and handed Mandy one of the two glasses of iced tea he'd carried over from the counter, and Carl the other one before going to get one for Michael and himself.

"Thank you, Harry."

He nodded as he handed Michael the other glass, then sat with his own. Sunny sighed and went to get her own glass, and Harry stared at Carl and Michael expectantly, as though he'd never seen other people before.

Maybe he hadn't.

"Their mother drank a lot when she was pregnant," Mandy said, her expression a mix of love and sadness. "I arrived here five years ago, right before her liver failed, and the kids… well, there was nowhere for them to go. This is all they've ever known. And since their mom had already established this as a bird sanctuary, and what I needed to do was track down some birds—"

"You met a need," Carl said, and Michael wondered how hard it was to have such a polite conversation when there were years and years of things they each wanted to know.

"So," she said, sounding for all the world like a woman in a restaurant, "did you ever catch those car thieves?"

Carl chuckled. "Took me two tries," he said, his eyes going sideways to Michael, who grinned because he knew the story. "But yes, they're currently rotting in a prison in Hungary, which is good because they were not nice people." He inclined his head. "I take it you were sent on assignment while I was gone?"

She gave half a shrug. "It was supposed to be no big deal," she said, and only the sadness in her eyes told Michael that this five-year-old ache had changed her life. "There was a vineyard that had reported losses due to difficulties with birds. The company sent me to simply estimate how much of the crop had been eaten and then made a recommendation to compensate the winery on the condition that they try something new in the way of pest control."

"Falconry," Carl said.

Mandy inclined her head. "You've done your research."

"I had to get a whole new crew to make up for your loss," he said, and his hand sought Michael's, and he twined their fingers. Michael squeezed back and realized that for all this polite back-and-forth, this sipping iced tea in the kitchen coziness, Carl felt for the bright-eyed girl who seemed to have been living a wealth of sadness since he'd seen her last. "So, Matteo di Rossi?"

Mandy grimaced. "So I looked into this new version of 'pest control,' as the company called it. The wineries in Napa have been using it for *years*, so I came here, and I ran into Matteo. He was playing big cheese at one of the wineries, and we got…." She swallowed.

"Close?" Carl asked softly.

She nodded. "Close. And I told him that we were looking at renting falcons to help keep the crows away. He got very, very serious and told me that I had to be very careful. Most of the falconry outfits were legit. And purists, in fact, who thought of their job as sort of a religion.

Bonding with birds, training them—that takes a full-time commitment. Those people get intense. But apparently, more recently, somebody at Serpentus had wanted shortcuts." She grimaced. "You know how that company likes shortcuts."

"Results," Carl said, his voice arid. "They don't look for answers. They look for results."

"Well, their result was to hire a gene-splicing lab in Mexico—because there were laws here, whether or not they were enforced—and there weren't there. Not five years ago. And their results were…." Mandy gestured furiously toward the mews outside. "They were a big fucking mess is what they were."

"Is that why you disappeared yourself?" he asked.

She blew out a breath. "I went down to Mexico and discovered they'd sold two birds to a prince in Qatar and thirty-six of those things to someone in California to be set loose into the wild. That included four breeding pairs. God, Carl, do you know what kind of damage they could do?"

At that moment, a cry that could rend metal permeated the house. Sunny looked up, her face blank, and said, "Kill it now?"

"No," Mandy said, but her grim expression told Carl that sometimes the answer was yes. "We try to domesticate them. They're scary intelligent, but they're also—" She made helpless gestures with her hands.

"Flying dinosaurs?" Michael hazarded, because God, that thing's cry had rattled his bones.

"Pretty much," she said, nodding. "So I went down to Mexico, saw what was happening, and sent word to Matteo. He'd been up here, working with legitimate breeders, trying to develop a new breed of houbara that was resistant to a pathogen that was killing off the species in the Middle East. His work was legitimate. He'd put his own money into it, and he'd cleared it with customs. But we hadn't realized two things."

"Tell me," Carl said as the hybrid outside screeched again.

"Well, the first was that the pathogen had been lab-cooked. I didn't discover that until about three years ago, the last time I left this place for more than a trip to buy supplies. There was—*was*, mind you—a prince from Qatar who was trying to instigate a coup, and he thought that the way to do it was to kill off the food source of the royal birds. He actually bought two of the super-predators and released them in Qatar. It was symbolic, really. For show."

"Like when King Henry VII had the dogs fight the lion," Carl said.

Mandy's smile made her years younger. "Yes, exactly!"

"He sent the dogs to be killed?" Michael felt bad for derailing the conversation, but he was appalled.

"Worse," Carl told him soberly. "The lion was old and sick. The pit bulls killed the lion, so the king hung them in the square the next day. The prince in Qatar, I would guess, wanted to kill off the bustards so there would be nothing to bring the tribes together to talk. He could backstab and undercut the older leaders in the country without them ever realizing that the reason their falcons could no longer hunt was that he was a greedy asshole who had no respect for the ways of his country."

Mandy nodded, her mouth twisted in a grim smile. "I'd forgotten how quick you were," she said. "God, I've missed a lot of people. My mother, my sisters, the guy who used to deliver Chinese takeout to my apartment. But I'd forgotten how much fun you were too."

"I knew," Michael said, determined to contribute something, even if it was only possession.

Her eyes gentled as she acknowledged him. "Smart boy," she said softly.

"So Matteo was doing legitimate work," Carl said. "Why was there no paper trail? And what happened?"

She swallowed angrily. "Besides the fact that the lab he was using burnt down the day after he died? The best I could figure is that *I* happened. Like I said, we were lovers. But I still had a job to do, and I thought I was working for the good guys, no matter how often you told me we weren't always and to use my best judgment. So his contacts sent me to Mexico, I discovered the flying velociraptors, and the first thing I did was tell the people back at Serpentus."

"Ginger Carson," Carl said.

Her face bleached white, and the hands that held the iced tea glass trembled as she set it down carefully on the condensation ring on the table. "Is she still there?"

"Yes, she is."

"Does she know I'm alive?"

"Possibly." Carl shook his head. "I asked about Matteo, and she shut me down, so we hacked her files and found an old photo from about three years ago."

"Mexico," she muttered. "The one lousy time I went back. I had to see how many more predator birds had been released and to make sure they weren't breeding. I absolutely had to visit the lab again."

"Are they?" Carl asked, and Michael echoed his alarm. "Breeding?"

"No." Mandy shook her head. "There were three pairs that ostensibly *could* have, but so far, no nests have been spotted." She let out a breath. "The *good* news is that they seem to age faster than their counterparts. A falcon or an eagle can live between fifteen and twenty years, but these guys seem to be getting creaky at five. There's hope that they can die out before they obliterate the small bird population of the state."

"Yikes," Carl muttered, shuddering, and Michael nodded in agreement.

She gave them a grim smile. "So how'd you end up here?"

"I'm not stupid!" Carl gave a laugh and finished off his tea. "Like I said, we hacked Serpentus and realized that you and Matteo had both been 'killed' at about the same time. Then my hacker went searching for you, found a picture in San Diego—did you stop there on the way to Mexico?"

"I did indeed," she said grimly. "The fact that Serpentus knew that is terrifying by the way, but go on."

Carl shrugged. "Since we were looking around the wineries already, we tracked you down. A bird sanctuary wasn't too much of a leap. So you told Serpentus, because you still believed in Santa Claus, and they—what? Why would they have Matteo killed?"

"I don't know. The best I can figure is that Matteo figured out what Ginger was doing and that it was illegal. Because *I* might not have. Serpentus wasn't putting their name on anything. *She* was. It wasn't until after his death that I realized Serpentus—or somebody slapping their name on things—might be involved in the giant fucking birds," Mandy said bitterly. "I told her about Matteo because—" She swallowed a lump of fury that Michael could only imagine. "—because I knew she had contacts at the DOI and thought she could help his quest to repopulate the bustard population. I was going to take leave and assist him after my trip to the lab where I found out about the birds. I left Nayarit and took a plane to rendezvous with Matteo at the yacht, and the night after I arrived, the crew warned me that men were coming—bad men. They hustled me overboard, and there I was, treading water, hoping there weren't sharks or oil spills, when I saw the company logo. It was *our* guys, Carl. Our fixers. The ones who look like police but don't have any real authority? They boarded the yacht and came out with all of Matteo's paperwork and computers and stuff." She wiped her eyes with the back of her hand. "I swam ashore and walked away with the clothes on my back and a few contacts that wouldn't rat me out. And Matteo was…. He was dead. I heard that much when I was disappearing myself. I—"

"You tracked the monster birds," Carl deduced, "because you had nothing else to do."

She let out half a sob. "Five years, and I haven't been able to tell a soul that story. Who would believe me?" She shook her head and wiped her face on her shoulder. "One of my contacts had a sister out here who ran a bird sanctuary. She'd written to him about the fucking velociraptors because they were killing all her peregrines and harriers and pretty much decimating their food sources. I came down to check them out and… and she was dying. And she had Sunny and Harry, and this is the only place they've known. The place makes its money on online donations, and that keeps us alive and keeps us hunting the damned birds."

She wiped her face again. "And now you're here, and I don't know what it means!"

Carl released Michael's hand under the table and captured hers where it rested on top. "It means you're not alone, for one thing. We're here working for Matteo's brother and his son—"

"His son?" her voice squawked indignantly, and Michael felt a little vindicated. Possessiveness was a *thing.*

"The son he never knew about," Carl said, his voice soft.

"Oh." Mandy's eyes grew bright. "His father…. He told me his father was a very bad man."

"Yes." Carl nodded. "So was the girl's father. Keeping the boy's parentage hidden was a safety measure."

"Why'd he go looking now?"

Carl breathed out through his nose. "Matteo's son got ill," he said softly. "His uncle—Matteo's brother—was… God, he was thrilled to find out about the boy. Jumped at the chance to help him out. But then he told us about the circumstances behind Matteo's death and—"

"And you wanted to know more," Mandy said softly. "What brought you to Napa?"

"Monster trucks and bustard eggs," Carl said, and Michael remembered Danny and smiled "And falcons. And suspicions."

Some of the sadness in Mandy's eyes eased up, and she stood for a moment, stretching her hands over her head and popping her spine. "Here," she said. "You boys can stay in here and rest, if you like. Or cook dinner if you want to make yourselves useful. We've got to go feed the raptors, and if we wait too long...." She shuddered.

"We can throw some food together," Carl said, standing. "We've eaten up a lot of your afternoon."

"I'd appreciate it."

"So would I," Michael said apologetically. "I'm starving."

Carl grinned at him and nodded. Then he turned to her. "Do you have a landline we can use? There's no cell service here—"

Her mouth hardened. "Carl, we can't be caught out here. I don't even know how you drove in. We let the road stay washed out on purpose."

"Ha!" Michael muttered. "I knew that was insane."

"Chuck would have thought it was fine," Carl said, and Michael rolled his eyes because there was a reason neither of them were with Chuck and he knew it.

"I'm calling a hacker," Carl said. "With the world's most secure and encrypted phone. Someone with as much to lose as you if the company figures out what we're doing and why we're here."

She looked skeptical. "Hackers are famous for being bought," she warned.

"This one's got his own fortune. And if I don't make contact with him, he's going to send in the cavalry. And I'd rather he didn't because right now they're checking out wineries to find the monster truck that killed Matteo."

Her mouth fell open. "One of the wineries was behind his death? I always thought it was Ginger."

"She may have had something to do with it," Carl said. "But one of the trucks was used to herd him into a cliff, and two of the wineries have events using the damned things, and also hire falcons to guard their livestock. We saw the eggs, figured falcons, and saw the truck and figured—"

"Wineries." Mandy paused in the act of grabbing her shotgun from the doorway. "Can't fault your logic," she said, and for a moment, Michael's heart froze as he thought, *This is it. We've given her everything, and now she's going to kill us and feed us to the birds.*

But she didn't. She just grabbed the gun and nodded to the young people.

"Carl, the phone's in the living room, back in the corner. There's a pen and paper there too. C'mon, guys. We've got work to do, and they're going to make us dinner."

"I like hamburger," Sunny said, picking up her gun.

Harry didn't say anything, but together they all trooped out to complete their very unusual mission, leaving Carl to call Stirling and Michael to fix dinner.

A HALF hour later, Carl came out of the living room looking relieved and surveyed the meal under construction. Ground beef and onions were browning in a skillet, and a big glass casserole dish sat filled with pie crust that Michael had made out of flour and shortening.

"Anything I can do?" Carl asked, washing his hands at the sink, which told Michael he was serious.

"Yeah. There's bags of frozen peas and carrots in the chest freezer." Michael gestured with his chin to the thing in the corner. "Could you grab one of those and spread it in the casserole dish after I put the meat in?"

"Roger that." Carl did as he was told, and his chuckle at the chest freezer told Michael he'd encountered the white-butcher-paper packets marked Murder Bird in black grease pen.

"Yeah," Michael said, spreading the ground beef and onion mixture over the crust while Carl wrestled with the chest freezer. "I figured nobody would want to eat something called Murder Bird, so I left those alone."

"Predators in general taste terrible," Carl told him. "All the nasty stuff the herbivores and omnivores eat goes right up the food chain. I saw one study where scientists theorized that if we could go back in time and eat a T. rex, it would make us sick."

"Well, the damned murder bird's the size of a velociraptor," Michael muttered. "I would imagine those aren't much better. Ready with the peas and carrots?"

"Yup." Carl stepped in and spread the vegetables over the meat Michael had added to the casserole while Michael toweled out the skillet. When Michael was done, he stepped forward and pulled up the envelope of pie crust he'd flopped over the side of the dish and started to scrunch its edges together to turn the concoction into a hearty meat pie. Carl saw what he was doing and started to help him from the other side.

"Did you talk to Stirling?" he asked while they worked.

"He threatened to send the cavalry. Twice." Carl grunted. "I don't think Stirling trusts the world much."

Michael snorted. "I think that's a sage observation," he said, and was startled by Carl's big, wide-palmed hand on his own.

"What's wrong?" he asked.

Michael let out a sigh and reminded himself for the umpteenth time that Carl had been super supportive of his ex-wife and kids, who were coming to visit in the summer—and that Michael was going to visit during Christmas—and the fact that Michael had pretty much willed Carl into a long-term relationship with his awesome mind powers alone.

"I didn't have much to contribute to the conversation," Michael said, trying to keep his jealousy out of it, but Carl saw right through him.

"There's nothing between us. You know that, right?"

Michael shrugged, not meeting his eyes. "You seem to have history with a lot of people," he acknowledged. "And I am feeling… small."

Carl's snort made him look up. "Not all that many," he said, looking aggrieved. "They just all seem to be coming together in this case. And it's not fair. I'm still trying to impress you, you know."

That brought a small smile to Michael's lips. "That *was* some pretty fancy driving."

Carl laughed softly, and when Michael met his eyes, they were fastened on Michael's face. "I want so much for us," he confessed, his voice low. "I wouldn't screw it up now. Just remember—Mandy's an old friend, and she's been through a lot."

Michael nodded. *That* much he knew. "Yeah. That's why I didn't say anything," he confessed. "It seemed petty and small, considering what she was dealing with. It was just weighing on my heart some." He gave a shrug. "I'll get the hang of it, this idea of being with someone

I haven't known since we were in diapers. Now to the most important thing. How in the hell are we going to get out of here without calling on Stirling and the cavalry?"

Carl shook his head. "Here's hoping Mandy has some ideas," he said. "I don't think I can make that road again. That was some hairy shit."

"Right?" Michael hefted the casserole dish with the now completed meat pie in it. "Unlike this, I hope, which should not be hairy at all."

He tucked it in the stove and started cleaning the kitchen, pleased when Carl helped him without being asked. As they were finishing up, Carl asked, "How long do we have for that to cook?"

"At least an hour," Michael told him. "Why?"

"Want to go see the live murder birds up close?"

Michael felt a slow smile start. "I thought you'd never ask."

WHEN THEY got out to the cage, Mandy was in the middle of throwing pieces of goat into the three giant mews, and Michael gave a shudder. He'd grown up on a two-acre plot of land—he could slaughter livestock by the time he was ten, not that he liked the job any. He wondered if Carl realized how fresh those furry legs might be.

Carl was under no illusions.

"How big's your herd?" Carl asked as they approached. He gestured with his chin to the furry things on the side of the nearest hill, and Michael realized they'd moved a little closer while the time had passed. He could see them move, see the lack of fleece, and realized they were indeed goats.

Mandy gave him a grim look. "About two-hundred head, after the spring birthing season," she said. "We try to kill off the old ones first, but these fuckers go through a full-grown billy in about three days." The mews all had bi-level doors, and she swung open the top half of the door to the closed mew and threw in a chunk of goat.

Michael watched as one of the birds snapped a leg bone in its powerful jaws and gulped down the meat, bone, skin, wiry hair, and the hoof at the end.

"That's fucking insane," he said, not even sure the words had come out of his mouth.

"These are the ones we could keep contained," she said. "The first one Sunny and Harry's mom caught in a snare *ate* the four-by-four posts that made up the mew. He was going after the kids when I took him out with a shotgun." She shuddered. "I mean, kids get hurt in rooster attacks all the time—it doesn't make the news. But these things? They can kill you. Many large predatory birds have that capability, but they also don't see the need. These assholes don't need a practical reason. They'll do it for free."

"So," Carl said, frowning as if he'd been thinking about this for a while. "Serpentus just tried to forget about these creatures. I mean, speaking of not practical."

Mandy looked at him sharply before moving her bucket of dripping red meat to the next cage. "You're right," she said, as though it had just occurred to her. "But I don't have any other explanation. I found the facility, a contact told me they'd been commissioned to breed these fucking murder birds, and then the commission ended. That's all I know."

"Not to excuse Serpentus," Carl said, gnawing his lip, "because they obviously have some responsibility here and I want to see them get nailed, but like I said before, I think there was another player."

"What makes you say that?" she asked. "And could you hold that part of the door open? This one's tricky." The mews were constructed with pig wire and four-by-four wood posts, and Michael could see the pig wire was bent on the top door of this one. Without someone to hold it, it fell out of position, and as Michael watched the other two birds gulp their supper down, their movements lightning fast and almost synchronous, he could understand how having to run in front of the opening to reposition the door to the mews before fastening it could make someone feel mighty vulnerable.

"Instinct," Carl said. "Incongruity. You're right. Serpentus has their little fascist cop group, and they're scary and all mercenary trained, don't get me wrong. But you know what they don't do?"

"They don't kill people by pushing them into a cliffside in a monster truck," she surmised.

"No they don—watch out!"

Mandy leaped back right when the bird in the mews lunged for her, ignoring the haunch of goat she'd just thrown into its quarters. Carl threw himself forward, slamming the pig-wire gate shut a caught breath before the bird thrust its head out the opening. The gate clanged off the bird's beak, and it let out an indignant shriek, but Carl was busy fastening the three hook-and-eye locks that held the gate shut.

The bird eyed him coldly, ignoring the dinner lying at its feet, and let out a slow, meaningful "*braaaaaaaaawk*" sound that loosened Michael's bowels and made him have to pee.

"That bird," Mandy said distinctly, "is going to want to kill you."

Carl kicked the mews hard enough to make it ring around the bird's head. "I'm finally in a good place in my life," he said. "That bird can fuck right off." He smiled over his shoulder at Michael. "Think dinner's ready yet?"

"Yeah," Michael said weakly. "I'll go check it." He looked at Harry and Sunny, who were staring at the cage with flat affect, neither frightened nor surprised. "You two come inside and wash your hands," he said. "We've already set the table."

"Hamburger?" Sunny asked.

"It's got hamburger in it," Michael said. "Let's get cleaned up."

# Risk and Escape

CARL LAGGED behind with Mandy, wishing he could take her shotgun and cold-bloodedly kill the three creatures that shrieked in the cages behind them, but he couldn't. They hadn't asked to be hatched, and if they did die, they should be studied, if for no other reason than so people wouldn't have an excuse to do something like this again.

"Thanks," Mandy said weakly. "My big fear is that I'll die here and the kids won't have anybody to take care of them."

Carl let out a breath. "Does Harry speak?"

She shook her head. "He might have if their mother had gotten them some early childhood intervention, but she didn't. He's pretty content to do what I ask him, and Sunny too, but back in civilization they'd need social workers and lots of intervention care. Sunny might enjoy it, but Harry dislikes change. I'd love to give it a shot, though." She shuddered. "Going away for a day to get supplies is scary enough as it is."

He thought of the emergency conversation he'd had with Danny. "I spoke to my sources. We can start by getting an education specialist out here to simply live with them for a week and evaluate them as they work. If nothing else, that will give you some time where you're not out here alone. We can also—if you let me give coordinates—get you some supply deliveries, if you tell me how you get in and out."

She snorted. "Small aircraft, Carl. Can you manage that?"

Carl felt stupid. "Of course!" He looked out over the property again, taking in the outbuildings, including a large red structure with a giant double door. "The big barn. I was thinking hay, but if your herd is grazing off the hills—"

"We do have some hay," she said. "But since I have to mow the property once a year to get it, mostly it's grazing. I don't know about all these new people—"

"Mandy, we're going to get the bastards who killed Matteo. And we're going to nail Serpentus for allowing this abomination. And Ginger Carson for whatever her role was in it too. If you believe nothing else, believe that those of us who want to avenge Matteo's death are not going to let you rot out here." His voice softened. "Particularly since you were special to Matteo di Rossi as well. I know it's rough, but—" He gave a crooked smile. "—that young man in the house just cooked hamburger pie for you and your friends based on my say-so alone. That's the level of good works we're talking about here."

She gave him a sideways look. "Judging by the way he was looking at you, he would have done all that for you anyway."

Carl tried not to look too stupid about this and probably failed. "Well, yeah. But trust me. His heart? That sweetness? That's what we're talking about here. Help us get out of this valley and back to the vineyards and we'll try to find the names to take and the asses to kick. In the meantime, you don't have to be alone here anymore." He let out a grunt of frustration. "If you don't have faith in me, you need to have faith in him."

"I don't know him," she said after a moment. "But I do know you." She let out a sigh. "Still, I have to admit, he is awfully cute."

Carl grinned. "Right? I have no idea what he sees in me. It's the damnedest thing. He just started to look at me like I was special."

She laughed. "Oh, Carl. I used to look at you like that all the time. Then you went off to catch car thieves in Hungary."

"See? I'm not that bright."

She laughed again. "Shut up. I'm about to have a meal I haven't cooked myself, which, believe me, happens about once every three months. When you're done, we can figure out how to get you out of here."

"Are you sure there's not a road?" he asked.

"There's a goat track," she told him frankly as they neared the front door. "An off-road vehicle could probably make it, but you might as well write your rental off now."

"Maybe not. You've got tools, don't you?"

"Of course." She gave him a look that indicated she couldn't possibly have survived the past five years if she couldn't change her own goddamned oil.

"My friend's a mechanic by trade. Give him a day to work on the Cherokee and let me take the plane in and out, and maybe we can come up with a plan."

She stared at him, and he could see the girl who had looked at him with such worship in her eyes so long ago. "You have a pilot's license?" she asked.

"Oh, I didn't say that...."

HE'D BEEN afraid Michael would protest being left behind to modify the Cherokee while Carl attempted to fly the plane back to the landing strip Hunter had used earlier that day.

He was right about the protest but wrong about the reason.

"You're going to fly the plane?" Michael asked.

"Well, yes."

"But... but I've seen you fly a plane!" Michael's voice squeaked, and his fork clattered to the table. "You weren't that good at it!"

"Everyone needs practice," Carl said, trying to sell it. He'd never really batted his eyes at anyone before, but he was discovering it was harder than it sounded.

"But why? Why would you want to fly the damned plane and leave me here to fix the car, *maybe*? Why?"

Carl grimaced. "Because," he said heavily, "you're right. I'm not that good. I want to make contact with Stirling and the others, but I don't want you in the plane in case it's a really bad idea."

Michael's brown eyes got really huge, and he stared at Carl helplessly. "Unbelievable!" he said. "Why can't you wait for me to finish the damned Cherokee! Or at least try. I can't promise shit, but if she's got the right tools and some spare parts, I *might* be able to get that fucker over the hills and through the woods and to goddamned civilization. At least give me a couple days to try."

"For one thing," Carl said, giving Mandy an apologetic look, "we don't have a couple of days. We gave ourselves a few extra days to look around before we're expected at the Aerie, and given what Mandy told us, we *really* need to make that work. Also, I really don't want to leave a trail someone else can follow back here. If I land a plane in the middle of nowhere—"

"Or crash it!" Michael reminded.

"Or crash it," Carl accepted, "Nobody has to know where I took off from. But if we come driving out of the underbrush in a tricked-out Jeep Cherokee, I'm thinking we just made Mandy's life a lot more dangerous. I'd rather fly out, come back with supplies, and then fly out with you before we start our big detective thing at the Aerie, and leave the rebooted rental car as a last resort. But I don't want you in the plane the first time in case it turns out to be a really bad idea."

"*It's already a really bad idea!*" Michael protested, his hands shaking as he dragged them through his glossy dark hair.

"How do you know?" Carl shot back, hurt. "It could be the best idea I've ever had."

"If it was the best idea you've ever had, you'd let me sit in the plane with you," Michael told him, crossing his arms. "And that's that." He looked apologetically at Mandy. "Sorry, Mandy. Also...." He sat up straighter, as though this had just occurred to him. "*Also*, if I take a look at what Mandy's got, when we return, we can bring the *right* stuff to trick out the Cherokee so it's not held together with bubblegum and a prayer. I know you've been watching all the wrong movies, but I'm not suddenly going to convert that perfectly conventional vehicle into a monster truck with tractor parts, okay?"

"I don't want you in the plane," Carl said, trying to be reasonable. "Not the first time, anyway."

"The first time?" Mandy spoke up. "You said you could—"

"My first solo flight," Carl said, glaring at Michael and daring him to contradict. "I had... instructors for my first takeoff and landing. Landing*s*." He added the plural belatedly.

"Were they good instructors?" Mandy asked dubiously.

"The best," Carl said.

"No, they weren't," Michael snapped, and then they glared at each other.

"I feel confident I can do this," Carl told her, trying a smile that said exactly that.

"Then feel confident enough to take me," Michael insisted.

"*You* are a father of three, and you'll be missed if this goes tits up, as Chuck would say," Carl retorted, and they glared at each other for a moment now that he'd said the thing that should be perfectly logical but Michael had apparently not conceived of yet.

Michael blew out a breath. "Well, *you* are my reward for two years of prison and a lifetime before that of thinking I was gonna be trapped straight in Texas my entire life, and I'm not watching you blow off or up into the wild blue yonder without me."

Carl gasped and rubbed his chest. "Dammit," he muttered. It was suddenly hard to speak, much less argue. "That's not—you can't use that as an argument."

"Then don't make me," Michael said, his brown eyes obstinate and not sweet at all. "If Mandy will take me out to see what I've got to work with, I'll make a list of shit we need to bring back."

"Hamburger," Sunny said out of the blue.

Carl, Michael, and Mandy all looked at the young woman in surprise. For the most part, their conversation had gone by the two young people like wind around twin mountains. The words might have weathered them a little, but it would take a lot more talking to make an impact. They were certainly not expecting input.

"What?" Mandy asked, sounding disconcerted. "Sunny, what about hamburger?"

Sunny gave them a sweet smile. "Put it on the list," she said. "Hamburger is some of the shit you need to bring back." She took a bite of her pie. "This is good. I want it again."

Carl let out a held breath and Michael did the same, and they both remembered that they were having their first fight in front of other people.

"Fine," Carl muttered. "I'll talk to Hunter and Chuck tonight after I take a look at the plane."

Michael smiled. "You'll do good," he said with the same level of confidence he might have had if Carl was drawing up a brief. "I mean, you're not gonna crash if I'm in there, right?"

"No," he said, his chest getting tight again. "I might have a heart attack, but I definitely won't crash the plane."


LATER THAT night, after Mandy and the teenagers had watched some television—the kids were partial to sitcoms—and Carl had scoped out the plane while Michael had made his list for the Cherokee, Carl used the landline again. It was an old-fashioned desk phone, drunk-piss yellow with a long curly cord and a rotary dial. Carl had nearly broken his finger on the dial because it was stiff from disuse—both the dialer and the finger, apparently. It sat on a small black-lacquered secretary that came with pens and paper and stood in the corner of the room by the television and an armchair—inconvenient when kids were watching TV, fairly convenient for doing business Carl was used to doing on a laptop.

The furniture was indicative of the entire farmhouse. Apparently built in the eighties, the builders probably thought it was a pioneer sort of place—a precursor to a land boom like much of California experienced. But the road proved to be difficult, and a series of floods and then long years of drought had made the low hills a financial risk for nearly any sort of building, and so the house sat in its little valley, alone.

Mandy had told him that the reason they had grazing land for all the goats was that the water table in this part of the Napa Valley was still reasonably functional, whereas much of the rest of the state had already sunk into dust.

Carl, thinking about the feathered abominations in the mews outside, gave a groan. "Why are humans?" he asked rhetorically, not wanting to even broach the subject of what had been done to the planet.

"Because bonobos got busy?" Mandy retorted with a straight face, and Carl had chuckled.

Now, picking up the landline and calling Stirling, he sort of wished they hadn't.

"You're not back yet," Stirling growled, and in the background Hunter said, "Give me that!"

"Hey!"

"Carl?" Hunter said, voice brisk, "Give us the sitch before Stirling's circuits fry. I didn't realize how fond he'd gotten of you, but you're apparently one of his people now, so we need you to not explode and die."

"Uhm, yeah," Carl said, looking nervously at Michael, who sat glaring at him on the stuffed brocade couch that faced the television. "About that. We've got a plan."

Carl outlined his idea, which was mostly that he would fly the Cessna 206 that was Mandy's connection to the outside world to the airfield Hunter had landed in earlier that day.

"Why can't Mandy fly you out?" Hunter asked, sounding aggrieved.

"She can't leave the stock unattended—or the special-needs teenagers," Carl told him. "Apparently she needs to prep everybody and everything for a good week before she goes on a supply run. Right now, she doesn't have time for the prep work it would take before she left. She was going to go next week, and she can't take the plane out without coming back with some of the shit on her list."

Hunter grunted. "That's… unfortunate. So you land the plane and nobody dies. What happens next?"

"We need to send it back with supplies," Carl replied. "I have a list. Then Michael needs Chuck so they can fix the damned Cherokee up so they can drive it out down a goat track."

"Well," Hunter said, sounding put out. "You just took a difficult assignment and made it more interesting. If you hadn't discovered the damned velociraptor birds and the missing piece to our investigation, I'd say you liked to start trouble."

"Ha, ha," Carl retorted sourly. "Look, someone needs to tell Torrance Grayson where to dig on this. Serpentus had monster birds manufactured and then released into the ecosystem because they're fuckers and they need to be brought down. Or there's another explanation that involves them. And someone at the wineries is definitely using murder birds to police their grapes—or they were—and had Matteo killed to cover it up. Mandy is proof this is happening, but she can't tell a soul until we make sure she's safe and the bad guys are taken care of, you understand?"

"Yeah. yeah. You're bragging because you cracked the case. Don't you want to know what Grace and I discovered?"

Carl blinked. "Sure. Hit me."

"We discovered that one glass of wine makes Grace spin around in a thousand circles and throw up. It's a bad idea. Don't do it."

"Helpful," Carl said, failing to keep the laughter out of his voice. "What about Chuck and Lucius?"

"Well, they discovered that Jesse and Jewel are—and I quote Chuck on this—'Super fun people who wouldn't hurt a fly,' which of course helps nobody, but he also discovered that they may run the odd monster-truck event on their property, but they mostly lease their name and business connections out to the outfit Molly's working for, and *that* business does most of its work at the stadium at the Aerie. We'll keep an eye on them, but Chuck is pretty sure the person involved in Matteo's accident would have to be more than a little acquainted with the vehicle or they would have ended up in their own blood puddle at the end of the maneuver."

"So the Aerie?" Carl asked, grimacing.

"You saw the picture, Carl. All those smiling white people can't possibly be up to anything good."

Carl grunted. "You know, I swear someone in that picture looked really fucking familiar. If there was anything like internet out here, I'd take another look. So we're pretty sure Jesses and Jewels is on the up-and-up because Chuck thinks they're 'super nice.'"

"His people sense is usually right on. Don't tell him I said that, by the way."

"I'll skywrite it when I fly in tomorrow. Just for you."

Hunter let out a sigh. "Are you really going to fly?"

"It's our only option. The Cherokee won't make it without modifications, and it would take us a day, maybe two, through rattlesnake country, to hike out of here."

"We need you tomorrow," Hunter said grimly. "Before Michael's bird gets us kicked out of the fucking hotel room."

"Did you feed it?"

"Yes, moron, we fed it. And we kept the hood on, and we smuggled in old mattresses to soundproof the bathroom. But it smells, man. Predator poop is something special."

"You should smell the murder-bird shit," Carl agreed, tamping down on the gag reflex that had been threatening to give since he'd first gotten out of the Cherokee. "So bad. *So* bad. But yeah, there's early bird check-in for the bird training events. We can check in Michael's bird tomorrow, but it's gotta be us."

There was a silence over the line.

"What?" Carl asked, suspicious.

"Did you just say early bird check-in for the murder-bird training?"

Carl blinked. "Fuck you," he said pleasantly. "Are you going to tell me how to fly the damned plane or not?"

Hunter took a deep breath. "I'd rather make bird jokes," he said. "Murder bird. You gotta admit, it's got a nice sound."

"That's because one of them didn't try to eat you," Carl muttered.

"How big are they?"

Carl thought about it. "Four feet, toes to nose, and probably a fourteen-foot wingspan, maybe sixteen on a good day. They could eat a California condor for breakfast." Carl shuddered, thinking that the condor had only recently come back from near extinction. The murder birds could have wiped them out again.

"Are you *shitting* me? Why don't you just put a halter on one of those fuckers and fly it over!"

"Because it would spend most of its time eating me. And then when it was full up on art lawyer, it would move on to mechanic. I'm serious. I've seen these birds in action. They can break your arm with one snap of the beak. It is not funny."

"I believe you. I'm going to have nightmares ab—"

At that moment, two of the birds began shrieking, the tones ripping through the mews, across the considerable yard, and into the house.

"What in the hell is that?" Hunter asked tonelessly.

"That would be a murder bird. Two of them." Carl fought the sudden urge to pee.

"How far away from the house are they?"

"About a hundred yards, if not more."

"Bwah!" Hunter let out the sound someone made after a shudder. "So, a Cessna 206, right?"

"Yeah."

"Let's get you the fuck out of there."

"Don't get too excited. Someone's going to have to fly back."

"Well, let it be me and Chuck, then. I want to see the thing that made that noise."

Carl looked at Michael. "He wants to see the thing that made that noise."

Michael scowled. "Tell him I'll cook him up a piece of it if he wants, but maybe he should leave the live ones alone."

"But that would make him sick...." He took in Michael's look of disgust with Hunter's daredeviltry. "Oh." He spoke into the phone. "Don't eat them," he said seriously. "They're probably toxic and taste bad. And Michael just offered to cook up some meat to feed you, so maybe don't tease him about the murder birds. They're a little scary."

Hunter gave a low chuckle. "So's the idea of you flying the plane. Now, Stirling pulled up some schematics here, and I've flown one of these before, so I'm going to have you write down a preflight checklist, then a takeoff protocol, and then a landing protocol. Stirling can track you in the sky because I don't want to know how, so we can steer you. But dude, this is a terrible plan."

The murder birds shrieked again.

"And yet here we are," Carl said dryly. "From the beginning...."

As he put his faith in Hunter, Stirling, and about halfway through, Chuck, who knew the plane better, Carl's stomach fluttered, but not from fear. This was the same feeling he'd had when he'd gone after the car thieves in Hungary and when Hunter and Molly had tried to maim him because he'd spotted Danny across the room.

It was the feeling of adventure and of purpose, of excitement, and he realized that this time it was better because—even over the phone—he was with friends.

THE NEXT morning, just after sunrise, he, Michael, and Mandy were prepping the plane. Mandy had steered the thing to the straightaway through the goat field that she used as a takeoff and landing strip, and was busy checking the gauges for him to make sure they conformed to Chuck's specifications.

"You guys have your lists?" she asked, sliding out of the pilot's seat, and Michael patted his pocket as he slid into the copilot's.

"Yes, ma'am. One for the Cherokee and one for supplies. The guys should have the shit on the ground when we get there."

Mandy nodded and then grimaced at Carl. "I can't believe I'm letting you do this," she muttered. "If you crash my plane while I watch, I'll never forgive you."

Carl grimaced back, but part of that was trying to fit his broad shoulders and long legs into the teeny cockpit. It was like the time he'd driven a friend's MG in college—doable but not fun. "Yeah. I left Stirling's phone number in case that happens and we have to change plans."

She swatted him on the back of the head. "My God, you're stupid." She turned a sympathetic look toward Michael. "Good luck with him. Thickest, most asinine man I've ever met."

Michael grinned at her. "He's pretty great, isn't he?"

"Pretty great at being an asshole." She rubbed the back of Carl's head. "Take care of yourself. You're the closest thing to hope I've seen in five long damned years."

"We'll get you some help, Mandy. Trust us."

"Fine."

And with that, she climbed out of the plane and put up the walkway, making sure the hatch was secured and patting the side of the plane to let them know.

Carl let out a sigh of relief as she walked away.

"She was making me nervous," he muttered to Michael, wishing that their night together hadn't been spent on the uncomfortable couch and love seat in the living room, covered in extra blankets. It wasn't that he thought they were going to die or anything, but if they *were* going to die, he would have liked to make love one last time before it all went dark.

"Yeah, well, let's do the checklist thingy." He pulled it out of the pocket of his hoodie. "That'll make me happy. Number one, check the fuel."

"Half full. Check."

"Number two, check the tire pressure."

"No worries. Check."

And one thing at a time, Michael walked him to the part where he had to press forward on the accelerator, then check the speed, then pull up the flaps, then pull back on the stick.

For a moment, he had to wrestle with the controls, because the plane *wanted* to go back down to the ground, like breaking the accustomed laws of gravity was too much for it.

"Getting close to those trees," Michael said, not panicked or anything. He sounded as though he was mentioning the weather.

"I see them," Carl muttered, pulling back on the stick harder.

"What are those? Not pine."

"I think they're oak," Carl said, yanking back some more.

"Nice of the goats to get out of the way."

"Yup." God*dammit*, why wouldn't they go any higher?

"Maybe, you know. More on the flaps?"

Oh! Fuck fuck fuck fuck fuck! He hit the switch that moved the flaps up, and suddenly the plane stopped fighting him and shot up, not quite vertically but with excessive force, which was good, because they could hear the scratching of the oak leaves on the fuselage.

"Good," Michael said, voice a teeny bit thready. "Keep going up, 'cause, hey, there's another hill in front of us and it's higher—"

Carl adjusted the flaps again, pulled back on the stick, and suddenly, they were free and clear, with nothing but sky in front of them.

Carl could feel sweat coating the palms of his hands, sliding between his arms and flanks, down his neck, and down between the crack of his ass in his jeans. God, even his feet seemed to squelch in his shoes.

"You check the altimeter?" Michael asked, and Carl did, letting out a sigh of relief when it read the height Chuck had given him.

"Yup. Time to call the guys and let them know we're not dead."

"Sure." Chuck glanced at him and saw that Michael was a bit pale and his teeth were clenched together. "You okay?" he asked.

"You know, I never thought this would be a thing to put my money in, but I'm wondering if it's too late in life to invest in adult diapers."

Carl let out a bark of a laugh. "I don't know. Let's see how my landing looks before we take extreme measures."

Michael turned to gaze at him, and his face had gained a little color. "I must absolutely love you, because I don't think I'd be that excited about dying in a fiery plane crash with anybody else but you."

"You love me?" Carl asked, his chest aching with a combination of fear and joy that he was pretty sure had nothing to do with the plane.

Michael's smile was the intoxicatingly sweet expression that had caused Carl to fall for him in the first place. "Pretty sure," he said soberly. "But we may have to see what the landing looks like to be certain."

Carl grinned, chilly now that his sweat was drying, sticking his clothes to his body. "Well, in case it goes badly, you should know I love you too."

Michael closed his eyes and held his face up to the sun. "We gotta land good now," he said. "I'm pretty sure that means there's more to come."

# Landings Rough and Smooth

HE WAS coming in too low.

As awful and seemingly endless as the trip *into* the winding hills had been—including those terrible, perilous moments when Michael had seen his life flashing before his eyes and only his faith in Carl had kept him from leaping out of the vehicle—the actual flight *out* of the hills had only taken around twenty minutes.

Which wasn't long enough to prepare Michael for landing.

It wasn't that he didn't have any faith in Carl Cox. He was in the plane, right? He'd *argued* for his right to be there, to put his life in the hands of a guy he knew for a fact had only flown a couple of times and whose last landing had been less than ideal, to say the least.

But the closer they got to the landing strip by Napa, the more he remembered the bounce. The bone-jarring, tongue-biting, terrifying bounce that had happened when Carl had come in too hot, bounced the plane, and then set it down.

He figured he could live through the bounce again, but the more he waited, the more anxious he got. Chuck's voice over the headset sent relief coursing through his body.

"Carl, buddy, how you doing?"

"Fine," Carl said. "I can see the landing strip. I'm approaching head-on."

"Good. Perfect, actually. What we're going to do is raise the nose and lower the tail just a bit. So what do you do with your flaps?"

Carl told him and then did it and tugged gently at the stick. And still the runway was getting closer and closer, and they seemed to be getting closer and closer to the ground, and it was going faster and faster, and—

Michael wasn't aware he'd closed his eyes in panic until the wheels caught on the tarmac and he let out a little moan of relief. His eyes flew open, and the plane didn't bounce once as Carl slowed it to a graceful stop, almost a perfect distance from the hangar.

For a moment the silence was deafening, and then Chuck's voice came through again.

"Nicely done! You're practically a pro now. You can take a shift the next time we go cross-country!"

"Sure," Carl said weakly before discarding the headset and leaning wearily back against the seat. He turned to Michael and gave a thin smile. "See? It wasn't an awful idea."

Michael started laughing semihysterically, and he felt a sudden surge of affection for the man next to him. "You know what?" he said. "The thing I love about you is you get the job done. You keep saying you're not flashy, that you're the second up. That's not it. You just wait until you're needed and you get the job done. Well, you did it. Here we are. You got the job done."

Carl's smile increased in wattage and amperage. "I'll take it," he declared. Then with a hopeful, almost flirty little wink, "Do I get a kiss now?"

Michael was out of his seat and practically in Carl's lap, and as their mouths met, he made a little groan. Carl answered it, his big, broad-palmed hands sliding under Michael's shirts, and even though they were both a little sweaty, they were suddenly electric for each other.

"Don't we have a room to ourselves?" Michael asked breathlessly, pulling back with reluctance.

"God yeah."

"We're gonna have to do something about that," he said.

"I'm saying." And then Carl pushed up to kiss him some more, and that was about all Michael could manage until Chuck's voice—in person this time—intruded on their thoughts.

"If you two could wait until you get back to the hotel...," he said delicately, and Michael pulled back so quickly he hit his head on the low ceiling of the cockpit.

"If you insist," Carl told Chuck. He nudged Michael and gave a nod, and Michael sighed and extricated himself so he could get to the ramp. He looked back, but Carl had paused to ask, "Do you have all the supplies you need?"

"They're incoming," Chuck said. "Hunter and Grace are on their way with the load from Walmart as we speak. My job is to stay here and make sure it gets loaded on and then fly this thing back while you two go reassure Stirling you're alive, shower and change, and then take the bird for check-in at the Aerie."

Carl let out a yawn. "Then can we nap?"

"If that's what the kids are calling it." Chuck's deadpan expression told Michael, at least, that Carl was fooling nobody.

"It is," Carl said decisively. Then he sighed. "C'mon, Michael. No rest for the wicked."

"And no wickedness either," Michael grumbled. His mouth still tingled from the kisses, and his nether parts weren't far behind. He found his stomach muscles clenching without his say-so and his... his *hole* was right there with it.

God, he wanted to be touched there again. Not hard but *decisively*. The way Carl did things, with commitment and care.

It was the first time Michael ever thought consciously that he wanted *that* sort of sex, as long as it was with the right person. But boy, did he want it. He wanted it *bad*.

BUT HE was a grown-up, and he had to wait.

Stirling didn't exactly throw himself in Carl's arms like a child, but his face became animated in a way Michael hadn't seen unless the guarded young man was talking to his sister, or to Josh, or to Danny. After that first burst of what was apparently joy, he scowled ferociously.

"No more risks like that," he snapped.

"Okay," Carl said. "If it bothers you, I won't."

Stirling looked at him suspiciously, then at Michael. "Not... you know. You're old."

"I know," Carl said, mouth twitching. "I'm probably too old for Michael too, but he's okay with it. It's fine, Stirling. You and me are friends. We got tight when we worked with Lucius back in July, and we're good friends now. I don't work well with a lot of people. I'm glad we found each other."

Stirling let out a long breath. "Thank God. You get me. You can't go out and get yourself killed."

"Understood." From the bathroom in Stirling's room came a muffled shriek. Given that it wasn't coming from a big scary murder bird, the falcon's cry almost sounded sweet and soulful, but Michael was very aware that was only because it was surrounded in padding.

"We need to change before we get the falcon out of your hair," Carl said.

"Take your time." Stirling shook his head. "I double-checked on the drop-off time for your friend there, and they don't take early birds before 2:00 p.m. You've got a couple of hours to nap."

Michael growled. "Fucking Chuck, man. He made it sound like we had to get back on the road again."

"He's mad too," Stirling told him, surprising them both. "You scared everybody. You said 'Hey, we're going to check out this random lead,' and then you disappeared. It wasn't cool."

Carl rubbed the back of his neck, looking abashed, and met Michael's eyes. "I didn't think we'd be missed," he said, and Michael nodded in agreement.

"Me neither," he confessed. "Now we know. No more adventures without checking in with the family. Understood." And then he yawned. Mandy's living room furniture hadn't been comfortable in the least, and God, those birds had not shut up.

He thought glumly that they might actually spend their nap time napping, and that irritated him no end.

"Well, Hunter radioed while you two were driving here and told me to have you wait until he and Grace get back. You've got until three, but I'm thinking we should meet for lunch at one."

Carl chuckled. "You know, I keep thinking it's twelve or one or something. It's only 9:00 a.m. That plane trip was the longest half hour of my life."

Michael found himself laughing too. "One o'clock for lunch sounds fantastic," he said.

What he was really thinking was that he and Carl had time to be naked together after their shower. The thought was starting to dominate his every brain cell.


CARL TOLD him to shower first because he had phone calls to make, and he was ready to step in as Michael stepped out. He looked preoccupied, Michael thought, and he realized that yes, Carl's brain was probably on the job, and on Mandy, and on calling Torrance Grayson and moving falcons and on stupid velociraptor murder birds.

Michael, who was usually very good about putting practical matters first, suddenly wanted his full attention.

Carl was under the spray, wetting his hair, and Michael moved to the bedroom to dry himself off. He wrapped a towel around his waist and went to his suitcase—or Carl's suitcase, since Carl had luggage and he did not—and was sorting through his clothes when a puff of air from the vent danced across his shoulder blades and he was made abruptly aware of his nakedness.

And how much he wanted Carl's attention.

Michael cocked his head and listened to Carl, grumbling to himself in the shower, and thought about how badly he wanted to be touched. Then he pulled the lubricant from his shaving kit, where he'd tucked it, just in case, and set it on the end table of the king-size bed, making sure it was in plain sight. They'd discussed their status before this, and they were both negative. Michael had been put on PrEP in prison after his first visit to the infirmary, so they both knew condoms wouldn't be needed if they took that next step.

And he really wanted to take that next step.

He had wicked, sinful thoughts of lying naked, legs spread lewdly, cock in his fist, while he fingered himself, but although they made him wiggle with arousal—and grow more than a little bit hard—he wasn't sure he was brave enough to follow through.

However, by the time Carl emerged from the bathroom, toweling his hair dry, another towel knotted firmly around his waist, Michael had managed to be under the covers, hair combed, underarms deodorized, all creases dried off and ready for action.

Carl paused in the act of going through his own suitcase—the big brother to the one he'd loaned Michael—and took note of Michael lying on his side, propped on his elbow and looking hopeful, obviously naked underneath the sheet.

Michael watched as Carl blinked once, all the busy thoughts in his head appearing to stop. He blinked again, and it looked as if his mind was yanking itself back on the track Michael needed it to be on.

One more blink and he was wholly, completely in the same room with Michael, and the realization that they were both naked, both alone, and they had a couple hours to kill seemed fully upon him.

A slow, sultry smile curved his lips.

"You have some plans, Mr. Carmody?"

Michael nodded. "You have a problem with that, Mr. Cox?"

"Not in the least," Carl said, still smiling. He grabbed a comb from his suitcase and dragged it through his thick blond hair, which was probably a good idea since if it dried tangled, it would be a mess. Then he draped his two towels over the back of a nearby chair and moved to Michael's side of the bed so he could bend down and offer a kiss.

Michael took the kiss and raised the passion, sitting up and scooting back until Carl was on the bed with him, their mouths feverish, their hands sliding smoothly on clean, soft skin. The kiss went on and on, their lovemaking confident now, and Carl moved to Michael's nipples, sucking and nipping until Michael moaned and rolled to his back, spreading his knees and giving himself over.

He knew what it was like to trust someone with his body now. He wanted things from Carl that he'd never willingly taken from any man, and the thought of receiving them made him shiver from pleasure, not fear.

Carl kissed his way back up, along Michael's neck, nibbling his jaw and earlobes until Michael let out a hum of arousal.

"Michael," he whispered, and Michael shuddered from hearing the name *he'd* chosen said intimately in the shell of his ear.

"Yeah?"

"You got out the lubricant. Was there anything you wanted?"

He moaned. "Yes."

Carl reached below the covers, caressing the soft skin of Michael's stomach before going lower, grasping his cock for a smooth, long stroke.

"You're going to have to say it," Carl murmured, licking delicately around his earlobe.

"I want—" Michael said, right before Carl squeezed his cockhead gently. "Augh!"

"Want what?" Carl whispered again, cupping Michael's balls before starting his next stroke.

"Want you to fuck me," Michael rasped a little desperately. His hips were thrusting and receding, and if Carl hadn't been fondling his balls, he might have gone facedown on the bed, knees up to his chest in blatant invitation.

"You're sure?" Carl asked, his fingers drifting lower, and Michael spread his knees and lifted his ass, begging him silently to take the hint.

"Please?" Maybe not so silently.

Carl's low chuckle told him he'd do anything Michael asked. He slid down to the bottom of the bed again, stripping away the sheet so they were both naked in the unmerciful light of the hotel room.

Michael didn't care. He could trust now, and it didn't matter about the scars and imperfections that life had left on his body. Carl had seen them all, touched them, owned them for Michael, and Michael wasn't afraid.

When Carl fitted himself between Michael's spread knees and lifted his hand imperiously for the lubricant, Michael turned it over without a qualm.

Carl took it but didn't use it right away, parting Michael's cheeks first, licking, rimming, stretching, while Michael lost himself in the sensation, loving it even more now that he'd performed this act and had seen Carl come apart from the feel of his tongue and fingers.

*Fingers.*

Carl had snicked the lid already, had dripped some lube on his fingers, and was tracing lazy figures across Michael's hole. Trace, tease, slip in for a moment, slip out. One finger, in, out, in, out. Two.

None.

One.

Michael clawed the sheets, digging his heels into the mattress and arching his hips, allowing his body to respond, not caring about the begging noises—he'd heard himself make them before, and Carl never let him beg for long.

Oh God. Two fingers again, scissoring, stretching, every atom of Michael's body exploding outward, then stopping. He gasped, caught his breath, and moaned some more.

Three fingers, stretching.

"Please," he begged, the word coming easily. "Please. I want it. All. Please. Please."

Carl pulled his fingers away and paused to engulf Michael's cock all the way to the root. Michael cried out, but Carl sucked hard, pulling back until it slid out with a pop, and he was bereft, his entire body aching for possession but not a finger touching him.

Then he felt Carl's cock, poised at his entrance, and Carl's harsh whisper.

"Look at me."

Michael's eyes flew open, and he whimpered.

"Still want this?" Carl asked, and Michael nodded.

"Please."

Carl slid in slowly, very slowly, and Michael didn't even think to be afraid. He wanted this, craved it, and Carl filled him long, strong, and hard.

Michael gave a little gasp when Carl's cockhead pushed in, and then his shaft kept going, wide and full.

"More," he whispered, aching for it all, shuddering when Carl thrust in the last bit until his hips were flush with the backs of Michael's thighs. "Yes," he hissed. "*Yesssss....*"

Carl stayed there for a minute, resting, giving him a chance to adjust, and as Michael relaxed into the mattress, melting into the joy of being possessed, Carl began to move. First he pulled back, and Michael's greedy asshole clenched down, not wanting him to go.

Then he thrust forward, and Michael's head fell back as sweat popped out on his forehead, his entire body flushing hot and cold with the ache of submission.

"More," he begged again, and Carl began fucking him, hard, slow, making every thrust count.

Oh wow. Michael couldn't move, couldn't play with his nipples or grab his cock. His entire being was consumed with what Carl was doing. One more electric zap of his nerve endings would send him rocketing into the stratosphere without a net.

And Carl kept fucking him, harder and harder, until every breath felt like a climax, until Michael couldn't think anymore from the combination of desire and arousal.

Then Carl's fist closed on Michael's cock as he thrust, and Michael cried out, his entire body coming off the bed as he came.

He clenched down on Carl's cock as he jetted come all over both of them, and Carl cried out too, rutting hard inside him, setting off a series of aftershocks that Michael couldn't control and didn't want to.

Then he felt the pulsing of Carl's cock, filling him hotly, and he shuddered, his limbs splaying out as he collapsed weakly into the damp sheets, Carl on top of him, hips still pumping as though he couldn't help himself.

For a moment the only sound in the world was their harsh breathing, the little moans and grunts of orgasm that had never completely faded.

"You... good?" Carl asked, still lodged solidly inside him.

"So good," Michael managed to say. He was falling asleep, his body limp and exhausted, Carl's come drizzling down his crease and coating the back of his thighs.

It was an amazing sensation.

"Good," Carl whispered, embracing him hard. Michael tried to hug back and mostly succeeded, but then his eyes were fluttering closed, closed, his entire body buzzing with climax and white light.

He'd wanted Carl to pay attention to him. He hadn't expected that attention to electrify his bones, his skin, his flesh.

He would want this again, he thought muzzily. Again and again and again.

Best thing he'd ever done.

"Love you," he mumbled before his mind went dark.

"Love you back," Carl told him, and that gave him the peace he needed to sleep.

"WHAT'S WRONG with him?" Chuck asked suspiciously.

Michael caught Carl's quick puzzled look before Carl replied, "Nothing. Nice place, by the way."

They had taken over the patio of a small restaurant outside of Napa, not too far from the hotel. The restaurant itself was sided with faux rock walls, and the patio was fenced in with white-washed timber, bougainvillea draped over the struts and the also white-washed wire between the posts. Both the inside and outside were paved with polished stone, and the tables and chairs were sturdy farmhouse-style affairs that looked like they could hold two of Carl on a rainy day.

Michael approved of places that looked sturdy—he'd grown up with his brothers roughhousing around him, and the idea that furniture could break had never been very far from his mind.

"No, no, something's wrong with him," Chuck replied, still squinting. "Michael, are you feeling okay?"

Michael gave him a serene smile, not even trying to come down from the sexual buzz Carl had given him. "Peachy," he replied, before trying to study his menu. He touched Carl's arm. "Do you mind if I have a beer?"

Carl shook his head. "Doesn't bother me," he said. "Beer was never my drink anyway."

"What was?"

"Vodka and gin. Clear stuff that tasted like cooking oil. Fabulous."
He glanced up at the patient waitress. "I'll have a sparkling water with
the chicken salad. Michael?"

"Craft beer?" he asked, thinking about what a luxury it was to
order something that would taste wonderful and he didn't have to drink
a six-pack of.

"I'll get you the house brew," the woman said. In her thirties,
dressed in black pants and a white shirt, she was the type of woman who
turned waiting tables into an art form of customer care and empathy.

"And a hamburger, rare, thank you." Michael beamed at her, and
she went around the table.

Lucius ordered a glass of pricey white wine and a steak, Chuck
ordered the same beer Michael got with steak, as did Hunter, and Grace
looked at the menu and then looked at Hunter and said, "Know what I'm
not gonna get?"

"Wine," Hunter said dryly.

"Believe me, I'm as surprised as you are," Grace muttered,
sounding incredibly contrite.

"He'll have a whole pitcher of soda," Hunter told the waitress, who
tried hard to hide her smile. "And a chicken sandwich, no bread, no
mayo, nothing but chicken, lettuce, and pickles."

"You know me," Grace said, beaming at him.

"I'll have soda," Molly said regretfully, rolling her eyes. "Because
I have to work my shitty job." She sent Stirling an evil look. "And a
chicken sandwich with everything." She glared at Grace. "Because I
don't have to crawl through drainpipes."

"I'll have soda because I'm not twenty-one yet," Stirling told her
blandly. "And a hamburger because they're delicious."

"Two months," Molly said grimly. "He's got two months, and then
he can stop bragging about being the youngest."

"Josh is the youngest," Grace said quietly. "He'll be twenty-one in
December."

They all took a deep breath, and the waitress, seeing that she'd
taken everybody's order, scurried discreetly away.

"Is Torrance meeting us?" Carl asked.

"Yeah." Hunter checked his phone, which was sitting on the table
in front of him. "He wants us to put in an order for chicken too. I'll wait

until she gets back." He glanced at Michael meaningfully. "And Chuck is right. Look at him. He's practically luminescent. What happened to him? Were there murder-bird hormones in the water or something?"

Chuck shuddered. "Bwah!" he said, shaking like a dog. "Y'all, I got a good look at those things, and they were *not* friendly. I thought Carl was exaggerating, but no. If anything, he understated their absolute ugliness and ability to haunt a man's dreams."

"They've got a face like a California condor after an accident with a cheese grater," Carl said matter-of-factly, and Michael nodded. "You got Mandy the supplies, right? And the things Michael's going to need to trick out the Cherokee?"

Chuck nodded. "Yeah. I figure you two drop the bird off at the Aerie this afternoon. Then Michael and I can go back this evening and spend tonight and tomorrow getting that thing ready to roll. We'll put extra parts and tools in the back, so if it breaks down on the way down the mountain, we can maybe fix it without killing ourselves." He paused as though realizing this was a new bit of plan. "You good with that?" he asked Carl.

"As long as we're good to check in tomorrow at three," Carl said. "I mean, I can probably check us both in by myself and say he got hung up in travel or something, but, you know, we're doing a romantic getaway thing. Gotta sell it."

Grace, Hunter, and Chuck all turned to Michael like their heads were on swivels.

"What?" Michael asked, feeling singled out.

"That's it," Grace said in wonder.

"I think you're right," Chuck agreed.

"What?" Carl asked, staring at him, but friendly-like so Michael didn't flinch. "What's wrong with him?"

"He looks all lit up inside," Grace told him happily. "Like someone shoved a lightbulb up his ass."

Michael's face went hot. "Well," he said with dignity, "it was a little bigger than a lightbulb."

A shocked silence washed over the table, and Carl covered his eyes with his palm.

"Hey!" came the cheery voice of the dapper, handsome Torrance Grayson as he stepped through the patio gate. "What'd I miss?"

He had to wait a long time—and wade through a lot of laughter—before he got an answer to that question.

FINALLY THE laughter died down, and by the time they all had their food, they'd brought Torrance up to speed.

He lingered thoughtfully over his chicken and vegetables, asking them all questions and more questions, eking out details and making notes in a legal pad he'd brought with him.

"Wow," he muttered, pushing his plate back and leaning his elbows on the table. "You guys have the most interesting games. So as far as I can tell, we need to do three things." He drew a big one on his pad. "One, we need to find out who killed Matteo—who was driving the monster truck and the vehicle behind him, but most importantly, who was giving the orders."

"We're on that," Carl said, nodding with Hunter. "We're checking into the vineyard hotel tomorrow, and we've pretty much narrowed it down as the one we think is responsible."

"I'm working for the monster-truck outfit," Molly said, checking her phone. "In fact, I've got to leave in about five minutes. Anyway, I've got three drivers in my sights who have a direct link to the Aerie. One has a girlfriend who works there—I'm thinking no because he's a total sweetheart and super smart, so not the type. One's got a grudge against Jesses and Jewels, and he's just generally an asshole. And the third is decent enough, but he's the grandson of the owner of the Aerie. I'm thinking if he was ordered to do something, he'd probably do it. I know in the pictures that family is all happy and functional, but you can smell the dis in the function if you know where to look."

Torrance Grayson looked up from his pad. "Elaborate?"

Molly grimaced and shook back the hair cascading from the half ponytail drawn up on the top of her head. She was dressed in skintight jeans and a white T-shirt that showed off her cleavage, and Michael had to admit she looked exactly like the NASCAR groupies he'd grown up with. She'd even done her makeup super bold, with bright blue shadow to make the illusion complete. "Can't. We need to catch up for dinner, sweetness," she said. "I've got to go or I'm gonna get fired, and there goes our connection."

She blew them all a kiss and said, "Seeya! Stirling, fight for the check for me!" before running out the gate.

All eyes turned to Stirling, and Lucius gave a feline half smile. "Feeling lucky today, young man?"

"No," Stirling said, clearly assessing his odds. "But don't worry. I'll get in there when you're not looking."

"Good choice," Chuck said, laughing. "Particularly since a lot of us ordered alcohol and you're not twenty-one."

Stirling's mouth twitched up at the corners, and Michael knew the young man had something planned that would probably take Lucius by surprise. He realized he liked this game, seeing who could pay for the check first; it was a good-natured sort of thing, unlike his brothers' naked attempts to fleece their victims for as much as they could.

"Okay," Torrance said, writing furiously. "At least we have leads. We also need proof that the birds are illegal hy—" His phone pinged, and Chuck looked up from texting him pictures he'd probably taken that morning. "Oh dear God," he said weakly, taking in the enormity of what the birds were.

"Yup," Carl said.

"That's terrifying. It looks photoshopped."

"We've got an ice chest full of monster meat on its way to a crime lab that says different," Chuck said.

Michael looked at him in surprise. "I didn't even think of that," he said with admiration. "How long will it take to look at the DNA?"

"We had Felix make the call and fill out the request," Chuck said. "The lab was in Bakersfield. While you guys were—" His eyes narrowed. "—stuffing lightbulbs, we flew to Bakersfield, dropped off the chest, and flew back. Since it's under Salinger and has no connection to Napa *or* the conservancy, I think it's safe."

"What did you say it was?" Carl asked.

"Said it was a bird that was harassing my livestock," Chuck said, "and that it looked fishy to me. I asked Mandy, and she said she hadn't dressed the birds, just broken them down so they'd fit in the freezer and wrapped them in butcher paper, mostly for this reason. It was one of Mandy's secret weapons in case somebody threatened her or her proof escaped. Murder-bird meat in the freezer."

"God," Carl muttered, shaking his head. "She had better not be in danger."

"I hear you," Chuck said. "And now that I've met her and seen her situation, I can understand why you were so worried. It's one of the reasons I told her I'd return with Michael. I want to see what we can do to tighten security."

"Good deal," Carl said. "I can come back with you and help—"

Chuck shook his head. "No you can't. Torrance, tell him why."

"Because we need data mining," Torrance said. "We need to look at things like bird attacks on livestock and the effect they have on endangered species populations. Before we call your contact at the DOI, we need to make a case for these things being the monsters they are. If we're going to have this done by the time you find the missing pieces—who killed Matteo, who ordered it, why—I'm going to need some help." His gaze flickered to Grace and Hunter. "You guys—"

"Not so much. We'll go help Mandy," Hunter said. "I'll take the plane back later tonight, and Chuck and Michael can drive in."

"I'll ask around Jesses and Jewels," Lucius said. "Chuck and I don't think they have anything to do with Matteo's death, but I hadn't thought about the livestock angle. If there are monster birds flying around picking up small children, some of the people working in the vineyards would have heard of them."

"So that's two things," Carl said, frowning. "Who ordered Matteo's death, as well as who carried out the order, what environmental impact the birds have had—and we can assume it's been considerable—and what's the third?"

"Why? What started this whole thing? There's got to be an underlying purpose here, but given that the guy in Qatar who bought one of the mating pairs has been dead for three years, I don't think it's him. Why is Carl's insurance company—or *who* at Carl's insurance company—is so hell-bent on hiding this? What is being hidden?"

The table went quiet then, and Michael chewed his lip. "When you put it like that, it makes me think…." He felt stupid when everybody looked at him again, and not because now they knew he'd been having really good sex.

"What?" Carl prompted softly.

"Why didn't I tell the insurance people that my brothers were stealing from me?" he asked. Carl blinked, and so did Chuck.

"Because you didn't want to put those two assholes in jail," Chuck said thoughtfully.

Michael nodded. "Yeah. Because they were family, even though they were making my life miserable. It's the same dumb reason I picked up a gun and went to rob a bank. 'Cause family. I'm just saying, all those dumb things I did—they look like I got no reason and I got no sense, but there was an underlying thing there, a thing nobody talks about but everybody understands." He looked at Carl, begging him to get it. "Like you were saying, there's things we don't talk about but rules everybody understands. There's no good goddamned reason for these birds to exist, for someone to go to all this trouble to have them made, and then to go to all the trouble to hide them. There's no good goddamned reason except—"

"Family," Stirling said, surprising him.

"Yes!" Michael cried. "Yes! You see it? I wasn't sure I was making any sense at all."

Stirling rolled his eyes. "Grace, remember Justin Henson?"

Grace chuckled like a horror movie villain. "Yes."

"Remember what happened to his hair?"

Grace shrugged. "I have no idea. Turned green, fell out. Whatever. Ninth grade. Shit got weird."

Stirling gave Grace a dry look.

"Justin Henson put my face in the toilet and gave me a swirlie," he said, his voice matter-of-fact. "And my sister never left my side for the next two weeks. Then, suddenly, Justin's hair turned green and fell out, and they discovered his shampoo had been tampered with, and wasn't that a shame. Couldn't have been Molly, though. She hadn't left my side, remember? Must have been someone else."

Grace's smile curled up the sides of his mouth. "Josh's formula," he said, looking pleased. "I snuck it into Justin's house. Ah, youth."

Stirling looked at Michael and nodded. "Like your brothers and the insurance guy. Like you robbing a bank. With family, things can go sideways. Hunter keeps saying all those smiling faces on the webpage give him the creeps. There's something there that went sideways."

Torrance nodded. "Now *that's* what I'm talking about," he said. "We can data mine, and we can investigate, but until we find that missing motive, we don't have a story."

Everybody at the table nodded. "Well, now we know what to look for," Carl said decisively. "And we all have a job to do."

"Sure," Torrance said, finishing his notes with a flourish and tucking his tablet back into his battered leather messenger bag. He paused and looked around. "But can we have dessert first? I had to fly commercial to get here today, and God, I'd just really like to sit and chill."

"Certainly," Lucius said, cocking a self-satisfied eyebrow at Stirling. "But since everyone else has a time commitment, how about if you and I linger while everyone else scatters. How does that sound?" And then before anybody could answer, he signaled the waitress with his credit card and had her put everything, including the dessert Torrance Grayson was about to order, on his tab.

"Tough luck," Michael said to Stirling as they were making their way out to the SUVs to go back and fetch the falcon from the Residence Inn.

Stirling chuckled. "You think?"

"What did you do?" Carl asked, sensing something was up before Michael did.

At that moment they heard Chuck's footsteps as he caught up to them. "Nice move," he said to Stirling. "Lucius wants you to know it's game on, though, so you'd better be on your toes."

Stirling gave a catlike smile. "I hope he enjoys paying for Torrance's dessert," he said, swinging into the back of the SUV.

Chuck's hearty laughter was only cut off when they all yanked their doors shut.

"And only Torrance's dessert?" Carl asked, starting up the vehicle.

"Molly took care of the bill on her way to the bathroom before she left," Stirling told them smugly. "Telling me to fight for it was misdirection."

"Now see," Michael complained. "I don't know how you knew that. How would you know that's what she meant?"

Stirling paused a bit before answering. "Foster care was... challenging," he said. "For us both. But she'd been fighting in the system for two years before I came along. That first day we met, we were in a big, impersonal place, and some kids tried to bully me. She put me behind her and beat them bloody and told me that I would never ever have to fight like that if I didn't want to."

It took a minute for Michael to get it. "And she told you to fight for the check," he said.

"Which meant she'd already fought for me. I *have* gotten into fights since then, and she taught me how to take care of myself. But she's very protective. It gives us a solid code."

"You are so lucky," Michael said, meaning it. "I mean, I know you lost your parents—twice—but I gotta tell you, parents aren't the acid test in the family lottery. I had two brothers who would rather I was dead than gay, or even happy, or even right, and my ex-wife had to put out a restraining order on my mama when she was moving the kids out of state. You got your sister. Man, she's worth twelve of every relative I've got put together."

Stirling made one of those sounds then—a laugh sound that only people who knew him would hear as a laugh. "I know *I* wouldn't trade her," he said modestly, and Michael thought that was how you knew the boy was raised right.

# Lost Connections

"So, UHM, the *falcons* stay here," Michael said, looking around the bird sanctuary building for the Aerie.

"Looks like." Carl glanced around the place for the umpteenth time. He'd be tempted to whistle in appreciation, but falconers sometimes used whistles as cues, and, well, there were a *lot* of birds in the building.

About half the size of the horse barn that also sat on the property, with bird enclosures instead of stalls, it lacked the majesty and gravitas of the Souk. But maybe that's because, in true American fashion, the "sport of kings" had been transformed into a "growth enterprise," and there was no room for gravitas when dealing with the sheer stinking practicality of shoving as many birds into one area as possible.

Even clean, the building reeked of predator poop.

And it *was* clean. The straw at the bottom of the wooden enclosures practically sparkled, and Carl wondered if it was changed more than once daily. The birds sat, hooded and mute, one bird per enclosure, making those sharp, minute movements that gave lie to the illusion that they were posed, frozen until roused. The fact that the enclosures were stacked, one on top of the other, in two column by two column formation, with walking space between the groups, made Carl think of a vast computer bank, with every twitch of a bird equivalent to a new data stream being transmitted through the barn.

"Not a friendly place, really," Carl muttered, keeping his voice down so as not to disturb the birds. There was plenty of activity in the place—at least one helper for every eight birds, he estimated, but they all moved gracefully and quietly between the cages as well.

Carl longed to take Michael to Qatar, if for nothing else but to see a place where birds were treated with mystery and reverence, not as cogs in some great machine.

The young, unsmiling man with the long, freckled face who greeted them as Michael dropped off the bird was hyperefficient, taking down their names and reservation number in his tablet and taking notes as to the bird's condition and requirements before he placed Michael's rescued falcon—none the worse for its stay in a shower cubicle surrounded by mattresses—in one of the guest mews. Those were made special by velveteen padding on the four-by-four posts. Carl was not impressed.

"So, the bird's name?" the young man inquired. His nametag said "Roger," and Carl wanted to laugh because he wasn't sure anybody in their twenties had been *named* Roger at this stage in the game.

"Uhm, Scooter?" Michael said, cocking his head at Carl.

"Yeah, I think that's what we decided on," Carl told him, keeping up the pretense that they planned to keep this bird. Michael hadn't wanted to name it because he felt like that would imply ownership. He'd told Carl on the plane that he considered himself as nothing but a stepping stone on the bird's journey to own the world again. Naming it felt inappropriate.

But they were expected to give it a name because they were masquerading as falcon hobbyists, and Scooter was as good a name as any. Also it was the name of Michael's hated older brother, which told Carl he was *really* not intending to keep the bird.

"So, Scooter," said Roger, sounding bored. "And do you know how long until its wing has healed?"

"He hasn't had any pain there for a couple of days," Michael replied, surprising Carl. He hadn't realized Michael had checked. "I would have taken the sleeve off before we left, but I know traveling would get him all riled up, and I didn't want him to hurt it again on the cage."

Roger made a notation in his tablet. "We have a certified veterinarian visit before the falconry classes. I'll have her give Scooter a sweep with the portable X-ray. If he's close to flight ready, it will make your training experience much more exciting."

"Sure," Michael said, sounding bemused. "That would be awesome."

Roger handed him a card. "I'm Roger Meyers-Bartlett. I'm your certified falconer, and if you have any questions about your animal or just want to check on it while it's boarded here, give me a call or a text. My job is to make sure your animal has as much fun at the winery as you do."

The words were excited, but the tone of voice not so much. That didn't matter, though. They were supposed to be a couple on a romantic getaway, which meant making small talk and presuming intimacies was completely allowed.

"Oh!" Carl gushed. "Roger Meyers-Bartlett. Are you any relation to the people who run the place?" He grinned, willing a dimple in his cheek to pop to life that he was pretty sure had never existed before.

"Calvin Meyers is my grandfather," Roger said, sounding bored and put upon. "And his son, Connor, married the daughter of my great-aunt Maisy's sister-in-law, who is married to her husband's brother. Her husband is Abel Bartlett."

Carl's eyes crossed. "I, uh, would need a genealogy chart—"

"Don't bother," Roger told him shortly, wrinkling his little pug nose. "It's a fucking nightmare. Frankly, birds are easier. You track which birds fucks which bird where, count the eggs, make a notation, and never let those eggs meet those birds again."

"That's for birds bred in captivity," Carl said. "Do you ever capture eggs in the wild? I know it's legal in some states."

Roger stared at him with undisguised horror. "Legal, yes, but you'd have to climb cliffs, and those people *kill* each other for undisturbed nests. No. Just… no. Captive breeding, you get the bird you want when you want it. So much easier." It was the most genuine thing Roger had said so far.

"Do you ever tinker with them?" Michael asked, his voice full of wonder and disingenuousness. "'Cause, you know, they're a fun animal, but wouldn't it be cool if you could make them not so *loud*!"

Roger looked around, making sure all his coworkers were engaged with things like ripping apart roadkill and cleaning up bird shit. "No," he said. "We don't do that here because—" He shuddered. "—bwah! But there are some *monster* birds that fly around here. I don't know where they come from, but they do *not* look like condors, and they are *definitely* not eagles. They go after our birds here, man. I watched three birds working in different parts of the winery get together to hunt in a squadron to ward off an attack from one of these assholes, and they barely escaped with their lives. And falcons are killing *machines*. So yeah. We wouldn't do it—not here. But somebody has, because *dude*!"

"Are they a nuisance?" Carl asked, sounding properly surprised. "Because I know *your* birds are bred and trained to keep pests away from the grapes. But something bigger than a regular falcon, wouldn't that be a danger to small livestock?"

"They're a danger to Labrador retrievers!" Roger yelped and then looked around again and kept his voice down. "But my boss—who is also my great uncle, and no, don't try to figure that out again—won't even let us take pictures of them. He says he's afraid the 'government people'"—he used air quotes—"will come shoot them or something. But I'm serious. If the government shoots those things down, it's because they're alien aircraft."

Roger stopped talking and took a step back, chest heaving and eyes shifting as though he realized he had gotten worked up about something he was not allowed to talk about.

"Anyway," he said, trying hard to adopt his regular bored tone, "genetic manipulation of predatory birds is frowned upon in falconry circles and outright illegal in many countries. It's bad for the environment." He gave a bland smile before turning away to dismiss them.

"Bad for the environment?" Michael said as they were walking away. "What about the Labrador retrievers?" And from the corner of his eye, Carl could see Roger Meyers-Bartlett nodding in wholehearted agreement.


CHUCK WAS planning to fly back to the bird conservancy around six, so Carl and Michael had a couple of hours to kill. On the one hand, Carl was tempted to go back to the Residence Inn and try a repeat of that morning, but his sense of responsibility wouldn't let him. Instead they drove back to Napa and stopped for ice cream. Then they went to the local grocery store for a few staples, followed by a trip to the hardware store for better gloves for Michael to use with the bird and to the local feed store for two pairs of coveralls. Finally they got gas for the rental car and sodas.

And with every stop, the two of them struck up random conversations with the locals, talking about the weather, the sky, the mountains on the near horizon, and, oh hey, lookit that bird!

The reports were grim from nearly every quarter.

From missing chickens to a missing Chihuahua—and a couple of very rattled house cats—to two small-plane crashes nearby in which the survivors had *sworn* that giant birds had flown purposefully for the windows of the aircraft, pretty much everyone in town had a story about the "big bird problem."

Carl documented every incident on his phone, sending the notes to Torrance Grayson when they were done.

"I don't get it," Michael said, slurping his soda appreciatively as Carl drove the rental Hunter had provided after they'd landed. "If these birds were engineered in Mexico, what in the hell are they doing raising so much ruckus here?"

Carl had wondered when someone would ask that question.

"They were engineered *for* somebody here," he said thoughtfully. "That would have put a few birds in Mexico for Mandy to find— prototypes and extras—and hence that photo op in San Diego that was the file from Serpentus—and then the rest were shipped to the places the birds were intended." He gave a humorless snort of laughter. "What was it Mandy had said? A chinchilla farm in France?" He paused. "That *was* in her notes, right? A chinchilla farm in France." He grunted and pulled out his phone. "Here, text Stirling. Have him tag Leon di Rossi and tell him some of the birds might have been sent overseas."

"Why's that important?" Michael asked, taking his phone and doing as he was asked.

"Because if Leon can confirm it, that's our in at the DOI. That's international. It *must* be reported. And that means Serpentus isn't only subject to US laws, which are frequently not as strict."

Michael finished and then set the phone down and picked up his giant soda again. "You sure do seem excited about nailing your company," he said thoughtfully.

Carl grunted. "Fourteen years of carefully nursed grudges," he conceded. "They make a good cover—and they do make people a lot of money—but they are not really on the side of good."

Michael chuckled. "If you manage to sic the Department of the Interior on them, I'm pretty sure your gig with them is over."

"Whatever." Carl realized that with every risk assessment he'd made, whether for Felix, for Michael, or for himself, about what would happen if he was caught by Serpentus, he had made his peace with the fact that he had better things to do with his life. He glanced at Michael, drinking from a swimming-pool-sized plastic cup and looking out into the rolling hills and cultivated wineries of the Napa countryside, and thought God, he was sweet. Excited. Happy like a little kid, capable and emotionally vulnerable like an adult. Wherever Carl landed, he wanted to be the guy who made Michael Carmody happy.

And that would be so much easier to do if he threw his much-loathed employer to the wolves.

WHEN THEY reached the airstrip, Chuck was leaning against the little plane, a small knapsack over his shoulder. "We raided your room, and I have an extra change of skivvies and some sweats for you," he said, nodding at Michael.

Carl held up a bag from one of their stops. "And we got you coveralls," he said. "I figured nobody here brought their shitty clothes for fixing cars."

Chuck grinned. "Wow. Way to think ahead. I am impressed." He looked over to where Lucius was approaching, looking as casual as Lucius ever got in khakis and a button-down, the wind in his hair and the sun at his back. Trust Chuck to fall in love with a guy who looked like he should be on the cover of *James Bond Magazine*, even when on assignment.

"There's bedding in the plane," he said as he drew near. "I understand the couch and love seat aren't comfortable in the house. And Hunter ordered more supplies, including clothes for the young people after meeting them this morning. And cage lights. Wasn't that something you said you'd need?"

"Yeah, Scotty Brice," Chuck said with a wink. "Now come here and gimme a kiss before I take this bird up and fly away from you."

Carl ignored them as they said their brief goodbyes and turned to Michael, troubled. "I am not happy about this," he said, looking to where the sun had sunk below the hills. The day was still bright around them, but the long shadows were casting a chill.

"It's a good plan," Michael said. "We can drive the Cherokee back, Mandy gets supplies, and you stay and work on information. You gotta admit, it plays to my strengths." He smiled brightly, and Carl wrapped his arms around those slender shoulders and held him tight.

"I love you. That's not going away," he said after a moment.

"Good," Michael mumbled, relaxing completely. "Me too. I mean neither. I mean, I love you, and it's not going away."

Carl kissed the top of his head, and then, when Michael raised his face, Carl kissed his lips, gently at first and then with some passion.

They parted with a sigh, and Carl nodded to Chuck as he lowered the stairs. "You two take care of yourselves," he said.

"You worry about yourself," Chuck said. "We got the monster birds—you got monster people somewhere. I'll have him at the Aerie before dinner tomorrow."

"Fair enough," Carl said, waving.

He was still troubled as he and Lucius watched them take off, though, and Lucius asked him what he was thinking.

"I'm thinking we need to see a family tree of the Meyers-Bartlett clan," he said, remembering Roger the bird caretaker. "And we need to see finances on the Aerie, which I can't believe we didn't think of before."

"We've missed Danny and Felix on this one," Lucius told him. "They are, in a word, brilliant at this sort of thing."

"Yeah, well, we need to be brilliant too if we're going to crack this." Carl grimaced. "You going back to Jesses and Jewels?" he asked.

"Yes, why?"

"Because we spent hours today asking the locals about giant birds, and we got a lot of great answers. Maybe you can ask the locals about the Meyers-Bartlett clan and see what you get in terms of history. I'm thinking local legend might have more in it than the computer at this point, and it would be a shame to let that pass."

"I think you're right." Lucius grinned. "And you know, if we clear this case early, we might have time to actually, you know, vacation. Right?"

Carl laughed a little. "I think if we clear it early, we don't tell Julia and Leon, and give them a chance to do exactly that."

"You have a devious mind, my friend, that is belied by your awesome stolidity."

Carl snorted. "And you are a good match for Chuck's bullshit. Drive safe, Lucius, and seriously, watch out for the fuckin' birds. They seem to be everywhere."


WHEN HE got back to the hotel, Carl dropped all his purchases in his room, almost disappointed to see room service had visited. He would have rather liked to have returned to a scene of debauchery, with rumpled sheets and towels on the floor, just to remember the sheer joy of having Michael in his arms like that, free and unafraid.

He didn't linger on the feeling, no matter how much he wanted to. The conversation with Roger Meyers-Bartlett had exacerbated that itch he had every time he thought about the happy, smiling Meyers clan. He'd once had a case of poison ivy as a kid, and his mother hadn't been the "Oh, baby, have some calamine" sort of mom. The rash had spread to his neck, his back, his ears—God, even his asscrack—before the school nurse had taken pity on him.

This sensation of knowing that he *knew* the final link in this picture, the thing that connected the birds to the company, the company to the location, the location to Matteo di Rossi's senseless death and Mandy's current situation—it burned as bad as untreated, festering, chafing poison ivy.

Except Michael was out there in Murder Bird Central, trying to trick out a Jeep Cherokee to help make sure everybody involved in this mess was all right, and that made it burn worse.

He grabbed his secure laptop and went next door to Stirling's room, wanting the company and knowing there were very few situations in which Stirling couldn't help.

Torrance was there too, dressed casually in yoga pants and sitting cross-legged on one of the beds while Stirling worked at the desk. They both looked up as Carl entered.

"Welcome to Research Central," Torrance said with a grin. "Where I am taking all of those good leads you sent me an hour ago and running with them."

"Excellent," Carl returned. "Stirling, what are you working on?"

"Hacking the DOI to see if they knew about this beforehand and are just playing dumb. And checking out your friend Tamara Charter to see if we can trust her with our info."

"What's the consensus?" Carl asked.

Stirling held his hand up and tilted it. "Maybe?"

Carl grunted. That hadn't been what he'd expected to hear. "Why maybe?"

"For one thing she's been there through two administrations, one of them not particularly friendly to the environment. That takes some political maneuvering right there. And for another, her record of action regarding wildlife is iffy—but part of that could be, again, the people she was working for. Shit rolls downhill, and so does blame. For all we know, the reason things weren't worse was that she was there working with the environmentalists trying to protect the environment. But then, she could have been straddling the line between the planet killers and the next administration."

"She seemed so solid," Carl said, thinking to himself. "And after watching Ginger lose it, go psycho on me, it was a relief, I guess, to trust someone up the food chain."

Stirling cocked his head, temporarily distracted when he was usually a single-minded entity in front of the computer.

"That's not… in character," he said at last. "You usually seem to act so independently. Independent of your job, independent of Felix and Danny. You've spent your entire life as an outsider. Why would you trust somebody now?"

Carl swallowed, suddenly feeling naked and seen when it was true—but while he'd been the outsider, he'd also been trying to be the quiet boy in the principal's office, safe and invisible and secretly in the know.

"Because it's the environment," he said after a moment. "We want to think that there's a grown-up in charge."

Stirling nodded, face grave. "What do we do if there's not?" he asked after a moment. "What do we do if the reason Ginger freaked out so bad was because she knew Charter was bad news?"

Torrance chimed in, not even looking up from his research. "Expose Charter, send evidence to the head of the DOI, keep Ginger out of it."

"And if it's Ginger?" Carl asked, suddenly desperate for that grown-up, even if it was in the guise of a slick news-tuber in sweats and a hoodie.

Torrance stopped clicking. "What made you think it was Ginger in the first place?"

Carl thought about it. "Because she's high up in the company— and loyal. And I've had to work around her a couple of times to do the right thing. Instead of changing the company's culture or trying to look at something besides the bottom line, she would rather toe the line, and covering up genetically engineered predators sounds like something Serpentus would do."

"But would they order the birds made?" Torrance asked.

"No."

That came out before he could think about it or censor it, and once again he had to stop and analyze where the instinct came from.

"Not out of any sense of decency," he said after a moment. "Out of a sense of liability. They could look into the viability of hiring falcons to protect their interests. That makes sense: environmentally friendly, good PR, lots of potential. They'd have to insure the birds, insure the property, insure the handlers—so much money to be made. But creating the birds illegally? They have interests all over the world, including Mexico. Doing that put them potentially at odds with a foreign country. Mexico has laws. They're different from ours, but there are still regulations. The company itself, with all its corruption and venality, won't go out and actually seek ways to break the law. So they'll cover up the consequences...." He thought of Matteo di Rossi's tragic death.

"But they won't set the whole thing into action," Torrance said thoughtfully. "You're looking for someone who had a vested interest in this area, because I've run queries, and these birds are localized here. I think your boyfriend was right. This is sideways because it's personal. Whoever is behind it has a personal connection."

Carl nodded, missing Michael but enjoying hearing him referred to as "your boyfriend." He'd never really had that. It implied continuity, a long relationship—permanence.

"We haven't really run Ginger's or Tamara's personal backgrounds," he mused, remembering his conversation with Lucius. "Or the Meyers clan's financials. You know, I think it's time to do that."

"What do we want?" Stirling asked.

"Any connection to here," Carl replied smartly. "These are people I met a long way from Napa Valley. Let's see if either one of them is a long way from home."

The answer, when it came, was simple... and frightening. And as Carl suspected, it had its roots in that happy, smiling, freckle-faced family that had so captured his attention.

Torrance, Stirling, and Carl all looked at the side-by-side yearbook pictures on the computer screen and whistled.

"They look different now," Carl said, looking at the green eyes, the round cheeks, and the teeth with the braces. "But I can see it. Particularly around the eyes."

"What are you going to do?" Stirling asked, gnawing his lip.

"What do you mean what am I going to do?"

"These two women want to kill you!" Stirling exclaimed. "You can't check into the scary family hotel when the spawn want you dead!"

Carl kept his arms crossed and shook his head. "Only one of them," he said. "We still don't know which one. And we don't know if they really want me dead. We just know they're related. Sort of."

Napa wasn't that big a place, it turned out. In the same way Roger Meyers-Bartlett was related to the falconers and the vintners, Ginger Carson was the grandchild of Deanna and Calvin Meyers, and Tamara Charter was Calvin's niece and Ginger's cousin.

Either one of them had motive. Either one of them had means. Both of them wielded power. But which one had wielded it to cover up for family? Which one had known about Matteo di Rossi's death?

Or had both?

"But they *know* you!" Stirling protested, and Carl smiled soothingly at the younger man.

"It's okay, Stirling. What do they know? They know that I'm on vacation. That's no big deal. They know I was asking about Matteo di Rossi. They don't know what I know. And there's no reason for either one of them to be here! They're both based in Washington, DC, remember? No, we do the same thing we were planning on doing yesterday. I check in at three with all the luggage, Michael gets there in time for dinner, and we poke around and see what's what."

"I don't like this," Stirling muttered.

"Don't like what?" Molly asked, swinging into the room. "Torrance, get off my bed."

"Fine," Torrance grumbled. "Carl, can I use your bed?"

"Michael might eat your balls for breakfast," Molly said. "But sure. You do that."

Torrance thought consideringly. "He's small. I could take him."

"He grew up being beat on by his brothers, Scooter and Angus," Carl said. "Something tells me he's a lot more dangerous than he looks."

"If you're not going to get off, at least let me lie down," Molly complained, flopping backward onto the bed. "There. Work around me. And tell me why Stirling looks like he's been sucking lemons."

"You know both of Carl's handy sources?" Stirling asked bitterly. "Turns out, they both have ties to the place where the bad birds might be coming from."

Molly popped up. "Show me pictures." She looked at the computer screen and scowled. "*Current* pictures. Don't test me here, guys. I'm telling you, I have been fending off redneck hands on my ass all day. These guys think that all they have to do is drive a truck and the rest of the work falls to me. Just because I take tickets, I'm also responsible for resetting cones and fueling the vehicles and filling the tires and every other damned thing that needs to be done when it says in my contract that none of that bullshit is my job. It's theirs. I hate them, I hate you, and I hate everybody with a penis right now. So if you're telling me that these two women want to hurt Carl, you need to tell me what they look like so I can rip their eyebrows off."

"Even though Carl has a penis?" Stirling asked. "We assume."

"Michael told us himself it was bigger than a lightbulb," Molly retorted. "Now show me pictures." She paused. "The women, not Carl's penis. Ew."

While Stirling pulled up current photos and Carl ignored the part about "Ew," Torrance said, "And by the way, about the financials on the winery?"

"Yeah?" Carl was more than interested.

"About six years ago, they reported a massive loss. Almost their entire growing season was devastated by a flock of starlings. The falcons were overwhelmed. Apparently it was a bumper crop year for the invasive little beasties, and a lot of wineries took a hit. It was written off once as an act of God, but after that, the insurance company changed the policy."

"Typical." Carl could have predicted it. "So that makes sense. The family business is going under, their usual methods dealing with pest control aren't working, and they get desperate."

"But they're luckier than most," Torrance murmured, drumming his thumbs on his knees. "Because *they* have an in. Somebody in their family has contacts. They can breed a better pest-control predator."

"And they do," Stirling added, still typing. "They breed wonderful predators in Mexico, because the local labs won't do anything like that."

Carl smiled at him, liking the way the young man had begun to relax into the thought flow that seemed to rebound so easily throughout the crew. "And somehow, Matteo di Rossi stumbles on the project. He's doing his own breeding—except he's using a nearby lab, probably because there are falcons and falconers also nearby and readily available genetic material for the bustards." He thought for a moment. "There had to be testing of the bustards and their meat. You wouldn't want your genetically tweaked bustards to poison your falcons, would you?"

"Ooh…," Torrance muttered, just as Stirling said, "On it!"

"I like this kid," Torrance told him, his grin looking less professional and more "little boy with a toy." "He's very useful."

"He's the nephew I never knew I needed," Carl said dryly, earning a far more evil grin from Stirling before he went back to his keyboard. "So, Mandy is sent to Mexico to check out the suspected breeding of the predatory birds. But she and Matteo are lovers, and she's told Matteo everything. And Ginger Carson too. So when Matteo stumbles across the birds here, he knows what they are, and that they're bad. He's already scheduled and outfitted the trip to transport the bustard eggs to Africa. He and Mandy were going to reunite in Mexico after he transported the eggs cross-country. But somebody gets the significance of Mandy's trip to Mexico and Matteo's newfound knowledge and boom!"

They all let out a collective sigh.

"Literally boom," Molly said sadly. "Matteo into a cliff with a batch of soon-to-be baby bustards. And Mandy back here, hunting and trapping flying velociraptors with two special-needs teenagers to help."

Carl rubbed his mouth with his hand in thought. "Life's weird sometimes," he said after a moment. "You think you've managed to come to terms with chance and fateful cockup, and suddenly you're…." He smiled.

"In love with an ex-convict auto mechanic who wouldn't hurt a fly?" Molly ribbed.

"Yeah," Carl said, grinning at her. "That."

"Aw," Torrance said, at first sounding smarmy and ironic. Then he said, "Dammit! Why? Hunter, Chuck, you. What's wrong with me?"

"You're too good-looking," Stirling said dryly. "It's terrifying."

Torrance glared at him sourly, but the young man was still typing industriously away. "I'm not going to stop moisturizing to get a mate, if that's what you mean."

"Sure. That's the problem. Moisture."

Carl choked back a laugh. "Don't spar with him, Tor—he's sneaky and he cheats." Suddenly tired, he sank onto the bed *not* occupied by Torrance and Molly. "It's all here," he said. "We only need two things. The labs they both used so we can get confirmation, and whatever Matteo stumbled over. Who did he hear talking? What did he see happening?

What tipped him off to the connection between what Mandy was investigating and something terrible and illegal going on in his vicinity?"

"Uhm, guys?" Stirling said, sounding supremely unhappy. "I've—well, I've got one of the things, but it's not going to help."

Once again, there was a gathering around Stirling's computer.

"Aw, dammit," Carl muttered. "I'm going to sit down again." Dimly, in the back of his mind, he remembered Mandy saying something about this, and he cursed himself for not taking notes.

"Yeah," Molly said with a yawn. "This was *not* worth getting up for." She sprawled on the other bed, but they both cast baleful glares at Stirling's computer, where a news story from five years ago was featured prominently. It detailed a fire at a local university lab, one that specialized in gene splicing and editing to protect crops and livestock. It was nearby, attached to the University of Davis, but closer to San Francisco. It would have been a perfect place for Matteo to get his bustard eggs and someone from the Meyers enclave to attempt to engineer falcon eggs—or send a request and be denied. But there was obviously no proof.

Stirling was right. He'd found one of the things, but it wasn't going to help.

"All the records?" Carl asked, making sure.

"The server was at the lab," Stirling confirmed. "It happened the day after Matteo died. If he hadn't been killed in another state, somebody might have made the connection."

"Do you have a list of employees?" Torrance asked, making Carl glad they'd grabbed him and begged him to help.

"I do not," Stirling said, grunting. "And that's worrisome. It indicates that someone has wiped this off the university server. So yes. Between killing Matteo and burning down the lab and making sure nobody could track down any employees, we are facing somebody extremely smart."

"Dammit!" Carl muttered. "It should *not* be that easy to hide a link to illegal birds that are eating the family dog!"

Suddenly Molly, who had been sprawled on the bed with her arm over her eyes, sat up. "I'm the dumbest bitch in the history of dumb bitches," she said, and every man in the room turned toward her in shock.

"I... uhm, Molly?" Stirling sputtered.

"No. This is unconscionable. I can't believe this. There I am, working my ass off as a clerk and part-time mechanic in this penny-ante enterprise, and I have completely forgotten what I'm there for."

"You're there to get a bead on the truck that helped run Matteo off the road," Carl said. He stopped. "Hey, whoever is running the Meyers/Bartlett financials, see if you can find a sale or insurance claim on a *fast car* that could have herded Matteo toward the monster truck before he got run into the cliff."

"Sure," Torrance said. "After Molly's done talking, because right now my brains are scrambled by that first thing."

"You don't get it," Molly said. "I'm looking at the trucks. That's *all* I'm looking at. But you know what I'm *not* looking at? I'm not looking at the *outbuildings* that are a good football field beyond the track and the stadium. What was it Danny said? 'I wonder what the birds think of the noise?'"

"Yes," Carl muttered, slowly getting it.

"Well, what if they're *drowned out* by the noise. Because there's *never* a time in that area where there's not an engine going and it's not loud and awful. My ears are still ringing, and I left an hour ago. A lot of the guys wear ear protection, and that even makes it better. You said Mandy had captured a couple of the monster birds, right?"

"Yeah," Carl said, his blood thrumming, much as it had when Roger Meyers-Bartlett had mentioned the Labrador retriever.

"What if they have birds too? We have two days off after every race. What if that's when they let them out to fly, to do the predator thing."

Carl caught his breath. "You know, the mews we visited today were very… mass produced. And that bothered me. They were very clinical, very clean, very much for public consumption. What if that's on purpose? The Bartletts fly the public falcons, make a big deal about using them for the winery, but—"

"But two days a week they fly the big ones: let them exercise, steal stock, harry small children." Torrance sounded almost salaciously excited by that idea, and Carl had to shake his head.

"Sure," he said, "but why risk it? Why not just destroy them? I mean, it's heartless, yes, but they've committed cold-blooded murder already. What's destroying a couple of super scary birds that could ruin their reputation, their business?"

Torrance shrugged. "Well, maybe for the same reason they were created in the first place—they still needed the predator."

Carl nodded decisively. "Yeah, we should definitely check out the buildings. How big would you say they are, sweetheart?"

"A couple of them are toolshed or pump-house sized, but one of them is as big as a good-sized horse barn," Molly responded. She was staring into space, obviously visualizing the area.

Carl thought about the horse barn that housed the "recreational" falcons and nodded. "That sounds about right," he admitted. "Are they guarded?"

"No," Molly said thoughtfully. "But the only people I've seen go in there are clan, you know? Etni, his older brothers, their parents or aunts and uncles. There's no parts or anything related to the trucks in them. They're far enough away that I think people forget about them, treat them like part of the winery itself."

Carl nodded. "Good. Think anyone will be out there tonight?"

Molly frowned. "Like, *tonight* tonight?"

"Yeah. I want to take a look out there before we check in to the hotel. If they don't have birds, we can rule them out and concentrate on the main falconry business." He rubbed his stomach, remembering the day he'd helped Stirling hack Serpentus. "I've got a gut feeling about this, though," he said. "I think it's worth checking out. Isn't there a rally tomorrow night?"

"Yeah," Molly said. "Lights, noise, a crowd—I mean, you probably could still sneak out there, but tonight I'm pretty sure the area's empty."

Carl yawned. "Okay, everyone. I'm going down for a nap, then grabbing some dinner. I'm thinking of driving out there around eleven, long after anybody tending stock would be in the area. I can go myself, or ask Hunter or—"

"I'm in," Torrance said.

"I'll get Hunter to come with you," Stirling said.

Carl grimaced. "You know, if Torrance is coming, give Hunter his night with Grace. We don't need to bother them."

"Can I come?" Molly begged.

Everyone in the room snapped, *"No!"*

"If this doesn't pan out and we get caught, Molly, you would have lost a valuable cover."

"So will you!" she protested.

"Yeah, but I'm the only one here who's seen these monsters before," Carl replied reasonably. "I know the difference between a velociraptor and a condor and a vulture. It's not always easy to spot."

Molly's brows lowered, and it looked like she was going to argue, but he had an ace up his sleeve.

"I also know Ginger *and* Tamara. I can send out a signal flare to the company and get everyone involved if shit gets dire. And while they're dealing with that, you can still be working on the monster-truck angle. Trust me—this is for the best."

She shook her head, eyes narrowed. "Yeah, fine. But I'm breaking the wrist of the next cowboy in a giant gas-powered penis who grabs my ass."

"I wouldn't have it any other way," Carl replied gravely. Then he frowned. "Do they all do that?"

Molly shrugged. "Some of them are okay. Etni—I mentioned him? He's okay."

"Etni?"

"Yeah, whatever. It's California. Anyway, he's sweet. A little sad. Perfect gentleman. Scares the other guys off me. But yeah, lot of rednecks who like my ass in jeans."

"Feel free to hurt those people, sweetheart," Carl told her seriously. Maybe because she was the lone girl surrounded by gay uncles, but the rule was that nobody touched Molly. "Now I'm going down for that nap. I've got a king-size bed, and I swear I don't snore. Anybody want to join me? I promise I will leave your ass unmolested. Michael will never know you were there."

Torrance yawned. "I'll take you up on that," he said. "And I'll come with you tonight."

"And I'll sleep here," Molly said happily, burrowing into the bed she'd co-opted. "Stirling, you're on for ordering takeout before everything closes."

"Deal," he said, yawning himself. "Naps all around. Everybody break."

# Fortune's Rescue

MICHAEL HAD forgotten how easy Chuck was to work with. And how much fun. Now that the sex thing was off the table and that pit of loneliness that had been eating Michael alive all that time ago had been filled, Michael could enjoy his bullshit and swear along with him almost in concert.

And together the two of them, fueled by lots of iced tea and lemonade brought out by the two kids who thought they were super interesting and fun to watch, made good time tricking out the Cherokee so it could get through the rough rocks and forested terrain that sat between them and the wineries.

"You know," Chuck said, his head under the hood, "after taking a look at that so-called road, I'm fairly impressed Carl got this thing out here, and even more impressed he had the good sense not to take the same road back."

Michael shuddered. He was working from under the car—easier for him to fit because he was small—but that terrifying floating feeling of the wheels spinning in thin air while Carl used momentum and prayer to get them over the washed-out part of the road wouldn't leave him alone.

"I know, but I gotta tell you, I thought he had more sense than that when we hooked up."

The sounds of Chuck's wrench abruptly stopped.

"You're not having second thoughts, are you?" he asked anxiously, peering down at Michael through the gaps in the engine block.

"No!" Heaven forbid. "God no!" Michael took a breath and checked his work. Seeing that the part they'd just replaced was securely bolted to the chassis, he stopped to think about the question. "It's just… it's funny. How you think you're looking for one thing your whole life, and then it turns out you're looking for something completely different."

"What'd you think you were looking for?" Chuck asked curiously.

"Someone to keep me safe," Michael answered. He'd said it over and over again; it was why he'd thought he was so attracted to Carl.

Chuck grunted. "As I could not do."

"That's not what I'm talking about." Michael shot himself out from under the Cherokee, partly because he was ready for a break and partly because he didn't want Chuck to feel this anymore. "You did what you did *to* keep me safe. And that's what I *am* talking about. Because Carl wasn't trying to keep me safe when we came over that road. He was trying to fix things. And he didn't weenie out because I was with him. He assumed—and rightly so—that I would be more interested in fixing a wrong than I would be in freaking out about a little bit of washed-out road. But he's not a daredevil. He'll stop when it's too rough. And he's not a thrill-junkie like some people I know."

Chuck gave a bit of a wolfish smile. "You're welcome."

"It's well earned," Michael said with dignity. "But that's the thing. Carl's like me. He wants to fix a thing, and he just keeps working on it until it's fixed. And he'll go sideways if he has to and over and around, but he'll get it done. I mean, I'm not proud of picking up that gun, and I'm really not proud of walking into that bank, but I wanted to keep my family from getting thrown out on the street, and I couldn't see any other options. And that's the thing about Carl. He *could* see the other option. I don't know what it would have been, and I bet you don't know either, but Carl would have. And I think that's why I love him. 'Cause he don't give up, and 'cause he thinks I'm an equal, and 'cause he keeps his promises and does his best. He's not brilliant like all them kids that hang out at the Salinger place—and I gotta tell you, Felix, Danny, and Julia are fuckin' *terrifyin'*—but he just keeps working to find the best possible solution. You gotta admit it, Chuck. The world's pretty fucked up. A man that can see the good and the beauty and keep walkin' toward it? And wants to hold your hand while he's goin'? That's gotta be a man you'd follow."

"It is," Chuck agreed. He'd stood by now and wiped his fingers off on a spare rag on the tool bench they'd set up in the garage. "But I think the safe thing helps."

Michael gave a shy smile. "It's a perk," he agreed.

Chuck nodded. "I know I'm with who *I'm* supposed to be with. But you two seem to belong together, and that makes me happy."

Michael chuckled. "You know, it's funny. I know you think you're the big slutty one, but Carl seems to have tapped a few himself, right?"

"He has!" Chuck laughed. "But nobody saw him like you do, I think. There was always the assumption that he was too stolid. Too boring."

"He's not," Michael said. He dropped his voice. "Have you ever heard him talk about art?"

"No, I have not." Chuck gestured for him to go on.

"It was like *love poetry*," Michael told him. "I swear to God, it gave me a *boner* just hearing him."

"Passion," Chuck said, his eyes going far away. "What you're talking about is passion. Which people confuse with lust, but it's not."

"No, it's not." Michael drained the last of his tea. "Passion's got feeling. Heart feeling. And you think, 'If this guy has this heart feeling for a statue or a piece of art—'"

"Or a company, or a cause," Chuck said, his mind obviously on his own boyfriend.

"Yeah. Something important. You think if he's got this heart for that, what could he have for me?"

They met eyes then, and all traces of their former relationship were gone, drowned in the deluge of feeling they had for the people they were with now.

"And if he's got that feeling for you," Chuck added softly, "you'd follow him to the ends of the earth. You'd die for him. Because you know that's special there, and only a fool throws that away."

"We're smarter'n we sound," Michael said, thinking Chuck's Texas had come out a lot in their conversation.

"We're smarter'n anybody ever thought we could be," Chuck agreed, seeming to snap to the present. "We know when to hold on to someone good."

They had a quiet moment in the lengthening shadows of the late September afternoon, and then Michael set his empty glass down.

"You ready to do the other side now?" he asked. They were halfway there.

"Damned straight."

THEY KEPT working.

Mandy and the kids brought them out a tray of food—hamburgers and tater tots—and Michael and Chuck thanked both the kids profusely.

Sunny said, "You're welcome!" with a lot of enthusiasm, and Harry nodded and smiled. After Mandy shooed them away back to the house, she turned to them.

"How's it going?" she said. "Also, thank you. Not just for the supplies but for being nice to the kids. I was afraid, you know? All the new people in and out. But you've all been really kind."

"Apparently being nice to kids is my thing," Michael told her seriously, and Chuck laughed.

"He's got three of his own," he said. "And you're welcome. As for how it's going?" He grimaced and held his hand out, wobbling it from side to side.

"Some good, some bad?" she guessed.

They'd started the engine and driven it about five feet before some of their bodywork failed, and they'd had to hook it up to a winch and drag it back into the barn to jack the damned thing up and see if they could weld it back together.

"Another two hours," Michael surmised. "I want to get it done tonight so we can double-check it in the morning before we take off."

"You do know we're only about an hour overland from where you're supposed to be tomorrow, right?" Chuck asked. "I know it took you three, four hours to get here, but the way back is *way* more direct."

Michael glared at him sourly. He'd figured that out from the short plane ride.

"Yeah," he said, rubbing his stomach. "I just... I got an antsy feeling. They can't text us, and Carl and the others have had a lot of time to go investigating. I just...."

Chuck sucked air in through his teeth. "Yeah. That group of people could get into a lot of trouble without us."

"I am sayin'."

"So yeah," Chuck said to Mandy. "Give us a couple of hours out here—"

He was interrupted by a scream from one of the birds. The beasties had done that periodically, not enough to get on their last nerve, but enough to thoroughly scare the shit out of them once they thought the birds had settled down.

The scream was followed by the unmistakable sound of a hard beak trying to tear through the metal Mandy had used to reenforce the big cage.

They all stopped for a moment and swallowed. Even Mandy, who should have been used to that sound by now but obviously wasn't.

"Urgency," she said tersely. "I can feel it too." She blew out a breath. "Okay, then. I was going to invite you in for dessert, but I'll bring some cookies out here for you."

"That's a kindness, Miss Mandy," Chuck said, his Texas coming out like it did for women. Michael couldn't even roll his eyes because he knew Chuck only did it to make them feel comfortable around his tall, broad-shouldered frame. Carl didn't have that same easiness, but he did have sincerity, and that seemed to count for something.

"If you could listen for the telephone?" Michael asked fretfully. "I know they can't text us or call us, but if they call *you* at least, we'll know what's going down."

"Why don't you go in and call?" Chuck asked. "Since we're taking a break. Get my sweatshirt from my duffel while you're in there—it's getting chilly out here."

"Good idea," Michael said. "That way you don't have to bring the cookies out to us," he told Mandy with a smile. She smiled back, and together they trooped in while Chuck resumed work on the Cherokee.

When he got to the living room, he used a clean rag to hold the phone receiver while he dialed Carl's number. When he got shunted off to voicemail, he frowned and called Stirling instead.

"Michael?" Stirling asked, obviously recognizing the number from earlier.

"Yessir. Just checking in. Carl's not answering."

Stirling made an unhappy sound. "No. He and Torrance went to check on some outbuildings by the monster-truck arena. Molly spotted them, and we thought if the Meyerses and Bartletts *had* engineered the velociraptors, that would be a good place to keep them."

Michael felt his eyes go big. "So they've got a lead and they just *left*? Without backup? What about Hunter? Shouldn't Hunter be with them?"

The silence on the other end of the phone was not encouraging.

"He should be," Stirling said thoughtfully. "They told me to let him and Grace have a night, but I may have to call him."

"*Ya think!*" That roiling in the pit of Michael's stomach had gotten way worse.

"Okay," Stirling said, decision in his voice, "I'll call Hunter. Thank you. I'll get off the phone now. Don't worry. We'll call you if anything happens."

Michael opened his mouth to say, "Sure," while not meaning it at all when the line went dead.

"Fucking fantastic," he muttered to himself.

"Anything wrong?" Mandy asked, coming in from the kitchen with a box of Oreos and a plastic pitcher filled with milk.

"My boyfriend is dumber than a box of hammers," Michael muttered unfairly. "And if he gets himself killed after promising me the world, I'm gonna hunt him down in hell and drag him back by the hair."

"Okay, then," Mandy said, eyes big.

Michael shook himself. "Sorry," he said before taking a deep breath and holding his hands out. "Go ahead and hand those over. Chuck and I are going to need some sugar if we're going to get that thing ready in time to go bail Carl out of the fucking fire."

"I'll bring glasses," she said with a sigh. "But you know, give Carl some credit. He used to do dangerous stuff all the time when I knew him. Made it look easy, like crossing the street."

Michael shook his head, so irritated he couldn't even meet her gaze. "In my part of Texas, those are the people we call road waffles," he said before stalking out to give Chuck the bad news.

AT ONE in the morning, they were still working, and Mandy came out of the house, dressed in sweats with an old plaid robe around her shoulders.

"Guys?" she said uncertainly. "There was a phone call. Someone named Stirling said, 'Tell Chuck and Michael they've disappeared.'"

Michael barely avoided scraping his face on the underside of the car because he was on his way up before the wheeled dolly had gotten completely out from under the truck.

"They who?" he asked, at the same time Chuck said, "Hunter too?"

"He didn't say," Mandy told them. "He sounded sort of freaked out, and there was a girl in the background hollering something about calling their uncle—"

Without another word, Chuck took off running for the living room while Michael tried to assess the situation.

"And one more thing," Mandy said, causing Michael to focus his eyes on her pale face.

"I don't even want to know."

"He said, 'They found the bird cages, but some of the birds were gone. Do not, repeat, do not let Chuck and Michael fly back.'" She swallowed. "Because that was my first thought too."

Michael cocked his head at her. "Oh, this is bad," he said.

She nodded. "Even I know that."


## MEANWHILE…

The outbuildings had looked small and forgotten beyond the monster-truck arena, the lack of streetlamps and anything but the ambient illumination from the faraway city setting them like tiny teacakes iced in silver starlight.

Carl and Torrance followed the service road past the arena and on toward the largest building—a barn, like Molly had told them—and probably painted tan in the daylight.

That in itself was odd. The grapes were watered regularly, but the outlying pastureland and fallow fields were not. The surrounding rural areas tended to be grasslands before the rains kicked in around October, so tan barns sort of faded into the landscape.

These three buildings were meant to hide in plain sight.

Carl followed the gravel service road behind the largest one so they couldn't be seen from the main track to the arena, and killed the engine.

"Well," Torrance said next to him, "this isn't spooky *at all.*"

Carl grimaced. "It's a little unsupervised, yes," he said. He pulled out his phone to check the charge and grimaced. "A little more supervised than we'd planned." Although they didn't have service out here, much like they hadn't at Mandy's, the text had come in while he and Torrance had been en route, as well as a phone call from Mandy's number. He sighed. He couldn't answer Michael now, but the other thing he had to acknowledge.

"Hunter just told us to sit tight and wait for him and Grace."

"Why? Doesn't he trust us?"

Carl shook his head. "I don't even know how he found out. Whatever." He blew out a breath. "I'm not waiting. This isn't supposed to be a party. I just want to see what's in there, that's all. If it's nothing, there's no sense in all of us trespassing for bupkes, you know?"

Torrance slanted him a canny reporter's look in the dim light. "You don't think it's bupkes," he said.

Carl shook his head. "No. I should have known when I saw Mandy's caged birds. The only way for them to be *here* instead of where they were bred would be if they were shipped here. Some of them flew away, and Mandy caught them. Some of them—and God knows why—have been trained like falcons and used. I'm not sure—"

Whatever he meant to say was cut off by a scream like shattered glass, only louder, so sharp it felt like it should have torn the metal siding of Torrance's rented SUV.

Carl's bowels froze, and he and Torrance met eyes.

"Visual confirmation," Carl said roughly. "Pictures."

Torrance nodded hard, once, and shuddered. "We're going to need them," he said. "Nobody's gonna believe this without pictures."

Together they slid out of the SUV and walked toward the small door on the side of the barn. Carl reached into the back pocket of his jeans and pulled out his lock-picking kit, which was, as far as gifts went, the best and most important thing Danny Lightfingers had ever given him. He paused as they neared the door, and nodded toward the two cameras he saw, one on each corner of the building.

Torrance pulled out a handy little gizmo that flashed as he pushed a button, and the green lights on each camera went out completely.

"Jammer," Carl murmured. "Very nice. Think it worked on the alarm?"

"It didn't need to," Grace said, emerging from the far end of the building, the side facing the mountains instead of the road. "Because I disabled the cameras on the other side and the alarm from the pump house, which houses the generator that feeds all this shit. The hell are you two doing out here without us?"

"Did you hear the bird scream?" Carl asked, getting busy with his lockpicks.

"Yeah. Not sure my balls are going to drop for at least a week after that."

Carl shuddered, almost dropping the secondary pick but keeping hold of it out of sheer desperation. Grace was so very good at this, but he really didn't want to be shown up. "Mine are pretty much lodged under my sternum. We need some shots of the birds," he said, keeping his voice down. "One or both of my contacts might be corrupt, so Torrance needs something independent he can use to raise a stink." He thought of Stirling's comments about how there weren't any grownups coming to their rescue. "We have to assume we're on our own."

Grace grunted, and just when Carl thought he was going to start giving Carl shit about being slow, Carl felt the give in the padlock that would let them in.

Still moving quietly—and using the sleeve of his hooded sweatshirt to wipe off the lock—he undid the door and slid in, counting on the others to follow him.

He wasn't disappointed.

The barn opened up like a vault. Giant aviary-sized cages stretched nearly from wall to wall, with a three-foot space on each end for caretaker passage and eight feet between.

Carl glanced around, seeing the security lights that should have been on sensors. Normally, this much movement would have meant illuminating the entire place, and he was grateful for Grace and Hunter's interference.

But he wasn't willing to leave without getting what they'd come for.

"They're not all full," Torrance murmured in his ear, and Carl nodded. About half the cages were open. They had fresh water—and fresh bone piles—inside, so Carl assumed the cages were occupied but....

"They really must be handled and flown," Carl murmured. "Get footage of the ones still here."

It made sense. There were six cages altogether, and three of them were empty. Somewhere out in the night, three falconers wearing cast-iron jockey shorts were probably hefting twenty-pound birds up in the air to go get prey.

And they were apparently okay with what those birds might be coming back with to eat.

Torrance grunted and walked toward the other end of the barn, a sudden flare of light indicating a handheld light source to help him film. Not subtle, no, but if he could escape with that footage on his camera, they had something to use as leverage and proof that this fantastical crime was taking place under the nose of every agency supposed to help the environment.

Carl wandered to the far side of the barn, where he realized that each cage had a corresponding trapdoor opening on the side of the building. The ground next to the foundation had been dug out by about six feet, the better to give a large bird room to take flight before landing. He got it. The side with the human-sized door was for humans. The side with the six-foot-wide trapdoors were for birds. Again—hidden from the arena.

Carl wondered how often the birds were let out to hunt.

He was staring out one of the open trapdoors when he sensed movement in the direction he and the others had come from. He looked up to see Hunter sliding in, silky as a shadow, and breathed a sigh of relief.

He may have resented Stirling's call to Hunter and Grace behind his back, but he apparently felt a lot safer with the two of them here, didn't he?

And then they all heard the loud, unapologetic "*braap-braap-braap-braap*" as a car bigger than it was supposed to be, with a tricked-out exhaust system and way too much torque, approached from the road.

"Someone's here," Carl said quietly, knowing the sound would travel. Their cars may have been hidden slightly by the angle from the outbuildings, but they weren't invisible. Anybody coming out to the barn would see they were there.

Everybody nodded grimly, and Carl's brain went into overdrive.

"Hunter," he said sharply, "get Torrance out of here. Grace, go with him!"

Hunter grunted. "Grace, in the rafters. Torrance, with me!"

He and Torrance sprinted for the human-sized door, and Carl stood to the side and looked out the trapdoor toward the arena.

"Monster truck and SUV," he said. "Two vehicles at least. Take the SUV overland now!"

"Why aren't we going, Mr. Suit Man?" Grace hissed from right over Carl's head. Carl glanced up, unsurprised to see Grace hugging the rafter, all but invisible in the dim light and certainly not easy to spot if you didn't know someone was there.

"Because they've probably seen our car," Carl said bitterly. "Wherever you guys are parked, it couldn't be seen from the road. If they catch us here, we give the others a better chance at escaping." He glared upward. "But you were *supposed to go with them*."

Grace let out an exasperated breath. "No," he said smugly, and they both heard the quiet vroom as Hunter's SUV engine opened up and tore out of there.

"Shit," Carl muttered. "If I really wanted to be a diversion, I'd find some way of turning the lights on."

"Hm…," Grace murmured. "Downside to doing my job too well. We could always let loose a bird."

"So it could rip my face off?" Carl said, just as one of the monstrous birds let out another cry. Carl looked in their direction, taking them in again, and realized they were hooded, with jesses that were tied to their perching posts, which were made of wide-diameter dowels.

"Wait right there," Grace said, and before Carl could make sense of what he was seeing, Grace ran lightly across one of the beams suspended near the roof of the barn and stopped when he came to the corner, where Carl could see the cables for the outside and inside lights were joined through a small hole in the barn and then secured down the side, tucked up against one of the visible support beams.

Working quickly with a tiny set of electricians tools and lockpicks, Grace pulled out an even tinier flashlight and removed the battery, and then jimmy-rigged the battery to one of the stripped cables.

A beam of light from the sensor illuminated half of the barn, and Carl would wager it did the same thing outside.

Then, without even preening, Grace ran lightly across the beam again, took his perch in the darkest corner of the barn, and crouched there, invisible.

"Don't say a word," Grace warned him. "You go be all noble and captured, and I'll make sure our guys know where you are."

Carl nodded. He'd figured. "You stay out of sight," he cautioned. God, better him than any of the kids.

Better him than Michael.

Quickly he pulled his phone from his pocket and texted, *Love you— pretty sure I'll see you soon*, thinking that if whoever came through that door transported him outside this particular service blackout, Michael would get the text when he needed it.

After that, there wasn't much to do besides lean up against the trapdoor and try to look nonchalant when the door burst open.

Carl took his time, unsurprised at the first figure who strode in. The young man behind her was a stranger, but he would imagine Molly would recognize him as one of the many Meyers/Bartlett younger generation members. He was wearing jeans, a denim jacket, and a "People Eater" hat featuring a stylized truck on the front, so odds were good he was one of the drivers or mechanics from the monster-truck enterprise that had hidden this entire cache of illegal birds from plain sight.

The two people—obviously related, now that he saw them together—both had freckles, green eyes, and reddish hair.

Although much of Ginger Carson's came from a bottle these days, he guessed, because it had probably gone brown as she'd aged.

He shifted on purpose so they'd see him, and waved.

"Carl?" she asked, sounding shocked.

"Ginger," he said, not surprised in the least. He'd had it right the first time. She'd been the one in on it. Tamara may have helped the family cover it up, but Carl didn't think it was her idea.

"What are you doing here?" she asked, still shocked.

"I could ask you the same question," he said. "I mean, I know why *I'm* here, but last I knew, you were in DC."

Her eyes hardened. "My family needed me," she said in obvious evasion. "That doesn't explain—"

"They needed you to do what, Ginger?" He was busted, dammit, and he wanted some answers. "To come hide your mess?"

She stiffened. "This isn't *my* mess. The damned starlings were killing us, you understand? And did the government help? No. The Small Business Administration wanted us to give all our profits—plus sell a big chunk of land—to help recoup our losses. And everybody knows those fuckers take two or three years to pay out. We didn't have that long. My parents would have had to give up land our family has held for generations."

"So," Carl said with a swallow, "yada, yada, yada, you Frankensteined some giant birds together and let them ravage the ecosystem?"

Ginger gave a sniff. "Now you sound like Tamara." Her eyes narrowed. "Did that bitch put you up to this? I swear to Christ, listening to her whine about the environment almost sent me over the edge last time."

"We wouldn't want you to be responsible for murder, now, would we?" he asked acidly, and to her credit, Ginger looked away. Tamara had known about it, he realized, but she hadn't *liked* it. He got it now. If Carl investigated and then alerted her agency, she could move in and right the wrong. But until somebody besides her family contacted her, she was caught, trapped between family duty and duty to her job.

Like Michael had said—sideways.

"That… you don't understand," Ginger said, her eyes flickering to the young man who'd come in after her. He was stalking restlessly around the cages, looking for someone else in the shadows. The barn itself was clean, with a concrete floor and plenty of straw in the enclosures; if Grace hadn't killed most of the lights, there wouldn't be many corners to look in, and Carl felt sweat pop out on his forehead in an effort to not dart his eyes to Grace in his hiding place like Ginger had just looked at her brother.

And that quickly, he got it. Things went sideways because of family. "You hadn't planned to kill anybody," he said, his voice softening. "Sure, you'd kill the entire ecosystem to save the family business, but that was desperation talking. You weren't planning to kill Matteo di Rossi. In fact"—her eyes, wide and green and, at first hard, had softened now, and her lower lip quivered—"you were trying to stop him."

She looked over her shoulder to where the young man—in his early twenties now—looked away.

"Your brother?" he asked softly. Molly had said there were a couple of Meyers-Bartlett clan boys working at the monster-truck franchise. She hadn't been able to keep them straight, and the noise, he thought, would have made her job even harder. But if it was this one, this kid, he would have been in his teens, maybe sixteen? Seventeen? Not very old when he'd been party to driving Matteo di Rossi into a cliff.

"He didn't mean to," she said, her voice shaking. "Matteo had a test flock of bustards near the lab," she said. "We hadn't built the barn yet. Abel and Maisy hadn't figured out how to handle the dragons—"

Carl let out a surprise bark of laughter. "You call them dragons?"

She gave him a stony look. "They carry off small sheep."

"Yeah, I know. I've been calling them velociraptors. 'Cause they're fucking terrifying. But go on. Maisy and Abel didn't know what to do with the giant fucking birds you had engineered in Mexico, and it was all Matteo's fault because he had a food supply?"

"No!" Her voice rose, and her brother turned away from the corner of the barn where Grace was crouched—thank God—and strode to where Carl and Ginger were speaking. Carl hadn't determined if either of them were armed yet, but he was betting that people who had to work with giant murder birds were prepared to defend themselves.

"He was just there," the boy said.

"Etni, no," Ginger said softly, putting her hand on the denim sleeve of the boy's jacket. Ah, Etni, of the original name and the sweet disposition, Carl thought. It was all falling into place.

Etni shook her off. "He was a nice guy and all, but he was there at the labs when someone brought a dragon in. They'd shot it in their backyard and… and the lab guys talked to Matteo because he knew about falcons. He'd seen the crates at our place. They said Birds and were really big. He put two and two together and then showed up at the house, asking Abel about the dragon at the lab, where it came from." Etni looked away. "He was supposed to leave the next morning, but when Abel told him to go fish, he said he'd be back."

"And you knew where he was going," Carl deduced. "You knew his route through the desert."

Etni shrugged. "He was a nice guy," he said. "Had lots of time for someone who ain't never been out of Napa. Said I reminded him of his nephew."

Carl felt anger and grief welling up. "I've met his nephew. He misses the shit out of his Uncle Matteo."

Etni swallowed, and Carl's chest hurt.

"Etni didn't mean to," Ginger said pleadingly. "He… see, I found out he'd taken the truck to go head Matteo off, and I was going to catch up to him and explain and—"

And Carl could see it now. So clearly. "And it really was an accident," he said, bitterness lacing his voice, dripping to the floor. And then anger again. "But you made it worse," he told Ginger. "You used the company's research contacts to make the birds, so it was easy to use those same contacts to cover it up, to destroy Matteo's itinerary, to exile Mandy—"

"I don't know what happened to Mandy," she retorted. "She'd left by then. I…." She let out a little whimper. "She and Matteo had been so happy. I thought maybe she'd just disappeared to grieve."

The words hung in the air, and Carl's stomach growled again as he realized he'd damned near given away Mandy's vulnerable position. No, Ginger and Etni hadn't committed cold-blooded murder *yet*, but with everything hanging in the balance, people had a tendency to double down. Right now, while he had an ally watching who would report back to his backup, he had to find out how far they'd be willing to go.

"Maybe she did," he said, voice hard. "But that's not where I'm going."

And with that, he headed for the door.

He didn't see a gun or other weapon in their hands, but they must have had something, because as soon as he cleared Etni, the searing pain smacked the back of his head, his knees gave way, and he crashed to the cement floor of the barn.

HE CAME to on a cold, hard floor in a very familiarly shaped enclosure, with the barest hint of gray morning light seeping through tiny sandwich-plate-shaped windows.

A plane? He was on board a cargo plane?

His head gave a mighty throb, and he tried not to vomit. He was on board a cargo plane with a concussion.

And someone was messing with his hands, which were secured tightly behind his back. He started to wriggle, and Grace whispered harshly in his ear.

"Stop it, suit-guy. I'm almost through."

The rough loops of rope binding his wrists burst, and his shoulder came forward in a flash of entirely new pain. "How long," he gasped as Grace went to work on his ankles, "was I out?"

"Couple of hours," Grace murmured. "There was about an hour of 'What do we do now?' along with, 'I don't know, Etni, you clocked him!' and then there was tying up and dragging you to the back of her SUV." He chuckled. "Etni followed in the giant truck. Riding in the back of that thing sucked. I'll be coughing exhaust for a month. You're welcome."

"Thank you," Carl said sincerely, waiting until Grace stepped back to wiggle his feet. The wash of fire and pain was anticipated—but not welcome. "Where's everybody now?"

"Ginger and Etni—is that his name? Anyway, they're in the control tower trying to bribe the guy bringing planes in to tell them when Leon di Rossi gets here. Apparently they got wind of him flying to Napa, and that's why Ginger caught the red-eye, to beat him."

Carl grimaced. "So she tracked Leon. God, that was bothering me. It makes sense. She's going to try to convince him it wasn't her, maybe try to blame Mandy. So, what's the plan?"

Grace shrugged. "We, uhm, get out of the plane, sneak around like thieves, and catch a ride back to the hotel?"

"We can't do that. We have to *stop* them somehow!"

Grace stared at him nonplussed. "Because why?"

"Because if that kid doesn't see some sort of owning up to what he and his sister did, Leon di Rossi only has one option," Carl said harshly. "He can't afford to let an insult like this toward his brother go. He's worked for the last six years to fix his name, his reputation, save his kids—we can't let him flush that down the toilet!"

Grace blinked golden eyes at him. "This is why you wear a suit, right?"

"Yes, Grace, this is why I wear a suit." He looked down at his scuffed jeans and tennis shoes. "Usually." With a grunt, he pulled his aching pins-and-needles-on-fire feet underneath him and pushed up to stand, leaning heavily on the sloped side of the plane. "If you can lower the steps, I can get the fuck out of here," he said, and in short order, he was stumbling after Grace across the tarmac and toward the small tower in the same airfield Hunter had landed them in.

"Do you think Hunter knows where we are?" he asked as they ran past the dozen or so planes parked in the corner of the airfield that Ginger was apparently going to taxi out of.

In response, a black-clad arm snaked out from behind the tail of the Cessna they were passing and pulled Carl into an awkward crouch by the wheels.

"Hunter!" Grace said happily, going in for a kiss. "You found us!"

Hunter scowled at him—after the brief kiss. "Yes, I found you. I tracked your phone. Did you think to *text* me, moron? I thought you'd been *captured*!"

Grace smiled at him happily. "I was in the back of the monster truck. It was like riding a giant smelly vibrator. I didn't think I could text."

Hunter worked hard to school his expression. "You didn't want to *drop* your phone and have it break," he said, eyes narrowed.

"I totally could have held on to it, especially when he went skidding over the off-road part. So easy. At no time did I bounce up into his line of sight, only saved from discovery by the fact he was trying not to drive us into a ditch."

Hunter's eyes got big, and Carl's chest went cold.

"We need to not tell Josh that," Carl rasped.

Hunter shivered and pulled Grace in for a solid one-armed hug. "No. We need to tell Josh that. And Danny. And Felix and Julia. Holy God."

Carl gave them a minute so Hunter could pull his shit together, and then the sense of urgency compelled them all. "Where is everybody?" he asked.

Hunter blew out a breath. "Stirling and Molly are at the hotel. Lucius is on his way out to meet Leon and Julia, so he should be here shortly because this is where they're coming." Hunter grimaced, and Carl's chest, which had just warmed up enough after his retroactive fear for Grace, went about a thousand degrees colder.

"Michael? Chuck?" he asked a little desperately.

"They... well, they're on their way," Hunter said. "Obviously not in a plane, because hey, somebody's flying giant velociraptors—"

"Dragons," Grace told him. "The bad guys call them dragons."

Hunter snorted. "That's stupid. There's no such thing as dragons. Velociraptors are real."

Carl squinted at him, tempted to try to parse what was wrong with those statements—and there were many things—but he concentrated on the important part.

"They're driving the Cherokee?" he asked. "Do they even know where we are?"

"I would imagine so," Hunter told him. "He called Stirling about an hour ago at sunrise and said they were ready to go. They needed directions. Stirling did something with your phone, and then there was more talking about where the dead spot in the coms ended and there's a reason Stirling does what Stirling does."

"He misses Josh," Carl said, remembering how busy he'd been and how tired. "What about Torrance?"

"Mr. TV?" Hunter snorted. "He's putting together a full-fledged— heh—segment. He says he just needs some live footage of the birds in flight and he's ready to go."

Carl scrubbed his face with his hands, trying to think. Go live. That would mean Serpentus would be completely exposed, and Carl would probably be out of a job.

Best news he'd heard all day.

But he had to make one phone call. With a grunt, he pulled his cell phone out of his back pocket, only to have Grace sniff in disgust.

"They left it on you?"

"They're not pros," he said, feeling for Grace. Grace was a far smarter criminal than either Ginger *or* Etni. With a sigh, and a glance toward the tower to see if Ginger or Etni were on their way out, he punched in Tamara Charter's phone number.

She must have known something was up, and thank God for the three-hour time difference because it was nine a.m. in DC.

"Carl?" she asked, sounding surprised.

"I'm in Napa," he said. "I know everything. We're about to blow it sky high. Ginger and Etni are going to need to face the music, but I don't think you did anything but cover it up for your family after the fact. If you want a chance to clean this mess up, you need to get out here now."

"Dammit!" she muttered. Then, after a weighted, almost emotional silence, she asked, "Why did you call me?"

He let out a breath. "You were, when all was said and done, trying to protect your family. Not your job—your family."

"Etni is Ginger's kid brother. My cousin. You have to believe I didn't know what they were doing until Ginger called me out there five years ago." Her voice broke. "Carl, what Leon di Rossi could do to that kid—"

"Is something you will force him into if you do not arrest Etni," Carl said harshly. "He's not a monster, Tamara. He's just like you. His family forced him into a tight spot, and he did what he had to in order to keep the youngest members safe. He can't be seen as weak, but if Etni owns up to what he's done and does some time, he won't be. Do you understand?"

"How do you know?" Tamara asked, but not harshly. More like she was begging for some hope.

"I've met Leon. He has children. We can come to an agreement, I'm sure," he said, hoping they weren't wrong, hoping Michael had been right. Family sent things sideways. But being the best person you could be so your kids would grow up proud—that was a powerful thing. It was what had attracted him to Danny and Felix, Julia and Josh, in the first place.

It's what had brought him back to them, and eventually back to Michael, and had given him a chance to do something with his life that was purposeful, not accidental, and that he was proud of.

"I'm trusting you," she said, her voice shaking. She sighed. "I'll be on the first plane out."

She hung up, and he checked the message he'd sent to Michael the night before to see if it had been received.

It had been—about half an hour ago, which meant they were close.

"Chuck and Michael are on their way," he said to Hunter and Grace. "And Tamara will be here in about six hours. But in the meantime, we're on our own."

"So," Hunter said, "what are we going to do?"

Carl stood up straight. Ginger and Etni had just strode out of the tower, looking upset and frightened, and Carl remembered how this all started when he, Hunter, Chuck, and Liam had gone to extreme measures to talk to someone about doing the right thing.

"You guys are going to stay hidden," he said, looking beyond the airfield toward the main road. "Lucius is going to join me in a few minutes, and we're going to talk to the enemy like human beings. When do Leon and Julia arrive?"

"About two hours from now."

"Maybe reverse that order—you stay hidden, and we try to have Leon and Julia talk to them," Carl said. He took a deep breath. "And you know, if these idiots pull guns, make sure I don't get shot."

With that, he went striding across the tarmac like his head wasn't going to pop right off his shoulders, and his shoulders weren't aching like a sonuvabitch, and like he could actually feel his feet.


*MEANWHILE...*

Mandy hadn't wanted to part with any of her shotguns, and having seen the murder birds in action, Chuck and Michael wouldn't have asked her to. But she did pull out a surprise friend for them to take on their trip.

"Is that a crossbow?" Chuck asked, handling the thing with sure—albeit inexpert—hands.

"Gimme that," Michael said, checking the angle of the sight bridge, the psi of the trigger, and the power of the spring on the latch. "You got bolts?" he asked. The crossbow itself was smallish—the kind with the stock and trigger made to look like a gun's—and he was relieved at the almost full quiver of shortish, sturdy wooden bolts. "Good," he muttered, almost to himself. "A metal bolt'll tear through a car. This, though, will pierce a wing and bring one of those things down if we need it."

"You're not afraid of bad guys?" Chuck asked. "Remember, it's family that made Carl disappear."

"Well, yeah. But this'll stop a man too, if I shoot it through a leg. I'm just sayin'. These can be more accurate if shot right, you know? I mean, I grew up hunting with crossbows and guns." He smiled tightly at Mandy. "Don't worry, hon. This is all we're gonna need."

"That and the last fuckin' weld to hold," Chuck muttered direly.

"And sandwiches and water," Mandy added, all practicality. "I've got the food in the fridge—help me grab the water for your trip."

Which was a nice sentiment, but Michael didn't know who that woman thought was going to eat. They'd worked pretty much through the night, with periodic updates from Stirling on the house phone. They'd finished about two hours before dawn, but Stirling had begged, telling them they knew where Carl was heading and they had eyes on him. Please, *please* wait until they had some daylight to traverse the rugged terrain through the woods and then through unpaved fields to the airstrip.

Then Chuck had mentioned goats and sheep and fences that might not be on Stirling's map, and Michael had given it up. His head hurt and his heart hurt and his knuckles ached like fire because he'd bashed them more than once as they'd been working.

But as Chuck had pointed out, he had more than Carl to think about: he had his kids, who had just gotten their father back and who would not be happy if anything happened to him now.

God, it was irritating when that man was right. But Michael figured this was the same thinking that had gotten him two years of prison instead of shot and a fortune in stolen money and legal investments to take care of his family instead of the heartache of knowing he'd left them destitute.

It wasn't comfortable thinking, but it sure did beat the consequences of not doing it.

They hadn't bothered with the bedding they'd brought—two hours didn't seem worth it. Chuck's alarm went off at five thirty, and the two of them rolled off the backbreaking couches, washed their faces, used their fingers on their teeth, and grabbed the granola bars Mandy offered them before they were pretty much out the door, crossbow and sandwiches in hand.

Then there was nothing to do but hold on to the oh-shit bar and pray for deliverance, because once Chuck Calder got behind the wheel of a vehicle, not even Satan himself could get between Chuck and his goal.

That didn't mean the terrain wasn't fierce, though. They'd raised the suspension and made it independent, each wheel with its own spring, and they'd reinforced the chassis and put on tractor wheels, so the damned thing could get them over rocks and down gullies, over downed trees and around the slalom of upright soldiers that had survived several years of heartbreaking forest fire. At one point Chuck hit the gas, and the Cherokee bounced so high Michael couldn't tell where the deer trail was beneath them, and they hit so hard, all four wheels jouncing at a different time, that he thought he knew how Carl must have felt when he'd landed that airplane the first time.

Michael didn't dare take his phone out, and he wasn't going to say a word to Chuck, who was scowling at the lightening terrain like he was reading code and didn't like the message God was sending him. All he could do was hold on to the chicken stick, close his eyes, and pray.

And he tried—he did. But all that came to him when he opened his mouth to ask God to get to where they were going in one piece was the look in Carl's eyes when he'd slid to the side after they'd made love and Michael was all dreamy and floaty and tender and happy.

Those eyes been wide and serious—pretty, because Carl's green eyes weren't ever going to not be pretty—but he'd been looking at Michael like he was precious and perfect and he wanted to make sure his touch had been worthy.

And all Michael could think of while he was hanging on for his life was that he'd never find another person who could look at him with that reverence in his pretty eyes, and please, oh please, God, don't let anything happen to that.

"CARL, GET in the plane!" Ginger almost shrieked, and Carl wasn't surprised to see the small-caliber pistol in her hand. He fingered the lump on the back of his head gingerly—he'd been out for hours after Etni had used that thing the first time. He imagined things would be even worse if she *shot* him with it.

"No," he said shortly. "And put that thing away. I've got friends watching you, and if you pull that trigger you'll have worse things to worry about than the police."

"Like what?" Etni asked, and now that it was daylight, Carl got a good look at his face. The kid really couldn't be more than twenty-one, twenty-two, but he looked thin, haunted, his big green eyes enormous in a pinched face. He'd been living with a murder and a death sentence over his head for the last five years, and nobody—probably not even Ginger—had known how to take it off his shoulders.

"Like you'll have nobody to talk to Leon di Rossi for you, to explain that you didn't mean to kill his little brother," Carl replied, looking at the kid steadily. "Di Rossi knows me, likes me, in fact. If I talk to him and *you* turn yourself in to the authorities and face some consequences, he might not have to kill you! But if you hurt *me*, well, di Rossi may like me, but his kids think my boyfriend walks on water. He'll already be pretty upset about his brother, but that'll ice his cake right there, you think?"

"I can't!" Etni moaned. "I can't go to prison. I... God, I can't. I'd rather die!"

"Etni, no!" Ginger turned to him, gun forgotten as she comforted the boy. "You'll survive. We can help you. You were a minor—I wasn't. You'll get a reduced sentence. You'll serve less time than I will!"

She swallowed, and Carl could see it hit her then, what her actions five years ago had cost them both. "I-I've been living with it for the last five years anyway," she said, her voice breaking a little.

For a moment, Carl had hope that the boy would give himself up, show contrition, and this would be easy, but then Etni's shoulders stiffened, and he backed slowly away.

"I can't," he said again, voice growing stronger. "I can't." And then he spun on his heel and took off running for the truck, shouting, "*I can't!*"

"He's fast," Carl said dispassionately, watching as those long legs ate up ground. The truck was maybe two hundred yards away, but the boy was getting there quickly, boots and all.

"All-State track in high school," Ginger said, a little hysterically. "Jesus, I've got to call my parents."

"Do they know?" Carl asked gently.

Ginger shook her head. "No." Her voice choked up. "They think the birds were legal. You're right. I used my connections at Serpentus to have them engineered—and the fire at the lab was a goddamned coincidence, I swear to Christ. Neither of us were even here then—we were still in Nevada screaming 'What are we gonna fucking do?'"

Carl blinked. Well—one mystery solved. But Ginger wasn't done with her half-sobbed confession.

"Maisy and Abel were ecstatic about being able to work with them, and my parents were so grateful." She gave a little snort. "Tamara isn't going to talk to me ever again, though. She was furious. Everything she believed in, and I shit all over it."

"She helped you, though," Carl said.

"She won't again." She paused, squinting, sounding lost. "Oh, look. Somebody's coming down the road."

Sure enough, just as Etni leaped into the truck, a luxury SUV—probably Lucius—turned off the main highway onto the narrow track toward the airfield.

"Where in the fuck does he think he's gonna go?" Hunter asked, drawing near Carl's side, Grace with him. He was obviously talking about Etni, who had the choice of either crashing into Lucius at this point or going overland.

"I've got no idea," Ginger said, wiping her face with her palms. "He's so scared. He's been so scared for five years. The family said, 'Help us, Ginger, we're going to go out of business!' and I dropped everything and came, and I fixed the problem. And then Matteo figured everything out and...." Her voice broke again. "And the accident. I swear to God it was an accident, Carl. I was trying to catch up with him, and Etni was supposed to head him off. We just wanted to explain, and... I don't know. But he was furious. All he could talk about when he tore out of the winery was the ecosystem and how invasive the birds could be, and when he saw I'd caught up with him in Nevada, he kept going faster, and I kept going faster, and Etni showed up and...."

Reluctantly Carl found himself putting an arm around her shoulders. He figured Michael would forgive him. "You're going to have to own up," he said, thinking about Mandy and the kids. "There are other people paying for your mess."

"No, seriously," Hunter said, getting their attention. "Where in the fuck does that kid think he's gonna go?"

Etni, whose impulse control had apparently not improved much in the last five years, had seen Lucius's SUV heading his way over the one available access road and taken off overland. There was nothing but bare stubble field as far as the eye could see, bisected by an irrigation ditch, and the view didn't change until the field ran right up to the base of a series of foothills covered in woodland.

"Does that thing have enough gas to even get to the trees?" Carl asked, and then he took another look at the trees. "Wait a minute." Something was emerging out there: a vehicle, coming from seemingly impassible terrain. Surprised, Carl stared at the pinpoint of metal and raised suspension, his suspicions of who that might be hammering at his chest.

"Do you think that's—"

"A souped-up Grand Cherokee driven by a bat out of hell?" Hunter supplied.

"It's like you know who's driving just by how insane it looks on the ground," Grace agreed. "I mean, that was fast. That was *epically* fast."

Carl pulled out his phone and was just about to punch in Michael's number when something else caught his eye, sweeping off the horizon, too small to be a plane, too big to be much else, going impossibly fast. A visceral shudder started behind his knees and swept past his thighs to his balls, then settled in the pit of his stomach, causing even his hands to shake.

"Jesus God," he said, even though he'd seen them up close and personal. "Are they all that big?"

"That's Brunhilda," Ginger told him, her voice soft with awe and a sort of affection. "She's the biggest. She *really* doesn't like the trucks. We put them out in that area for secrecy. It's the most outlying stretch of property we have. We didn't count on the effect all that noise would have on the birds."

Carl swallowed past a dryness in his throat as he watched Brunhilda—God, her wings must have spanned sixteen feet if they spanned an inch—sweep toward Etni's truck with what even an onlooker had to admit was malevolent purpose.

"His window is open," Ginger rasped. "He hates driving with it closed. There's an exhaust leak. He only does it for showtimes. Oh God, Etni, turn around!"

"Call him," Carl urged, only to be met by three "Are you stupid?" gazes.

"Loud. As. Fuck." Grace nodded his head for emphasis. "You can't talk to him. He's on his own."

They stood, helpless to do anything, watching as the prehistoric bird swept toward the monster truck and the souped-up Cherokee started a path to intercept. As Carl gazed into the distance, trying to figure out how deep the irrigation ditch was off to the side of Etni's truck—and how dangerous it might be—his phone started to buzz in his hand.

It was Michael.


"DO YOU want us to get this guy or not?" Michael shouted into the phone, watching the giant perversion of gas and metal jouncing its way overland. Monster trucks were not really off-road vehicles—they bounced too much, they made too much noise and let out too much exhaust to be legal in most wilderness areas. And while they could, indeed, just mow over a lot of obstacles, they could not maneuver for shit. Michael had, in fact, wondered at the wisdom of trying to run someone off the road with one; it seemed to him like that would take more dumb bad luck than evil intention.

Carl's voice—what he could hear of it—was a wee bit panicked for a guy watching all the action from nearly half a mile away. Yeah, Michael knew he was with that small knot of people by the airstrip. Stirling had given him Carl's phone-tracking code, and Michael had never been so grateful as when Carl's message from the night before had transmitted. Blessed, blessed technology, telling him his boyfriend was probably not dead.

"Don't hurt the idiot kid!" Carl hollered. "But don't let the bird get him either!"

"Bird?" Chuck asked. "Holy shit, do you see that irrigation ditch?"

"Maybe don't test the suspension out on that!" Michael warned. Loudly.

"I hear you. Did he say bird? Where the fuck is the bird?"

Michael was the small one in his family, which made what he was about to do sort of expected if you grew up with brothers like Angus and Scooter.

"Hold on a sec!" he shouted, dropping the phone and hitting the switch to roll down his window. "Let me see!" With that, he unbuckled his seat belt and reached into the back of the SUV for the crossbow and bolts.

The jouncing was particularly savage as he hauled himself one armed out the window of the SUV to perch on the door, and holding on to the crossbow wasn't easy. The wind stung his eyes, and he wrapped the seat belt around his ankle and up to his knees so he didn't fall out while wishing mightily for a helmet to protect his fragile noggin. Squinting, he raised his head to the horizon and spotted the raptor, heading straight for the window of the monster truck with—if Carl was right—an idiot kid behind the wheel.

He let go of the SUV frame to load the crossbow, relieved when he felt Chuck's strong hand wrapped around his ankle while he drove one-handed, the speed of the Cherokee unchanged.

Jesus, that man was fucking nuts.

While Michael was wrestling with the crossbow, the bird made its move, diving for the open window of the monster truck, screeching loud enough to be heard over the wind and the engine noise from this distance. The bird struck hard and wheeled, not getting tangled up with the window frame and shooting straight up in the air with mighty heaves of its vast and powerful wings.

The kid must have been either scared or hit, because the truck veered. Right toward the irrigation ditch. He was going fast enough for the front end to lift, almost like he was going to jump the maybe fifteen-foot span, but his foot must have slipped as he went, because instead of jumping the rift, the truck went nose first into the water with a splash.

Chuck slowed the Cherokee nice and easy, coming up alongside the ditch and braking, giving Michael the opportunity to scramble out of the window and get his feet on the ground. Both of them looked up in time to see the bird wheeling, wings outspread, eyeballing its target. From the ditch they heard a moan as the kid—and he *was* a kid— behind the wheel fell out his own open window and started flailing in the water.

"Shit," Chuck muttered. "That thing's heading right for him. He's bleeding."

"I'll get the bird," Michael said, eyes steady on his target as he took aim with the crossbow. "You get the kid."

He ignored Chuck then, figuring Chuck would know to trust Michael the way Michael had trusted him all that time ago when Michael set out to be arrested for a robbery he had no intention of committing. All he saw was the bird, the giant fucking bird, which had pulled its wings in enough to start a dive but had not yet committed enough to tuck them right against its body, creating a twenty-pound projectile with razors on one end.

Bird. Wing. Aim.

Breathe in. Let it out. Squeeze the trigger.

He heard Chuck telling the boy to calm down, Chuck was going to help him out of the damned ditch, right when the bird screamed, aborting its dive, a crossbow bolt lodged solidly through its wing.

Michael didn't take his eyes off the thing until it had flown in for a clumsy landing, about a football field away, and stood, disconsolate, holding its injured wing out and muttering in secret bird language about the fuckers on two legs with loud fucking trucks.

Once he saw the bird was safe—or rather, that the humans were safe from the bird—Michael dropped the crossbow inside the Cherokee and ran to the side of the irrigation ditch. He got to his knees to haul out the kid, who had big bleeding gashes on the left side of his face and his shoulder.

For a moment, it was all about heaving that kid like a sobbing, flopping fish out of the water so he could flop and sob about on the dry stubble of the field. When the kid was safe and not going anywhere, it was all about giving Chuck, who was six inches taller than Michael and outweighed him by a hundred pounds, the same sort of assist.

For a moment, Chuck and Michael sat on their knees in the stubble field, breathing hard and looking dazedly at each other.

"Kid?" Chuck said over the young man's mewling. "Do you have any idea why in the hell we did that?"

In the silence of the back field, without the hellific grinding of the two powerful engines and the roaring of the wind, they could hear him through his sobs.

"I'm the one who killed Matteo. It was me. It was my fault. And now Leon di Rossi's gonna kill me."

Chuck and Michael met eyes in relief.

"Oh thank God," Michael said. "At least you didn't just steal a car."

THE SILENCE in Hunter's SUV as Hunter piloted it over the stubble field was tense and deafening. Lucius was behind them; Hunter had fishtailed in front of him as he'd been about to turn into the airstrip, and Carl had waved him to follow from his open window. He wasn't sure if Lucius had *seen* Chuck's daring rescue, but he was pretty sure Lucius would expect Chuck to be the center of any trouble involving an automobile.

About two minutes into the ride, when he got tired of hearing his breath in his own ears, Carl heard his own voice from far away. "Did you see that?"

"I did," Hunter said.

"I got it on film," Grace said, and Carl did a slow pan to the back seat, where Hunter's boyfriend was looking at his phone with great enjoyment.

"Wow," he said, impressed. Then, while his synapses were functioning, he remembered, "You're sending it to Torrance, right?"

"I sent it to Stirling—does that count?"

Carl let out a breath and sagged against the seat. "Yeah. We just need it somewhere it can hit the airwaves. Torrance is editing his segment right now."

"Well, that's it," Ginger said, staring out the window hungrily to see if Etni was okay. "There goes my career, my life. I'm finished."

Carl didn't want to feel sympathy for her, but he did. Sideways. Family made you do things sideways. Maybe his greatest gift as an investigator had been the ability to see the sideways part. He hadn't had any of it growing up, had always been a solitary tree in his family's yard. He could see the connections that forged the art forgers, that bred the fear for a legacy, that made people commit crimes for their loved ones that they would not commit for themselves.

Since Danny, he'd always thought his greatest gift as a human had been his ability to balance the retribution with the need—and the harm. Ginger and her brother had done great harm. They would have to pay for that.

But they hadn't done it out of malice or entitlement, but out of desperation, and maybe that got Ginger some kindness at this moment, as all humans should be given.

"Your life's not over," he said softly. "Your career, yes. And I do see you doing time. But you'll have a good lawyer. Your family will still love you. And your heart is obviously here in this place. Maybe in the end, you'll get to come home and that will be enough."

Ginger let out a sound then. Not angry or bitter but full of grief, honest and real. "Maybe," she said. In the rearview mirrors, they could see that someone in the tiny tower had called first responders, probably when they'd seen the monster truck go into the ditch. Then, as though realizing something, she said, "Oh shit. I need to call Maisy and Abel to come get the bird."

She pulled out her cell phone and started talking, and Carl turned his head away from the tableau of Michael, Chuck, and Etni on the muddy bank of the irrigation ditch and saw the bird pacing fretfully with the bolt in its wing.

He smiled a little to himself. "Would you look at that. I think he wounded her on purpose, you know."

"Your boyfriend is batshit," Grace said disgustedly from behind them. "You assholes say *I'm* crazy!"

But Carl didn't think wounding the bird as opposed to killing it was crazy.

He thought it was very, very Michael.

Hunter came to a stop, and the lot of them flurried out of the SUV. Carl made a beeline for Michael, hauled him off the muddy ground and into his arms.

"You," he gasped, shaking, "scared the living shit out of me."

Michael's muffled chuckle against his chest was nothing short of miraculous. "Jesus, Carl, where the fuck did you go?"

Around them, Lucius was demanding an explanation from Chuck, Ginger was tending to her brother, and then the rescue squad arrived and the chaos was complete.

THE DEPUTY was a self-important man, a little on the short and round side, who had a way of squinting at everybody at the scene that told Carl at least that they were all foreigners on his turf.

"Miss Ginger?" he asked, eyeballing them suspiciously, "did these men try to hurt you or coerce you in any way?"

Across the crowd, Ginger met Carl's eyes with grim determination.

"They were bringing me to justice, Deputy Reyes. I think you should wait for my cousin to arrive to take their statement. In the meantime, Etni belongs in a hospital under guard, and I'll stay there with him, if you don't mind."

"Ginger?" Deputy Reyes looked at her, legitimately shocked, and she gazed back at him helplessly.

"I did a bad thing," she said, and to her credit she didn't cry or evade. "I did a very bad thing. And so did Etni. And it's time for us to face the music. But it needs to be a real atonement—I need it to go on record, not just with you, but with my company and with the county and state DA. There needs to be a full accounting. So if you don't mind, I'll accompany my brother to the hospital, but you need to put me under arrest, and him too. Handcuffs, Barney. I'm serious."

Reyes's eyes went red and shiny, and Carl could imagine him knowing her back when they were kids. "Jesus, Ginger, what did you do?"

"It's a long story," she said. "Wait for everyone." She looked at Carl. "The tower said their plane should land within the hour."

Carl nodded. "Well, then. Lucius, if you could greet them, explain things, and we can get Chuck and Michael to the hotel to get cleaned up?"

"You've got blood on the back of your head, Carl," Hunter said dryly. "I'm pretty sure that's you too."

That quickly, Carl's knees got wobbly and the world went a little dark. "Four hours, then," he rasped. "Somebody give this man the directions to the Residence Inn."

"Oh, Carl," Ginger said, her polish doing her well in this moment as she accepted the cuffs in the front. "If Barney will let me use the phone and you give us another hour, we can show you more hospitality than that."

So it was that a little before noon, Carl sat down with the sheriff, the DAs, and Tamara Charter in the private dining area of the Aerie and spun a fabric for them consisting a little of fact and a little of fiction. And Matteo di Rossi's death was finally put to rest.

# Old Ghosts Sleeping

MICHAEL HAD never been so proud of someone he knew as he was when he heard Carl spinning his web of sunshine and bullshit to the police in the sumptuous—*vacated*—eating area in the Aerie. Ginger *had* called her parents, and apparently Carl and Michael were still going to stay in the nice winery for a week, even though they'd wreaked havoc all over the family. Michael was grateful. The natural-cut wood tables with the thick layer of lacquer and the deep-cushioned chairs made the restaurant area his kind of place. The bay window opened up on a view of the winery—the pretty part, with stand upon stand of grapevines lined up in chaotic order for what was sure to be a stunner of a purple-and-gold sunset—and Michael had fantasies of him and Carl, seated and wearing their nice clothes, eating steak and drinking mineral water and saying sweet things to each other while looking out that window.

But first, Carl had to spin the bullshit.

"So you see," Carl said expansively, looking very legitimate in a sleekly cut gray suit that made his shoulders wide and his waist trim, "the birds were engineered and then transported to California. That's a crime, but as I understand it, Tamara, the Department of the Interior is going to be responsible for pressing charges?"

"Yes," she said, looking pale but composed. "Because I'm family—"

"Although you didn't know anything about this five years ago," Carl emphasized, and Tamara nodded, accepting the lie, albeit unhappily.

"No, I did not," she said, and she closed her eyes in a way that said she knew Ginger would lie for her and so would Etni and so would everybody else involved. She'd been dragged sideways by family—it didn't make her bad at her job. "But I am still recusing myself from the investigation. My cousins will definitely face charges: Ginger for trafficking exotic animals and manslaughter, Etni for second degree manslaughter." She looked at the state and county representatives of the

DA's office. "My office can assume those duties if you'd rather. We can hammer it out later."

Both reps—an older woman, close to retirement, who represented the county, and a young, fiery man of Mexican descent who was obviously ready to leave his mark on the state attorney's office—nodded.

"Since the crime took place in Nevada," said the state attorney's rep, "we'll have to talk to them—but yes, I think this all needs to fall under the same umbrella, and those charges seem to cover the bases." He paused, looking at her seriously. "We won't offer much in the way of leniency, you understand. The boy committed his crime as a minor, but your cousin—"

"Is prepared to accept a reasonable sentence," Tamara said, before compressing her mouth. "But that's all I have to say on the matter. As I told you, I'm recused."

All the law enforcement brass looked at Carl and Michael. "You two gentlemen have done us a service," Jorge Padilla told them. "But I think the rest of the discussion needs to take place between those of us here."

Understanding that they had been dismissed, Carl and Michael both rose, and Carl steered him through the dining room toward the entryway of the hotel itself.

"Where to next?" Michael asked, yawning. Dealing with the authorities had taken nearly three hours. After that, they had about enough time to shower—and for Michael to double-check that Carl had gotten the blood out of his shiny gold hair and to lament the gash that probably should have had stitches but was apparently going to close over the goose egg on the back of Carl's head without any help whatsoever. And then they'd changed, and Hunter had piloted them to the assigned meeting place, along with their clothes, so they could check in for their week.

Danny and Felix hadn't gotten *everything* from Stirling's harried, busy face-to-face call, but they'd insisted on that. Yes, the case may have been solved, but nobody—*nobody*—was coming home early.

As Michael asked the question, Hunter—who was slouching on the couch in the rust-and-green decorated foyer—popped up like someone had lit a fire under his ass.

"Next, we go meet Leon and Julia at Pensive. Don't worry. I think with this interview, you'll get food."

"Oh thank God," Carl muttered. His stomach growled loudly, and Michael checked his phone.

"It's only eleven in the morning, but I'm starving and exhausted," he said crankily. "It had better be some breakfast."

And it was.

Leon and Julia had apparently commissioned a full brunch for everybody upon their arrival, and the much more refined, delicate dining room was filled with the Salinger crew—Stirling, Molly, Lucius, Chuck, Torrance, Grace, Hunter, Michael, and Carl—and, on a computer that Leon di Rossi had propped up near the head of a banquet table—Felix, Danny, and Josh, who were all crowded into the picture on the monitor.

There was a lot of chatter and a lot of eating off one another's plates as people filled up from a buffet that included things like shrimp sandwiches on croissants and finely sliced strips of tenderloin served upon eggs made to order.

Finally, when everybody's plate was full and they'd sat at the table long enough to touch base—and to check to make sure the others were all right—Felix called the meeting to order.

"So," he said kindly, "I think Carl gets to start this one, and the rest of you need to wait until he's done to add your parts."

Carl took a bite of sandwich, swallowed, and then set it down regretfully. Michael resolved to have something boxed up for him before they left if he didn't get a chance to eat any more than that.

"So," he said, his voice clear and steady, in spite of the lines of weariness under his eyes, "allow me to tell you all a story about a winery with a long family tradition behind it and farm property that had been handed down for generations, and how it was all threatened by a freak crop of starlings that not even traditional falcons could take care of."

And with that, Carl spun the story again, but this time, it was complete and without embellishment. He talked about how Ginger had been called to the winery by her parents, desperate and hoping their daughter, with her connections to the insurance world, could find a way to keep their winery—and their legacy—safe. He told them how she'd first asked a nearby lab to create the birds, but they'd declined, and how she'd gone to Mexico and transported the birds back up to California, although one of the mating pairs had been bought by the now-deceased prince and released in Qatar, where they failed to breed and were hunted down before they did much damage. Even the prince's bustard virus had proved ineffective. Matteo may not have made it to Qatar with the virus-resistant bustards, but he'd sent his notes to the naturalists there, who had managed to save the population.

But that was incidental to what Leon di Rossi really wanted to know.

Carl told di Rossi that his brother had fallen in love with Mandy Jessup, and she had loved him back, and how he'd been in Napa to create a disease-resistant strain of bustard to replenish the population in Africa and to continue the long, proud tradition of falconry during the bustard migration that had united princes and kept the possibility of eventual peace alive in the Middle East.

He recounted how Matteo had stumbled upon Ginger's secret, and how Etni had taken the big truck—he'd found out from Tamara that it had been the only vehicle Etni had known how to drive at the time—to head Matteo off and try to talk to him about not reporting the birds. And how between his and Ginger's desperation, the unthinkable had happened.

"He was afraid of your reputation," Carl said near the end, looking Leon di Rossi in the eyes. "He'd looked your brother up and saw who you were. Your father's competitor had just died, and Etni was...." He grimaced.

Di Rossi nodded. "Afraid of getting blown up," he supplied bitterly.

"Indeed. So Ginger and Etni came back, and their family used the birds as they were intended, I think. But they're not tame animals. Falcons aren't as a whole, and there's no guarantee a falcon won't just decide to fuck off and desert their handler in a fit of pique. So the velociraptors—"

"Murder birds," Michael, Chuck, and Hunter all said in concert.

"Pterodactyls," Molly said primly.

"Dragons," Torrance added.

"Giant hybrid predators," Carl insisted, "didn't all stay in the same place. Mandy worked her way up from Mexico on the reports of the giant birds, and she found the little shoestring bird conservancy, and the last five years of her life have been grieving your brother and trying to control the by-blows of the giant Frankenstein bird experiment."

Leon blew out a breath. "That," he said after a moment, "is some tale. What happens now?"

Carl met Michael's eyes before answering di Rossi. Michael could tell this was the part he was worried about. "Ginger and Etni go to jail, sir. Ginger was quite firm about that. They've owned up and confessed to what they've done. Torrance's piece on the birds will go live tonight, and there will be no covering up what happened to your brother or why. And as for the birds? I think, short of destroying them all, and that may happen, although I rather hope they don't, this is the place for them to be. I think if Tamara's people can come in and make sure the animals don't spread—and don't harass local livestock—we can let the birds die out on their own. I got a chance to speak to Maisy and Abel Bartlett as they came out to get the bird Michael took down. The birds can be taught— and they can bond—but Maisy and Abel confirmed what Mandy told us about how the birds apparently age much faster than other birds of prey. They're showing signs of decline already. There's no reason they can't live out their lives and die, a footnote in history to be studied."

Di Rossi let out a sigh and nodded. "I can see your concern for your friends—"

"More like acquaintances," Carl said, with a sideways look at Michael that made Michael smile. "But it's more than that. Etni was young. And stupid. And he made a mistake. And a lot of us have done the same. He's going to do time, sir. Hard time. And it's not a picnic."

"I can vouch for that," Michael said softly, feeling like he had to stand up for the young man. "If you're thinking he's walking into a country club, sir, you're very much mistaken." He shuddered, and Carl clasped his hand before placing a gentle kiss on his temple. "There will be scars from prison," Michael continued bleakly. "He's not getting off easy."

Di Rossi nodded again. "You're asking me to let it be," he said, his voice devoid of tone.

"We are," Julia said, and it wasn't until Carl blinked several times, his eyes growing red-rimmed and shiny, that Michael realized how much this meant to him.

To them both.

"Indeed." Leon di Rossi gave a smile then that was nothing short of miraculous. "You all have trusted me with this—and given me closure, even knowing who I am and who I was. I am tempted to exact revenge. I cannot lie. I'm not a saint. I loved my brother very much. But you all have risked so much." His eyes sought out Carl and Michael before moving to Hunter, Grace, and Chuck. "You've risked your lives. And you gave me this information with the trust that I wouldn't abuse it." He nodded sincerely. "I will not." And then, probably without meaning to, he darted his eyes to Julia's. "Is that satisfactory?"

"You didn't promise not to harm them," she said without mercy. "Your brother got a second chance. Everybody around this table has gotten a second chance. It would seem the height of hypocrisy not to grant one to this young man."

Di Rossi let out a breath. "Since you need to hear the words, no, I will not harm them. I may even"—he grimaced—"have to protect the boy in prison, because I cannot say the same for some of my employees. But I'll make it clear he's protected. Is *that* enough?"

Like a little boy hoping for a cookie.

Julia didn't let him down. She granted him a warm smile and a graceful touch on his sleeve. "Thank you," she said, stately as queen. "It's good to know young Etni will have another chance to be a better man."

There was the quiet murmur of assent around the table, and then Josh's voice, rough but sound and alert, came over the computer.

"Are we all going to forget the fact that I've got footage of Michael hanging outside the window of an SUV while he aims a crossbow in the air? Is nobody going to tell me about that?"

"Oh, let *me* tell you about that," Chuck drawled, calling all attention to himself before launching into the grand tale of the Jeep Cherokee and the epic ride from the place that had no road.

Michael grinned, pleased to let Chuck tell the story, and surreptitiously handed Carl the rest of his sandwich.

"Eat," he said softly under the chatter from the table. "'Cause I have the feeling we're both gonna sleep through lunch."

Carl smiled, tired, but he tore into the sandwich. "You take good care of me," he said after a couple of bites.

"Good," Michael murmured. "I'd like that to be a permanent position."

"Me too," Carl said, and they glowed quietly at each other while they finished their breakfast and everybody's stories were told.


THEY DID eventually make it back to their room at the Aerie to sleep through lunch, as predicted. Michael woke first and rolled over to watch the big warm man in his bed take even breaths, in and out, for a few moments before he opened his eyes.

"Are you watching me sleep?" Carl asked muzzily.

"Yeah. It's probably a little creepy, huh?"

"Naw."

Carl had put on a soft gray T-shirt with his old college logo on it to sleep, and with his hair tousled, the sun coming in through the curtain over his shoulder igniting his blond hair like a halo, he looked young and a little defenseless. Michael reached out to brush his fingers over Carl's lips, just to remind him that they'd been together. They'd made love. Michael had been possessed by this amazing male body.

Carl kissed his fingers, and when Michael gasped, he slipped in a little tongue.

Michael bit his lip, smiling shyly when Carl rolled that wide-shouldered body over and covered his, moving from Michael's fingers to his mouth, taking him over, devouring him in a sure, gentle possession.

Michael didn't mind. He'd already given himself over, body and soul. The kiss was sweeping, possessive, grand, and they were both breathing hard when Carl pulled back a bit.

"Did I tell you," he asked breathily, "how scared I was, seeing you hang out of that window?"

"Chuck couldn't see the bird," Michael said, grimacing. "I couldn't get a good shot with the car moving, though."

Carl laughed softly. "Be careful with what's mine," he murmured before taking Michael's mouth again.

This time, Michael pulled back. "You're the one who got bonked on the head!" he protested, moving a tender hand to feather along the bump. "That was not cool! There I was, trying to trick out that fucking Cherokee, and you're knocked out and kidnapped?"

"I was fine," Carl told him with a quick peck on the lips.

"Were not," Michael grumbled before kissing him back.

"Grace had my back." This kiss was longer, harder, and Carl undulated his hips so his groin pressed up to Michael's. They were both growing hard by now, and the ache that started in Michael's balls, the need, was getting powerfully urgent.

"'S fine," Michael muttered. "Grace can have your back. As long as it gets you back to me."

This kiss kept going, on and on and on. Carl's hands skimmed Michael's flanks, his thighs, up his chest, and the next time he reared back, it was to haul Michael's T-shirt over his head, followed by his own.

Michael hummed, moving his palms along Carl's flat stomach, his chest, heavy with muscle, his solid biceps. "You look good in a suit," he said admiringly, "but you're even better without clothes."

"I'm gonna get fat in middle age," Carl warned.

Michael pushed up enough to capture his hard pink nipple with his lips. He sucked and played and pleasured until Carl tangled his fingers in Michael's hair and groaned.

"I'll let you fuck me then too," Michael teased, flicking out his tongue for one last taste.

"You want it?" Carl asked, pleased. He pushed Michael flat again and began the grand tour, kissing his way down Michael's sensitive stomach, stripping off his briefs. His tongue, dragging the length of Michael's cock, sent a shudder of hard want down Michael's spine.

"God yes."

Before they'd fallen into bed, Michael had deliberately placed the lubricant on the end table. He'd been making a statement, he knew, about what kind of vacation this would be. Sure, there'd be falconry lessons and wine tasting—for him—and a trip to the beach.

But he'd just gotten comfortable with Carl's hard, amazing body inside his, and he wanted more.

Carl engulfed his cock in one swallow, and Michael groaned and fumbled for the lube.

He wanted *much* more, and he wanted it *now.*

He grabbed the little bottle and pushed it against Carl's shoulder, moaning again as Carl sucked his way up Michael's length. Carl looked up, eyebrows raised, cock stretching his lips as he took the bottle.

"Yes," Michael hissed. "Yes, I want you to stretch me and fuck me. You broke me in, I'm yours, now ride me, dammit!"

Carl's low chuckle was even filthier because it rumbled around the head of Michael's cock.

He kept his mouth there, his tongue stroking, the suction hard, as he snicked the lid on the bottle and dumped slick on his fingers. Gently he slid two fingers in immediately, and the teeny bit of bite made Michael shudder.

"Oh *hell* yes! More!"

And again that filthy, arousing chuckle as he slid his fingers in and out, scissoring, stretching, getting Michael ready.

"Oh my God—oh!" Carl had bobbed his head down and up while thrusting in and out, and Michael almost came.

"Now!" he begged. "Now, now, now, now—oh God, Carl, please, now!" He spurted some then, and Carl pulled away and pulled his fingers out at the same time, leaving him hard and aching and needy while Carl shucked his own briefs and moved back to cover Michael's body with his own.

When Carl possessed his mouth with a hard kiss, Michael tasted his own precome on Carl's tongue and moaned. And then, before he could beg again—and he would have begged, he would have bent over the bed and pleaded—Carl's cock was big and thick, slicked up and ready, pushing gently against Michael's entrance.

Michael moaned and pushed back, welcoming Carl's thrust into his body with a sigh of completion.

Yes. Carl's cock, deep in his asshole, bursting at his skin—it was all he'd ever wanted, all he'd ever dreamed of in a lover, in a man in his bed, in a man in his *life*.

Carl rocked forward and back, thrusting, receding, and Michael lost himself in the motion. Thrusting like waves capping, pleasure surging in his loins, his heart—his ass! And then receding, giving him a chance to breathe, a chance to need, a chance to beg.

And again, and again, and again, and harder! Carl's head was thrown back, the cords in his neck tight, sweat trickling along the fair line of his hair on his forehead, and Michael's body tingled from hard use. Michael gibbered, incoherent, so close to the precipice, half afraid to go over, when Carl growled, "Come for me! C'mon, baby, *come*!"

That—*that* was all he needed. Carl's mouth crashed down on his, and he screamed his orgasm into their kiss, his entire body clenching into a knot that broke, sending them both flying and free into the void.

They came to, and Michael felt Carl's come trickling between his cheeks, down his thigh, and he smiled in a very animal pleasure.

He was full of his lover's come.

Carl was sprawled on top of him, trusting Michael's slender, wiry body to take his own massy weight, and Michael welcomed every pant of breath into his ear.

"Good," Carl gasped eventually.

"Great," he said softly. And that was all that was spoken for a while.

Finally Carl rolled off him, and with some scooting around, they were face-to-face again, like children under the sheets telling secrets, and Michael smiled at Carl's rumpled hair, the glaze around his lips, his hooded eyes. He didn't look innocent in sleep anymore. He looked replete and sexed up.

Michael found he liked that look.

They were just smiling into each other's eyes when Michael remembered a question he'd been meaning to ask.

"What was that?" he said. "That thing you were saying to Leon right before we left. You looked pretty serious."

Carl's eyes grew intense and focused. "We were talking about a gift," he said. "For you. He wanted to give you something for caring for his children, for being part of the adventure, for hanging out the window of a Jeep Cherokee to maybe shoot a bird with a crossbow."

Michael rolled his eyes. "Everybody else helped too."

"Yes, but you're special. What can I say? Chuck's probably going to get more suits, Hunter's going to get more weapons, nobody gives Grace anything, and Torrance is going to get more equipment. Di Rossi likes to give presents."

"What's he want to give me?"

Carl's smile was wicked. "A house."

Michael half sat up in bed before Carl nudged him down again. "A *what*?"

"I told him we'd been staying in the apartment in the city, but your job was really an hour or so outside at the airstrip. And you needed a house—probably in Glencoe, because, you know, family. Not mansion-sized, but big enough for three kids and a dog, with a yard and some play equipment and maybe some referrals for a nanny so you're set for when the kids come to visit." He looked very pleased with himself. "And, you know, an office for your big dumb boyfriend, and maybe a closet so he can keep his suits separate from your work clothes." Carl hadn't heard from Serpentus, but even if he did get fired, Michael had no doubt Carl's skills as an investigator would forever deem him a man in a suit.

Michael swallowed. The vision of a house in the suburbs where his kids could come live for part of the year and Carl could do his job when he wasn't traveling, and he could have a family, with extended family nearby, and a dog—oh God. It was everything he'd ever wanted, and Carl had just asked for it. For him. For Michael. And Michael wanted it to be complete.

"Will he be living with me?" he rasped hopefully. "The big dumb boyfriend with the suits? 'Cause it might be lonely without him."

"If you're ready for him," Carl whispered. "It's been quick, you know. Maybe you want me to stay in the apartment in the city some more and—"

Michael shook his head, his eyes burning as he stopped that noise with a kiss. He pulled back and tried not to sniffle. "We grow up fast in Texas," he said, trying to sound worldly and wise. "We make our decisions quick, and we live by them. I pretty much chose you after that first meeting. You smiled, shook my hand like an equal, and were kind to me, and I liked the look of you. And after a lifetime of not trusting my gut, I trusted it with you, and you turned out to be better than I could have imagined. I'm trusting it now. I'm trusting *us*. You and me, we're gonna live in that house, and my kids'll meet you over the computer, and it'll be fine. You'll see. We're gonna be just fine."

Carl nodded. "I'm taking your word on that," he said soberly. "I never thought of having a happily ever after or a family, not until you. You're the one who knows how to raise kids. You're the one who knows what a good family looks like. All I've got to go on are the Salingers, and they're a good example, but they're not stepkids and a house and a dog."

"All you gotta worry about is coming home to me," Michael told him. "You landed a plane with a few half-assed lessons and two assholes screaming at you from the cabin. You and me are gonna do okay."

With that he kissed Carl, quieting his doubts, his fears. He didn't want doubts and fears in their bed, not now. Not when he could see it all so clearly, the future of his dreams. Carl returned the kiss, and Michael knew that, while it might not be smooth sailing all the time, Carl was right there with him.

They worked just fine apart, but they were so much better together. Michael thought he would make it his goal to see they were together as often as possible.

And life couldn't get much better than that.


THAT NIGHT, they really *did* see the sunset over the winery, but not from the dining room.

When they'd awakened from their sleep, there had been a message on the phone to report to the falcon mews as soon as they were able. The vet had some exciting news for them.

Roger Meyers-Bartlett was there, along with a smiling woman around Carl's age with a few gray streaks in her long black hair and crinkles in the corners of her eyes. She introduced herself as Dr. Saunders, an avian specialist, and took them to the falcon mews to see "Scooter," the falcon Michael had named after one of his irritating do-nothing brothers.

Scooter, apparently, was ready to hit the skies again, and Michael and Carl were in a conundrum.

"Now," Dr. Saunders said, "I know you told Roger that you'd planned to fly this falcon and train him, but I also understand that might have been sort of a… uhm…."

"Ruse?" Carl suggested.

"Flat-out lie," Michael supplied. "We were going to use Tom Cade's method of introducing him into the wild."

"That's very sound—and very humane," Dr. Saunders said kindly. "And in fact, Maisy and Abel have landings across the property. Do you see them?"

She turned and pointed to the three platforms, each one higher up than the last, on the very edges of the grape field the mews occupied.

"You might not want to release the bird in California," she said, "but if you like, we can test his wings a little so you can see if he's ready to be released back where you came from."

Michael felt a little pang of sadness, seeing his friend the falcon go, but on the other hand….

"Like a test flight? Would he come back to me?"

"I was thinking we'd give you jesses to hold and just test his wings. You could see if he's a domesticated bird now or if he really is meant to go back into the wild. I mean, since you're here and you have experts to consult, it's an idea."

Michael nodded. It was a good idea and sound reasoning, and he'd like to see his friend whole and healthy before they flew him back to Chicago to set him free.

"So right now?" he asked.

Right now.


A HALF hour later, they were loaded into a Chevy Expedition with a custom-made back end outfitted with a cage, Scooter screaming irascibly from within. It was funny how irritating the bird had been when locked in the shower at the Residence Inn, but compared to the shrieks of the genetically engineered hybrid birds, he practically sounded like a house wren.

The sun was just starting to touch the hills to the west, throwing long shadows across the valley, when they came to a stop within fifty yards of the shortest of the platforms. Once they'd disembarked, Roger took off for the platform itself, an insulated container over his shoulder, while the veterinarian handed Michael a pair of staunch leather gauntlets.

"Would you like to do the honors?" she asked. "Put your arm in the cage—up to the gauntlet only—and see if he'll perch."

It didn't take long. With a little prompting from Michael, who made sure the bird's feet could feel the new perch while the hood remained, he eventually stood up straight, the bird's scant three-pound weight almost featherlight on his forearm. Carefully, wearing her own leather gloves, Dr. Saunders reached over the bird's head, pulled off the hood, and made sure Michael had the jesses tucked under his thumb. The bird looked around sharply, but his cold eyes didn't seem to recognize Michael anymore. Maybe that had just been in the mews back at home. Michael had meant food then.

Michael swallowed. "What do I do now?" he asked.

"We're just going to get him to spread his wings," she said. "So you're going to lift your arm and see if he extends his wings fully and then retracts them, that's all. We're going for full extension by the end of the session."

"What if he's not ready to go when we get him back?" Carl asked.

She gave a one-shouldered shrug. "Some of them enjoy humans. They choose to stay. Those are the ones it's good to train and to fly. The ones who hate captivity—no amount of kindness can convince them to stay. It is up to the bird. They can be trained—to an extent—but they can never be mastered. Not really."

Michael turned toward Scooter. "You ready, buddy?" he asked. "I mean, the cage can be comforting, but I gotta tell you, life outside can be all you ever dreamed and more."

The bird gave a shriek, and Michael took that for "go." He raised his arm partway up and let it drop slowly, happy when the falcon spread its gray-and-black wings and flapped to keep its balance. Michael did it again, and this time, the bird flapped some more, with more lift.

"All right then!" he said, happy to see the wings work. "Let's do that again! One, two, *three*!" And he gave the bird another heft, hoping to feel the lift of the wings as he lowered his arm, but instead, the bird gave two powerful swoops with his wings and jerked hard against the jesses. Michael gave a squawk worthy of a chicken and worked to untangle the jesses from his fingers. When the bird shrieked again and flapped, the knots around the bird's feet were loose enough for the jesses to slip off, and they fell uselessly to the ground.

One more hard flap and the bird was borne aloft on wings that were obviously strong enough to carry him.

And carry him they did.

"Oh no!" Michael exclaimed. "Scooter, come back. Man, we were gonna let you go back home!"

Dr. Saunders was watching the bird fly off with absolute surprise on her face. "Well. Uhm. I guess maybe he *is* home?"

"Is he gonna be okay?" Michael asked her. "I didn't want to just ditch him here. It's not Chicago at all!"

She grimaced. "It doesn't seem to bother him. We'll try to keep an eye out during your stay, but sometimes wild animals do what wild animals do. There are plenty of peregrines in California. Maybe he feels at home."

Michael eyed the bird unhappily, but Scooter seemed oblivious to all the rules of man he was breaking and intent on exploring this new horizon.

"I guess a bird's gotta bird," Michael said finally. He and Carl watched in awe as the bird went up, up, far beyond the feeding platform, circling above it once, twice, and again, probably to scope out the land.

"I don't think you have to worry about that one coming back," Carl said softly. "He seems to like his freedom just fine."

Michael sought out Carl's hand with no hesitation, wanting his heat, his presence, as they watched as the bird finished its third circle, gave a shriek, and flew off, west toward the ocean, every sweep of its wings bearing it higher and farther away.

Carl's hand squeezed his as the bird disappeared into the horizon under the shadows of the lowering sun.

"That was pretty," Michael said. "As long as he's gonna be okay here, that was worth all the trouble, that's for sure."

"Yeah," Carl replied. "Birds are so damned cool."

Michael turned toward him and grinned, remembering how Carl had caught his attention with that the first time Michael had dared to get him alone to see if maybe the attraction Carl held for him might someday be reciprocated.

And now look at them, just like the bird. Escaping the cage of loneliness and past mistakes they'd each lived in and flying off into the sunset together, into a whole new world.

"Yeah," he said softly. "Birds are really cool."

They were quiet for a moment, and then, almost as one, they both gave a shiver.

"And it's getting *cold* out here," Carl said, that practicality Michael loved at the forefront. "Are you hungry? I could eat."

Michael raised up enough to kiss him, brief and hard on the lips, before turning toward Dr. Saunders and a disgruntled Roger.

"I climbed the damned ladder for nothing," he muttered.

"Yeah," Michael agreed. "But did you enjoy the view?"

Roger's pursed mouth softened. "How could you not. It's why my family stays." He sobered and leaned forward. "Thank you, guys, for what you did for us. Most guys might not think being elbow deep in falcon shit is their dream job, but I tell you, I wouldn't do anything else."

"Neither would we," Carl told him, and Michael nodded enthusiastically.

As they got back into the Chevy, the smell of damp earth and the faraway salt of the ocean strong in the air, Michael realized that Carl was right.

He couldn't imagine anything better than going off into the sunset with this man by his side.

Keep reading for an exclusive excerpt from
*Fish in a Barrel*
Fish Out of Water series, Book #7
by Amy Lane
Coming soon!

# Apple Picking Weather

JACKSON HAD to hand it to the woman; she claimed she was shy and nonconfrontational, but she didn't seem to be afraid to express an opinion.

The courthouse in Sacramento was a newish marble-and-glass structure, the rooms inside were carpeted, and the seats were lined. It wasn't exactly designed for comfort, but there wasn't a thunderous echo either, which was helpful when the witness who saw the crime in question hadn't wanted to testify in the first place.

But she had finally agreed because, she said, it wasn't right.

"So, Mrs. Kleinman," Ellery said, looking decisive and articulate in his best suit. "You say you are absolutely positive that the person you saw holding a gun to the victim's chest was not, indeed, the defendant, Mr. Ezekiel Halliday, seated." Ellery gestured to Halliday in the defendant's seat, still thin from the hospital, dressed reluctantly in a suit that was tight at the shoulder joints and knee joints but loose everywhere else. He had dark curly hair and a close-cropped beard, mostly because it was easier to trim the beard than to shave by himself, and his brown eyes didn't always track the proceedings, although Jackson knew without a doubt he was listening. His narrow face was capable of great joy—Jackson had seen that—but not today.

"Absolutely," Mrs. Kleinman said. Her face softened as she took Ezekiel in. "Zeke wouldn't have known what to do with a gun if he had one."

Ellery nodded. "We'll get back to that. It's important. But how can you be so sure. The police identified Ezekiel after one canvass of the neighborhood. What makes you say it couldn't have been him?"

She gave a *harrumph*. "Well, for one thing, I'd passed Ezekiel about a block before I came to the mouth of Harmony Park, where the incident happened. He was sitting on the sidewalk, holding his foot up to his mouth to suck on a wound."

Ellery had been prepared for this answer—he and Jackson had spent some private time in their office giving voice to the "oogies" as their paralegal, Jackson's sister, called the intense visceral reaction to something gross. But Jackson still saw his wince of dismay when Mrs. Kleinman said it.

"That doesn't sound… hygienic," Ellery said delicately. "Why would he be doing that?"

The woman was plump and doughy, in her fifties, with graying hair and everything from bad ankles to bad knees to a bad back. None of that stopped her from walking three obnoxious Pomeranians two to three miles a day in her little suburb, and apparently Effie Kleinman didn't miss a trick.

"He'd run away from his care home the day before," she said, shaking her head. "His shoe had come off, and he'd stubbed his toe. Zeke's joints aren't properly formed—it makes him very flexible but not very stable on his feet."

"Did you offer Mr. Halliday help?" Ellery asked.

Effie sucked air in through her teeth. "Well, that's tricky. I've got the number for his care home by my desk in my house, but I didn't have it on my cell. I talked to him for a bit, and he was feeling fractious, so I told him I'd call Arturo—that's the man who usually comes to get him when he's gotten out—and left him to go on my way."

"So that's the last time you saw Mr. Halliday," Ellery responded.

"That day, yes," she said with a grimace, "because then I was walking through the park entrance, and that asshole with the gun was screaming, and I was trying not to shit my pants."

Jackson watched Ellery as he slow-blinked, trying to digest what she *actually* said as opposed to what they'd been *coaching* her to say for a week.

After a stunned silence in the courtroom, Ellery asked, his voice dry as toast, "Were you successful?"

Effie gave an embarrassed snort. "Not entirely. I did feel a powerful need to go home and change my britches, which is one of the reasons I didn't stick around and talk to the police. Besides," she added, sobering again, "I really wanted to call Arturo. If there was a lunatic loose in the park with a gun, I didn't want Zeke out in that."

"So you didn't stick around to answer any questions?" Ellery reinforced.

"No sir. Not my scene." She gave a shrug. "Witnesses like me are invisible to police anyway. Just another fat brown woman with too many dogs. They didn't want my opinion."

"So what made you decide to come here and testify?" Ellery prodded, and Jackson let out a breath. They had to make this clear now or the prosecution would turn it into a "gotcha" question on the cross.

"Well, your man there," she nodded toward Jackson, who waved, "got my name from one of the other witnesses. When he told me they'd fingered poor Zeke, I had to come forward. I'd called Arturo, and he was going to come get Zeke, but Arturo's got no obligation to me. He hadn't told me Zeke was in jail, which was the stupidest thing I'd ever heard of."

Jackson Rivers had known Ellery Cramer for nearing on nine years now, and they'd been sharing a bed for over a year of that. Ellery had slick brown hair and sharp features—nose, cheekbones, chin—along with hard, flat brown eyes.

Jackson knew Ellery's every expression, including when those narrow lips went slack and bruised with passion and his brown eyes went from hard to limpid with need, and he knew that if he hadn't known Ellery down to the last nuance, he might have missed the fury he was suppressing as they covered this next line of questioning.

"Could you explain why it's a 'stupid' idea to think Zeke should be in jail for holding a gun to the victim's head?" Ellery asked, keeping that fury in check.

"Objection!" Arizona Brooks, the ADA in charge of prosecution stood up hurriedly. "This witness is not a medical professional, and she is hardly qualified to tell us what conditions the defendant may have had that would hinder his ability to perpetrate a crime."

Ellery and Jackson stared at her. Arizona was a fit woman, known for her zero tolerance for bullshit, who sported a spiky gray buzz cut, big silver earrings, and liked to wear white men's cut suits when she was in court.

She was sharp, surprisingly compassionate for an ADA, and willing to deal for the good of the victim and the perpetrator if she saw injustice being committed in the name of the law.

And she never, ever made a mistake.

Until right now.

"Your honor," Ellery said, yanking his gaze to the judge in the front of the courtroom with an obvious effort, "besides having been a teacher of the moderate and severely disabled for over twenty years, Mrs. Kleinman has taken a compassionate interest in our defendant for several years and has an established relationship with his caretaker. While we will call Arturo Bautista, who runs the Sunshine Care Home, as our next witness, Mrs. Kleinman can speak directly to why it would have been impossible for the defendant to be where the police claimed he was at the time of the crime."

"Overruled," the judge said reluctantly, and Jackson caught the glare the man sent Arizona.

And he didn't like it.

Judge Clive Brentwood *looked* like everything a judge should be— tall, broad-shouldered, distinguished, with the tanned skin of a tennis or golf aficionado and a lion's mane of gray hair tamed by the stylist's comb. Brentwood *looked* like he should be wise and educated and fair. His courtroom presence was formal and impeccable, much like the man himself.

But Ellery had groaned and cursed his luck when he'd seen that he'd drawn Brentwood to try the case in front of, because whereas much of Sacramento was progressive and most of the judges were fair and had the best interest of their constituents in mind, Brentwood was conservative down to his Ronald Reagan leather-soled oxford shoes.

And he was not afraid to let his politics get in the way of a fair ruling.

The look he'd aimed at Arizona Brooks had not been friendly, although technically Brooks had done nothing wrong. Her mistake had been in giving Ellery a chance to voice Mrs. Kleinman's qualifications as a judge of Mr. Halliday's condition, and Ellery had taken full advantage.

Jackson eyeballed Arizona, who managed to put an apologetic face on things, but who didn't—to Jackson's eyes anyway—look sorry at all.

In fact as she sat down, Jackson saw her give Effie Kleinman a look that bordered on hope. Like she *hoped* Mrs. Kleinman was the answer to Ezekiel Halliday's prayers.

But Ellery was already questioning their witness, and Jackson's attention was pulled—as it always was—to the magnetic personal force that was Ellery Cramer.

"So," Ellery said, rephrasing for Arizona's sake, because she was a colleague, "could you tell us why it would have been impossible for Mr. Halliday to have been the perpetrator who took Annette Frazier hostage?"

"Well, like I said, Zeke was sitting down, tending to his foot when I passed him. He was bleeding, and it looked like a fierce cut there, and Zeke doesn't move well anyway."

"Could you explain 'doesn't move well'?" Ellery prodded.

"He's got something wrong with his muscles and joints—I think Arturo said it was caused by brain damage at birth, so cerebral palsy of some sort. He's very flexible but not very strong and not very coordinated. If he was the dickhead with the gun who terrorized Annette Frazier, he would have needed to pass me up on the park pathways, and he did not. And he would have needed to have gotten a gun from somewhere, and then done all of the things the witness for the prosecution said he did: wrap his arm around Annette's throat, hold a gun to her head, threaten bystanders. His speech isn't clear enough to threaten bystanders, and if he wrapped his arm around somebody's throat it would be to help himself stay standing. I was there. I saw the guy they were looking for. He was young with brown eyes and brown hair, but that was the only resemblance. Zeke Halliday was not him."

The silence in the courtroom was electric, and Jackson saw the witnesses for the prosecution looking at each other and grumbling. Jackson managed to let out a breath he hadn't known he'd been holding for a month, ever since Arturo Bautista had contacted them on Zeke's behalf to try to get his charge out of jail.

"Why do *you* think Zeke Halliday was arrested?" Ellery asked Effie, and Jackson's eyes darted toward Arizona Brooks to see if she'd object to the question. She should have—it called for speculation on facts Ms. Kleinman could not know—but she didn't, which told Jackson all he ever needed to know about how excited Arizona had been to prosecute this case.

"I think the cops got lazy," Effie said, obviously hurt. "I think the bad guy got away, running through the park's underbrush and down the irrigation stream, and whoever followed them encountered Zeke on the pathway and thought, 'Hey, this guy's obviously homeless. Nobody will give a crap if we arrest him, and that way we can say we tried.'"

Effie's words rang throughout the courtroom, bitter and very true, and once again Jackson looked toward the prosecution to see if there would be an objection.

This time, when Arizona remained stubbornly silent, Ellery met Jackson's eyes in question for a brief second before he turned his attention back to the stand.

"One more thing," Ellery said, before turning the witness over to the prosecution. "You said Mr. Halliday had a wound on his foot. Was he wounded anywhere else?"

"No sir," Effie said, her eyes seeking out the officers sitting behind the prosecution's desk waiting to be called in rebuttal.

"Were there any bruises on his face, neck, or on his arms?"

"No sir."

"Was there any blood besides his foot?"

"No sir," she replied, eyes narrowing.

"Objection," Arizona said belatedly. "Where's this leading?"

"We'll have to talk to the next witness to find out," Ellery said smoothly.

"Withdrawn," Arizona snapped out smartly, and again, that glare.

Brentwood had been going to sustain, but Arizona hadn't let him.

Interesting, Jackson thought. Very, very interesting.

The cross-examination went smoothly, and Arizona pretty much stuck to the script, testing Effie Kleinman's testimony in the places it could—potentially—be weak. Could Mr. Halliday have run through the underbrush in order to take a shortcut to where the incident had taken place?

No, Effie had insisted, he could not have. Between the injury to his foot and his lack of physical coordination, Zeke Halliday couldn't have beat her to the park's entrance where the incident had taken place.

Then Arizona had done more of Jackson and Ellery's work for them. Why, she asked Effie, if Zeke Halliday was disabled, would he be allowed to stand trial?

"He's not *stupid*," Effie had protested. "His IQ is very functional, and I understand he really loves audiobooks—he apparently loves to discuss them. But his body makes it difficult to parse his sentences and difficult for him to be self-sufficient. He's cognizant and able to stand trial, but he's not physically capable of committing this crime."

Then Arizona Brooks had put the nail in the coffin of her own case by asking what sounded like a "gotcha" question—but it got the wrong side.

"You say you were going to go home to call a resource for Mr. Halliday," Arizona said, her voice measured, as though she were weighing every word.

"Yes, and I did. I called Arturo as soon as I got home."

"But there were resources all over the park. The police were already there. Why didn't you call them?"

Effie Kleinman visibly recoiled. "Have you ever *heard* the police roust the homeless? Have you *heard* the way they talk to the transient population in my neighborhood? It's dehumanizing as hell, and it's certainly not help of any sort. No, if I'd realized they were going to come get Zeke, I would have sat down next to him and told them to fuck off when they tried to arrest him. I certainly wouldn't have thrown him to the wolves."

And before the judge could call order, Arizona proclaimed herself done with the witness, and Ellery was up to call the next one to the stand.

Arturo Bautista was a trim man in his midfifties with a square brown lined face and a sweet smile. His family ran several adult care homes off Stockton Boulevard, and while the places weren't posh, they were clean, the residents felt safe, and the staff knew everybody by name and talked to them like human beings. Arturo, who'd been sitting next to Jackson during Effie's testimony, gave Jackson a nervous smile as he stood.

"You'll do fine," Jackson said, and Arturo gave a here-goes-nothing sort of shrug.

After being sworn in, he sat, both feet on the floor, and regarded Ellery with bright, alert eyes and a sort of calming presence. Jackson had seen him in action at the care home. Arturo had a big job, taking care of nearly forty residents, each with an assortment of mental and physical disabilities, but he dealt with the challenges using compassion, humor, and a solid dose of common sense.

"Mr. Bautista," Ellery began, "you are the proprietor of the Sunshine Prayers Care Home off Stockton Boulevard?"

"The Sunshine Prayers Care Home for the Moderately Disabled," Arturo clarified. "Sunshine Prayers is the company name. There are different homes for different needs."

"Thank you for the clarification," Ellery said, and Jackson had to keep from smiling to himself. Ellery had originally scripted different wording during witness prep, but once, when he'd been tired, he'd simply left off the remainder of the name. Arturo had made the clarification then, too, and Ellery had liked the way it sounded—as though Arturo was a professional who knew his business and made sure there was no confusion.

"So," Ellery continued, "you're responsible for Ezekiel Halliday?"

"Well, his family is responsible for him," Arturo said wryly, "but we provide the day-to-day care. It's often difficult for a family— particularly one with low income—to provide a suitable peer-interactive environment for an adult with special needs."

Ellery nodded and began to question Arturo about the day-to-day operations of the care home. Jackson's stomach knotted, expecting Arizona's objection at any moment, but none came. In a way, it was a relief; sometimes the prosecution spent the entire trial trying to disrupt the defense's rhythm, or vice versa. But as Ellery's questioning—designed for one exclusive purpose—continued, Jackson started getting jittery. When was the other shoe going to drop?

"So your facility sounds very organized," Ellery said. "But that begs the question. How was it Ezekiel Halliday was in the park that day unsupervised?"

Arturo looked sorrowful, as he had during witness preparation. "Zeke's smart," he said with a sigh. "And he gets bored. Some of the residents are cleared to leave unsupervised. They need very little help and are close to being independent. Ezekiel has been begging for the same privileges, but—" Arturo took a deep breath. "—he's easily injured," he said, meeting Ezekiel's eyes in apology. "And his speech is unclear, so it's difficult for him to ask for help."

"How long had Ezekiel been missing from your facility on the day of the incident?" Ellery asked without commenting on the Arturo's explanation.

"Two days."

"Is this common, Mr. Bautista? For a resident to be missing overnight?"

"No," Arturo said grimly. "In fact with any other resident, we would have been on the phone to every authority in the book to find him. It's not safe for him to be out there."

"Then why not this time?" Ellery lowered his voice, made it soft, almost invisible, because he wanted everybody to hear the answer. Jackson hated the answer, but it wasn't any less true because Jackson hated it.

"This was his third such incident in two years," Arturo said. "When it happens too often, social services moves residents to a different facility."

"Wouldn't a different facility be a better fit?" Ellery asked. He'd asked that question during preparation, just to find out why Ezekiel had been in the park that day.

"The state-owned facility is horrible," Arturo told him, voice shaking. "Too many people, too many problems. He could get assaulted, have his possessions stolen, be force-fed medication. He's vulnerable on his own, but that is not the place for him. Neither is jail. There's not a violent bone in his body. He just… was in the wrong place at the wrong time."

"So you didn't call the police because you were afraid of what they'd do?" Ellery asked.

"Yes."

Ellery pulled a folder from his desk that featured 8 x10 photos that Jackson had taken when they'd managed to bail Ezekiel out of jail.

"Is this what you were afraid of?" he asked.

Arturo's voice broke. "Yes."

Between the time Effie Kleinman had seen Ezekiel sitting on the sidewalk and Arturo had gone to the jail with Jackson and Ellery to post his bail, Ezekiel had been badly beaten. His face was puffy—one eye swollen almost completely shut—and his jaw had been broken as well. He'd lost two teeth, and there were bruises on his neck and shoulders that showed clearly the outline of hard-soled boots.

Not the soft-soled crocs given to prisoners.

"Objection?" Brentwood asked, looking at Arizona Brooks.

"Of course I object to seeing a man badly beaten," Arizona said smoothly. "And so should you."

"But the pictures are irrelevant," Judge Brentwood protested.

"To why the defendant had a legitimate fear of the police?" Arizona responded. "No sir, I think they speak very clearly as to why the defendant and his caregiver didn't ask the police for help. It is not your place to object. It's mine. And I don't. I think the defense should continue on."

Brentwood gaped for a moment before looking at Ellery in confusion.

"Mr. Cramer," he said, gesturing vaguely.

"Thank you, sir," Ellery said smoothly, but Jackson could see that Ellery was as boggled as he was. Arizona Brooks was a topflight attorney. Much of the testimony, including the damning pictures that spoke to a painful beating at the hands of the authorities, should have been a tooth-and-nail fight to get admitted.

Arizona was doing everything but leaning back and taking a nap. In fact she was going one better. She was actually putting on her hip waders and helping Ellery cut through the bullshit.

Jackson wondered why. He wanted to excuse himself to go make a phone call or two, but he'd promised both Effie and Arturo he'd be there for the two of them. Effie was sitting next to him now, clenching his knee with stress.

Jackson patted her hand until she let go with a sheepish look, and together they watched as Ellery finished with Arturo's testimony and turned Arturo over to Arizona.

She looked at Arturo reluctantly and continued to give him a very mild cross-examination. Toward the end, she paused and took a deep breath, as though fortifying herself.

"Now, Mr. Cramer showed us pictures of the defendant, and he looked in bad shape. Did you ever, at any time, see one of the officers seated behind me lay a finger on Ezekiel."

"No ma'am. I didn't see it happen."

"Then why would we assume that the police are responsible for the bruises?"

"Because when I asked Ezekiel what happened, he said 'the bad policemen'," Arturo said, not backing down.

"But I thought Mr. Halliday couldn't talk!" Arizona was feigning surprise—and not bothering to hide it.

"It's difficult to understand him," Arturo told her. "But not impossible. He knows who to be afraid of."

Arizona nodded slowly. "Good," she said. "It's good somebody does. No more questions for this witness."

The judge looked at the clock. "It's getting close to quitting time. Let's resume testimony tomorrow, nine a.m. sharp."

"All rise!" intoned the bailiff, and Brentwood exited the courtroom, followed by the jury.

Arizona didn't look at them as she packed her briefs into her suitcase and turned to speak to the officers who had been ready to be called as witnesses. The conversation didn't appear to be going well.

The officer in charge, wearing his full blues, hat tucked under his arm, was doing his best to use his full six-foot-plus height to loom over Arizona's five eight or so.

True to the woman Jackson and Ellery knew, she sent him a killing look.

"If you didn't want it brought up," she said icily, "maybe you shouldn't have authorized it."

"He fought back!" said a younger officer bitterly. So fair his neck was turning purple with agitation, his voice rang with injured adolescent dignity.

"You were *beating* him," Arizona retorted. "I don't know which part of that you don't understand. I told you this would happen, and I warned you they would introduce the evidence in the criminal trial so they could use it in the civil trial. Well, they have. And when this kid gets let off, expect Cramer's partner to come after you in the most celebrated civil suit in the city. This isn't going away."

"Well, not from anything *you're* trying to do," snarled the taller, dark-haired officer. "I swear, it's like you want him to get off!"

"Because even *I* know he didn't do anything," she snapped back. "Now if I were you, I'd go try to find the real perpetrator, or Rivers and Cramer are going to do it for you and make you look even worse. Now go."

They all stared at her and then looked over at Jackson and Ellery speculatively.

Jackson bared his teeth at them in what was definitely *not* a smile. They were working on it. Of *course* they were working on it. But the state was hell-bent on cramming this case through the system, trying their defendant while the bruises from his police beating were still visible and his jaw was still wired, rendering him all but mute.

The witnesses for the prosecution visibly recoiled from Jackson's expression, and the silence in the courtroom thudded like a lead gavel on flesh.

"*Go!*" Arizona shouted, and the clot of cops left, grumbling, leaving a nearly clear courtroom.

"Arizona…?" Ellery began, but she shook her head and held up her hand.

"Win this one," she said, "I can't have any more off days or Brentwood'll declare a mistrial. You know that. See you both tomorrow."

And with that she was gone, leaving Jackson with the distinct impression she was crying.

Ellery met his eyes then, and they had a complete silent conversation that started with "Okay, that was weird," and ended with "We'll talk about it when we get rid of the civilians."

Arturo had already gone around the table to grasp Ezekiel's wheelchair and begin pushing him down the aisle between the banks of seats, and Effie followed him slowly. Arturo, Effie, and Zeke had all come in Arturo's van—he'd been given custody after Zeke made bail, and suddenly Zeke was having to deal with locks on the door to his dormitory and hourly checks to make sure he hadn't tried to fly the coop again.

Jackson got the feeling that after meeting the "good" guys, Zeke wasn't going to want to fly the coop again for a very long time.

Award winning author AMY LANE lives in a crumbling crapmansion with a couple of teenagers, a passel of furbabies, and a bemused spouse. She has too damned much yarn, a penchant for action-adventure movies, and a need to know that somewhere in all the pain is a story of Wuv, Twu Wuv, which she continues to believe in to this day! She writes contemporary romance, paranormal romance, urban fantasy, and romantic suspense, teaches the occasional writing class, and likes to pretend her very simple life is as exciting as the lives of the people who live in her head. She'll also tell you that sacrifices, large and small, are worth the urge to write.

Website: www.greenshill.com

Blog: www.writerslane.blogspot.com

Email: amylane@greenshill.com

Facebook: www.facebook.com/amy.lane.167

Twitter: @amymaclane

Follow me on BookBub

# The Mastermind

## AMY LANE

A Long Con Adventure

Once upon a time in Rome, Felix Salinger got caught picking his first pocket and Danny Mitchell saved his bacon. The two of them were inseparable… until they weren't.

Twenty years after that first meeting, Danny returns to Chicago, the city he shared with Felix and their perfect, secret family, to save him again. Felix's news network—the business that broke them apart—is under fire from an unscrupulous employee pointing the finger at Felix. An official investigation could topple their house of cards. The only way to prove Felix is innocent is to pull off their biggest con yet.

But though Felix still has the gift of grift, his reunion with Danny is bittersweet. Their ten-year separation left holes in their hearts that no amount of stolen property can fill. A green crew of young thieves looks to them for guidance as they negotiate old jewels and new threats to pull off the perfect heist—but the hardest job is proving that love is the only thing of value they've ever had.

**www.dreamspinnerpress.com**

*The Muscle*

AMY LANE

A Long Con Adventure

A true protector will guard your heart before his own.

Hunter Rutledge saw one too many people die in his life as mercenary muscle to go back to the job, so he was conveniently at loose ends when Josh Salinger offered him a place in his altruistic den of thieves.

Hunter is almost content having found a home with a group of people who want justice badly enough to steal it. If only one of them didn't keep stealing his attention from the task at hand….

Superlative dancer and transcendent thief Dylan "Grace" Li lives in the moment. But when mobsters blackmail the people who gave him dance—and the means to save his own soul—Grace turns to Josh for help.

Unfortunately, working with Josh's crew means working with Hunter Rutledge, and for Grace, that's more dangerous than any heist.

Grace's childhood left him thinking he was too difficult to love—so he's better off not risking his love on anyone else. Avoiding commitment keeps him safe. But somehow Hunter's solid, grounding presence makes him feel safer. Can Grace trust that letting down his guard to a former mercenary doesn't mean he'll get shot in the heart?

# www.dreamspinnerpress.com

# The Driver

## AMY LANE

A Long Con Adventure

Hell-raiser, getaway driver, and occasional knight in tarnished armor Chuck Calder has never had any illusions about being a serious boyfriend. He may not be a good guy, but at least as part of Josh Salinger's crew of upscale thieves and cons, he can feel good about his job.

Right now, his job is Lucius Broadstone.

Lucius is a blueblood with a brutal past. He uses his fortune and contacts to help people trying to escape abuse, but someone is doing everything they can to stop him. He needs the kind of help only the Salingers can provide. Besides, he hasn't forgotten the last time he and Chuck Calder collided. The team's good ol' boy and good luck charm is a blue-collar handful, but he is genuinely kind. He takes Lucius's mission seriously, and Lucius has never had that before. In spite of Chuck's reluctance to admit he's a nice guy, Lucius wants to know him better.

Chuck's a guaranteed good time, and Lucius is a forever guy. Can Chuck come to terms with his past and embrace the future Lucius is offering? Or is Good Luck Chuck destined to be driving off into the sunset alone forever?

have to deal with their personal complications… and an attraction that's spiraled out of control.

# www.dreamspinnerpress.com